Praise for the novels

"Jo Ann Brown delivers a thrilling story details, plot twists, wonderful characte
—Patricia Davids

"Jo Ann Brown provides a lovely treat for readers with *A Wish for Home*, a delightful story of two opposites thrown together on a stormy night in Amish country. With a deft touch, Brown draws the contrast between Lauren, an ambitious advertising executive, and Adam, an Amish widower intent on raising his small daughter. Heartfelt and genuine, Brown takes readers along with her characters on the difficult and challenging road to home."
—Marta Perry, author of *A Springtime Heart*

"Jo Ann Brown's writing is both powerful and charming. She provides a respite from the cares of the day and gives the invitation to join her for a journey of peace that lingers in the heart."
—Kelly Long

"An Amish tale that is anything but plain and simple."
—*USA TODAY* bestselling author Vannetta Chapman

"A wonderful ride through Amish country filled with adventure and surprises. Jo Ann Brown's characters and story are sure to touch your heart."
—*USA TODAY* bestselling author Rachel J. Good

"A heartwarming, richly layered story of love and loss, betrayal and redemption with well-crafted characters. Readers of Amish fiction will love *A Wish for Home* by Jo Ann Brown."
—Mary Ellis, author of *Nothing Tastes So Sweet*

"In *A Wish for Home*, Jo Ann Brown weaves an intriguing story that readers of Amish fiction are sure to enjoy. A book about finding oneself, learning to forgive, and discovering the things that really matter in life—faith, hope, and love."
—Jennifer Spredemann

"*A Wish for Home* by Jo Ann Brown is a beautiful story of forgiveness and letting go of the past to return home. I really enjoyed this sweet, emotional story. I promise it will touch your heart!"
—Lenora Worth, author of *Seeking Refuge*

Also by Jo Ann Brown

Love Inspired

The Amish Suitor
The Amish Christmas Cowboy
The Amish Bachelor's Baby
The Amish Widower's Twins
An Amish Christmas Promise
An Amish Easter Wish
An Amish Mother's Secret Past
An Amish Holiday Family

Visit the Author Profile page at Harlequin.com for more titles.

A WISH FOR HOME

Jo Ann Brown

LOVE INSPIRED

INSPIRATIONAL ROMANCE

LOVE INSPIRED®

INSPIRATIONAL ROMANCE

Recycling programs
for this product may
not exist in your area.

ISBN-13: 978-1-335-92868-9

A Wish for Home

Love Inspired
22 Adelaide St. West, 40th Floor
Toronto, Ontario M5H 4E3, Canada
www.Harlequin.com

Printed in U.S.A.

For the three people who have helped make this series possible:
My agent, Jennifer Jackson, who suggested I try a longer book.
My editor, Tina James, who has been both teacher and cheerleader
with every book.
My husband, Bill, my beta reader who catches missing
and extra words...most of the time!
With my greatest appreciation for all of you!

For ye were sometimes darkness, but now are ye light in the Lord: walk as children of light.

—*Ephesians* 5:8

A WISH FOR
HOME

Chapter One

A sleepy, dark road in central Lancaster County was the last place in the world where Lauren Nolt wanted to be on a stormy March evening.

Or any evening, to be honest.

She peered through the windshield, trying to follow the road through the rain that funneled out of the darkness like a hail of bullets. The clatter striking the glass warned it might not be rain, but sleet. She leaned forward as if she could force the storm aside if she focused hard enough.

"Can this day get any worse?" she muttered to herself and slowed her car as she approached the crest of yet another hill leading toward Bliss Valley. In Amish country, it was foolish even on a sunny day to speed over a hill or around a sharp corner. A buggy could be on the other side, and there wouldn't be time to stop before hitting it.

She wouldn't even have been driving the back roads of Lancaster County tonight if she hadn't listened to the GPS. Half an hour ago, the calm voice on her cell phone had suggested she leave the main road near Gap at the eastern side of the county so she could avoid a long traffic delay ahead of her. Something more than rush hour traffic, she guessed, suspecting the storm was the cause. She hadn't bothered to check to see the length of the detour or where it went. She'd pushed the button to have the GPS reroute her, eager to get out of the storm and to her hotel in the city of Lancaster after the hour-long drive from Philadelphia.

Usually she loved driving the ancient light blue Beetle she'd bought with her very first bonus check from her very first job seven years ago. She'd named the car Ringo, and they'd logged a lot of miles together. But she wasn't enjoying driving Ringo tonight when the blinding downpour alternated between rain and sleet and snow.

The late spring storm wasn't supposed to hit until after midnight. That's what the weathermen had been repeating. If she'd known it was going to be nasty, she would have worn her boots and brought along a hat and gloves.

Her thoughts were interrupted by the approaching scream of a siren. More than one. From the top of the hill she'd just gone over, lights flashed like scarlet stars on the wet rear window. Moving the car toward the right shoulder, she winced when she heard the front passenger tire drop off the sharp edge of the asphalt. A guardrail prevented her from moving farther off the road. The small car vibrated as a pair of fire trucks raced past her as if the road were dry. They vanished into the storm, leaving a malevolent red glare in their wake.

A shudder arched across her tense shoulders. Were the trucks on their way to an accident or a fire? Was everyone safe? She couldn't imagine how horrible it would be to fight a big fire in the icy rain.

Lauren glanced at her rearview mirror, ready to ease her foot off the clutch and the car onto the road. She slammed her foot on the brake as an ambulance and a pickup truck with flashing red and blue lights in its grille erupted over the hill. As they sped past, she saw more vehicles with emergency lights coming toward her.

Putting the car into neutral while she waited for the end of the parade of first responders, she jerked the emergency brake. She reached for her phone, wondering if she'd need to find a detour from her detour. She didn't expect to see anything on her GPS yet, but she had to make a decision whether to keep going the same way or find another route through the winding roads among scattered farms.

She tapped the phone to life as cars and trucks kept rushing past, rocking her little car as if it were stuck in the highest branches of a tree in a gale. Frowning at the list of voice mails visible on the screen, she saw two from Cassie Varozza. Cassie was her number one competitor for being named the next partner at the public relations firm of Krause-Matsui-Fitzgerald. Cassie had attended all the right schools, from kindergarten to the big-name university where she graduated with a degree in communications, but her major truly had been meeting and befriending people with the connections to get her where she wanted to go with the least amount of effort.

Lauren hadn't learned how to do that because her parents hadn't been able to put her on the fast track when they didn't even know such a thing existed. The past had been working against her until now. She'd been sent to check out the two sites in the county where potential clients were interested in building a casino because, until shortly before her fourteenth birthday, she'd lived in the Amish community.

Her boss thought, since she'd grown up plain, she'd have an inside track on how the local Amish would feel about a new casino being built in their midst. Even if she knew the opinions of the local communities, she wasn't going to use any insider information because, if everything went as Lauren hoped, she wouldn't come into contact with a single person she'd known during her childhood. Her parents had been shunned by their family and neighbors when they'd chosen to leave the community for reasons they'd never explained to her. When she'd asked once during her first semester of college, she'd been told by her mother and father that they'd disagreed with a decision made by the bishop and could no longer stay. They never explained what that decision had been or why they'd been opposed enough to it that they gave up everything but each other and her, and she hadn't pushed when she saw how sad her question had made them. Because she'd been a child and not yet baptized, she hadn't been shunned, so no Amish door in the community would be closed to her. Yet, how could she schmooze the very people who'd turned their backs on her parents?

Maybe she hadn't understood when she was younger, but she'd noticed—in spite of her parents' attempts to keep the truth from her—how alone they seemed to feel. They didn't fit into the *Englisch* world. They now lived in a Bryn Mawr caretaker's cottage on the estate where her father was the gardener and her mother worked inside the big house as the cook. There weren't a lot of jobs out in the real world for people with no more than an eighth grade education, and her mother had been passed over for promotion to housekeeper twice because of it.

Once she made partner at Krause-Matsui-Fitzgerald, she'd be able to take care of her parents and give them the lifestyle she wanted them to have. She intended to buy them a house in Sarasota, Florida. That would allow them to escape the winters, which seemed to sap them more every year, as well as let them live near the plain community of Pinecraft where the rules governing the Amish were looser. Being in the Sunshine State might banish the shadows clinging to their eyes when they thought she wouldn't notice.

Then she'd be alone in Pennsylvania. Her folks had hoped she'd find a nice man and settle down by now. Her mouth twisted. Nice men didn't come into her life often. The few she'd met were already married or in a serious relationship. She'd thought she'd found one, but eventually came to see what everyone else had right from the beginning. He'd been using her connections to feed his ambitions in the public relations business. When she'd broken it off with him, his sole regret had been he wouldn't have access to her address book. At least, he hadn't pretended to care when she ended it.

Scrolling past Cassie's messages, Lauren saw one from a Lancaster number she didn't recognize. Was it from one of the property developers she was supposed to meet in the next couple of days? Opening it, she put the phone to her ear. Before she could listen to the message, the phone rang.

She nearly jumped out of her skin as the sound blasted her ear. Was she *this* nervous about these upcoming meetings?

Or was it being in Bliss Valley that had her on edge? She had good childhood memories, though some she wished she could forget. Most of those had to do with three boys who'd delighted in making her life and her best friend's miserable. She had no idea where Adam Hershberger, Joel Beachy and Samuel King were now, and she didn't care as long as she never had to see or speak to any of them again.

Glad she didn't have to answer either question, Lauren swiped to answer the call. "Lauren here."

"Thank goodness!" came her mother's familiar voice. "You're at the hotel already?"

"Not yet. I—"

"Not yet? I thought you'd be there by now. Is the weather bad? It's starting to rain here. Did you stop for supper?"

Lauren tried to answer one of the questions but couldn't before her mother threw more at her. Astonished at how wound up her mother was, she waited until Mom took a breath.

"What's bothering you?" Lauren asked.

"Is it that obvious? You didn't answer the phone while you're driving, did you? That's not a *gut* idea, ain't so? It's too dangerous, you know."

"Yes, I know, and I know something is bothering you." She didn't add that her mother never slipped into *Deitsch*, the language spoken by the Amish at home, unless she was upset. "What's wrong?"

"I got a call today."

She waited for Mom to say more, but it seemed her mother had run out of steam. Only the faint buzz in her ear told Lauren they remained connected.

"Mom?" she prompted.

"I got a call. For you."

"And?"

"They wanted to talk to you, *liebling.*"

She tried not to roll her eyes, but it was impossible. "I got that, but what did they want to talk to me about?"

"About you."

"They wanted to talk to me about me?" She took a steadying breath before her frustration burst out. It wasn't like her mother to be obtuse. "Is Dad there? Maybe I should—"

"No! I don't want him to know! Not yet! Not until we figure out what to do. *Du duh net verscheteh!*"

Lauren translated in her mind: *You don't understand!* She sat straighter, gripping the steering wheel with one hand so hard she heard it creak. Mom hadn't strung so many *Deitsch* words together in a row since they'd left Bliss Valley fifteen years ago.

"Mom, tell me what's wrong."

"They left a message on the answering machine. Is there a way for me to play it so you can hear it?"

"Not easily." She switched on the wipers as she tried to figure out a way to bring the call to a close without hurting her mother's feelings. The sleet was getting thicker. "Tell me what they said."

"They were calling from a lawyer's office. They wanted to talk to you. They want you to call them back."

She let her shoulders soften from the tension that had gripped them. "It's okay, Mom. I talk to lawyers all the time with work."

"This wasn't about work. This was…" Her voice shattered into sobs.

Lauren gasped. Mom never cried, not even when she'd cut herself so badly she'd needed a dozen stitches.

"Mom," she hurried to say, "it's gonna be all right. Tell me what the message was."

More sobs resonated against her ear before her mother said in a whisper, "They said they were trying to get in touch with you because your birth mother contacted them."

"Birth mother?" She must have heard wrong. Wasn't that a term used by someone who'd been adopted? She seemed to remember from some deep half-forgotten recess of her memory one of the obnoxious boys, Joel Beachy, using it. He'd been adopted as a tiny infant.

"They want you to call. As soon as possible. They said it was urgent, and you should have your birth certificate at hand when you call."

Lauren almost laughed out loud with relief. Her birth certificate? What? Not her social security card and her mother's maiden name, too?

"Take it easy, Mom," she said. "It's all a scam."

"It's…" Her voice dissolved into more sobs.

Lauren listened for a moment, frowning at the pellets of sleet on her windshield wipers. She needed to get to the hotel in Lancaster before the roads got too treacherous.

"Mom, Mom, Mom," she repeated, hoping to get past the weeping.

"Du duh net verscheteh," she repeated. "We so wanted a *boppli* of our own."

Lauren scowled. "Mom, what are you talking about? You had a baby. Me! Why are you letting a scam get to you? Those sleazeballs sit around and come up with ways to cheat people out of money and private information. Delete the message."

"I can't. I can't do that to your real mother."

"My..." This time, she couldn't repeat even the simple word.

"Not after the *wunderbaar* gift she gave us. We adopted you when you were only a few days old. We'd tried for years to have a *kind*, but God didn't bless us with a *boppli* until we were able to adopt you."

"What?" She struggled for another word. Usually she was the articulate one, the one who found the right words for a public relations campaign. All words had vanished from her head.

For a long moment, the only sound in the car was the rumble of its engine and the stoic swish-swish of the wipers. Her ears began to buzz as her vision contracted. She blinked. Hard.

She'd heard wrong. That was it. That had to be it. A glitch on the signal coming through the phone.

Trying to laugh, but sounding like a cackling goose being strangled, she said, "Mom, there must be something wrong with the phone line. I thought you said you adopted me."

"I did." Her mother's voice was suddenly as calm as a windless morning. "That's what I said."

Lauren's arm lowered the phone to her lap. The soft tap-tap-tap of the sleet on the windows and roof enclosed her into a private world where nothing felt real, her own private twilight zone with no connection to anything she'd known.

She was adopted? Was that what her mother was trying to say? Was that what her mother was so happy to have said that she now was her normal serene self?

Normal?

How could anything be normal when her parents had lied to her? How often had they scolded her when she'd tried to stretch the truth? They'd disciplined her for doing what they'd done without a hint of guilt at their hypocrisy.

"I've got to go," she said, then realized she wasn't holding the phone near her mouth. Lifting it, she didn't hold it to her ear as she repeated the words.

"Lauren—" Her mother's voice was distant and thin.

Like her grasp of the importance of not lying to her only child her whole life.

"I've got to go. The storm is getting bad, and it looks as if it's going to turn to snow at any moment. I can't afford to risk getting stuck. I don't even know where I could get a tow truck out here."

"Out here? Aren't you on Route 30?"

"No. I was detoured off."

"Then where are you?"

She didn't need this conversation right now. If she mentioned she was a mile or so from the Bliss Valley Covered Bridge, her mother would worry more than she had already. Lauren wasn't sure if she could hold it together herself much longer.

"I'll let you know when I get to the hotel. I need to get on the road. It's coming down hard. I want…" Her babbling hit a wall as she realized she had no idea what she wanted.

No, she knew what she wanted. She wanted time to rewind to a few minutes ago when she'd been ignorant of how her parents had lied to her every day of her life. No, not every day.

She must have spent some time with her biological mother, who'd abandoned her like a kitten by the side of the road and now wanted to intrude into her life.

Why?

What had changed after almost thirty years of silence? Of silence and lies.

"Lauren—"

For the first time in her life, Lauren hung up on her mother. Her *adoptive* mother.

She wrapped her arms around herself and shivered as great sobs roiled within her. They didn't come out, just built like a giant storm as her whole world shook beneath her.

Resting her head back against the seat, she stared at the dark curve of the car's roof. Her emotions swept over her, blowing away every bit of the sham her life had been and revealing the raw debris left in its aftermath.

The cold outside her became as strong as the ice within her, and she realized she couldn't sit by the road all night. She had work to do, a job that could be a stepping-stone to the next level of her career. Her breath caught. She'd been working so hard to get that promotion so she'd be able to help her parents, but what would their relationship be like now?

Pain cut across her forehead, and Lauren rubbed her brow with two fingers. She needed to get to the hotel before this headache became a blinding migraine. She tossed her phone onto the stack of folders on the passenger seat, then grimaced when it slid off. Stretching to pick it up, she was careful not to bump the gold folders. Each was embossed with the silhouette of an Amish buggy and horse superimposed over a pair of playing cards. Tomorrow, she'd hand them out to the first of two prospective developers. Each had a possible casino site in Lancaster County, but only one would be given approval from the Pennsylvania Gaming Control Board to build their casino. It was her job to make sure Krause-Matsui-Fitzgerald was chosen by the winner to handle their public relations.

Pressing the brake and clutch, Lauren lowered the hand brake in one motion. She started to ease the car onto the road, but halted as another vehicle went by, appearing out of the storm and disappearing into it too fast for the conditions. The black truck had been a shade darker than the road and the sky. Had its headlights been on?

Rolling the car into the right lane, she told herself to stop looking for trouble where there wasn't any. Of course, the driver had the headlights on. She hadn't seen the car and couldn't blame someone else because she was distracted.

Her attention returned to driving when the tires slid on ice. She concentrated on the road where the tire tracks from the truck were already fading. Sleet mixed with snow and fought the wipers' efforts to sweep it off the windshield. She wished she'd looked at the GPS app before she'd tossed aside her phone. She couldn't be more than ten or fifteen miles from her hotel, but it could take twice as long to get there tonight.

Her fingers tightened on the steering wheel as she descended a steep hill toward a covered bridge. It was over Bliss Creek. Most of the covered bridges in the county were only a single lane, so she must be sure no other vehicle was passing through it. She doubted many plain folks would be out in their gray buggies on such an inclement night, but she couldn't assume. Not after the bane of her childhood, Adam Hershberger, had lost his parents when a car sped through a covered bridge without checking that no other vehicle was inside it.

Adam and Samuel and Joel…and her one-time best friend Naomi Gingerich. She hadn't thought in years about any of the kids who would have graduated with her from the plain school. Were they still living in Bliss Valley? Regret clamped onto her. Though she didn't care what had happened to those three cruel boys, she should have made more of an effort to stay in touch with Naomi. The two of them had been inseparable until her parents had jumped the fence into the *Englisch* world a few months before eighth grade graduation.

She shoved the memories aside. Each memory made her think about her parents—her *adoptive* parents—and she couldn't deal with that. Not now.

Driving through the covered bridge gave her a momentary break from the storm. Her tires thumped on the wooden planks of the deck, the sound echoing against the walls. She slowed and gave her wipers a chance to clear the windshield. Again she kept her eyes on the road ahead of her. Looking at the interior of the bridge that she'd crossed often as a barefoot child would open her up again to the onslaught of memory and betrayal.

Ice pellets and snow struck the Beetle harder as she rolled out from beneath the bridge. Ahead of her, the road was untouched. The other car must have turned before crossing the creek. If the emergency vehicles had passed this way, their tracks had been obliterated.

Lightly touching the gas, Lauren drove toward the stop sign she knew was less than a quarter mile away. Even that slight acceleration was too much. Her tires slid. The car spun. She twirled the wheel one way, then the other, trying to drive out of the skid and away from the stone abutment curling away from the end of the bridge.

Then she hit something. Not along the road. In it.

The car bounced hard. First the front tires, then the back. The suspension protested with crunches and crashing sounds. Her seat belt caught, cutting off her breath. The wheel jumped out of her hands. She fought to grab it. The car headed for the guardrail and the creek beyond. She pulled the car to the center of the road. A strange thud came from the front as her wheels turned.

Everything but the storm stopped as Ringo slid to a halt. The snow continued to fall, and no lights were visible anywhere. Was the car all right? Was she?

Every muscle ached as if she'd been slammed from one side of the car to the other, and a heated path followed her seat belt over her shoulder and across her collarbone. She panted as adrenaline pumped through her like an oil gusher.

First, the conversation with her mother and now slamming into the world's worst pothole. What next? Didn't bad luck come in threes?

Don't put your faith in luck. Put your faith in God's will. When you do His will, all will be well.

"Get out of my head, Mom!" She groaned, hanging her head as another rush of sobs threatened to explode from her throat. "Why should I believe anything you've ever said?"

Pushing aside the serrated pain cutting into her heart, she told herself to focus on the issues at hand. She was parked in the middle of a country road while a storm raged around her. She glanced at the box on the passenger seat. The folders must be pristine when she handed them to the representatives from Carl Welsh Development and Pan-Lancaster Growth Initiatives, the two companies vying to build the lone casino that would be approved. She took another steadying breath. She was okay. The folders were okay. Now, how about Ringo?

Though she wanted to sit there with her eyes closed, she couldn't remain in the middle of the road. She sat straighter and eased her foot off the clutch to let the car roll forward and to the right so she was in the proper lane. For a second, she didn't feel or hear anything unusual. She dared to believe the car was undamaged.

Then she turned it onto the road curving up another hill.

The wheels wobbled, and she heard a dull clunk. She wasn't sure if the sound came from the wheels or the shocks or some other part, but hitting the pothole had damaged something in her car.

When she turned the steering wheel again and the sound grew louder, Lauren accepted the inevitable. Whatever was broken wasn't going to let her get to Lancaster. She needed to find someone to look Ringo over and repair him. She glanced at her watch. It was past six. Even if she could find a mechanic in a place where many of the vehicles were buggies with single horsepower, would the shop be open? As she turned the wheels to go around another curve, the strange thud warned her she didn't have any choice. She needed to get her car repaired.

A sign appeared out of the swirling snow.

"Frank's Auto Service. 1/4 mile ahead on the left."

Relieved, Lauren edged her car along the road. A battered concrete block building was ahead on the left. A trio of ice-encrusted cars were parked to one side and a dark house, that looked empty, was set behind it. Slowing, but not daring to stop, because she wasn't sure she could get the car going again, she wanted to cheer when she saw a light on inside. She pulled into the parking area in front and winced when her front passenger wheel dropped into another pothole. The thump from the front of the car was now accompanied by a grinding sound. Had she busted something else?

Grabbing her umbrella and purse, Lauren zipped her coat and pulled up her hood as she got out. She grimaced as she stepped into a puddle of icy slush. She winced at the cold, but after a quick glance at her car which *looked* okay, she rushed into the building.

Odors of gasoline and oil struck her as she entered the dim shop. Nobody stood behind the counter. Parts were stored in cubbyholes on either side of a door that must have led into the service bay. Through the door's window, she could see several cars, but the place appeared deserted.

There must be someone around. The door had been unlocked, and some lights were on.

As she pushed back her hood and shook water off one shoe and then the other, she noticed a sign on the counter.

"Ring bell. If nobody comes, look in the back."

That was at least clear.

She hit the bell. Twice. And waited, letting water drip off her umbrella. By the time the bell's cheery sound had died, she guessed nobody else had heard it. So she opened the door to the service bay.

"Frank?" she called.

"He's not here. Can I help you?" came a deep voice from beneath a pickup at the far side of the bay.

A man, who'd been lying under it, pushed his way out. Her eyes widened as his long legs emerged and she realized he was wearing broadfall trousers. The pants, which buttoned rather than zipped, were what Old Order Amish men wore.

What was an Amish man doing working on cars?

His worn light blue shirt was topped by black suspenders. A dark brown beard emerged, but not a long one, so she knew he hadn't been married for more than a few years. He pushed himself to his feet. As he bent to pick up an oil-stained cloth, he asked, "Can I help you? I'm Frank's assistant. Adam Hershberger."

She whipped her hood over her head and fought her feet that wanted to flee. She hadn't seen his face, so he might not have seen hers either. She'd been wrong when she thought the worst possible place to be tonight was the road leading through Bliss Valley.

The worst place was coming face-to-face with the person who'd tormented her during the most dreadful years of her life.

Chapter Two

Adam Hershberger wiped his hands on an already greasy towel as he took in the sight of the woman in front of him. Not that he could see much of her. The hood of her bright red puffy coat shadowed her face. A black tailored skirt matched her purse and shoes with high and narrow heels. She wasn't wearing gloves. Her slender fingers were burnished with red from the cold, which he'd felt nipping at him when she'd opened the door. He noticed, however, her knuckles were pale as she clasped her hands together.

She wasn't tall. The top of her hood would barely reach his shoulder, though he reminded himself an *Englisch* woman didn't wear a bonnet and starched *kapp* under the hood. She must be an inch or two taller than his original estimate. On the other hand, her high heels were a *dumm* choice for a stormy evening.

He watched as she clenched and unclenched her hands. She was eager to get out of there. Not many women wanted to spend time in a car repair shop. In fact, he'd never met one, which might have been the reason he liked coming to help his friend when he wasn't busy in his own small engine repair shop or working on his great-*grossdawdi*'s farm.

Or spending time with his daughter. A pinch of guilt reminded him he'd told Mary Beth that he'd be home tonight to tuck her in. She was four years old and still mourned her *mamm* who'd died two years ago. He knew he should be mourning, too, but he'd stayed stuck in numb disbelief that someone else in his life had died too young. It was easier to remain where he didn't have to feel too much, *gut* or bad.

He looked again at the *Englisch* woman. Maybe she was nervous about the storm. He glanced toward the garage doors at the other end of the bay. Sleet hit the dusty windows. He should have listened to *Grossdawdi* Ephraim. Ephraim Weaver was actually his great-*grossdawdi*, but everyone called the old man *Grossdawdi* Ephraim. He'd warned Adam that the storm tonight was going to be a nasty one. Once Adam found out what this *Englisch* lady wanted, he'd hitch his horse and head home. Sparks didn't like getting his hooves wet, and the old horse despised wintry weather.

"Can I help you?" he asked again, though what he wanted to ask was why she was hiding within her coat. Some *Englischers* felt uncomfortable around plain folk, and he guessed she'd been surprised to find him working in the shop. *Englischers* seemed to think because plain folk didn't use electricity in their house or drive motorized vehicles, they were as unaware of modern technology as someone from the Middle Ages.

"I need someone to look at my car." She wrapped her arms around herself. She spoke as if clenching her teeth to keep them from chattering with the cold, though it must be fifty degrees in the service bay. "I hit a pothole, and the front wheels are making a strange sound."

"What kind of strange sound?"

"Sort of a thud, like someone's kicking it."

"The engine?"

She shook her head. Or at least he thought she did, because her hood moved from side to side. Impatience sifted into her voice. "No! The problem is with one or both of the front wheels. Look, is Frank around?"

"Tonight's his night off. I can check it for you, if you'd like."

He waited for her to answer. Silence stretched between them like two desperate hands clutching each other on the edge of a cliff. He flinched. He hadn't thought of *that* day in years, though the memory of the day when, as a foolish kid, he'd eluded death continued to sneak into his nightmares almost a dozen years later.

"All right." Even though reluctance laced through her voice, he was grateful she'd spoken and scattered the thoughts he didn't want to have. The past was the past, and dredging it up was asking for trouble and pain and the grief haunting his every breath.

Adam tossed the cloth into a bucket beside the truck he'd been working on. "What are you driving?"

"A 1966 Beetle." She led the way through the door into the room where his friend greeted customers.

"Frank doesn't work on many foreign cars." He looked out the front window at where the small vehicle was almost lost in the mixture of snow and sleet, though it was parked close to the building. "Especially ones that old, but let me take a look. It may be something that can be fixed until you are able to get it to a mechanic who knows more about older Volkswagens than I do."

Her shoulders stiffened under her coat, and he wondered if he'd surprised her by knowing the manufacturer of her car. Did *Englischers* think plain people wore blinders so they were unaware of the world around them?

He went to the counter and opened a drawer. The flashlight that was supposed to be there was missing. Frank was a great mechanic, but he wasn't *gut* about, as his friend would say, putting his things away.

Grabbing his black coat and winter hat from pegs by the door, Adam pulled them on as he went into the storm. He was surprised when the woman followed him through the cold wind that tried to snatch his breath right out of his throat. Maybe she wasn't as finicky as her fancy clothing and high heels suggested.

Or maybe she didn't trust him to check the car.

Without a word, he dug into his pockets and pulled out his gloves. He offered them to her. Again time stood still as neither of them moved for what seemed like an hour. Probably only a few seconds passed before she took them and pulled them on, thanking him.

He had to admit she had a lovely voice. It wasn't high-pitched. Instead it was soft and low, very pleasing to his ear.

What was he thinking? He didn't want the entanglements of a woman now or in the foreseeable future. He had too many other important people in his life—his daughter, his great-*grossdawdi*, his two teen cousins who shared the old farmhouse—to deal with a woman's demands. Getting involved with an *Englisch* woman beyond fixing her car would prove how stupid he was.

When he turned to walk away from her car, she asked, "Where are you going?"

"I need a flashlight. I've got one in my buggy."

"You can use mine. I keep one in the car for emergencies."

"*Gut.* The less time we have to spend in the storm the better."

Letting her lead the way to the car, he stood aside as she opened the door and the glove compartment. She kept her hand on her door as the wind tried to snatch it away. Pulling out a flashlight, she switched it on.

He walked around the car and examined it. The beam was broken by sleet and snowflakes as he ran its light along the car's frame. "You said you hit a pothole, ain't so?"

"Just this side of the Bliss Valley Covered Bridge."

He grimaced. "That's a big pothole. Hard to miss."

Unsure how she'd react, he was amazed when she said, "The road was covered with snow, so I didn't see the hole in time. There should have been a sign to warn drivers."

"Everyone around here knows the pothole is there, so we avoid it."

"I would have driven around it, too…if I'd known it was there." Her chiding tone returned.

He was swept by the sensation he knew her, that they'd met before. As he thought about the *Englischers* living in and around Bliss Valley, no name came into his head.

Squatting, he aimed the flashlight in a slow circle around the front passenger wheel. He looked for a minute, then stood and without a word, walked around to the driver's side and did the same. He switched off the flashlight and handed it to her.

She stowed the flashlight in her car, then asked, "Do you think you can fix it?"

"We can fix anything if we can get the parts. From what you've said and a quick look, I'd say you've damaged the front struts. As I said, Frank doesn't work on foreign cars often, so I don't know if he's got parts for your Beetle."

"Is it drivable?" She grimaced as she hunched against the wind. "The roads are getting worse by the minute, but can I drive the car? At least far enough to find a place where they can fix it?"

"I wouldn't advise it. What you need is to get a full inspection of the suspension and the wheels." When she began to ask another question, he held up his hand. "Tomorrow we can get it on the lift and take a *gut* look. Until I can do that, we're spinning our wheels." He couldn't keep from grinning. "Sorry. I didn't mean to make light of your situation."

"I need to get to Lancaster tonight."

"I don't think that's going to happen. *Komm mol.* I mean, let's go. We can talk about this inside." He went to the door and opened it for her to precede him into the shop. Shaking snow and BB-sized ice off his shoulders, he set his hat on the counter and turned to her.

She pulled off his gloves and tossed them next to his hat on the counter. She sneezed, and her hood flew back to reveal her face. All color washed from it as his gaze crashed into hers as he was about to say, *Gesundheit.*

The word shriveled on his tongue, and he couldn't look away from her oval face. She was pretty with delicate features. Her light brown hair streaked with blond fell forward over eyes that were an amazing light purple.

Purple eyes, blond hair, headstrong, correct in everything she did and said.

His own eyes widened. Was it possible? Could the *Englischer* standing in front of him be a former classmate at Bliss Valley School?

Knowing he'd feel like a *dummkopf* if she said no, he asked, "Are you Laurene Nolt?"

She flinched, but replied, "Yes, but I go by Lauren now."

She didn't add more. She didn't need to. He could hear her accusing thoughts as if she screamed them. This beautiful woman standing in his friend's shop was the adult version of the young girl who'd been given the task of trying to tutor him when they were in their final year of school. She'd been cute as a fourteen-year-old, but time had enhanced the golden sheen of her hair and deepened her eyes' rich shade.

Scene after scene exploded out of his memory as he recalled the hours he'd spent with her. Each one buffeted him like a fist, more painful and humiliating than the previous one. Back then, the humiliation had been heaped on her. He'd made sure of that, but now regret threatened to drown even the simplest thought as he recalled what he'd put her through when she'd been trying to help him. She'd done her best, and he'd ridiculed her for it.

He'd thought that part of his past was dead and buried, but now it stood in front of him. Not it. *Her.* With her chin raised and cold disdain in her eyes, she was a living tribute to the foolish things he'd done in his life.

He guessed she wouldn't be leaving soon. Not when it would have been dangerous for her to try to drive her car with compromised struts. The storm would have the roads closed soon, if they weren't already. She was stuck in Bliss Valley at least for tonight, and he couldn't leave her stranded in the shop.

He owed her at least that much.

The urge to laugh clawed at his throat. He owed her so much more, but the best thing he could do for them—and for his family—was to get her somewhere safe tonight. Somewhere he could avoid her and the past she'd brought to life.

Where was a fairy godmother when she needed one?

Or a lamp with a genie ready to pop out and grant her three wishes?

Lauren knew what the very first one would have been. She wanted to be anywhere but where she was now. Stuck in a storm with Adam Hershberger instead of being at her comfy hotel in Lancaster, reviewing the materials for her presentation tomorrow morning.

She couldn't say such things to the man staring at her as if she were some bug. She doubted he'd understand. He'd get the urgency of preparing for her meeting, but not the fairy-tale references.

When her parents had jumped the fence and Lauren had entered a public high school, she'd had to take a crash course in the common cultural references everyone else took for granted. She'd read every fairy tale and watched endless Disney movies in an effort to figure out what her new classmates were talking about. Of course, she'd never believed those charming tales were true, but right now she sure wished one or two of them were. She could have used a magic carpet to fly her to Lancaster.

Explaining what had happened to her boss Patrick Giacchino—*Don't call me Pat!*—was something she didn't look forward to doing either. No one was ever supposed to bring him bad news. She guessed her rival Cassie filled his ears with everything he wanted to hear, so Lauren would have to choose her words carefully.

Her boss wasn't her problem now. Adam Hershberger was. She didn't lower her eyes as he continued to stare with his cool, brown eyes. He'd tried to intimidate her before, and she wouldn't let him do that again. Not with his steady gaze and not with his unexpected good looks. The last time she'd been in his company, he'd been a pimply-faced kid. His face hadn't been as sculpted. He'd seldom smiled. The few times he had was when he was about to do something to annoy her or Naomi. Or when he was exulting with his friends about what nasty thing one of them had done to aggravate her and Naomi.

She couldn't help wondering whom Adam had convinced to marry him. Though he didn't wear a wedding ring—no plain man did—his beard, which followed the strong line of his jaw, was an announcement to the world he'd spoken his vows with his chosen bride. Whom had he married? A girl from their district, or had he met someone from another district during a youth event? Maybe he'd married Naomi Gingerich.

Lauren shuddered at the thought. Naomi had been an adorable kid who was always smiling and trying to convince everyone else to do the same. She deserved someone better than Adam Hershberger, who'd been happiest when he was making Naomi and Lauren unhappy. The same went for his appalling buddies. She wondered where Joel and Samuel were now, but didn't care enough to ask and risk opening the door to that terrible time in her life when she'd had to stop every day after school at the outside pump and wash tearstains from her face. She hadn't wanted to let her parents know how the incessant teasing and remarks had torn at her soul.

I don't want to think about that, shouted a sensitive corner of her mind. Not that part of the past anyhow. Thinking about Naomi was something different. Shock rippled through her again when she realized it was likely her best friend was married. Most Amish women married when they were in their early twenties.

Pulling her cell phone out of her pocket, she tapped the screen. She'd had enough of Bliss Valley. Without looking up, she asked, "Do you know the name of the local cab company? There used to be one in Strasburg, but I don't remember its name." She waved a hand in his direction. "Forget it. I'll look up Uber."

"You're not going to get a taxi or an Uber out here," Adam said in a taut voice.

"The storm—"

"You know it's not just the storm." The condescension deepened in his voice. "This part of Bliss Valley has mostly plain farms, so the only drivers around are Keith or Madeleine Morris."

"They're still driving the Amish?" she blurted before she

could halt herself. When she'd been a kid, the married couple had seemed as old as the ancient trees along the creek. Plain people had used their service when needing to go farther or more quickly than a horse and buggy could.

"As far as I know." He leaned one hand on the counter. "You're not going to get them out on a night like this."

"I can't sleep here."

"There's The Acorn Farm Inn. It's a bed-and-breakfast. About a mile or so from here. They might have a room available tonight because it's off-season."

"I already have a hotel reservation in Lancaster."

"It looks like you're going to have to cancel."

She sighed. He made it sound simple, and his life was a lot simpler than hers. Off the top of her head, she could think of a half dozen calls she'd need to make because of the delay in getting to Lancaster. None of them would be easy calls, but she'd feel better once she was off the phone with Patrick.

"All right," she said. "I guess I don't have much choice. Point me in the direction of the B and B, and I'll be on my way."

"You plan to walk in this weather?"

A single look at the wind blowing ice and snow past the window kept her from retorting she was capable of walking a mile. She glanced at her heels. They were perfect for the office, but not for trudging through sleet and snow. Dismay dropped onto her shoulders. She almost laughed as she realized she hadn't thought about the extraordinary call with her mother since she'd gotten the bad news about her car.

When she didn't answer, he said, "I can drive you there."

The words *he didn't have to take her* burned on her lips, but she didn't speak them. If he didn't give her a lift, she'd be stuck all night in the mechanic's shop, which was getting colder by the minute.

"I guess I don't have any choice but to say thank you." The words emerged before she could halt them. She hadn't meant to sound snarky. He was doing her a favor, but she didn't want to be beholden to Adam Hershberger. It felt too much like doing a deal with the devil.

Again he stared at her for a long minute before he said, "*Komm mol.* No sense waiting for the roads to get worse. While you get your stuff out of your car, I'll get Sparks hitched up. Or do you need help getting your things from the car?"

"I'll be fine."

"*Gut.* Be as quick as you can." He grabbed his hat off the counter and tossed her his gloves again. As she grabbed them, he said, "You're a lot better at catching than you used to be."

Lauren thought of several sharp retorts, but not until after he'd left. Her mind was slow tonight. She'd had too many mental grenades thrown at her.

She jammed her hands into the gloves as she wished she had another option other than letting Adam drive her to The Acorn Farm Inn.

She didn't.

"This night is just getting better and better," she muttered as she stamped toward the exit.

The wind tried to rip the door out of her fingers, but Lauren forced it closed behind her. She half ran, half slid toward Ringo. Knocking her fist against the ice on the door handle, she was able to free it enough so she could open the door.

She grabbed her carry-on bag and looked at the box on the passenger seat. Several of the folders had fallen onto the floor. She checked to make sure they hadn't gotten wet. If the handouts for her presentations were ruined, the whole trip would be a waste.

Opening her coat, she shivered as the wind assaulted her. She pushed the folders under the left side of her coat, then zipped it closed. Pressing her right arm to her coat to pin the folders against her, she hefted her suitcase. It wasn't the first time she'd had to safeguard materials from the weather. She winced as cold water oozed through her heels. Her toes were freezing, and she guessed her shoes were ruined. She'd have to get a new pair before her first meeting.

Shadows coalesced into a dark gray buggy moving slowly toward her. She frowned when the metal wheels slid as Adam drew the horse to a stop a few paces away.

"Is it safe?" she asked when he jumped out and took her bag. She readjusted her arm so the folders didn't slide out.

"As safe as anything else is tonight." He opened the door on the passenger side and put her bag between the buggy's front and back seats. "We'll take it slow and hope anybody else on the road is being careful, too."

Lauren halted as she was reaching for a handle to help herself into the buggy. The vestige of grief in his voice touched a memory she'd long forgotten until earlier tonight. Adam's parents had been killed by a driver going too fast and slamming into their buggy. He'd been thrown clear and had been the only survivor of the accident. Left alone at ten years old, he'd come to Bliss Valley to live with Ephraim Weaver, his great-*grossdawdi*, and soon after began his reign of terror against the scholars in their one-room schoolhouse.

Deciding the best thing to say was nothing, she climbed into the buggy. She drew out the folders and settled them on her lap. She set her purse between her wet feet while Adam went around to the driver's side and got in. He reached past her to draw the sliding door closed, then did the same on his side. Flicking a couple of switches on the well-polished oak dash between them, he slapped the reins to command his horse to head out on the road.

The faint lights from the side of the buggy couldn't combat the storm, so the glow cut only a few feet in front of the horse's nose. Beneath the metal wheels, ice and snow crunched a warning. To go faster than a walk would be foolhardy.

A gentle warmth curled around Lauren's ankles, and she looked at a small heater connected to the battery that powered the lights and turn signals. Nothing much had changed with buggy design in the past fifteen years, but that wasn't a surprise. Any changes—and there weren't many—came slowly to an Amish community.

"Guess it's been a while since you've sat in a buggy," Adam said, his voice sounding deeper and more intimate in the close darkness of the buggy.

"Yes."

She caught the motion of his brows shooting up when she didn't reply, *"Ja"* as she once would have done. She was tempted to ask if he was the same guy he'd been the last time they'd seen each other, but she didn't need to ask. He was a married man. By now, he probably had a half dozen kids. Her lips twitched as she wished all those kids would give him as much trouble as he'd given her.

"What's so funny?" he asked.

"The story of how I ended up in a buggy tonight." She hoped he'd buy her half-truth. "It's not as if I came here to do the tourist things. I don't need someone to drive me around and explain about plain life, do I?"

"What *are* you doing here?"

"I've got meetings in Lancaster. I'm sure you've heard about the plans to build another casino in the county."

"I have." His words were clipped off as if he spoke them past compressed teeth. "You're involved in that?"

"Only one aspect. I work for a public relations firm." She took the box from beneath her coat and set it between them on the seat. "We work with the media to present a positive image of the companies we represent."

As Laurene went on, sounding as if she'd memorized a list of services provided by her employer, Adam stopped listening. He'd heard all he needed to. She was here to smooth the way for building a casino in Bliss Valley. She'd be working with the pushy, too-slick developers who'd been coming again and again to his great-*grossdawdi*'s farm in an effort to convince Ephraim Weaver to sell his land to them.

For a multistory parking garage.

First, the developers had tried a lowball offer because they thought his great-*grossdawdi* was a witless old man who didn't know the value of his land. They hadn't done that a second time. They must have learned that the Amish—especially Ephraim Weaver—were excellent businessmen and well aware of every penny of equity they had in their farms.

The developers had come back with another offer, this time a bit closer to the property's actual value and explained how they planned to leave one section of the land as it was for green space, as they called it. The rest, including where the barn and house stood, would be razed for the huge parking garage. For some reason, they'd made the offer to Adam, perhaps hoping he'd work with them to change *Grossdawdi* Ephraim's mind. He'd gotten them to leave by telling the two *Englischers* he'd speak with his great-*grossdawdi* about their offer.

He hadn't.

During the darkest days of Adam's childhood, Ephraim Weaver had taken a grief-stricken, angry, frightened *kind* into his home. Not once had his great-*grossdawdi* given up on him. Adam owed him more than he could ever repay, and keeping the vultures from the casino company away was a small way to even that debt.

He cut his eyes from the snow to the woman sitting beside him. She'd stopped talking, though he wasn't sure when. She was half-turned away in a pose that announced she despised the fact she was dependent on him to take her to the inn.

She had no idea, he knew, that if she'd been waiting all these years for a chance to get vengeance against him for all he'd put her through, she'd found the perfect way.

Chapter Three

Lauren wasn't sure if she would have known which road they were traveling on, even if the storm hadn't hidden every landmark. Adam had made three right turns and four lefts. At one point, they reached a low spot where water rushed across both lanes. He turned the buggy around and tried a different route. Still, they seemed to have gone way too far for what was supposed to have been a trip of around a mile. Though she was curious if he'd missed a road, she didn't ask.

Even in the shadowed buggy, she noted how stiff his shoulders had become. She must have said or done something that bothered him, but she had no idea what it was. Everyone in Lancaster County must know about the plans to build another casino. Such a plan wouldn't be popular among the deeply religious plain people, but nobody was asking them to patronize the casino when it was built.

If it was. There was no guarantee ground would ever be broken for the project. Until the gaming control board made a decision, everything was a what-if.

Her fingers ran over the logo on the top folder. She hadn't been bothered by the image of the Amish buggy and the playing cards when the art department first displayed it in the Krause-Matsui-Fitzgerald conference room. Now she was uneasy at using plain people as a selling point for the casino.

Why are you being so ridiculous? demanded the small voice in her head. Plain people were accustomed to having their lifestyle put on T-shirts, cups and every possible tchotchke. The image of a horse and a squared-off buggy was instantly identifiable.

Because the most horrible person she'd ever met was doing something decent was no reason for her to question the project. She wondered if she was trying to avoid thinking about the call she needed to make to her boss once she was settled in her room at the B and B.

The horse's hooves and the wheels on the icy snow battled with the shriek of gusts to counteract the uncomfortable silence in the buggy, but she said nothing. She couldn't think of anything to say. No, that wasn't true. She could think of a lot to say. However, asking Adam why he'd been so awful as a kid wouldn't have been the best way to start a conversation. Should she consider asking him why he, as a plain man, was working on cars? She told herself it was better they didn't dig into each other's life.

When Adam drew back on the reins, she wanted to shout with glee. They'd reached the inn. Its bright lights seared away the storm, holding it at bay as the buggy turned up a circular driveway toward a wide porch where rocking chairs would welcome people on a warm summer night.

He lifted her bag as if it weighed no more than one of the snowflakes. Telling her to wait where she was, he got out and came around to open the door on her side. Wind swirled around him to sweep icy pellets into the buggy. She flinched and noticed the horse did, too, as if a swarm of flies taunted him.

"Let me take that." Adam, who acted impervious to the storm, held out his hand for the box of folders. When she gave them to him, he looked at them. His mouth tightened into a straight line.

She knew he'd seen the logo, but she wasn't going to apologize. She couldn't imagine why he'd care one way or the other if another casino opened in Lancaster County. It wouldn't be the first.

Stepping out, she said, "Thanks for the ride." She took the box of folders and reached for her suitcase.

"I've got it." He turned on his heel and walked up the steps to the porch.

Lauren blinked as another light came on when he went to the door. It must have been motion activated, and she winced as the glare struck her eyes. Climbing the steps with care because the wood was slick with ice, she frowned at his back.

It was obvious Adam Hershberger hadn't changed in one important way. He still thought he knew more than everyone else. When Millie Hausman, their teacher that last year, had insisted Lauren tutor Adam, he'd sabotaged every effort she'd made to help him. He'd given her a big dose of attitude that suggested what she was doing was stupid and he didn't need her assistance.

"I can take it from here," she said as she grabbed the handle of her suitcase. "Thanks for the ride. I'll stop by in the morning to talk with Frank about my car. If I can't get a ride from someone, I'll wait for the plows to go through. Once the roads are clear, I can walk out to the garage."

He didn't release her bag as he leaned forward to push the doorbell. "We need to see if there's a room before I leave. What will you do if they're full?"

"Sleep on a sofa?"

"Or I could take you home with me."

"What?" She reached past him and rang the doorbell again. He'd made some crude remarks when they were teens, but she hadn't expected him—as a married Amish man—to proposition her.

"Stop blushing," he chided, but he smiled. "I wasn't suggesting anything inappropriate. We've got extra rooms at my great-*grossdawdi*'s house."

"You live with Ephraim?"

"*Ja*. Where else would we live?"

It was a reasonable question. Most Amish farms had several generations living under the same roof. To cover her embarrassment at forgetting something so basic about plain life, she asked, "How's Ephraim?"

"I'd say he's slowing down, but he wouldn't." His voice lost its hard edge when he spoke of his great-grandfather, and she understood why. Even when Adam had been at his most atrocious, Ephraim had treated her with kindness.

Adam started to add more, but halted when the door opened.

Brighter light spilled out onto the porch, making the floor glitter as if a handful of diamonds had been scattered across it. "Welcome to The Acorn Farm Inn. How...? Adam, is that you?" asked an elderly female voice. "What are you doing out on a night like this?"

"Can we come in?" he asked.

"Of course. Get in here and get warm."

Adam motioned for Lauren to lead the way into the house. Releasing her bag, she went inside. She wasn't going to linger outside in the cold and sleet while they argued over which one of them would carry her bag.

The front hall was decorated with country items city decorators would pay big bucks for, but Lauren guessed they'd been in the house for a long time. Paint was chipped and designs were simple, showing the age-browned samplers had been made by young women who had stolen time from other responsibilities to work on. She was careful to maneuver her box of folders so it didn't strike the primitive bench that looked as if it'd been taken out of an old New England church.

"Close the door, Adam!" called the woman. "I know for a fact you weren't raised in a barn."

Lauren tore her eyes away from the charming collection in the foyer to look at a woman who was sitting in a wheelchair with her right leg propped out in front of her like a battering ram. A heavy cast covered it from ankle to where it disappeared beneath her simple dark blue dress and black apron. Her thinning snow-white hair was pulled back in proper Mennonite style beneath what looked like a round, crocheted doily.

Shock raced through Lauren. The woman in the wheelchair was Sylvia Nolt, her great-aunt. Sylvia had married Lauren's father's uncle, a Mennonite. Though she'd been raised Old Order Amish, Sylvia had left to join her husband's church in nearby Strasburg. She hadn't been baptized, so, unlike Lauren's parents, she hadn't been shunned by the plain community.

As her eyes were caught by a steady gaze, *Aenti* Sylvia—the *Deitsch* word came instantly to mind—gasped and stretched out a hand. "Laurene? Is that you, *liebling*?"

Abruptly tears wanted to flood out of her eyes as she heard her aunt use the term Mom often had when talking to Lauren. *Liebling.* Sweetheart. How many times had her parents called her that? Countless, but each time they'd said it while knowing the secret they'd hidden from her.

At that thought, her eyes became dry as if someone had pulled a plug in a drain. A frisson of pain and betrayal slithered down her spine. When she made the mistake of looking toward Adam, she couldn't help wondering if his blatant teenage cruelty had been as awful as her parents lying to her throughout her life.

His brows lowered, and puzzlement burned in his dark eyes. What had he seen in her expression? She shifted so she faced her great-aunt and avoided giving him another chance to seek any chink in the armor she'd learned to build around herself since she'd been his easy victim.

"It is, *Aenti* Sylvia," she said with the best smile she could find. Bending to give her great-aunt a quick hug, she asked, "What happened to you?"

"A broken leg, as you can see." She tapped her knuckles on the heavy cast. "It was a nasty break, so I've got to keep weight off my leg for a few more months. Next time I need a trunk taken to the attic, I'll call a strong, young man like Adam. Thankfully, the girls who work here have been able to help me while I'm imprisoned in this chair and relegated to being the greeter."

"When did you open this bed-and-breakfast?"

"About ten years ago." She wagged a playful finger at Lauren. "You should come and visit more often to keep up on the goings-on in Bliss Valley."

Adam intruded to say, "Her car hit that big pothole by the Bliss Valley Covered Bridge, and it's going to need work. Do you have room for her tonight?"

"*Ja.* I've always got room for you, *liebling.*" She raised her hands to silence Lauren's next question. "You won't pay me a penny."

"She's here on business," Adam said. "I'm sure her company will cover the cost."

Aenti Sylvia frowned. "Stop talking nonsense! Laurene is family, and my family doesn't pay to stay under my roof." Her bright blue eyes sparkled as she motioned for them to follow her into a large living room filled with more antiques. "If you were out by the covered bridge, Laurene, did you see the fire?"

"I saw a lot of fire trucks and volunteers heading north."

Her great-aunt nodded as she turned her wheelchair to face them. "That makes sense. The fire was at the Lowe farm out on Willow Road."

"Which one?" Adam asked.

"Nettles John's farm."

Lauren didn't recognize the name, but the simple explanation clearly meant something to Adam whose mouth tightened at the nickname. With dozens of Lowe families in the county and more than twenty or thirty where the head of the household was named John, the nickname identified a specific John Lowe.

"House or barn?" he asked.

"I don't know," *Aenti* Sylvia said. "I was hoping you knew. Before I could hear much, the power went off."

"It blinked at Frank's shop, but never went out."

"It was out here for about ten minutes. By the time it came back on, the alerts were over." Her brows arched. "Aren't you a fireman, Adam?"

"My cousin and I are still in training. We won't get pagers to be called out until we've passed the last few tests."

"I'll call Dean Crofts tomorrow. He'll know."

Adam chuckled, surprising Lauren. "He should. He's the fire chief." His good humor vanished. "Let me know, will you? Whether it was the house or the barn, we'll need to get a plan together to raise them a new building. This is the sixth fire in the past three months."

"Six fires in three months?" Lauren asked, astonished. "In Bliss Valley?"

"*Ja,*" Adam replied.

"Don't you think that's suspicious?"

Aenti Sylvia replied, "The authorities are looking into each fire, but they haven't found anything to suggest the fires are connected. That's why, after the third one, I got the police scanner so I could hear what was going on."

"We're getting too *gut* at replacing what's been destroyed," Adam said with a sigh.

"That's right," *Aenti* Sylvia said as Lauren unzipped her coat because the house felt as hot as a blast furnace after being out in the bone-gnawing cold. "You're the deacon for this district, ain't so?"

Lauren halted with her coat half off. Adam was the district's deacon? Was this some kind of great cosmic joke? If so, she didn't appreciate God's sense of humor. When there was a need for a replacement minister or deacon, any married man in the congregation could have his name included in the lot. Who would have suggested Adam for such a position? It would have taken three members of the congregation to add his name in as a possible deacon. Who had memories so short they'd forgotten the trouble Adam and his partners in crime had caused?

"Are you staying the night, too, Adam?" her great-aunt went on.

Lauren stiffened at the thought of seeing her nemesis across the breakfast table in the morning. She hurried to finish taking off her coat so she didn't have to look at the others. When Adam said he needed to get home, she managed to keep her sigh of relief silent.

"It's not that far if I cut through your cornfield," he added.

"*Ja*," *Aenti* Sylvia replied. "Ephraim and Mary Beth will worry if you don't come home tonight."

Was Mary Beth his wife? Lauren couldn't remember anyone with that name when they were growing up.

"I'll leave the buggy here, if that's okay with you, Sylvia," he said.

"Certainly. There's room in the old barn if you want to pull it in."

"I may."

"And your horse?"

"I'll walk him across the field behind the inn. Safer on a stormy night, and Sparks likes sleeping in his own stall."

Her great-aunt nodded. "Don't let us keep you, Adam. I'm sure you and Laurene will have time to catch up while you're fixing her car. Wait a minute." She wheeled herself out of the room so quickly Lauren was surprised there weren't skid marks on the hardwood floors.

An awkward silence followed her departure. Her great-aunt enjoyed talking about anything with anyone. She was the complete opposite of her late husband. *Onkel* Bruce seldom had said more than hello when someone arrived and goodbye as they left.

Knowing she should say something, Lauren cleared her throat. "Thanks again for bringing me here. You were right. I don't think I could have found my way here without your help."

He nodded, but didn't speak until her great-aunt returned with a plate covered in foil on her lap. She offered it to him with a smile.

"I know how Mary Beth likes my triple chocolate chip cookies," *Aenti* Sylvia said. "Ephraim, too!" She flashed a smile at Lauren. "Don't worry, *liebling*. There are plenty in the kitchen still."

He took the plate. "*Danki*, Sylvia. I'll stop by in the morning to see how you're doing."

"We'll be fine." She waved both hands toward the door. "Get your horse and yourself home before you freeze. Take a lantern with you. You don't want to trip over stubble in the cornfield."

"I'll do that."

When Adam bent and gave *Aenti* Sylvia a quick kiss on the cheek, Lauren was astonished. It was clear her great-aunt had a good relationship with him and his family. She was relieved to hand Adam his gloves before he bid them good-night and left.

"Let's get you settled, Laurene," her great-aunt said as the front door closed in his wake.

"All right." It would be useless to tell her great-aunt she went by Lauren now. Once *Aenti* Sylvia set her mind on something, nothing changed it. "The inn is full tonight, so why don't you take my bedroom upstairs?"

"I don't want to put you out of your room."

"I'm not using it." She slapped her hand on the wheelchair's arm. "This won't do steps, so I'm using the extra room out beyond the kitchen. Use my room. It has a nice view." She laughed. "Not that you'll be able to enjoy it tonight."

"I've got a few calls to make to rearrange the meetings I was supposed to have tomorrow. I'll make them upstairs, so I won't bother you."

"You can't be a bother no matter how hard you might try." She seized Lauren's hands and held them between her own. "It's so *wunderbaar* to have you home again, Laurene. I wish Wayne and Ida had never taken you away."

She didn't know how to respond. When her parents had secreted her and themselves out of Bliss Valley in the middle of the night, she'd been heartbroken to leave behind family and grateful she didn't have to endure any more bullying from Adam and his friends. She'd become accustomed to an *Englisch* life. To her life. True, there were some things she didn't like about it. She'd spent so much time trying to get ahead at work her social life was nonexistent, and she despised that competition seemed to be the hallmark of her job. No life was perfect, right?

"I should make those calls, *Aenti* Sylvia."

"Go. There's *kaffi* and cookies in the kitchen, so help yourself."

"Do you need any help tonight?" She looked at her great-aunt's casted leg and wondered how she got in and out of bed.

"I'm fine, *kind*, but you're a *gut* girl to ask. After two months of being in this chair, I've learned how to take care of myself." She waved Lauren away as she had Adam. "Go and take care of your business. Then get a *gut* night's sleep. You'll be up early tomorrow to check on your car. You never were a patient girl." As Lauren reached for her suitcase to haul it upstairs, her great-aunt added, "It was kind of Adam to bring you here on such an awful night."

"It was." Again she found herself compelled to ask, "How far does he have to go to get home?"

"His great-*grossdawdi*'s farm backs up to this place. He doesn't have to go more than a quarter mile." Her face dropped into a worried frown. "I hope I put that foil on tightly enough. Mary Beth wouldn't ever forgive me if a single cookie is lost." Her expression lightened again. "Oh, maybe you don't know. Mary Beth is his daughter."

Wondering how many more revelations there could be tonight, Lauren kept her own face serene as she often had to do when someone asked a stupid question during a presentation. "It's nice of you to send cookies to her, *Aenti* Sylvia."

"She's a sweet *kind*, and since her *mamm* died—"

"Adam is a widower?" she blurted before she could halt herself.

"*Ja*, his wife died a couple of years ago. So sad, leaving that darling *kind* in a house filled with men who don't have any idea how to raise her. Don't get me wrong. Adam, Ephraim and the boys—" she didn't pause to explain who "the boys" were "—love her, but it's not the same as having a woman there."

Though questions caromed through her head, Lauren bid her great-aunt a good night. She balanced the box of folders as she toted it and her suitcase upstairs. Walking along the beautifully decorated hallway to the last door, she went into a dark room. She flipped on the lights and stared at the canopied bed and the furniture that looked as if it'd been handmade several centuries before.

Sleet tapped against the large window. When she went to close the gold-and-white-striped drapes, she saw a movement near the point where the storm swallowed everything.

It was a light. Squinting, she made out the forms of a man and a horse. It looked as if Adam had caught a vagrant star and held it in his hand as he led his horse across the snowy field. She saw him glance back more than once to make sure Sparks was all right. That didn't jibe with the boy who'd driven hell-for-leather whenever he and his friends got their hands on a buggy. How many vehicles had they "borrowed" and wrecked on their sprees? She could remember at least four, including her family's market buggy.

"Who are you, Adam Hershberger?" she asked. "Who are you really?"

Adam patted Sparks on the nose, then picked up the lantern and plate he would return to Sylvia in the morning. He doubted the cookies would last more than a few minutes once Mary Beth and his cousins realized what was under the foil.

"*Danki*, old friend, for being cooperative," he said. "I know how much you hate nasty weather."

The horse nodded his head as if agreeing with him.

With a laugh, Adam stroked the horse's nose again before leaving the barn and heading into the storm that showed no signs of abating. Why couldn't humans be as simple to understand as a horse or a gas engine? A horse wanted to be acknowledged and fed, and it would work hard pulling a buggy or a plow. An engine needed only to have its parts maintained or replaced, and it would work as it was designed to. People were far more complicated, especially women.

His *gut* humor faded when he heard the warning creak of ice-laden twigs rubbing against each other. If the storm lasted all night, there would be plenty of cleanup in the aftermath. Branches and even trees could collapse under the weight of the layers of sleet and snow.

Every tree in the woods along the edges of the property would have to be checked, and it was a task he couldn't leave to his young cousins. Though Simon was sixteen, on this chore, Adam wasn't willing to depend on Simon and his younger brother. Or to put them in danger. Broken branches got hung up in a tree and would later fall without warning. That could be deadly, one of the reasons they were labeled widow-makers. Sending the two boys to check the woods—even with stern warnings to be cautious—could end in tragedy.

That was something none of them needed. Again.

Bowing his head into the wind, he wished it would scour away his emotions. Most of the time he was able to submerge his feelings in the detachment that had settled on him after Vernita's death. He'd avoid feeling *gut* things if it kept him from having to suffer from the bad ones.

That hadn't worked tonight when Laurene—he needed to remember she used the *Englisch* name Lauren—Nolt burst out of the past. He shoved his hands into his pockets. The warmth left by her skin was gone from his gloves, but he couldn't forget how her slim hands had looked in them.

He forced her from his thoughts as he strode to the farmhouse. It was dim, unlike at Sylvia Nolt's house, because inside his great-*grossdawdi*'s house, there were only propane lamps.

Some hung from the ceiling. Others were floor lamps. He preferred the softer light to dazzling electrical fixtures.

Shrugging off his coat in the mudroom, he hung it and his black wool hat on the empty pegs next to the washing machine. He ignored the stacks of dirty clothes on the floor. Once the storm was past, he'd remind the boys to do the laundry. It was a job none of them liked, but it had to be done.

Adam carried the foil-wrapped plate into the large kitchen, which smelled of the leftover stew he'd told Simon to heat up for supper. His stomach growled, and he'd grab a few of Sylvia's delicious cookies after he tucked Mary Beth in.

He looked around the room and felt worry fall from his shoulders. Coming home did that for him. Stress had started piling up on him when he'd vowed to himself—and to God—that he'd do everything he could to keep a casino from being built next door to the farm. This was home as no other place had ever been, and he didn't want to watch as his great-*grossdawdi* was run off his land by greedy developers.

The scene in the kitchen was the same as it was most nights when he walked through the back door. His young cousins, Simon and his fifteen-year-old brother, Dale, had the newspaper spread across the table between them as they tried to read the sports section at the same time. *Grossdawdi* Ephraim was half-asleep in the rocking chair by the woodstove, his large German Bible open on his lap as it kept a thin quilt over his knees.

Dishes from the evening meal sat in the drainer while the teapot steamed on the cooking range. It always was ready in case someone wanted a cup of tea or hot chocolate.

Where was Mary Beth? Not one night in the four years since she'd been born had his daughter ever gone to bed without protest, so he guessed she wasn't in her room upstairs.

He knew it wasn't the usual way to do things. After Vernita

had died, Adam had returned to the family farm with Mary Beth, and instead of his great-*grossdawdi* moving into the little house that was connected to the main building by a sunporch, they all lived in the main house. That way, *Grossdawdi* Ephraim could continue to live where he had since he was born, and Adam's cousins could keep an eye on him while Adam was gone. Not that the boys were inside often, because they had jobs and chores and the other things that kept young men busy.

Adam's jaw worked at the thought. Simon was already debating which *rumspringa* group he wanted to join, and Dale would be making the same decision next year. Without his cousins suspecting anything, Adam had to figure out a way to steer them toward a very different group than the one he and his friends had joined when they were sixteen. When he'd thought he knew everything he needed to know.

Now he knew he didn't know anything.

Mary Beth's habit of staying up later than she should was his fault. After Vernita's death, he hadn't been able to deny his daughter anything. Yet now, when Mary Beth would be going to school in another couple of years, he needed to find a way to persuade her to go to bed earlier. No schoolteacher, especially one as strict as Teacher Millie, would be willing for Mary Beth to show up for school at noon.

He sighed as he gazed out the window at the frantic storm. It was a parent's job to train up a *kind*, and he'd let that task slide for too long.

His cousins looked up as he crossed the room. Like him, they'd come to live on the farm after they'd been orphaned. They could have been twins except that Simon had blue eyes and Dale brown. Both had the broad shoulders they'd inherited from their *daed*'s family. They could handle the hard work on the farm with the ease of a full-grown man. However, Adam had overheard enough of their conversations to know neither boy was interested in taking over the farm. Simon had been working in a neighbor's woodworking shop in between doing his chores on the farm, and Dale was interested only in training horses.

"We thought you'd gotten lost," Simon said with a grin.

"I had to stop by The Acorn Farm Inn to drop off a customer whose car broke down." For some reason, he was hesitant to say more.

Both boys looked at the counter where he'd left the foil-covered plate, and their eyes brightened.

"Cookies?" they asked at the same time.

"You can have two each."

"Just two?" asked Dale.

"Would you rather you had one?"

His cousins rolled their eyes, but grinned as they each snagged two cookies from beneath the foil. Eating them as fast as possible, the boys went back to debating which baseball team would have the best season.

Pausing to check his great-*grossdawdi* was asleep, Adam pulled another thin quilt off the sofa and draped it over the old man. His fingers lingered on his great-*grossdawdi*'s shoulders that weren't as powerful as they'd been a few years ago. *Grossdawdi* Ephraim had saved him from throwing away his life. It was time for Adam to repay his great-*grossdawdi*.

He would, even if he had to find a way to booby-trap Laurene Nolt's plans for the casino.

"Where's Mary Beth?" he asked his cousins.

Dale pointed at the ceiling.

Adam poured himself a cup of *kaffi* from the other pot on the stove and took the plate of cookies before heading upstairs. Boxes he'd never gotten around to unpacking lined the walls in his bedroom. He'd planned to unpack soon after they moved in, but the idea of going through the possessions he and Vernita had received as wedding gifts halted him every time. After a few months, he'd gotten used to having the boxes there and no longer paid much attention to them.

"What are you coloring?" he asked when he walked into his daughter's room.

Mary Beth was stretched on her stomach on the rag rug his great-*grossmammi* had made years ago from worn and torn clothing. His daughter looked at him, her dark brown eyes serious as they always were. She smiled more than he did, but not as much as a four-year-old discovering so much new and exciting about the world should. Again he blamed himself. He wasn't sure how to convince *himself* to change, so how could he help her?

Her blond hair had loosened from her braids and stuck out in every possible direction. He didn't do a very *gut* job of braiding, but he'd try again in the morning. There were so many things he hadn't ever guessed he'd need to know as a *daed*, but now he was both *daed* and *mamm*...

"Die zeit fer ins bett is nau," he said as he did each night when he reminded her it was time to go to bed.

Without a word, she gathered up her crayons and coloring book. She stood and put them on one of the boxes. She already wore her nightgown, so he waited while she brushed her teeth after she finished her two cookies, said her prayers and got into bed.

Her bedroom had space for a single bed and a small table. Her clothing was in his dresser and closet...and most of his was still in boxes. She remained silent as she waited for him to pull up the covers.

As he did, she asked, "Did you have fun tonight, *Daed*?" She asked him the same question each night he worked for Frank.

"Not as much fun as I would have had if I'd stayed home with you and *Grossdawdi* Ephraim," he replied as he did every time she asked that question. "What did you do for fun tonight?"

"Read Noah." Her nose wrinkled. "Why God gots spiders on the ark?"

He smiled in spite of her somber tone. "It's not our place to question God's plan. It's our place to be grateful He's made us a part of it."

"But spiders, *Daed*! They're yucky."

"Did you ever consider that God loves yucky creatures as much as the non-yucky ones? Don't forget. He made them all."

Mary Beth considered that, her brow furrowing with thought. "Guess so." Without a pause, she said, "Read me a story, *Daed*."

He fought to keep his smile in place. "It sounds as if *Grossdawdi* Ephraim already did, and you're trying to squeeze out a few more minutes before you go to sleep."

"That was Noah. Read kittens." She reached under her pillow and pulled out the book that he'd bought for her the last time they'd visited the Gordonville Book Store north of Paradise. "Please, *Daed*."

Taking the book, he sat on the edge of her bed. He opened to the first page and stared at the picture and the words beneath it. The painting of a *mamm* cat wearing a blue dress with white polka dots and an apron made more sense to him than the letters under it.

Holding the book so they both could see the illustrations, he told her the story he guessed the words might tell. He wondered how many more nights he'd have before his daughter discovered the secret he kept from everyone. He couldn't read. The words made no sense to him.

His fingers gripped the book harder when he thought of how Laurene had tried to help him with his schoolwork and of how he'd made fun of her so she didn't find out he'd never learned the most basic skills every other scholar had mastered. His wife hadn't suspected, and neither did his customers at the small engine repair shop. When he worked with Frank, he let his friend look up parts in the catalogs kept behind the counter, always finding a way to have grease on his hands when a customer needed something ordered. Using his cousins to make up invoices and deal with payments at his own small engine repair shop, he'd been able to hide he was as stupid and useless at math as he was with reading.

His older cousin now had a job. His daughter would soon go to school and learn to read herself. And Laurene Nolt was back in Bliss Valley. Somehow, he was going to have to keep them from destroying the fragile web of lies that hid the truth.

He wished he had some idea how.

Chapter Four

The insistent ring sliced into Lauren's sleep. Groping for her cell phone, her fingers found nothing but air. She forced her eyes open, irritated that she couldn't do as she'd often said she could: find her phone in her sleep.

Darkness met her eyes. For a moment, as the phone rang again, she tried to determine where she was. The streetlight opposite her bedroom window had kept her awake the first week after she'd moved into her apartment. She'd grown accustomed to how it lit her room even with the blinds drawn.

But it was dark at—she stared at the clock that was on the wrong side of the bed—4:31. Who called at such an uncivilized hour?

She groaned when the phone stopped ringing. Why hadn't she put it on silent before she'd gone to bed? She remembered. After a frustrating hour of calling the participants of the scheduled meetings to let them know the date and times had to be rescheduled and getting nothing but voice mail, she'd wanted to know right away when someone responded.

Stupid idea, but she'd been determined to make sure everybody got the message the meetings were being postponed, so they didn't attempt driving through the storm and ending up crashing as she had.

She groaned as she remembered the sound of Ringo's suspension as the tire hit the pothole. Her poor little car!

Groping for her phone, Lauren waited for the soft ding that would announce the caller had left a voice mail. She tried to get her eyes to stay open and focus on the screen.

"C'mon," she muttered. "Finish your message, so I can get back to sleep."

Instead of the signal for a voice mail, the phone began to ring again. She tilted it so she could see the screen. It was unchanged.

For a moment, she could only stare; then understanding dawned.

It wasn't her cell phone ringing. It was another phone, but whose?

She tried to see through the darkness. That was impossible, so she pushed herself up to sit and listened hard. The sound was coming from her right. In the direction of the clock. She thought she saw a faint outline beyond the bright red numbers. Her fingers settled on the old-fashioned arch of a desk phone that had been out-of-date when her grandparents were young.

Picking the receiver up, she hid her astonishment at how heavy the piece was. She put one end to her ear and croaked, "Yeah?"

"I'm sorry to wake you, Laurene." *Aenti* Sylvia's voice sounded chipper. "I know you're a guest, but I could use some help."

Lauren pulled the heavy quilt closer as cold struck. "What do you need?"

"As you've noticed by now, it's still snowing."

"Uh-huh." She hadn't noticed because she'd been looking at the inside of her eyelids, but, for some reason she couldn't explain other than her great-aunt's cheerful voice, being asleep at half past four made her feel guilty.

"The girls who prepare breakfast won't be able to get over here through the snow. Can you...?"

"Let me get dressed, and I'll be right down."

"*Ach*, you're a *gut* girl, Laurene. I knew I could count on you. Use the back stairs. You'll see the doorway to the right of my door when you come out into the hall." Without a pause, she went on, "Oh, and, Laurene, my guests will expect you to look plain while serving breakfast. You and I aren't too far off in size. Get a dress from my closet. There's a black apron there, too, you can use. You'll find a *kapp* in the top drawer of the dresser. *Danki*."

Aenti Sylvia expected her to wear plain clothes? Lauren hadn't worn the simple style of dress since her parents had woken her in the middle of the night and insisted she leave everything behind her and come with them in the van they'd hired. How ironic that the first time she wore one of the dresses again she'd been awoken in what felt like the middle of the night!

Muttering something her great-aunt must have assumed was the end to the call, Lauren heard the other phone click off. Did *Aenti* Sylvia have some sort of switchboard inside the inn? How else had she called from downstairs?

Deciding it didn't matter, Lauren yawned. "You can't sit here forever," she murmured to herself. "*Aenti* Sylvia is expecting you to help."

She grimaced as she slipped from beneath the warm quilt into the cold air that had claimed the room. Curling her toes into the rag rug by the bed, she bit back a groan when she stepped onto the icy hardwood floor. She didn't want to wake her great-aunt's guests.

Turning on the single light over the bed, Lauren half expected to see icicles hanging on the wall. She careened, still more than half-asleep, to what she guessed was the closet. She hadn't opened it last night because she'd found the bathroom on her first try.

A string hung at the right, inside the door. She pulled it, and a bare bulb assaulted her eyes. Holding up her hand, she stared at the neatly hung clothes. Simple, dark-colored dresses and a few lighter ones, all in the same simple cut that once she'd considered normal. How quickly she'd tossed aside plain clothing for stylish *Englisch* clothes!

She reached for the closest dress, a dark purple one, then yanked her hand back as if she'd grabbed a beehive. What would her parents think if they saw her dressed plain after they'd given up everything when they'd left?

Everything including the truth.

The soft words in her head were as bitter as the cold searing the soles of her feet. Somehow, and she blamed it on being routed out of a deep sleep, she'd forgotten about the call from her mother last night. The truth that she'd been adopted crashed over her like a tsunami, drowning her in grief and anger and betrayal and more emotions that were too primitive to have names.

"Why?" she whispered, too overwhelmed to speak louder, even in the empty room. "Why did you keep the secret? Did you think I'd love you less?"

No answer came for her questions.

Maybe her great-aunt would know. A teasing memory reminded her that *Aenti* Sylvia had always been an integral part of the Amish grapevine. A smile tugged at her lips. A grapevine sounded so much more pleasant than the truth of how rumors rushed through the community in spite of the plain-est residents having no phones or other modern technology in their houses. Gossip over a fence or a clothesline might have gone out of fashion for the rest of the world, but it remained an efficient way for news to flit from one farm to the next with the speed of a hawk diving toward its prey. Time spent in the phone shack, the small building that looked like an outhouse at the end of a farm lane and was shared by multiple families, could obtain someone plenty of gossip, though no one ever admitted to listening to messages meant for others.

None of that explained why her parents had kept the truth of her birth from her. Had it been shame that kept them from being honest with her? Shame because of themselves or shame because of her? Joel Beachy was the only person she'd known was adopted when she was growing up, and his family had never made a secret of it. Though that might have been, she had to admit, because they wanted to distance themselves from his ever-increasing series of crimes that began with stealing a pie from a windowsill and escalated to helping himself to an *Englisch* neighbor's car. She wondered if he'd changed his ways or if he'd jumped the fence, moving into the *Englisch* world, as he'd vowed he'd do once he was old enough not to be returned to his parents.

She was stalling for time. Taking a dress from the closet, she hurried to change. The skills she'd learned as a child to get dressed on a cold morning stood her in good stead when she slipped the nightgown partly off, then pulled the dress over her head. She closed the snaps along the front of the dress be-fore smoothing it over her hips at the same time as she stepped out of her nightgown.

A drawer in the dresser held black socks, and she could wear her own sneakers that were the same color. Going to the closet, she found a dark brown sweater on a shelf to wear over the black apron that fit over her shoulders and was pinned along the back of her waist. It wasn't a combination of colors she'd ever consider wearing to the office, but it would work for serving breakfast.

Getting the pins on the apron in place took longer than she'd expected, because her fingers were clumsy after years of no practice in reaching behind her back and slipping the pins in the exact spot. She was relieved when she finished after stabbing herself only a half dozen times; then she looked into the mirror over the dresser.

What was she going to do with her hair? No self-respecting plain female would appear in public without her head covered and her hair hidden beneath a *kapp*. She couldn't remember a time before her family left Lancaster County when she hadn't worn something on her head. Either an organdy *kapp* over her hair that had been twisted into a bun, or a bandanna tied at her nape beneath her braids.

Now she wore her hair in a stylish bob that curled on her shoulders. She recalled the day when her hair that had reached below her waist had been cut. She'd felt as if she'd lost five pounds, and her head no longer ached from having her hair pulled tightly into a bun.

How was she going to pretend to be a plain woman when she looked like what she was: a young businesswoman?

A quick search of the room didn't find anything to help. She was about to sneak into the kitchen and ask her great-aunt for help when she opened a drawer in a small dresser in the bathroom. She sighed with relief when she found a box of bobby pins. From the big dresser, she selected one of the round, white *kapps* her great-aunt wore. She lifted out one. It was much smaller than the heart-shaped *kapp* Lauren had worn while attending school. Placing it on her hair, she frowned. It sat farther back on her head, and she'd have to figure out a way to hide the bobby pins holding her short hair. Would anyone notice if she put her hair into a French twist?

Hoping nobody looked too closely, she twisted her hair along the back of her head. She jabbed in enough hairpins to keep it in place, then set the *kapp* on her head.

The image in the mirror shocked her. She could have been her mother as Lauren remembered her from her childhood.

She whirled away. No, not her mother. Her *adoptive* mother. A sob broke in her throat. How she wanted to curl up in bed and sob as if she were five years old!

Not giving in to the yearning, she crossed the room, pausing by the window. She raised the dark green shade and looked out. Through the swirling snow, she could see the faint glow of lights in what she knew must be the barn on Adam's great-grandfather's farm. *Grossdawdi* Ephraim. The name burst out of her memory as if she'd last spoken it yesterday. The man, who'd seemed so old then, had always made a point of speaking to her after church Sunday services. On the few occasions she'd gone to his house to study with Adam, the old man had made her feel as welcome as family.

Now, as she had then, she wondered how such a kind-hearted man could have a great-grandson as cruel as Adam had been. Not that she'd complained to *Grossdawdi* Ephraim or Teacher Millie, who'd insisted that she help Adam, or even her parents, though it'd taken almost every bit of her strength to keep from dissolving into tears each time she'd come home after one of the so-called study sessions. She'd kept the truth of those horrible hours to herself, not wanting to burden anyone else, especially her friend Naomi who also was the target of the trio's cruel comments and pranks.

Hearing a toilet flush elsewhere in the inn, Lauren knew she must not linger. Her hair was already coming out of the bobby pins, so she avoided looking at the mirror before going into the hall. A nearby door was labeled for employees' use only. She closed it behind her before hurrying down unadorned steps, drawn by the unmistakable scent of apple muffins.

Brighter light welcomed Lauren as she opened the door at the base of the staircase. Red-and-white gingham café curtains hung on the windows, and rag rugs in the same colors were scattered around the room. The cabinets and counters were made of oak. Hinges and knobs looked as if they'd been hand-crafted by a blacksmith and matched the pair of hanging lamps with black punched metal shades. Two things didn't belong. The huge commercial gas range stood out along one wall. A double-door refrigerator/freezer claimed another wall. The stainless steel glittered in the light from the overhead lamps.

Her great-aunt rolled her wheelchair into the room and around the old oak table in the middle of the room, smiling. "*Danki*, Laurene. I know those clothes might not be comfortable for you, but it's what my guests expect."

"It's not a problem," she lied. Ignoring the guilt clamping around her, because she didn't want to become like her parents who'd been false with her, she hurried to add, "I work in public relations, and I know perception can be everything when dealing with customers. How many guests will be at breakfast this morning?"

"An even dozen."

"If you tell me what you want to serve, I'll do my best to cook—"

"I'm handling the cooking." She gestured toward another table at the far end of the kitchen. It was topped by a collection of small appliances including a toaster and an electric griddle and a waffle iron. A double coffee maker was waiting to be filled, but a percolator bubbled on the stove. "I can handle this, if you'll serve the food in the dining room."

Amazed at how her great-aunt had converted her kitchen

so she could prepare breakfast from her wheelchair, Lauren asked, "Where's the dining room?"

"Through that swinging door." She gestured at a door opposite the range. "Oh, I should tell you. We—the girls who work here and I—have developed a code so we don't bang the door into each other. When we're going into the dining room, we call, 'Out.' When we're coming back, we call, 'In.' Of course, we don't shout because that would disturb the guests."

"I'll try to remember that."

"It's not so important when it's the two of us." She grinned and rapped her knuckles on the cast. "Though I wouldn't want this to bang into you."

"Or me into it."

Aenti Sylvia became serious. "I know the situation is complicated for you, Laurene, but I've got to say I thanked God last night for Him blessing me with a surprise visit from you. It's been too long since I've heard from your family, and I hope we have time to catch up."

"I hope so, too." She didn't want to burst her great-aunt's bubble by saying that as soon as her car was fixed, she needed to go.

Where? Where should she go? She needed to hold her meetings with the casino development companies, and she wasn't in any hurry to get home. There she would soon come face-to-face with her parents, and she wasn't ready.

"What do you think of my mini kitchen?" *Aenti* Sylvia asked. "Ephraim Weaver and his boys came over to help rearrange things so I could manage."

"His boys?"

"Adam and his cousins. Simon and Dale. The younger boys live with Ephraim, too, since they lost their parents."

"Lots of that going around," Lauren mumbled.

"What?" asked her great-aunt.

Instead of answering the question, she went to a nearby window and looked out. "I didn't expect the snowfall to last this long."

"Every once in a while, we get a late storm." She rolled her chair closer to the appliances and took down a bowl. Stirring its contents, she sighed. "*Ach*, it's a shame. The crocuses were blossoming, and the daffodils were about to come up. All of them have disappeared now."

"Spring flowers are hardy."

Aenti Sylvia laughed. "That's true. There have been some years when the crocuses poked their heads aboveground and then slipped down several times before it was warm long enough for them to stay up and flower. Now, Laurene, here's what I need you to do."

For the next two hours, while dawn approached and the windows gave a view of the snowy fields, Lauren was kept busy acting as her great-aunt's hands and feet. She gathered ingredients for the hearty breakfast served each morning at The Acorn Farm Inn. Eggs would be made to order, but her great-aunt served orange juice and apple cider along with coffee—or *kaffi*, as *Aenti* Sylvia called it as the plain people did—tea and milk. Apple-cinnamon muffins needed to be arranged in baskets to be placed along the table, which also had to be set for a dozen guests. Waffles, hash browns and toasted raisin bread would be made just before the guests sat down at eight. Lauren insisted on helping with the cooking and used the range, which was fueled by a pair of propane tanks next to one of the windows, while her great-aunt worked with the efficient setup on the other side of the kitchen.

They had everything ready by the time the sound of footfalls could be heard from upstairs. *Aenti* Sylvia had Lauren squat beside her chair, so she could repin Lauren's recalcitrant hair into place.

Lauren drew in a quick breath when she stepped into the dining room, carrying a stack of the simple menus where her great-aunt had listed the variety of foods available that morning. She'd given the guests enough time to select their chairs before she emerged from the kitchen, and every eye focused on her when she pushed aside the door.

She looked at the fire on the hearth of the gas fireplace and reflecting in the glass covering the face of the tall case clock that ticked in the hushed room. Faint sunlight shone on the snow and past old glass bottles set on the deep windowsills. Above them, small panes in the mullioned windows had wisps of air webs and bubbles in the handblown glass. The pale sunshine wasn't strong enough to reach the ceiling laced with beams as thick as the mantel.

A long table, with room for at least twenty people, had been placed in the center of the room on the wide-board heart-of-pine floors. Silver candlesticks, set on either side of a silver acorn, marked the center of the dark oak table.

The walls were divided by a chair rail. Dark boards ringed the lower half of the room, contrasting with the pale pink paint above. The mantel around the hearth was several shades deeper and topped by a portrait of someone in colonial era clothing. Lauren knew it couldn't have been an ancestor because nobody in their family would have sat for a portrait, considering it a graven image forbidden by the Ten Commandments.

The painting wasn't the only aberration that wouldn't have been found in a conservative Mennonite home. Around the dining room were pictures of bank barns decorated with Pennsylvania Dutch hex signs. Many of the tourists connected those emblems that looked as if they'd been picked up off a quilt or a blanket chest with the Amish, but barns on Amish farms were painted white or occasionally red.

"Good morn—*gute mariye*," Lauren corrected herself as the

guests appraised her. She hoped the pins holding her hair beneath her borrowed *kapp* wouldn't give up their grip.

The guests grinned at her use of *Deitsch* as if her words were the opening to a play they couldn't wait to see. And wasn't it? She was playing a role to help her great-aunt.

"Are you new?" asked one of the men. His gray hair was coiffed as if he spent as much time on it as the woman next to him, whom Lauren assumed was his wife, did on her perfect makeup. "I don't think we've seen you before."

"I'm Sylvia's great-niece. Laur—Laurene." She hoped nobody noticed her stumbling over her own name. "I'm visiting, so I'm helping today when we're snowed in and everyone else is snowed out." She girded herself for other questions.

She didn't need to worry. At the mention of the white stuff piling up outside, the conversation at the table focused on the weather. Half the guests seemed thrilled with the snow while the other half were annoyed. However, everyone agreed nothing could be done except wait out the storm.

As she filled cups with coffee or with hot water for tea, the lights hanging from the beams flickered. Silence clamped on the table as every face, including hers, turned upward as the bulbs dimmed, then regained strength. Nervous laughter circled the table.

"Does the power go out often here?" one elderly woman asked.

The man beside her said, "You shouldn't be asking her. The Amish aren't hooked to the electric grid. Remember what we learned during our buggy ride?"

"Oh, that's right." The woman flashed Lauren an embarrassed glance. "I'm sorry, young lady."

"You don't need to apologize," Lauren replied. No truer words had ever been spoken, because in the years since her family had moved away from Bliss Valley, she'd become as accustomed as these *Englisch* tourists to having lights come on with the flip of a switch. Even so, she couldn't keep from adding, "The Amish are well aware of many things you take for granted like electric lights, computers and cell phones, though you won't see them in the plain homes around here. Maybe in businesses."

That set off the discussion about which shops the guests had visited and which they hoped to see. While Lauren took orders for waffles and eggs and toast, with many of the guests electing to have everything on the menu, the lights fluttered again. Nobody else seemed to notice as they discussed which shops had the best quilts for sale. They were on the same topic when she served the food and refreshed everyone's coffee.

Hurrying into the kitchen, and remembering to announce she was coming through the swinging door, she took a deep breath of the scents of cinnamon and apples from the oven where her great-aunt was baking pies while overseeing breakfast. "*Aenti* Sylvia, I'm going to make some more coffee. I—"

Whatever she'd been about to add went out of her head, forgotten, when the back door opened. Snow swirled in before a shadowed form appeared out of the storm.

She gasped. Even with a collection of scarves draped over a heavy coat, she recognized the stern set of his shoulders and his height before her great-aunt asked, "What are you doing here, Adam?"

Staring was rude. Adam knew that, but he couldn't stop himself. How many times last night had he reminded himself that Laurene wasn't the girl he'd known years ago? When she stood in the middle of her great-*aenti*'s kitchen with a pot of *kaffi* in her hand and a *kapp* on her head, it was as if she'd stepped out of the past.

It was an illusion. He could see where bits of hair, far shorter than a plain woman's, had escaped her *kapp*. Her dress must have been borrowed from Sylvia, and her sneakers had a bright logo that wouldn't be sanctioned by any *Ordnung*.

"I wanted…" Adam scolded himself for hesitating as if he were a thief who'd been caught trying to sneak into the inn.

Pulling his gaze away from the astonishing sight of Laurene—no, Lauren!—Nolt dressed once again in plain clothes, he closed the door after *Grossdawdi* Ephraim. Did she guess that he was almost as disappointed as she must have been that she couldn't hop into her car and drive away this morning?

Not wanting his thoughts to be visible on his face, he looked at her great-*aenti* as he added, "That is, *Grossdawdi* Ephraim wanted to make sure everything was okay over here."

"He did, did he?" Sylvia rolled her eyes, reminding him of his cousins when they thought he wasn't looking. "You're an old *dummkopf* who worries too much, ain't so?"

"I'd say," *Grossdawdi* Ephraim said, "I'm worrying the right amount. God gave me a certain capacity for worrying, and that's what I'm using."

Sylvia laughed. "Take off your boots, so you don't track water and slush through the kitchen."

"Trust me," Adam said. "Any mud out there isn't only frozen but covered by a couple of feet of snow."

"Even so, wet footprints across the floor can cause trouble. I'm keeping Laurene busy enough. She doesn't need to add mopping the floor to her to-do list."

At the mention of her name, he couldn't halt himself from looking at where Lauren stood in silence. There was no more expression on her face than on the *kaffi* pot.

"I understand." He had to wonder if the trite words were for Lauren or her great-*aenti*.

"How about a cup of *kaffi*?" Sylvia asked.

He didn't let her lighthearted question fool him. Sylvia Nolt was as intuitive as Lauren used to be. As she probably still was.

Realizing that he might be revealing far too much by looking at Lauren, he tore his gaze from her and turned to her great-*aenti*. Not even bothering to try to fake a smile, he said, "That sounds *wunderbaar.*"

"*Danki*, Sylvia," his great-*grossdawdi* said, aiming a frown at him.

Why? Because Adam hadn't thanked their neighbor for her offer? Or for some other reason? When the old man's eyes shifted toward Lauren, Adam pretended not to notice.

Sylvia began, "Laurene, will you—"

"I know where the cups are," Adam said, taking note of how Lauren's hand was clenched at her side. He didn't need to be a mind reader to know that she was annoyed he'd come to the inn.

Too bad, was his instantaneous reaction, followed by a quick supplication. *God forgive me for not caring what she feels.* The prayer surprised him as much as his unkind thoughts.

It wasn't as if he didn't recall far too many details about how he'd treated her when they were younger. He'd been cruel to her, taking out his frustration with his own inadequacies on her because she was the closest and easiest target. Shame rushed through him. He'd thought he had overcome those youthful tendencies to lash out at someone when he was upset. Seeing Lauren Nolt had brought them to the forefront again.

"I need to make more coffee," Lauren said into the strained silence after he'd interrupted Sylvia. "It'll be just a few minutes."

"Don't make extra for us," Adam said at the same time his great-*grossdawdi* said as he pulled off his glove and scratched at his hand, "We'll wait."

"It's no problem. *Aenti* Sylvia's guests will want more." She turned her back on him and went to the *kaffi* machine.

Her great-*aenti* glanced at *Grossdawdi* Ephraim with what looked like a conspiratorial smile. Conspiring about what? If, in some misguided attempt at matchmaking, Sylvia thought he and Lauren would pick up their relationship where it'd left off, she was wrong. He'd left that horrible kid behind.

Or at least he'd thought so until he'd heard the cruel thoughts in his own head. Were old habits so hard to break? He'd thought God had silenced that part of his anger, but it still simmered in him. It was an appalling realization.

Again he covered his discomfort. "We came over in the sleigh. That way, we were able to bring three hams, so you'll be able to feed your snowbound guests tonight."

"That wasn't necessary, Adam."

"Tell my great-*grossdawdi* that." His laugh sounded fake in his own ears.

Maybe not in Sylvia's, because she smiled and said, "You can be sure that I will." She wagged a finger at his great-*grossdawdi*.

Usually Adam found the verbal jousting between them amusing, but as his gaze kept slipping toward Lauren, he could tell how uneasy she was this morning. *Ja*, it'd been a shock to see her in plain clothing again, but he couldn't understand why she acted as guilty as he had after opening the gate and letting out a neighbor's flock of sheep one night with his friends.

"Put them in the refrigerator in the utility room, if you don't mind, Adam," the older woman said. "I'll keep one for breakfast tomorrow. Ephraim, will you come and check that curtain rod in the living room for me?"

The last thing Adam wanted was for his great-*grossdawdi* to climb a ladder, but he didn't get a chance to reply before Sylvia wheeled herself out with *Grossdawdi* Ephraim following.

Leaving him alone with Lauren, who had spoken only once to him since he'd walked into the kitchen.

Adam took a deep breath, drawing in the scents of baking pies and *kaffi* and bacon. He hoped she didn't hear his stomach grumble its demands to sample each one. "It's *gut* of you to help your great-*aenti*," he said, not wanting the tension to escalate again.

"It's the least I can do when she opened her home to me last night." She poured water into the *kaffi* maker, then slid the pot into place. She didn't face him. "How long has *Grossdawdi* Ephraim been sick?"

"Sick? He's fine."

"He doesn't look it. He looks pale."

"He gets that way in the winter. He'll look better once he can get out in the sunshine."

She still kept her back to him. "Are you sure? His hands looked swollen and as if he's got a rash. Has he been to see a doctor?"

"You know how he is, as stubborn as a brace of mules."

"If he were my great-grandfather…" She didn't finish her sentence. "Look. It's not my business, and I shouldn't be interfering. I guess I'm on edge about everything right now."

Adam was glad she'd changed the subject. He *was* worried about *Grossdawdi* Ephraim's health, but each time he'd asked, the old man had assured Adam that he was fine.

"I know you're upset," he said. "If it's because I was staring at you when we came in, I'm sorry." He couldn't halt himself from adding, "It was a shock to see the transformation."

She turned toward him, and he was pleased to see her faint smile. "You gawking at me isn't the problem. I couldn't believe my own reflection when I saw it in a mirror."

"If that's not the problem, what did I do to upset you?"

"What makes you think I'm upset because of you?" Her expressive brows lowered in a frown.

"Until now, you haven't said two words to me in a pleasant voice this morning."

She rolled her eyes and shook her head. "I know you think the whole universe revolves around you, Adam Hershberger."

"I don't. I—"

"I don't want to hear it." She waved him away as if he were a noxious gnat. "Give me a break, will you?"

He halted his sharp reply. She was right. He was pushing her as he had when they were kids. Were old habits so ingrained that even fifteen years later it was easy to fall into the same patterns? He wasn't the boy he'd been then, so why was he acting the same?

"I'm sorry. I know it's been tough with your car breaking down and being stuck here when you intended to be somewhere else today."

"That's the least of it."

"Least? Isn't that enough?"

"You'd think so, wouldn't you? But, no!" She flung out her hands as if washing them of everything around her, including him. He realized how mistaken he was to think he was part of the problem when she blurted, "No, that's not enough! I had to find out last night in the middle of the storm with fire trucks flying by at top speed that I'm adopted!"

He stared at her in disbelief. He'd heard her wrong. He must have. Everyone in Bliss Valley knew the story of how long Wayne and Ida Nolt had waited for a *kind* and how when they'd just about given up, God had blessed them with a daughter. He'd heard his own great-*grossdawdi* repeat those words. *Grossdawdi* Ephraim had told the story when Adam had been impatient with something in his life and resented God for not answering his prayers fast enough.

"I don't understand," he said. "Why didn't you know before this?"

Her lips tightened until the corners of her mouth were puckered with white. "That's the big question, isn't it?"

Chapter Five

A heavy hush consumed the space, and Lauren struggled to draw in a breath. She shook her head. Wasting her time wishing she could retract her words would be silly. For the first time, she wondered if anyone else in Bliss Valley had known the truth.

Not Adam. The shock on his face made that clear.

"I don't believe it," he said.

"It doesn't matter if you believe it or not." Hating how sharp her voice sounded, she took a steadying breath to center herself. "It's the truth. Apparently." She couldn't keep herself from adding the last word.

"So you found out last night?"

"Yes."

He rubbed his hands through the beard edging his strong jaw. "Why, after all these years, did your parents tell you now?"

"My mother told me that they got a call from an attorney—"

"Which they could have never told you about."

"My parents are honest with me!" she retorted, then faltered when she realized how stupid her words sounded. She was defending the indefensible. *That's the way to lose any negotiation*, came her boss's voice in her head. *When you're standing on slippery ground, grab onto facts and let go of everything else. It's the only way to win.*

Her parents *hadn't* been honest with her about her birth.

"We're not debating that," Adam said. "I want you to see the facts."

"What facts? Other than I'm apparently adopted, I mean." Why couldn't she stop using *apparently*? She didn't want to believe what she'd been told, but why would her mother make up a lie about her being adopted if she wasn't?

"Can't you see it from their side?"

She stared at him, searching for something to say that wasn't a lie.

"Don't you see what they could have done and how difficult the choice must have been for them?"

Why was Adam being the more reasonable half of this conversation? He'd never been the least bit sensible when they were younger. The times she'd tried to help him with his homework in the weeks before her parents had moved them away from Bliss Valley had been disastrous. Adam had done everything he could to disrupt her attempts to explain to him what he should understand and refused in the snidest tone possible to do something as simple as read her a short paragraph that laid out a basic math problem.

So many words burned on her tongue, but she refused to speak a single one. For all she knew, he'd found new ways to irritate her and had come over to inflict them on her. She felt the childish yearning to throw the past into his face. She almost asked if he'd been as petulant and cruel with his late wife.

Did he treat his daughter with the same disdain he'd shown her when they were kids?

No, she couldn't say that. Lowering herself to his level would make her as loathsome as he was. She'd always taken the higher ground with him.

...be patient toward all men, came the words into her mind. *See that none render evil for evil unto any man; but ever follow that which is good, both among yourselves, and to all men. Rejoice evermore. Pray without ceasing. In every thing give thanks: for this is the will of God in Christ Jesus concerning you. Quench not the Spirit. Despise not prophesyings. Prove all things; hold fast that which is good. Abstain from all appearance of evil.*

Even before she'd first met Adam and he became as troublesome as a nettle in her bare foot, her father had insisted she memorize those simple verses from 1 Thessalonians. He'd often read them during evening prayers along with the exhortation from Matthew always to turn the other cheek, telling her that if she followed those simple rules set forth by Jesus and His apostles, everything would turn out okay.

She'd struggled with obeying when tormented by Adam and his friends. She hadn't expected she'd face the same challenge now. She'd assumed—and hoped—she'd never have to talk to him ever again.

"I haven't had much time to consider everything, and there's a lot to consider," Lauren said, turning to the oven to check on her great-aunt's pies. They smelled as if they'd need to come out soon, and opening the oven door gave her an excuse not to look at Adam. "A ton of stuff has happened since I discovered the truth last night."

He started to answer, then like her, seemed to think better of it because he halted in the middle of a word. That startled her. The Adam Hershberger she'd known had been infamous among the scholars in their small school for spitting out the first thing that came into his head. If it'd been the right answer—which it seldom was—fine. If it hadn't been, he made sure that it was something sure to set off his cronies. Samuel and Joel had acted as if they thought Adam was the funniest person ever born.

She'd thought all of them were immature jerks, and she didn't care to find out if they'd grown up. It wasn't as if she planned to stay in Bliss Valley long. Once Ringo was repaired, she'd get out of here. She'd go...

Her fingers tightened on the oven door's handle. She needed to decide where she'd go once she finished the meetings in Lancaster. Not home to her parents, or at least not until she had her emotions under control and was ready to confront them about a lifetime of lies. Her own apartment wasn't much more than a place to eat and sleep. It'd never felt like home. All her mementos from her life after the Amish remained in boxes in her walk-in closet. She'd tossed a blanket over them after she'd moved in, telling herself she didn't want them to get dusty. Since then, it'd been simple to forget the boxes were there.

Telling herself not to fret about things that didn't matter when she had meetings to reschedule and a promotion to get once she nailed down a contract with the winning developer, Lauren peeked into the oven. The pies needed at least another fifteen minutes for the crust to become the perfect golden brown.

"Are you going to meet your birth *mamm*?" Adam asked from behind her.

Trust him to get right to the most painful aspect of the whole situation and then jab at her with his sharp question. Straightening and walking past him toward the dining room, she said, "I don't know." At the last moment she remembered to add in case someone was on the other side of the door, "Out."

"You don't..." He trailed after her. "How can you *not* know?"

"I don't know," she repeated again. "It's not simple."

"Why not? You either want to meet your birth *mamm*, or you don't."

"It must be so nice and comfortable to live in a world where you see everything in black-and-white." She picked up the stack of plates and headed toward the kitchen. "In!"

Again he followed her, holding the door aside as she went to the sink and placed the dishes in the sudsy water there. She grabbed the dishrag and started to clean them into the garbage disposal. A feeling of convoluted déjà vu struck her. She was in Bliss Valley in what appeared to be a plain house, but it was filled with appliances and electronics that hadn't been found in the home where she'd first lived with her parents. Yet, now, her parents had such conveniences in their small cottage in Bryn Mawr, though her mother seldom used anything like a garbage disposal or dishwasher at home. In the big house, her mother took advantage of the time-saving devices.

Her world was becoming a fun house filled with cracked and distorted mirrors, reflecting layer upon layer of disconnected images of people and places and situations in juxtaposition one atop another. Nothing felt real.

All she wanted to do was escape.

Wiping her hands on a towel and grabbing an empty tray, she said in a voice that didn't sound like her own, "I've got work to do."

She didn't give Adam a chance to answer as she rushed out of the kitchen, leaving the door swinging in her wake. She needed to escape.

To where?

Adam was dumbfounded, but put out his hand to keep the door between Sylvia's kitchen and dining room from slamming against the cupboards. Dents in the wood announced where the edge had struck it many times in the past.

I should come over and put a doorstop on it, so she doesn't have to worry about more damage, observed one section of his mind while the rest tried to figure out why Lauren was so different from the way he remembered her.

He was used to his brain working on two different problems at the same time. Multitasking was a way of life for him when he had to move from taking care of his family to overseeing work on the farm to the way-too-few hours he got to catch up with jobs at his small engine shop or at Frank's garage. Now Lauren was sneaking into his thoughts whenever he let his mind wander.

What had changed her? She used to be willing to rush in where angels feared to tread if she thought she could make a difference. Why else would she have put up with his efforts to end their tutoring sessions before she could discover the truth that he couldn't read? He hadn't expected the *Englisch* Lauren to be more timid than the plain Laurene.

When he went into the dining room, she scowled at him and said, "You're supposed to say 'Out' when you leave the kitchen."

"Why? There's nobody in the room but the two of us."

"You don't know that. If someone's standing on the other side of the door, they could get hit."

"*If* someone was there." With a pair of long steps, he moved between her and the table, making her stop as she gathered up more dirty dishes. "Look, if you don't want to talk about this whole adoption thing—"

"It's not an adoption *thing*. It's my life. I thought I knew who I was. Now I'm not sure."

Adam had to admit what she'd said made sense. Maybe she hadn't been as altered by her *Englisch* life as he'd begun to think. When he paused himself to consider what she'd been dealing with during the past twenty-four hours, he doubted he would have handled it any better than she was.

Edging away a half step to let her pick up another empty cup and put it on the tray, he said, "This must be a shock."

"You think?"

His brows lowered. "Sarcasm isn't going to help anything."

"No? It's the only thing that's making me feel the least bit normal now."

"You're usually sarcastic?"

He was shocked again. The Laurene Nolt he'd known never had a cruel word to stay to anyone, not even him when he'd irritated her, hoping her too-*gut*-to-be-real facade would shatter and show him she wasn't as perfect as she tried to be.

"No," she replied and walked past him.

"Then why...?" He waved aside any answer she might have given him while she glowered at him. "Okay, I get it. Your life has been turned inside out."

"You think?" She sighed and put the tray on the table. "I'm sorry, Adam. I'm not mad at you any longer. I need time to think about what I've been told."

He knew he should pay attention to everything she'd said, but a few of her words reverberated through his head. *I'm not mad at you any longer. Any longer.* How long had she been angry with him after she and her family had hightailed it out of Bliss Valley?

"I can understand that," he said, knowing he had to answer her. "I'm sorry to be pressing you. I've never met anyone who's been in your situation."

"Me neither. That's why I need to figure this out on my own."

"You don't have to do it on your own. Your great-*aenti*

would be glad to help, I'm sure." He didn't hesitate as he added, "I'd be glad to offer any advice I can."

"Thanks." Her tone made it clear she thought he was being polite. "I'm being honest, Adam."

"You always were."

A swift smile raced across her lips, gone almost before he'd realized it was there. "You believe that?" Again she didn't wait for him to reply. "I was honest when I said I didn't know if I'm going to speak with my birth mother. I won't know until I call the lawyer's office."

"So you're going to call?"

"I don't know." The words burst out of her in a half sob. "I know I should, but I don't know if I'm ready to face the truth yet."

Picking up the last few cups, he set them on the tray next to the ones she'd collected. "Can I ask you one more question?"

"Just one?" She laughed, this time without a hint of humor. "I don't know if you're capable of limiting yourself to one, but go ahead."

"Do you think your folks left Bliss Valley because they wanted to make sure your birth family wouldn't find you?"

"If they did, then it was all for nothing. My mother was contacted by the lawyer at home in Bryn Mawr."

"That's where you've been living all this time?"

"That's where they've been living. I was there until I went to college."

Now that might have been the first thing she'd said that hadn't shocked him. As much as she'd loved learning and reading and studying, he wasn't surprised she'd gone on to attend an *Englisch* high school and then to college while he'd finished with formal schooling a few months after she'd left. He'd gone to work with *Grossdawdi* Ephraim and had also done an apprenticeship in Wyman Richart's small engine repair shop until he could open his own business almost six years later. About the same time as Lauren had been graduating from college. That their lives had continued on such parallel paths unsettled him for a reason he couldn't name.

As she picked up the tray, walked to the door, announced "In" and went into the kitchen, he wanted to ask more questions. He didn't.

Instead she did as she put the tray on the counter. "Is your friend's garage open today?"

"Unlikely. He works plowing out people's driveways after snowstorms, so he'll be busy all day."

"Tomorrow?"

"*Ja*, unless the storm keeps going."

She pointed to the window behind him. "The sun's coming out."

"So it is." He was relieved to see a few lazy flakes wafting past the glass. "Looks like the worst is behind us. The roads should be plowed by tomorrow morning. I can come over and take you to talk to Frank." Not wanting her to give him a list of reasons why that wouldn't be a *gut* idea, he hurried on. "Why don't I stop by around nine—"

"No need. I'll give him a call."

He nodded, getting the message that she didn't want to spend any more time with him. "All right. I should get *Gross-dawdi* Ephraim and—"

"He's out by the sleigh."

"What's he doing out there in the cold?" Shaking his head, he reached for the knob on the door.

"Adam?" she called.

"*Ja.*"

"Thanks for bringing over the hams for *Aenti* Sylvia's guests."

"*Du bischt wilkumm.* I mean, you're welcome."

"I haven't forgotten *Deitsch*."

"I'm glad to hear that."

"Why?"

Another question he couldn't answer. Or didn't want to. She didn't have any reasons to remember her past—at least with him—with any warmth. There had to have been a reason her parents took her and left their lives in Bliss Valley. If he said he was glad she'd remained connected with her heritage, she might think he looked down on her *Englisch* life.

Right from the moment he met her, he'd admired Laurene Nolt. Her brains, her kind heart, her senses of humor and fair play...and her beauty. The cute girl had become a lovely woman, and it'd never been more evident than this morning when her cheeks were ruddy with her high emotions.

As he stepped out into the snow, he was grateful for the cold. It eased the heat that had swarmed through him when his gaze had swept over her delicate features and was caught by her *wunderbaar* purple eyes. He walked to the sleigh, knowing he might have been smarter as an attitude-filled teen than now as a man, because keeping Laurene at bay had been easier then than it was now.

One thing hadn't changed. He still hadn't figured a way to get her out of his mind.

Chapter Six

After taking the luscious smelling pies out of the oven, Lauren finished filling the dishwasher and cleaned the kitchen. Her skills probably weren't a match for her great-aunt's or of the girls who worked in the inn, but she did the best she could.

Why was Adam being so obtuse about his great-*grossdawdi*'s health? One look at the old man with his ashen skin and his swollen hands had warned her that he might be ill. Or could Adam be right, and it was simply the cold affecting *Grossdawdi* Ephraim?

Her mind was whirling in too many different directions. She stretched to hang a damp towel on the pole by the window. Something clunked in her apron pocket as it brushed a counter. She took out her phone and checked for any updates.

Fifteen minutes later, she still stood in the kitchen. In her right hand was her phone. She looked at the numbers she'd written on the page in her left. It was the phone number for Charles Satterfield, attorney-at-law. Her mother had sent it to her in the first of more than a half dozen texts Lauren had found on her phone amidst ones from her boss Patrick. There also had been almost as many voice messages. She checked most of them, but hadn't listened to the ones from her parents' number.

Instead she'd called Patrick and brought him up-to-date. The development companies were interested in meeting with her and promised to call her once they'd checked their calendars for the next few days. She'd thought that was good news. Patrick, however, had been furious.

Be grateful, Patrick had told her in his snippiest tone, *that the storm covered such a big area. Otherwise, they—and I—might not be so forgiving.*

Oh, how she wished she'd called him on her great-aunt's landline so she could have slammed down the receiver! Not that such histrionics would have done her any good.

They'd failed during her final call with Tobin Marlow. Her one-time fiancé had no longer cared about her at that point because he'd already stepped over her to get the promotion he wanted more than he did her. She knew her competition with Cassie had as much to do with Tobin as it did with her own yearning to prove she was the reason her ex had gotten his new job.

Paging through memories of her past mistakes wasn't going to get her anywhere. She'd done her due diligence with Patrick and wouldn't have to talk to him again that day. She wasn't going to call her parents. Not yet. She knew she needed to talk to them and clear the air between them, but she was going to ignore the voice mails a while longer.

That left only one message she needed to return.

Charles Satterfield, attorney-at-law.

She shouldn't put off making *that* call. She punched in the number before she found a reason not to contact him.

It rang once before a pleasant female voice answered with

the office's name and identified herself as Mr. Satterfield's assistant, Kai Provenzo. She asked why Lauren was calling.

For a second, Lauren almost hung up, but then explained who she was and how the lawyer had contacted her parents.

Kai said, "We have an opening tomorrow at noon. Will that work?"

No! she wanted to shout, but said, "Tomorrow at noon will be fine. I'll see you then. Should I bring anything with me?"

"Other than a picture ID, not at this time." She added a goodbye and ended the call.

"Tomorrow at noon," she repeated as she lowered the phone away as the swinging door from the dining room opened with a cheerful call of "In!"

Lauren's great-aunt wheeled herself into the kitchen and asked in the same upbeat voice, "What were you and Adam arguing about earlier?"

Instead of answering, she whipped off her splattered black apron and folded it over the edge of the sink. "I'm sorry our voices carried out of the kitchen, *Aenti* Sylvia. I hope none of your guests were disturbed."

She moved her wheelchair into the very path of Lauren's route to the stairs. "I'm not worried about my guests. You'd be astonished if I told you half of what I've heard from my guests. I'm worried about you. I couldn't hear your words, but your tones told me that you were at odds."

"You'd think after not seeing the man for fifteen years, he wouldn't still push my buttons."

"What buttons? That dress has snaps."

Lauren's irritation collapsed into laughter. "It's a saying, *Aenti* Sylvia. To say someone pushes your buttons means they know the right way to get under your skin."

"*Ach*, I can't keep up with the modern way of speaking."

"I can't either, even though it's part of my job to try." She wasn't going to explain that the expression had been around longer than she could remember.

"Adam Hershberger isn't the person you used to know. He was a wild, careless boy, but he's become a *gut* and careful man who cares about his family." She sighed. "Or what's left of it."

Sitting so she was on eye level with her great-aunt, she said, "Tell me one thing, *Aenti* Sylvia."

"Anything, *liebling*."

The dam holding back her tears nearly collapsed at the endearment. How many times had her mother used it before they left? Afterward, her parents had seldom spoken *Deitsch*, except for an endearment or two, as if they wanted to forsake everything in their past.

Focusing on the present, so she didn't surrender to her tears, she looked at her great-aunt. "You said Adam's wife was dead. Did he marry someone I knew? He didn't marry Naomi Gingerich, did he?"

Aenti Sylvia shook her head so vehemently that Lauren thought her *kapp* might come flying off. "No, Naomi married someone else and moved away."

Relief and regret warred within Lauren. Relief that Naomi wasn't Adam's late wife. Regret that she wouldn't get to see her friend.

"Once your car is fixed," Aenti Sylvia went on, "you could drive to Honey Brook to visit. It probably wouldn't take you more than an hour to get there."

"I don't know how much time I'll have." She longed to see her friend, but once her car was fixed and the meetings rescheduled, her boss would expect her in the city to report in minute detail what had transpired. Patrick wasn't a great boss, but he excelled at micromanaging.

"Naomi would appreciate seeing you, Laurene. She hasn't come here since her husband died."

"Naomi is a widow?"

Aenti Sylvia nodded. "It's sad. She would love to see you, *liebling*."

"I would love to see her." It felt good to speak from her heart. "I'll do my best."

"As you always have. Your parents taught you well."

"You know they weren't my real parents, don't you?"

"Not your *real* parents? They were there for you whenever you needed them."

"That's not what I meant."

"Are you talking about how they adopted you as a *boppli*?"

"You already knew?" She groped for the table beside her and grimaced when her hand hit a sugar bowl, sending it careening into two others. She jumped to her feet. Catching all three Depression glass bowls, she kept them from falling on the floor and breaking. If they'd shattered, she feared she would have, too.

"The attorney called here after speaking with Millie Hausman."

"Who's...?" Her eyes widened as she straightened the bowls. "Teacher Millie?"

"*Ja*. The attorney thought the best place to find out about *kinder* among the Amish would be to contact local schoolteachers."

"Millie is still teaching?"

The woman had taken over the one-room school during Lauren's final year. Teacher Millie had seldom smiled, not even at the youngest scholars who were cute when they lisped their ways through lessons. With an adult perspective and again having that sensation of being lost between broken mirrors, Lauren wondered if Millie's grim expression had more to do with the fact her husband had died the previous year, leaving her a childless widow.

"*Ja.*"

"Why would Millie give the attorney our names?"

Aenti Sylvia shrugged. "I don't know. You'd have to ask her. Maybe it was as simple as the attorney—what was his name? *Ach, ja.* Charles Satterfield. Maybe he was looking for *kinder* of a certain age at a certain point in time. Who better to know that than the schoolteacher? It was, at least, a starting place."

"Which somehow led to me."

"*Ja.*" Her brows tilted in a confused expression. "Why are you asking these questions now?"

Lauren explained about the call she'd gotten from her mother the previous night.

Aenti Sylvia listened before saying, "I always assumed you knew."

"Why would you assume that?"

"Why wouldn't I? You went to school with Joel Beachy, and you talked about how he was adopted as if it were the most common thing in the world. You didn't ask what adoption was, so I figured your parents had told you about your own adoption."

She almost choked as her stomach seemed to fall to her toes. The easy way her great-aunt spoke confirmed what Lauren still had hoped was a massive misunderstanding. She hadn't realized, until now, how she'd hoped her great-aunt would laugh at the joke Lauren's mother had decided to play for some ridiculous reason.

Reason didn't have anything to do with her unsettled feelings. How could she look at anything logically when her emotions were raw?

Somehow, as if from a great distance, she heard herself reply, "*Aenti* Sylvia, I was almost eleven years old when Joel Beachy's family moved to Bliss Valley. Of course, I knew what adoption was by then. I didn't know I'd been adopted."

Her great-aunt said something, but it didn't penetrate the buzzing filling her skull like a swarm of maddened mosquitoes. No, it wasn't in her head. It was her cell phone vibrating against the bobby pins she'd stuffed into her pocket.

Pulling it out, she sighed as she recognized the name of her contact at Carl Welsh Development. Back to the real world and trying to get the builder to contract their public relations with her company.

She waved toward the stairs, and her great-aunt nodded. She opened the door and began to climb as she answered the phone, sliding into the persona she'd built for herself. The competent, adroit and clever businesswoman who was eager to help a company find ways to enhance its profits while she filled the coffers of Krause-Matsui-Fitzgerald. It was her comfort zone.

The only one she had left.

The snow was already melting in a slow drip-drip-drip from the eaves of the rambling white farmhouse when Adam emerged from the barn after dawn the next morning. He'd just finished the milking with Simon and had spent extra time cleaning the barn. His cousins didn't like tending to details, and Adam had heard Simon mumbling complaints about having to remove dirtied straw by each stanchion where the cows stood while milked. Adam couldn't tell if his cousin was upset because he had to do the foul task or because his younger brother hadn't. Dale hadn't joined them in the barn that morning. The boy had complained of a sore throat, so Adam had let him linger in bed.

"How many is that?" asked Simon as they walked into the strengthening light.

Adam took a moment to savor the sunshine before he answered. It was a relief to have the sun come up earlier than it had in January. Doing chores in the dark in the morning and in the evening wore on even *Grossdawdi* Ephraim's spirits. Not that their great-*grossdawdi* had milked in more than two years, quitting as soon as Adam took over the farm after his wife's death. Lately, the old man had started reminiscing about barn work in a tone that revealed how much he missed spending time with the cows.

"How many what?" Adam asked when his cousin repeated his question.

"How many days has Dale convinced you to do his chores?"

"I don't know. I haven't been counting."

Simon scowled. "I have. Today's the fifth time in two weeks. Dale's playing you, Adam."

"Playing me what?"

"Playing *you*. It's an *Englisch* saying. I heard some of the guys using it over at the firehouse. Means he's got you *ferhoodled*."

"I'm not confused." Adam shoved his hands in his pockets. The weather was a bit warmer, but his fingers were chilled from using cold water to rinse out the pails after carrying the creamy *millich* to the dairy tank. "I know he's not being honest with me."

Simon's brows shot skyward. "If you know that, then why aren't you doing something? You're our deacon, Adam. It's part of your job to deal with troublemakers."

Stopping, Adam faced his young cousin. "How's he making trouble for you?"

"He's making you do his chores."

"That's trouble for me. How's he making trouble for *you*?"

Simon kicked a clump of snow that had rolled into the narrow walkway Adam and the boys had cleared yesterday. The clod exploded into white mist around them. "I don't like this, Adam. He's staying in bed while I've got to go out and milk the cows."

"Again, what difference does it make to you? Milking the cows already is one of your chores."

"You make it harder than it has to be."

"How? By insisting that we clean the barn every morning, too? That's something you and Dale should be doing, whether I'm there or not."

Whirling back to the barn, clearly wanting to get away from Adam, his cousin called over his shoulder, "It's not fair."

"What is?" Adam asked himself. Was it fair his daughter was growing up without a *mamm*? Was it fair after years of struggling to learn, he couldn't read the simplest words and numbers were as great a mystery as why one egg hatched and another didn't? Was it fair *Grossdawdi* Ephraim yearned to return to the life he'd once taken for granted?

Blessed are they that keep judgment, and he that doeth righteousness at all times. The verse from the one hundred and sixth Psalm was one Adam had used often in the years since he'd been ordained as the district's deacon. He quoted it when members of the *Leit* came to him with complaints about other members. It was a much nicer way of saying things weren't always fair, no matter how much someone tried to even the scales.

None of those complainers had wanted to hear it, and Adam knew his cousin hadn't either. Each of them, including Simon, should believe God would give them no heavier burdens than they could handle.

Adam halted in midstep. Did he still believe that? He wanted to, but the lesson he'd taught over and over no longer rang true for him. He'd been told that when his family died in the buggy accident. He'd been told that when his wife died. When he'd realized his great-*grossdawdi* needed help and his daughter did and his cousins did, he repeated the verse to himself. He'd also spoken those very words not only to his family, but to the *Leit* who came to him in times of trouble, because as their deacon he was there to advise them on issues beyond faith. Yet, everything in their lives revolved around their connections with God.

So why did his faith feel so flimsy?

He shoved his feet forward through the snow and grimaced when two icy drops of water fell down his collar by the door to the enclosed rear porch. Rubbing his nape, he sat on a chair that had been retired to the porch after years in the kitchen. He pulled off his boots and stuffed his feet into the moccasins he wore in the house.

The kitchen was warm because he'd stirred the embers in the stove and added more wood before going to the barn. He'd noticed during the past winter how the cold seemed to bother his great-*grossdawdi* more.

Adam heard a thump from the far side of the large kitchen. His great-*grossdawdi* was bent over his cane and gripping the molding on the door as if it were his last connection with life.

"Bischt allrecht?" Adam fought his first inclination to rush across the kitchen. The old man might have been getting frailer, but his vexation when someone mentioned that to him was as strong as ever.

Adam didn't get an answer.

"Bischt allrecht?" he repeated as he walked to his great-*grossdawdi* and asked him a third time if he was okay, a bit louder because the old man's hearing wasn't what it once had been.

Ephraim Weaver straightened to his full height, which was several inches shorter than he'd stood twenty years ago. His face was lined with pain, but he waved aside Adam's hand as he limped to a nearby chair in the kitchen.

"I'm fine," the older man said. "Pulled a muscle when I was helping the boys with the milking yesterday."

Adam frowned as he opened the refrigerator and pulled out

a bowl of the eggs he'd collected with Mary Beth the morning before the snowstorm. "I thought we'd agreed that Simon and Dale could handle the cows on their own. With a little of my help from time to time."

"You agreed. Not me." Lowering himself onto the chair, he sighed as he scratched at his reddened hand. "*Ach*, that's much better."

"How long has your hand been itchy?"

"All winter. Old skin is dry skin."

"Maybe you should see a *doktor* to make sure it's not something else."

"Don't you think I know dry skin when I see it? My eyes are old, but they can see as far as my hands!"

"*Grossdawdi* Ephraim, you should—"

The old man riveted him with a frown. "Don't start lecturing me, boy, with your 'shoulds' and 'shouldn'ts.' You need to remember you're Mary Beth's *daed*, not mine."

Adam sighed under his breath as he carried the eggs to the stove. It'd be worthless to remind his great-*grossdawdi* how they'd had a family discussion about which chores would be done by which person last month. The five of them, including Mary Beth, who'd insisted on joining them for the conversation, had agreed his cousins were to handle the milking and the barn chores while Adam oversaw the house and the fields. *Grossdawdi* Ephraim had been put in charge of babysitting Mary Beth when Adam was working. Even his daughter had been given the task of making her bed—or doing her best to do it—and picking up her toys and books at the end of each day. They'd spent two meals talking about little else but who would do what, and after a lot of compromise, had come to an agreement. Now, it seemed, his great-*grossdawdi* wanted to ignore it all.

"I'm worried about you," Adam said to cover his irritated

thoughts. "You seem to be having a lot of aches and pains lately."

"You'll understand when you get to be my age, boy."

In spite of himself, he laughed. "You've been saying that my whole life, and I'm still waiting for understanding to kick in."

"Sounds as if you're beginning to understand." *Grossdawdi* Ephraim guffawed, but the sound ended in a groan as he rubbed his right leg. "Don't look at me like the world's coming to an end. It's a cramp. I'm finding it takes me a little longer to get going in the morning, and if I try to hurry it, my muscles remind me I'm not a kid any longer."

"Now *that* I understand."

Frowning, the older man asked, "What's that supposed to mean? Are you feeling bad?"

"No." He realized he was kneading his lower back and halted. He'd shoveled Sylvia Nolt's place yesterday after his less-than-fruitful conversation with Lauren so he could get his buggy out of the barn. He'd helped Simon and Dale dig paths from the house to the barns on their own farm after that. His muscles were determined to let him know they'd been overworked. "Too much snow too late in the season."

"I could have—"

"Let's not argue about that again. The snow is our problem. Yours is making sure we've got lots of *gut* hot chocolate waiting when we're done."

"Mary Beth wouldn't let me forget that!"

"Wouldn't let you forget what?" asked his daughter as she skipped into the kitchen. She threw her arms around *Grossdawdi* Ephraim and gave him a kiss on the cheek before bouncing across the room to do the same to Adam.

He didn't think he'd ever seen Mary Beth walk if she could hop or skip or run. In that, she was much like him. He'd always been a fidgeting *kind*, especially in school where he grew bored when he couldn't comprehend what the teachers did or said. He sent up a quick prayer to thank God that, as far as he could see, school would be much easier for her than it'd been for him. He was grateful letters and numbers already seemed to make sense to her.

"*Gute mariye,*" he said as he picked her up and spun her. Her laughter was the best balm he could imagine for his aching back.

"More, *Daed!*" she begged when he set her down.

"A little later. *Grossdawdi* Ephraim will get grumpy if we don't get him his breakfast."

His great-*grossdawdi* raised his hands as if they were clawed and growled, which sent Mary Beth into more giggles.

Adam made breakfast with the ease of much practice. His great-*grossdawdi* was an admitted failure as a cook, and his cousins couldn't figure out how to turn the gas stove down from high and burned everything they attempted to make. He'd taken over the job because he remembered what it was like to be an impatient teenager.

The eggs, bacon and store-bought muffins he set on the table were eaten along with two bowls of applesauce. The *millich* Simon had carried in from the barn vanished. After a final prayer for the meal, his cousins and Mary Beth rushed away to do their chores.

Adam refilled his cup and his great-*grossdawdi*'s with strong *kaffi* and put them on the table. Sitting, he let steam from his cup rise into his face. Spending a few minutes together without younger ears to listen to their conversation was a custom they'd created after Adam had moved back to the farm.

"Did your cousins tell you that Old Leander stopped by and wanted to talk to you yesterday morning?" *Grossdawdi* Ephraim asked.

"No." He'd been expecting Leander Lowe, who was only

a year or two older than Adam but was the elder of two cousins with the same name, to talk to him after hearing the fire
the other night had been at the Lowe farm.

His great-*grossdawdi* sighed. "Some days, I wonder if those
two boys have a single brain between them. The only thing
Simon thinks about is girls. Dale spends his time coming up
with ways to convince you to let him skip his chores."

"I plan to talk to him about that."

"I thought you might."

After taking another sip of *kaffi*, he put his cup on the table
and locked his fingers together around it. "I haven't spoken
with the fire chief yet, so I don't know the extent of the damage."

"The shed is a total loss along with everything in it."

"*How* do you know that?"

"Your buddies from the firehouse stopped by. The *Englisch*
one and the plain one who are always with each other."

"Chip Weatherford and Mahlon Miller."

"*Ja*. They wanted to tell you about fighting the fire. From
what Mahlon said, Chip was the bravest man there. Chip acted
as if Mahlon was some sort of super-firefighter."

Adam grinned. "They're always joking about that." His
smile faded. "I'm going to have to talk with the bishop about
how to handle these fires. I've been deacon long enough to
know how much a single fire can cost the community, and
funds are being stretched thin with one fire after another."

"God will provide."

"*Ja*, I know." He gave his great-*grossdawdi* a grin. "Sometimes I wish He'd give me a bit of a clue how He plans to do
that."

"You know what lots of folks say? God helps those who
help themselves."

"Lots of folks say lots of things, but that doesn't make them true."

"Things like wondering why Laurene Nolt is back."

He huffed out what was supposed to be a laugh. It sounded like a distressed tractor engine. "I know what she's here for. Something to do with that new casino they want to build here."

"Really? I hadn't heard much about it, so I was wondering if they decided to build it somewhere else."

"It doesn't look like it if she's here in Bliss Valley."

"No wonder news of Laurene's return is swarming through the community."

"How can it be? She's been here for little more than a day, and we've been snowed in most of that time."

"Boy, you know that neither rain nor sleet nor dark of night, and certainly not snow, keeps rumors from rushing through the *Leit*."

"That's the motto for the mail, not for the Amish grapevine."

"True." His great-*grossdawdi* picked up his cup and winked over it. "The grapevine is faster."

As if to prove his point, Mary Beth skipped into the kitchen. "Have you seen her, *Daed*?" Her hair still hung loose. Adam needed to braid it before he went to work. Maybe today he'd get the two braids to match.

"Seen who?"

"The *Englisch* lady at the inn!" She folded her pudgy arms in front of her and gave him a look that suggested she wasn't in the mood to be teased.

"There are a lot of *Englischers* at the inn."

Whirling to look at her great-great-*grossdawdi*, she said, "Tell him! Please!"

"I don't need to," *Grossdawdi* Ephraim replied with a

chuckle. "Your *daed* found the lady—by the way, her name is Laurene—"

"Lauren," Adam corrected.

His great-*grossdawdi* sent him a warning glance. "Your *daed* found Laurene out in the storm."

"Was she frozen?"

Adam frowned over his daughter's head. "Of course not! She had car trouble, so I took her to Sylvia's inn to stay until her car's repaired."

"Let's go see her!"

"You're trying to keep from having to make your bed." Adam tried to sound stern, but he couldn't when his daughter grinned at him. How many times had *Grossdawdi* Ephraim told him Mary Beth was the spitting image of Adam's *mamm*? He had to take his great-*grossdawdi*'s word for it, because his own memories of his *mamm* had faded.

"But, *Daed*—"

"Listen to your *daed*," his great-*grossdawdi* said. "He's going to take Laurene to get her car when it's fixed, and he'll tell you all about it. Ain't so, Adam?"

When he'd been a kid, Adam had been amazed how his great-*grossdawdi* seemed to know things without being told. He was still astonished.

"At the inn? More cookies?" Mary Beth asked.

"You shouldn't expect Sylvia to send you cookies each time one of us visits," Adam replied.

She pouted for a moment, then her sunny smile returned. "Maybe she's got snow for you to shovel."

"And more cookies for you to eat?"

"Do you think she does?"

He ruffled her hair and was swept away, as he was too often, by the memory of Vernita plaiting their daughter's hair with such ease. Mary Beth's braids had been smooth then. Not like when he did her hair, and one braid seemed longer than the other or stuck out in an opposite direction.

"*Daed*, are you listening?" His daughter's impatient tone told him she'd asked that question at least once already.

"Of course I'm listening. You said you wanted to wash the dishes and dry them and put them in the hayloft."

She screwed up her face. "That's not what I said!"

When he chuckled, she did, too. He gathered her close as she flung her arms around him. How glad he would have been to remain at home with her! His responsibilities didn't allow that, and now he had one more.

Dealing with Lauren Nolt and whatever she was planning for the casino project and putting a stop to it, so his great-*grossdawdi* wouldn't be forced off the farm that had been in their family for generations.

Chapter Seven

Without her own car, which Frank had assured her would be repaired in a day or two, Lauren decided to call a limo service to take her to Lancaster to meet with Charles Satterfield, attorney-at-law. That was how she thought of him. Charles-satterfieldattorneyatlaw. All one word.

The limo dropped her off in front of a building that housed a café on the first floor. The attorney's office was on the upper floor, and she couldn't pull her gaze away from the windows as she got out of the car. The driver, a cheerful older man who'd talked nonstop during the twenty-minute drive into Lancaster, told her to call him when she was ready to be picked up.

As he drove away, Lauren looked around. She was a block from the Central Market, the indoor farmers market where plain people came to sell vegetables, meat and crafts. She went to the door with the number for the lawyer's office. In the small lobby, a list of offices was displayed in a glass case next to a single elevator. Thick carpet smothered Lauren's footfalls as she walked from the elevator to the door at the far end of a hushed hall edged by closed doors. The pebbled glass window had been painted with the name of the legal firm and listed the attorneys who worked there.

Inside the office, it was almost as quiet as the corridor. The faint echo of a car horn intruded, but otherwise the loudest sounds were bubbles from the aquarium that ran along the left-hand wall. The right-hand wall was decorated with large brass letters that spelled out the same names as on the door.

Lauren wondered why anyone would need to be reminded of where they were so soon after they opened the door. Then she thought about how many places the stylized logo for Krause-Matsui-Fitzgerald was scattered throughout their offices. Not on the wall in brass letters, which would have been considered gauche for a company pretending that clients needed it more than the firm needed them, but every desk held business cards with the partners' names. Each table in waiting areas was topped by brochures proclaiming the company's name in a bold font.

Walking to the receptionist's desk decorated by a vase holding four pink carnations and six red ones, Lauren waited until the young woman dressed in a white silk blouse finished her phone call. The woman, whose hair was a red nature must have envied, spoke in modulated tones and without a hint of impatience or boredom, though she rocked a pen between her fingers and rolled her eyes more than once as she listened. She halted when she noticed Lauren waiting.

"May I help you?" she asked in the same pleasant tone after she'd hung up the phone. It was the same woman Lauren had spoken to on the phone. Kai something or other.

"I'm Lauren Nolt. I've got an appointment with Mr. Satterfield at twelve."

"Mr. Satterfield is running a bit behind." Kai motioned toward a row of chairs along the wall, revealing the tattoo of a flower on the underside of her wrist. "If you don't mind waiting…"

"Thank you." She went to the closest chair and sat, wondering what Kai would have done if Lauren had said she did mind waiting.

She understood the time-honored ploy. Even though the offices were as silent as a tomb, save for Kai who was now typing information into a computer, Charlessatterfieldattorneyatlaw wanted to keep up the pretense that he was a very busy, very important man who could ask his clients to wait for him.

In spite of her nerves, Lauren smiled when she thought of her name for the lawyer she didn't want to meet. She kneaded her knees through her simple gray skirt until she realized what she was doing and stopped.

A tall, dark-haired man walked into the reception area from one of the hallways opening off it. Not as tall as Adam, but few men were.

Get out of my head, Adam Hershberger!

She doubted he would, because her memories of the past seemed to be coming faster and faster like a runaway truck on the interstate. How could she halt them when she needed to examine each and every one? There must have been *some* sign to reveal she was adopted, *some* look exchanged by her parents, *some* hint in a conversation that halted when she entered the room, *some* thing she'd missed.

There hadn't been a single one she could remember.

"Charles Satterfield." The hand he offered had recently manicured nails, she noted. His black hair was as stylish as his gray suit. The hints of white at his temples suggested a resemblance to a well-known actor who played an attorney on TV.

Coming to her feet, she shook his hand that was softer than her own. After working in the inn for the past two days, she could use a manicure before she met with the casino developers' representatives. Was there anywhere in Bliss Valley to get a mani-pedi?

Again, as she followed Mr. Satterfield toward a small conference room, she corralled her wandering thoughts. She needed to focus on *this* meeting, but it was impossible. She didn't want any of what was happening to be real. If everything from the moment her mother had called was a bad dream, surely it was time for her to wake up and let it fade away.

But it didn't.

The conference room could have been in any building in any city in the world. No windows offered distraction, and the walls were decorated with the innocuous artwork seen in hotel rooms. The fake cherry table was surrounded by upholstered chairs on casters. Even the carpet, a gray-beige mix, had been chosen to avoid causing any offense. A single pitcher of ice water sat in the center of the table along with four inverted glasses resting on paper doilies. It was professional and bland and aimed at keeping clients from lingering to talk longer to the busy attorneys.

Lauren sat and shook her head when Mr. Satterfield asked if she wanted water or coffee. She didn't trust her shaking hands.

He chose a chair facing her and opened a file in the exact position where she couldn't read it through the water pitcher.

Clever, she thought, but said nothing as she waited for him to speak.

Mr. Satterfield didn't waste time with pleasantries. First he asked for her license and got her permission to make a copy of it. After he'd handed it to Kai, who appeared with well-practiced efficiency, she hurried out and returned quickly. She gave Lauren's license and the paper copy to her boss before leaving and closing the door behind her.

Returning the license to Lauren, he said, "Thank you. I must inform you that I'm representing Gina Marie Tinniswood in this matter. If you wish legal counsel, I can suggest an attorney in this office or another, if you prefer that."

"Thank you, but I think I'll wait for now."

"As you wish." His warm voice didn't fool her. There were too many ways he resembled her boss, and Patrick used that tone when feeling out a potential client. It was ingratiating and self-assured at the same time. She'd witnessed Patrick employing it for his own benefit on several occasions, and she had to wonder why nobody else seemed to see through his unctuous patter.

"I assume Gina Marie Tinniswood is the woman who believes she's my birth mother." She kept her own tone as measured as his.

"Yes." He blinked once, then a second time, clearly startled by her serenity. "Mrs. Tinniswood has been searching for you. As you may or may not know, adoption records at the time of your birth were sealed and could be opened only with a court order. That often required duress. Several years ago, adoptees and birth parents were granted the right to petition the court for information. The process isn't a quick one, but it has led us to believe you are her daughter."

"If she was doing that, why did you contact my former teacher Millie Hausman in Bliss Valley?"

"We ran into some walls with the courts."

"Walls?"

"There was some confusion over which child we were looking for, so she—"

"Where is Mrs. Tinniswood?" she asked, tired of how he was couching every word as if running for political office. "I thought I was going to meet her today."

"No, I never said that."

"She isn't here?" Shock raced through her. "Then why am I?"

"I wanted to meet you and explain—"

"Mr. Satterfield, when—if—she wants to meet me face-to-face, you have my number." Coming to her feet, she saw his startled expression. She guessed most people didn't speak to him in such a brusque manner, but she was tired of being jerked around by people involved in events that had begun before she had any say about being handed off from one mother to another. "I look forward to hearing from you."

She thought he might try to call her back when she walked to the door and opened it. Had she shocked him catatonic with her straightforward words? If so, assuming she ever met Gina Marie Tinniswood, Lauren would suggest she hire an attorney with more backbone.

Nodding to the receptionist, she strode to the elevator and pushed the button. She pulled out her phone to call the driver and saw she'd received two texts within seconds of each other. The developers had agreed to meet with her and had chosen times far enough apart so she didn't have to worry about ushering one group out before the next came in. Neither had a problem with meeting at The Acorn Farm Inn.

Thankfully, something was going right.

"Miss Nolt?" asked Mr. Satterfield as he strode toward her. "I thought you'd like an answer to your question. I asked you here today because I wanted to make sure I met you before Mrs. Tinniswood did. She's been ill, and I don't want her health worsened by the stress of these circumstances."

"Why didn't you say that earlier?" Guilt flushed through her. Her mother—her *adoptive* mother—had scolded her often about leaping before she looked. Had she messed up any chance of meeting the woman who might be her birth mother?

"I didn't want to say too much before I had a chance to get to know you a little bit." He smiled. "I think a meeting with you will be the very best thing for Mrs. Tinniswood."

He had the decency to flush as he added, "She likes people who speak plainly."

"So when can I meet her?"

"Before there's a meeting, I'd like you to take a DNA test. Mrs. Tinniswood has already done so. The results from yours will tell us if you're her daughter or not." He pulled a card out of his pocket and handed it to her. "This lab can handle the test for you."

She took the card in numb fingers. What a joke she was! Walking out of the office like she was in control of everything when she was in a storm sweeping her along as if she were in Dorothy's house on its way to Oz.

Winter vanished as quickly as it'd returned. By noon the following day, the only snow remaining, other than the plowed banks by the road, clung to the shadows beneath bushes and on the northern side of the house. The crocus buds had re-appeared. In the sunniest spots, they blossomed, white and purple, eagerly welcoming spring. The green tips of daffodil stems poked through the soil. They wouldn't bloom for at least a couple of weeks, but seeing them was a promise that spring truly was on its way. The trees appeared to be asleep, but Lauren knew that, deep within them, they were awakening to the sun's warmth.

As she stepped out the back door to hang out the laundry, Lauren gazed across the fields spread before her like an array of paint chips. Each field was a slightly different shade of brown edging toward green. Plowing hadn't started because the ground was too wet from the freshly melted snow. The areas left fallow the previous year were the palest because the grasses and weeds that had grown over the summer had withered and twisted, sculpted by the winter winds.

Everything smelled of fresh mud mixed with distant smells

from the cow barns. Flocks of sheep already had claimed the sunniest spots among the rolling hills, and a pair of robins hopped across the yard. She heard the trill of others hidden by trees in a small copse near the old stone springhouse by the barn.

Lauren had forgotten how much she liked hanging up the wash. Though the sheets were stubborn and the corners wanted to fall on the ground if she wasn't careful, the aromas of laundry soap and bleach seemed the perfect complement for the lilting breeze. She pinned each into place on the large, spinning clothesline. Her great-aunt used the dryer for cloth napkins, tablecloths and kitchen wash, but her guests enjoyed the incomparable scent of line-dried sheets and pillowcases.

Finishing the job, she walked toward the road to get the mail. She smiled when grass squished beneath her shoes. A few more sunny days would dry out the ground. The earthy fragrance of mud and water grew stronger as she strolled across the yard past the barn and the farm pond beyond it. When she'd been small, she'd loved spending time at ponds. The reeds and tall grasses offered havens for frogs and harmless snakes. Many of them had ended up in her pockets, though she'd later set them free. As she'd gotten older, she'd netted tadpoles, put them in empty mayonnaise jars and watched them become frogs.

Her life seemed so distant from those simple pleasures.

A movement caught her eye, and Lauren glanced toward the fence that divided her great-aunt's land from Ephraim Weaver's farm. It was on the other side of the hot tub and pool which steamed in the morning sunshine. Her great-aunt had installed the heated pool to attract more guests, and the large tank that provided propane for the heater was hidden behind a thicket of blackberry bushes. She frowned when a bird popped out of the bushes, but nothing moved along the fence. Were her eyes playing tricks on her? Getting up before the sun was a definite change of pace, but she'd gone to bed earlier last night to compensate.

So why did she think she was seeing things?

As she started to turn toward the road, she saw the motion again. It was a little girl with hair the color of golden syrup and wide brown eyes. Freckles dotted her cheeks. She wore an odd collection of clothing with her simple dark blue dress. An unbuttoned coat had mittens stuffed in its pockets and her boots looked many times too big.

"Hello there!" Lauren called.

The child looked puzzled, then said, *"Wie geht's."*

Hello.

Of course, the little girl didn't speak English. Amish children spoke *Deitsch* before they went to school, and this child looked younger than six years old.

Lauren replied in the same language that she was fine and then gave her name.

The child looked disappointed.

"Was iss letz?" Lauren asked, wondering what was wrong.

The little girl explained she'd heard there was an *Englisch* woman staying at the inn and she wanted to meet her.

"I think I'm the one you're looking for," Lauren said.

"No. She's gots a name. Laurene. *Daed* said so."

"Well, I'm Lauren. Isn't that close enough?"

"Guess so." She grinned when Lauren asked her name. "I'm Mary Beth."

Could this adorable sprite be Adam's daughter? She appeared to be about the right age, and her eyes were as chocolate brown as his. What was a four-year-old doing by herself so far from home?

Lauren looked across the length of the field to the distant barn. For a second, she almost asked the little girl if her family knew where she'd gone. She halted herself as she recalled how she and Naomi had wandered the fields between their families' neighboring farms from the time they weren't much older than Mary Beth. Their mothers had had a single admonition: don't go near the creek. She and Naomi had listened for almost one whole summer before they dared to stick their toes in the water.

"Hi, Mary Beth," Lauren said with a smile. "I think you're looking for me."

"Are you *Englisch*?"

She almost laughed at the little girl's direct question. "I am."

Mary Beth eyed the plain dress Lauren had selected for serving breakfast to the few remaining guests that morning. "You don't gots *Englisch* clothes."

"I'm working for my great-aunt, and this is what she wants me to wear."

Climbing to the top rail, Mary Beth sat and tilted her head as she considered what Lauren had said. Then her face brightened. "Like ladies in restaurants?"

She smiled. "You're a smart girl."

"My *daed* says so." Her dark eyes twinkled. "*Grossdawdi* Ephraim says so, too. Know something?"

"What's that?" It was impossible not to like the effusive little girl.

"*Grossdawdi* Ephraim is my really great."

"You're right. He's a great guy. Everyone likes him, and—"

"No, no." Mary Beth shook her head, and her cockeyed braids bounced in two different directions.

Putting her hand on the top of the rail beside the child, in case Mary Beth started to fall off in her enthusiasm, Lauren said, "All right. Explain it to me."

"He's *Daed*'s great-*grossdawdi*, so he's my really great." Sitting straighter, she held on to the fence. "My really great-*grossdawdi*."

"Ah. He's your great-great-grandfather."

"No, he's my really great." She gave Lauren a pitying look as if the little girl couldn't fathom why a grown woman was so clueless.

Swallowing her laugh, Lauren said, "Now I get it. *Grossdawdi* Ephraim is your really great-*grossdawdi*."

"*Ja*. He is!" The little girl looked as proud as if she'd invented a cure for the common cold. "You gots cookies?"

"There are always cookies at The Acorn Farm Inn. That's what my great-aunt says." She'd make sure the child had a cookie and some milk, and then she'd walk her to her family's farm. "Would you like one?"

"*Ja!*"

This time, Lauren let her laugh loose. She held the child's hands to slow Mary Beth's jump to the ground. When the little girl kept holding one as they walked toward the rear door, Lauren's heart melted like the chocolate chips *Aenti* Sylvia put in her cookies. Mary Beth's smile and chatter were the perfect balm for the ache lodged there.

Adam jumped out of his buggy before it'd come to a complete stop. Simon and Dale had burst into his shop minutes ago, announcing Mary Beth had disappeared while *Grossdawdi* Ephraim had fallen asleep when he was supposed to be watching her. Adam had sent his two cousins to the farm to search the outbuildings while he headed for the one other place where his daughter might go.

Sylvia sat on the front porch in her wheelchair when he bounded across the lawn.

"Have you seen Mary Beth?" he asked.

"*Ja*. She's inside."

As he reached for the door, she held up a hand. "There's no reason to hurry, Adam. She's fine, and I wanted a chance to talk to you. It's been quite a while since you and I have exercised our jaws together."

"Sylvia, I should—"

"Sit and humor an old woman. Your daughter is fine and enjoying my cookies."

Shaking his head, he said, "I wish you hadn't given her any. She shouldn't be rewarded for running away."

"She didn't run away. She ran *to*."

"What are you talking about?"

Instead of answering, she gestured toward the closest rocking chair on her porch. He obeyed. "All right. I'm sitting."

"As I am."

"Are you waiting for guests?" he asked, realizing she'd been serious about intending to have a conversation. For a moment, he had to wonder why she was determined to keep him from going inside. He pushed that thought aside. Sylvia Nolt was a very outspoken plain woman, and she didn't play games.

Not like Vernita had.

Another thought he didn't want to deal with now.

"Bookings are always down this time of year," Sylvia said in a tone that suggested she didn't care one way or the other. "I don't have any guests tonight. There will be some coming in tomorrow for a long weekend. It's the same every year. Parents want to make sure their kids don't miss school before finals."

"I didn't think you let kids stay at the B and B."

"I don't, but parents won't come if they think their kids are going to get spring fever and play hooky while they're away."

"Maybe *Englisch* teens need some *rumspringa* time."

"From what I've heard from my guests, *Englisch* teenagers aren't interested in getting together for singings or making fudge and taffy." She cut her gaze to him. "Not that you were interested in such things yourself during your running around time."

"You've got a *gut* memory, Sylvia."

"It's easy to remember things from years ago. Things from a few hours ago are harder. I keep telling myself it's because the parts of my brain where memories live have gotten filled up."

The call from robins settling in the branches hanging over the porch made Sylvia smile. "They're getting ready to build a nest and raise a family. It's a tough job, ain't so?"

"*Ja.*" He was curious where she intended to go with this, because she and her late husband had never had any *kinder.*

"I can see that you're chomping at the bit to get your daughter. We'll have to have our conversation later." As he started to stand, she added, "It would be *gut* if you could take some time to speak with Laurene. She hasn't told me much about her visit with the lawyer yesterday, and I think she needs to talk to someone."

"She called the lawyer?"

"*Ja*, and went to Lancaster to meet with him."

"And her *mamm*?"

Sylvia's eyes dimmed. "From what she's said, no. There are procedures to go through first."

"She must be frustrated."

"That's the problem. I don't know how she's feeling. She tends to hide what she's thinking."

Adam almost asked, *What are you talking about?* From the moment she'd walked into Frank's shop, she hadn't concealed anything from him. She didn't like having him around and she was upset about learning she was adopted and what she wanted most of all was to leave Bliss Valley and him.

He nodded and opened the door, heading inside. He started for the kitchen but halted when he heard familiar laughter coming from the fancy living room Sylvia had set aside for her guests. Pausing at one side of the doorway that was draped with thick gold curtains running on a pole across the whole opening, he peered around them.

The room was overfilled, at least in his opinion, with all things antique and plain. Paintings on the wall depicted scenes of Bliss Valley with Amish farmers and their families tending to their fields and animals. Wooden, faceless people in plain dress were spaced along the high mantel of the fieldstone fireplace. Dolls with the same undecorated faces sat on ornate tables and overstuffed chairs in various shades of gold and white.

His gaze went to where his daughter was perched next to Lauren on a sofa that looked as if it had been carved from gold because sunshine made the gilded wood shine like a miser's cache. In front of them on a low table, crumbs marked the plate that had held cookies. Two glasses were drained empty of *millich*.

Mary Beth, her mouth edged with more crumbs, was talking at her top speed, a sure sign she was excited to be with Lauren. Her bare feet swung against the front of the sofa in rhythm with her words. Beside her, Lauren spoke haltingly as if trying out phrases she hadn't used in a long time. How long had it been since she last spoke full sentences in *Deitsch*? When his daughter finished what he guessed had been a long story about one of the newborn calves, Lauren gave her a hug. His daughter flung her arms around her and leaned her face, crumbs and all, against Lauren's light blue dress.

He watched, almost afraid to breathe and intrude on them, as his daughter closed her eyes and an expression of pure bliss lit her face. She whispered something too low for him to hear, but Lauren must have because she nodded and stroked Mary Beth's uneven braids. The motion was so tender, so honest, so caring the very sight squeezed his heart in midbeat.

Shifting away from the door, he leaned against the wall,

his head pressed against the wood and his fingers, too. He needed to be connected to something solid because the sight of his daughter being held with such kindness threatened to undo him.

He hadn't seen such joy on his daughter's face unless she was with him or *Grossdawdi* Ephraim. It was love, plain and simple.

A groan rose up from his heart. Lauren was going to leave as soon as her work was done, work that could well mean the destruction of the only home Mary Beth could remember.

He wanted Lauren to leave fast, and he wanted his daughter to be as happy as she was right now.

He couldn't have both. *Just as you can't have Lauren put her arms around you and hold you as she did Mary Beth.*

The unwelcome thought threatened to knock him off his feet. Where had *that* come from? It needed to go away and never come back. It—

"Adam?" Lauren's question was followed by Mary Beth's chirp of, "*Daed*, I finded the *Englisch* lady! She gots *gut* cookies."

Pushing himself away from the wall, Adam squatted in front of his daughter. One problem at a time, and Mary Beth was easier to deal with first.

"You know," he said sternly, "you aren't supposed to leave the house without telling someone where you're going."

"I tolds *Grossdawdi* Ephraim."

"He says you didn't."

She put her hands on her waist and stamped her foot. "I did! I tolds him and he said I should go and chase the dog. So I looks for the dog, but saw the *Englisch* lady instead. Do we gots a dog, *Daed*?"

"No," he replied.

"So why—"

Lauren interjected, "I think *Grossdawdi* Ephraim might have been talking in his sleep, Mary Beth. Grown-ups do that sometimes."

"It's happened before," he said as he pushed himself to his feet. "Go and get your coat and boots, Mary Beth. We need to get home and let everyone know you're okay."

"Me okay?" She giggled.

As his daughter hopped on one foot along the hallway, Adam gave in to his yearning to look at Lauren. His breath deserted him as it had when he'd seen her in plain clothing in the kitchen the other morning. She was lovely, even with her hair stuffed under her *kapp*. His legs urged him to step forward one step, then another, until he could gather her into his arms as she had Mary Beth.

Dummkopf! Hadn't she made it clear long ago he was the last person on earth she'd choose to spend time with? No matter how much he'd longed to pull her to him after seeing her hug his daughter.

Be careful. She'll be leaving soon.

At the warning thought, Adam pushed aside his others. He switched to English which was easier for her. "Frank asked me to let you know your car should be ready tomorrow. If you want, I can drive you out to get it."

"I've got meetings until about three tomorrow."

"I'll stop by about a half hour after that. All right?"

"Yes. Thank you."

"Are *you* all right?" He leaned toward her, lowering his voice so Mary Beth wouldn't overhear. "Sylvia told me you went to see the lawyer. How did it go with your *mamm*?"

"She wasn't there." She stiffened and stepped back, keeping an arm's length between them. "Only the attorney."

His brows lowered. "Why did he ask you to come in if your *mamm* wasn't there?"

"He was vetting me to see how I'd react to meeting her."

"What did he decide?"

"After I told him off for beating around the bush, he decided having a meeting for the two of us was going to be a good idea."

Shaking his head, he said, "Just when I think I understand *Englischers*, I hear something like this."

"Some of us are pretty candid with our opinions." She hurried on when he opened his mouth to reply. "I know you think that's a strange comment from someone who works in public relations and is trying to pull a fast one on the plain folks in Bliss Valley."

He held up his hands. "What's going on? Why are you mad at me?"

"I'm not mad at you. I'm mad at the world." She walked into the living room to get the dirty dishes. Halting, she spun to face him. "You don't understand, Adam! You don't know what it's like to have two women who want you to call them 'mother.'" Her face paled. Could she tell the very moment when an icy chill coursed along him as if the day had turned as cold as the depths of winter? "I'm sorry. I shouldn't have said that."

"Why? Because my daughter doesn't have a *mamm*?"

"You didn't have a mother either. Not after the accident. How old were you? Nine?"

"Ten."

"A little boy."

"That's not what I was told at the time. Everyone said I needed to be a big boy because I was the head of my family." He shook his head. "A family of one."

"You had *Grossdawdi* Ephraim."

"The one blessing granted me during that horrible time. He reminded me I wasn't alone." Again he felt the urge to laugh, though nothing was funny. "I couldn't complain. Everyone would have told me I wasn't alone because God was watching over me. I knew that, but I wanted flesh-and-blood arms holding me like my *mamm* had."

"You had someone else."

"Who?"

"Us. The other scholars." Her jaw tightened. "Or you could have if you'd have let us in. We were ready to be there for you, but you did everything you could to push us aside. Our teacher at the time... What was her name?"

"Bertha."

"Yes, Bertha Tice. She was related to my mother's family somehow. Fourth or fifth cousin. Anyhow, she told us we needed to be extra understanding when you came to our school."

"So you, being the *gut* girl, obeyed our teacher's orders."

She folded her arms so sharply he was surprised he didn't hear a snap. "That's not fair! You don't know why I tried to be nice to you. It could have been because it was the right thing to do."

"'*Ye shall not afflict any widow, or fatherless child.*'"

"Exodus, right? The old laws God gave Moses along with the Ten Commandments." She gave him a cool smile. "Don't look surprised. My father read the Bible and the *Martyrs Mirror* to me in the evenings as your great-grandfather read to you."

"So, like I said, you were the *gut* girl obeying the rules."

"While you were trying to break them?" Her icy smile sent another wave of cold along him. "I don't think I'm the one who needs to examine the past, Adam. I'm not denying you were hurt and had every right to be angry at us, at your parents, at God. You need to see the past from a different point of view, or you won't ever come to terms with what happened to your family."

Mary Beth rushed toward them, slowing every couple of

steps to readjust her feet in what looked to be a pair of his old boots. Where had she found them, and why was she wearing them?

More questions rushed through his head. Was Lauren right? Had he held on to his pain as a cushion against what he'd never understood about why his parents had died in that accident?

Or why he alone had survived?

A flush of the familiar guilt surged through him. People had a name for it. Survivor's guilt. A few members of the *Leit* had mentioned it and suggested he read up on the topic. Of course, they hadn't spoken of it in relation to his tragedies. They'd thought he was beyond the anguish of losing his parents and having his wife die before their daughter's second birthday. Their concerns had been raised in the wake of a horrific accident involving a van filled with Amish passengers from Central Pennsylvania.

God didn't make mistakes. He'd heard that over and over, so it couldn't have been a mistake he was ordained.

God, if none of this is Your mistake, it must be mine. I don't know how to fix it.

No answer flooded his heart with comfort as he picked up Mary Beth. One of his boots bounced across the floor. When Lauren retrieved it, she offered it to him in silence.

He took it the same way. His daughter called a farewell as he carried her out of the inn, but he said nothing. Anything he uttered was sure to be the wrong thing when he had to convince Lauren—and he had no idea how—to find a way to get the casino built somewhere far from his great-*grossdawdi*'s farm. He must figure out something and figure it out fast because the sooner he did, the sooner she'd be gone from Bliss Valley. Then he might be able to squash thoughts of Lauren Nolt and how *wunderbaar* it would have been to hold her close.

Chapter Eight

At quarter past three the next afternoon, Lauren took the whiteboard off its easel in the dining room. The two meetings that day had gone better than she'd had any reason to expect.

Part of that was, she knew, how delighted the developers' representatives had been to be welcomed to The Acorn Farm Inn. Picking up a handful of pens with the firm's name on them, she smiled. The representatives had oohed and aahed over the inn's architecture and its quaint warmth and the view. They'd asked questions about items displayed on tables and on the walls. They had been delighted to meet her great-aunt who insisted they have pieces of her oatmeal pie and cup after cup of her delicious coffee.

Aenti Sylvia had played the generous Mennonite host to the hilt, though she gave Lauren a conspiratorial wink when the representatives weren't looking. None of the businessmen and women seemed to recall, while they were complimenting her great-aunt on the delicious food, that The Acorn Farm Inn would be a competitor once the casino was open.

Collecting the extra folders from the dining room table, Lauren stored them in the battered box. Patrick was going to be pleased this evening when she sent him her report about the meetings. Both developers had been receptive to her ideas and had arranged for another meeting in a week where she would be expected to have more specific information to share about how Krause-Matsui-Fitzgerald could put a positive spin on a casino encroaching on Bliss Valley.

Her fingers tightened on the box as she reached for the lid. *Encroaching?* It was a good thing neither the potential clients nor her boss could read her mind. They'd be questioning if she was the right person to lead a public relations blitz focusing on the positive aspects of having a Las Vegas–style casino set amid a backdrop of cornfields and Amish buggies.

She looked around the pleasant room and tried not to imagine how it would look in harsh light from a towering parking garage that had been part of the plans shared with her. No! She was in Bliss Valley to do a job and reap the rewards when she succeeded. Then she could…

Pausing near the door to the kitchen, Lauren sighed. All her hard work had been aimed at helping her parents retire from the jobs that had worn them to the bone for the past fifteen years. Now how would they take the offer of her buying them a house in Florida? Would they think she believed she, because they weren't her birth parents, needed to buy their love? Would they think she was trying to get them far away from her?

"Stop it!" she said to herself.

She didn't need to look at her life from every angle and try to spin it in the best direction as she must with her clients and potential clients. Until the contract was signed and Patrick offered her that promotion, why was she worrying?

Because you feel guilty you haven't called Mom and Dad.

With a groan, Lauren pushed through the door as she said, "In." She rushed through the kitchen and around the ironing board set in the center, almost running into one of her great-aunt's hired girls who carried a large pile of sheets and pillow-cases. She called an apology over her shoulder as she opened the door to the back stairs and took them two at a time.

She glanced at the clock on the nightstand in the room she was using, then tossed the box of folders on the bed. Adam would be arriving soon, and she'd better get changed out of her business clothes. Not into plain clothes. Not today, when she was going to get her beloved Ringo back. Throwing her suit and off-white silk blouse on top of the box, she pulled on worn jeans, an oversize Philadelphia Eagles jersey and her black sneakers. She brushed her hair and wiped off her lipstick.

She picked up the box she'd tossed on the bed and pulled out her pages of meeting notes. Once she had her car, she'd run into Strasburg and have some copies made. Patrick liked to see them as part of her reports. She could have taken a photo with her phone, but it wouldn't have been as legible. To be honest, she wanted to stop at the Strasburg Country Store & Creamery and sample their strawberry ice cream. She'd bring *Aenti* Sylvia some of her favorite licorice.

Ready to go, she grabbed her coat off its hanger, picked up her purse, made sure her checkbook was inside, stuffed the pages into her tote bag, which still held a couple of her fold-ers, and opened the door. She started to close it, but halted. She picked up the clothes and hung them in the closet next to the other ensembles she'd brought with her. Old habits, ingrained throughout her childhood, wouldn't let her leave the room a mess.

If Gina Marie Tinniswood hadn't given her up for adop-tion and decided to raise her herself, would Lauren have been able to walk out of the room, leaving it a disaster? Who would she be now?

Again she shook the questions out of her head. Playing "What if...?" was an amazing tool when brainstorming with a client. Then, she had data and preferences to create a successful PR campaign, so she could craft what was required.

Now she had nothing other than her possible birth mother's name and an appointment to have her DNA collected tomorrow. Trying to look at possible scenarios was impossible. The number was infinite.

If you called your parents...

She silenced the small voice before it could finish. Until her head was on straighter and her thoughts under control, she would postpone the call. She didn't want to say something she didn't mean—or something she did, but phrase it wrong. That would make things more uncomfortable between them.

If possible.

Lauren went downstairs a little bit slower than she'd gone up. She waved to her great-aunt, who was on the phone, taking information for a room reservation. Stepping onto the porch, she saw a gray-topped buggy turning between the shrinking snowbanks at the end of the driveway. On time. For a man who didn't wear a wristwatch, Adam was incredibly punctual.

He'd dashed her hopes he wouldn't show up and she'd have to call a limo again. After he'd left yesterday in the wake of her blunt comments, she'd assumed—and been ready to believe—he wouldn't come back.

She hurried down the steps, her tote bag banging against her jeans. Water dripped from the roof, but she dodged it.

She didn't wait for Adam to get out. Skirting a knee-high snowbank along the drive, she slid aside the passenger door. She climbed in, knocking water and mud off her boots as she did.

Adam's face was shadowed by the brim of the straw hat he

wore instead of his black wool winter hat. His mouth was set in a straight line, and he sat stiffly as if he were a statue of himself.

When she greeted him, he gave her a curt nod.

"Set?" he asked as soon as she'd closed the door.

"Yes." She set her bag and purse between them.

Her bag tilted toward the floor. Steadying it, she shoved the contents inside.

She peeked through her lowered lashes at Adam, trying to look as if she weren't looking. He was such a handsome man when he smiled, but with his face so taut, he was intimidating. She wasn't going to let him tyrannize her. She wasn't that little girl any longer.

He picked up the reins and gave his horse, Sparks, the command to move the buggy forward. She couldn't help noticing how tightly he held the reins. He was as uneasy about the drive to the garage, she realized, as she was. As if he'd noticed her quick glance, he loosened his grip. She tried to relax against the seat and think of something to say when her thoughts focused on his ruddy cheeks and how the black coat flattered his coloring.

She went with the obvious. "Thanks for coming today to take me to the garage."

"I said I would."

"I didn't know—" Chiding herself for sounding like a nervous teenage girl on her first date with the big man on campus, she said, "I can tell you I appreciate it, can't I?"

"Of course."

When she waited for him to add something else, she realized he wasn't going to. The silence grew like a giant balloon, filling and then overfilling the buggy as it pressed against her chest.

She looked across the front seat. Adam stared straight ahead as if fascinated by his horse's ears. Her gaze dropped to his strong hands on the reins. He wasn't wearing gloves, though it was chillier today than it'd been yesterday. His hands were rough and chapped, the hands of a working man. She thought about Mr. Satterfield with his smooth hands. A few of the men she worked with in Philadelphia spent more time and money on manicures than she did. The idea of Adam sitting in a salon, soaking his fingertips in a bowl, was so ludicrous she struggled to smother a laugh.

He gave her a baffled frown, and she became serious. Again she searched her mind for a way to restart the conversation, but said nothing as two cars appeared, one coming toward them, the other catching up from behind. Adam needed to concentrate on driving. Even in the best road conditions, it was dangerous when a buggy was approached from both directions.

"There's a driveway just ahead," Lauren said, pointing to an opening in the gray snowbanks.

She'd assumed he would say, *Danki.* He didn't as he steered the horse across the driveway.

There wasn't enough room for the horse and the buggy, but he'd left most of the road for the cars. They sped past, spraying the buggy with filthy water from the road. The horse shook his mane, rattling the harness, and she guessed he'd been struck, too.

Adam reached behind the front seat and grabbed a towel. He didn't say anything to her as he got out and went to the horse. With care, he tilted Sparks's head down. She knew he wanted to make sure no salt or sand had gotten into his horse's eyes.

When he smiled and patted the horse's nose, she released the breath she hadn't realized she'd been holding. She shifted her purse and tote bag out of his way when he climbed into the buggy and pulled the door closed.

All without saying a word.

As he reached for the reins, she asked, "Why are you giving me the silent treatment? If you didn't want to pick me up, you weren't obligated to. I could have found another way to the garage."

He bent down and picked up a folder from the floor. She hadn't noticed it'd fallen out. She hoped it hadn't gotten wet from where the snow had melted off their boots. She didn't have many extras.

"This is what's bothering me," he said.

"My work?"

"Your work for those casino companies."

"I don't work for a casino company."

"You shouldn't have anything to do with that casino," he said in a clipped voice. "You grew up here, and you know building a casino here is wrong."

"Why's it wrong? I suppose you think a casino will ruin the peace and quiet." She pushed down a sudden surge of anger she didn't want to feel. It wasn't as if Adam Hershberger's opinion meant anything to her. Or it shouldn't have, but it did. "Weren't you the one who complained it was *too* peaceful and *too* quiet here?"

"When I was a foolish teenager, *ja*. Now that I've got a *kind* of my own—"

"Mary Beth is a sweet child."

"*Ja.*" He pressed his lips together, and she guessed he hadn't wanted her to take the conversation in a different direction.

Or did he think it was a big mistake for him to talk about his daughter with a woman whose parents were under the *bann*? She wouldn't put such a stupid idea past him. His ideas of what was right and wrong had always been skewed.

"You named her for your mother?" she asked.

"The Mary is for *Mamm*." He gave the command for Sparks to pull the buggy onto the road before adding, "The Beth is for my *grossmammi*."

"I'd assumed one of the names was for someone in her mother's family. I was named for my mother's great-great-aunt and my father's great-grandmother. Laurene Yvonne."

"It's nice to have a connection with the past," he said.

"It is, isn't it?"

She clasped her hands over the folder on her lap and raised her chin as they drove along the otherwise deserted road, past farms and fields reappearing from beneath the snow. She wasn't sure why she felt like she'd been through a battle with Adam. A battle with Adam that she, for the first time since she'd met him, had won.

Slowing the buggy in front of the garage where he worked part-time, Adam opened his door. He stepped out into a puddle and was glad he, instead of his daughter, was wearing his work boots today. Why Mary Beth had chosen to put on his boots instead of her own was a question he'd probably never get answered.

He looked under the buggy to check that the passenger door wasn't over another puddle. As piqued as Lauren already was with him, he didn't need her accusing him of parking where her sneakers would get soaked. He was treated to the view of slender legs stretching toward the ground in the jeans that clung to each line.

Before he could start recalling how nice the sight of her legs had been when a younger Laurene had rounded the bases during a softball game, he cleared his throat and said, "Be careful." A warning he should take for himself. "There's a puddle near the front wheel."

"Thank you." Her voice drifted to him, as light and pleasant as the spring breeze.

He led the way into the garage. The familiar odors of dust, oil and grease welcomed him. The front room was empty, and he heard the faint sounds of Elvis coming through the connecting door. A sure sign Frank was working.

Without a word to Lauren, he pushed through the door. He knew she'd follow because getting her car meant she wouldn't have to depend on him for a ride again.

The prick of dismay at that thought startled him. He wanted her gone from Bliss Valley and her public relations work with her. Yet, consternation at not seeing her anymore raced through him again.

He ignored it. Any feelings he had for Lauren, and he didn't want to explore them closely, had to be shoved aside to safeguard his great-*grossdawdi*'s farm. No matter how attracted he was to her and no matter how Mary Beth had talked about her yesterday and this morning, he must keep the casino from being built on their land.

Frank Collins resembled the Beetle he was standing next to. Short, round and without a hair on his head. His eyes, when he raised them from the engine to Adam as he came through the door, were even the same pale blue as the car.

Frank looked past him, his eyes widening. He wiped his hands on a stained towel and smiled. "You must be the owner of this car, my dear."

Lauren stepped around Adam. "Yes, it's mine." She was shrugging off her coat though it was cold in the garage. As she folded it over her arm, she added, "I'm Lauren Nolt. Adam told me you'd been able to fix it. I wasn't sure how much damage had been done by me making it limp here after hitting that big pothole over by the Bliss Valley Covered Bridge."

"Anything can be fixed," Frank said in his no-nonsense voice. "All it takes is time and money." He gave Lauren a slow wink so she couldn't miss it. "And a bit of experience and know-how."

Adam told himself he shouldn't be surprised Frank, who

paid more attention to cars than women, was flirting with Lauren. In Frank's eyes, she was one hundred percent *Englisch*. His friend was more than a decade older than Lauren, but he'd been dating all sorts of women since his divorce a few years ago.

Stay out of it, his mind warned him, but the rest of him didn't listen.

Stepping forward, he asked, "Frank, is the car set to go?"

His friend looked at him as if he'd forgotten Adam was there. "Just about. I can't remember the last time I saw one of these running." He ran his hand over the curved fender and focused on Lauren again. "1966, isn't it?"

"Yes," she replied.

"How long have you had it?"

"About seven years."

"You've taken good care of it." He wiped his hands again on the rag. "You and whoever had it before you."

"Ringo is a pretty special car."

Frank grinned. "So you're an oldies fan, too?" He gestured toward the radio still blasting from a shelf on the other side of the garage. "Nothing like a bit of the King to get the juices going, eh?"

"The King?" A flush climbed her cheeks. "That's Elvis, isn't it?"

"Yes. So I guess you like the Beatles more."

"I like some of their songs. To be honest, I named the car Ringo because it was the most 1960s name I knew. I thought a Beetle needed a Beatles' name."

Adam wanted to join the conversation, but he didn't know much about old *Englisch* music. He knew even less about contemporary popular music because he'd gotten rid of his radio and tape player when he decided to join the *Leit*.

Knowing he sounded rude, and not caring because he

wanted to put an end to the candid appraisal Frank was giving her, he asked, "Is the car ready for Laurene?"

They turned to stare at him. What had he said? Heat rushed up his face as he realized what he'd called her.

Laurene.

He thought he'd gotten past that mistake, though what he considered her real name slipped into his mind when he wasn't careful. In fact, remembering to call her Lauren was the smartest thing he could do. Laurene Nolt had been a part of their community, but Lauren Nolt was an *Englisch* woman. Splitting that hair meant he could admire her pretty face and the easy way she used her hands when she spoke without worrying a seed of attraction could grow into more. The divide between her world and his was as broad and insurmountable as between him and the sun.

That wasn't why he'd used it now. He wanted to put an end to Frank's bold looks and easy winks.

Frank said, "Sorry. I thought you said your name is Lauren."

"It is," she replied. "Now."

"You changed your name?" He leaned an elbow on the top of the car. "*That* is interesting. I guessed the moment you walked in here you'd prove to be an interesting woman. A very interesting woman." Without taking his gaze off her, he said, "Adam, fetch the file for good ole Ringo here, will you?"

Fetch? He'd never heard Frank use that word. Was Frank trying to impress Lauren? His friend was almost salivating as he stared at her.

"Hey, Adam," Frank called again, "while you're out there, get me that parts catalog, too, will you?"

He waited, knowing what would come next.

"The yellow one. I think I left it with the file on the counter in the front."

"I'll find it." He loped across the garage. At the door, he paused and looked over his shoulder.

Lauren was plying Frank with questions, and she didn't seem to have noticed Frank asking for the catalog by color rather than the distributor's name. His friend had become accustomed to using the cover color when he wanted Adam to get him a specific book. If he suspected Adam couldn't read, he'd kept it to himself.

Adam wanted it to stay that way. For Lauren to discover the truth now would be humiliating.

Chapter Nine

Lauren paced her great-aunt's bedroom that had become her impromptu office. Files were scattered on every flat surface, and stacks of notes and to-do lists were piled on top of them. More papers covered the quilt on the bed, and her computer was open on the pillows.

As she listened to yet another annoying repetition of her boss's taped voice saying again how important her call was and how he'd get to her as soon as possible and please don't hang up, she tapped the space bar on her computer to halt the screen saver.

For the fifth time.

That meant she'd been waiting for Patrick to pick up his phone for at least twenty-five minutes. *He* was the one who'd insisted she call him at ten this morning because he was busy, and he couldn't guarantee she'd get in touch with him if she didn't call at ten on the dot. *He* had assured her the conversation would be a quick one because he had a few items to update her on before she met with the casino representatives again.

Ten wasn't a convenient time at a bed-and-breakfast because it was checkout time, and she'd been helping her great-aunt by toting guests' luggage to their cars. At the same time, the housekeeping staff was piling bedding in the cramped laundry room. Washing and drying the sheets, pillowcases and towels had become Lauren's chore. She didn't mind, but if she was late getting the first load into the washer, the linens might not be ironed and on the beds before the next guests checked in.

Lauren had acceded to her boss's request. She knew some days at the office defined *hectic*. She'd rushed through serving breakfast and left before the dishes were done. Not that anyone had seemed too upset. *Aenti* Sylvia had said she understood, and Lauren suspected the two young women who worked for her had been glad when she wasn't underfoot any longer. Evonne and Kendra, who were Old Order Mennonite like her great-aunt, had been polite to her, but distant. She didn't know if it was because they were more than a decade younger than she was and thought she wouldn't be interested in what they had to say or if they were shy.

Glancing at the clock by the bed, Lauren knew she couldn't stay on hold much longer. She had to get downstairs and do the laundry. What would Patrick say if she told him that? He would either laugh or chew her out. He wouldn't waste a second sharing with the office what she was doing in Lancaster County to keep busy while preparing for the next meetings. Her boss sent his laundry out to be cleaned and pressed and ironed before being delivered to his door. How long would it take someone—and she guessed it would be Cassie Varozza, who would take advantage of the situation to grab the promotion that should be Lauren's—to create a meme that would fly through the firm like a new tidbit on the Amish grapevine?

Lauren stopped her pacing and stared at her reflection in the mirror. She'd never imagined she'd be thinking about memes while dressed in plain clothing with a *kapp* perched on the handful of pins holding her hair in place.

She'd never understood what someone meant when saying a person was caught between two worlds. She'd always been the decisive one. Consider the facts. Weigh the alternatives. Make a choice. No looking back once she leaped.

"Hello? Lauren, are you there?" Patrick's voice came from the phone.

Holding it to her ear, she said, "I'm here."

He didn't say he was sorry for keeping her on hold. She didn't expect him to. Patrick never apologized, though he expected anyone who reported to him to fall on their sword if they misplaced a comma in a contract.

"We've talked it over." He didn't bother to explain who "we" was. "We think it's best if you stay there, Lauren, until after the second meetings with Welsh Development and Pan-Lancaster Growth. I'm hearing Welsh has the inside track, because one of their principals went to school with a heavy-weight on the state committee."

"So you want me to focus on them?"

"No!" Patrick's scowl was obvious in his voice. "It doesn't matter which company wins the casino approval. All that matters is the winner chooses us to do their public relations. Of course, if while talking to them, you get some info that would tip the scales one way or the other, make sure you pass it to me ASAP. These guys are ready to play any advantage they can, and if they're grateful to us, that's good."

Lauren bit her lip to keep from reminding her boss that obtaining and using such insider information would be unscrupulous, if not downright criminal. Patrick wouldn't listen. In fact, he'd make fun of her for being a Goody-Goody Two-shoes. Those people, he'd reminded her often when she first was hired, were worthless losers who never got ahead.

He outlined the terms of the contract the firm would want to get from the victorious developer, though she'd drawn up the list he was reading from. Not giving her a chance to remind him of that or anything else, he said, "Keep me in the loop every inch of the way. Act as if your job depends on it."

"Because it does," she finished, but he'd already ended the call.

She sank to sit on the blanket chest at the foot of the bed. Disgust left her feeling as if a parade of slugs crawled across her skin. Use one company against the other to get the inside track?

Why hadn't Patrick's style of doing business bothered her before? She'd always nodded when he gave her what he believed was sage advice a mentor should pass along to a protégé. He'd said she'd be smart to sit at his feet and absorb the pearls of wisdom he tossed in her direction, and she had. She'd participated as a silent observer in his meetings as well as attending her own. She'd taken notes and then spent more time highlighting them and studying them.

Not once, until now, had she ever questioned his methods. The second thoughts she was having were ones she didn't like.

She needed to clear her head. To think. To remind herself how important it was to keep her eyes on the prize. Getting the promotion instead of Cassie snatching it away.

Everything else in her life had changed. She couldn't let plans for her career go off the tracks, too.

When, late one afternoon during the following week, Lauren came out of the inn to bring in the dried sheets, she wasn't surprised to see Mary Beth Hershberger perched on top of the fence separating *Aenti* Sylvia's land from the Weaver farm. Adam's daughter had come to the inn twice since her initial visit with Lauren, and each time Lauren had convinced her to return home before she was missed.

Today, the little girl's braids stuck out in opposite directions, and she wore boots that fit her. Mud edged the hem of her light blue dress and her... It took Lauren a moment, but she remembered the word for a little girl's pinafore. A *schlupp schotzli*. When the white garment was pressed and clean, it made a child look like a character from *Little House on the Prairie*.

Mary Beth's looked bedraggled and dirty.

"Have you been wrestling piglets?" Lauren asked in *Deitsch* as she put down the empty laundry basket and walked around the pool toward the fence. Her ability to remember words and phrases in the language she'd once spoken without a thought was growing every day.

"You're *ab in kopp*!"

Lauren laughed. "I'm silly, am I? If you weren't wrestling piglets in a sty, how did you get so dirty?"

Mary Beth looked at herself in surprise. "The field's muddy."

"I hope you left some of the mud in the field."

The little girl giggled. "Left lots."

"Well, we're going to have to get at least the top layers off your hands before you have one of *Aenti* Sylvia's snicker-doodles."

"Love snickerdoodles!"

"Me, too." In the same cheerful voice, she said, "Jump down, and we'll get you washed up. I'll send some cookies home with you."

The child shook her head. "No! Want to feed the ducks."

"I'll tell you what. You come sometime with your *daed* or *Grossdawdi* Ephraim and—"

"Want to feed them now." She banged her hands on the rail. "Now, please."

"Then you'll go straight home?"

"Cookies, too?"

Lauren had to fight her smile. The little girl negotiated with the skills of a disreputable used car salesman and had inherited her father's charm, something Lauren hadn't been able to disregard even when Adam had been filling her life with despair.

"Cookies, too." Holding out her hand, she said, "Let's go for a quick visit. Okay?"

"Okay." Mary Beth nodded and scampered down from the fence.

She didn't wait for Lauren as she began to skip toward the pond on the other side of the barn. *Pond* was a generous name for the small water-filled indentation in the field. Lauren guessed it was about ten feet deep in the center, but there were fish in it. There'd be plenty of bugs as the weather got warmer. Reeds bordered the water like an uneven lace collar, offering the perfect place for several pairs of mallards because they could nest among the reeds or in the high grass beyond the pond.

The afternoon sunshine danced in the ripples created by the breeze. Lauren caught up with Mary Beth and took the child's hand. Having the little girl rush right into the pond would make her clothes look even worse, and Lauren had no idea how much mud was on the bottom at the edge or where the pond dropped off into deeper water. Mary Beth began to protest, but Lauren bent and put a finger to her lips.

"The ducks will fly away if they hear us coming," she whispered to the child. "We've got to be quiet."

"Quiet." The little girl nodded, then held her lower lip closed with her teeth.

Straightening, Lauren led the way around the end of the pond farthest from the road. She had to bite her own lip to keep from laughing when Mary Beth walked on tiptoe.

"Stay right here." Lauren pointed toward the thick clump of grass on the opposite shore. "It looks as if Mama and Papa

Duck have built a nest over there, and they won't be happy if we get too close."

"I know."

"You do?"

"*Ja*. Eggs there." She grinned up at Lauren and held up a single finger. "One month for ducklings. That's what *Daed* says."

"That's right. It does take about a month for the ducklings to hatch. You're a smart little girl."

"Know 'bout animals. Me be a farmer one day. Like *Daed* and *Grossdawdi* Ephraim."

Knowing few Amish women would ever oversee a farm, unless they were widows, Lauren wondered if this little girl would be more accepting of the role she must take in a plain community than Lauren had been.

Was that the reason my parents took me and left? The question refused to remain silent, but she still didn't have an answer for it.

She couldn't recall any time when she'd spoken with her parents about what she hoped to do in the future. Other than teasing them to take her to the public library where she could find books on subjects not taught at the plain school, she'd never mentioned a single word about her dream to attend college and to travel the world. Higher education wasn't something a plain person, especially a girl, should aspire to.

Her parents never had mentioned her eclectic reading choices. They must have seen the titles of the books piled on the table in her room. Had they found the other books, which she'd hidden in the depths of the cedar chest under her window? Books about high school and college and choosing a career. She'd vacillated between becoming a teacher or a nurse. While she could have found a position teaching in an Amish school once she finished her own schooling at fourteen, the training she'd need to be certified as a nurse would require a high school diploma and college.

She'd decided, shortly before they left, she no longer wanted to teach. Working with Adam had soured her on the idea.

"See *bopplin*?" Mary Beth asked, pulling Lauren from the past.

Translating the question to mean the little girl wanted to see the ducklings when they hatched, Lauren said, "I'll keep watch on the nest. Once there are new ducklings, I'll let you know. Okay?"

"Okay." Her happy grin returned.

"Now, we need to get some cookies and get you home."

Mary Beth started to let out a cheer, then put her own finger to her lips.

With a smile, Lauren took her hand again and led her to the house. Going to the back door in the only section of the house, other than the front porch and trim, not built of stone, she stopped long enough to unpin the few pieces of laundry from the line and throw them in the basket. She left the basket in the laundry room and herded Mary Beth into the kitchen. It was empty, not surprising when *Aenti* Sylvia's hired girls went home around four, so they could help make supper for their own families.

"In," came the call from the dining room, and the door swung hard.

Lauren rushed over to hold it open for her great-aunt to steer her wheelchair through the narrow space. *Aenti* Sylvia was becoming more proficient with her chair every day. On Sunday, Lauren had attended services at the brick Mennonite meetinghouse in Strasburg with her great-aunt. Her plans to drive *Aenti* Sylvia in her Beetle hadn't worked because there wasn't room for the chair. A neighbor gave them a ride in her much more spacious car, and *Aenti* Sylvia had managed to steer her chair between the narrow rows of wooden pews.

Her great-aunt hadn't seemed bothered by the stares as they went in, but Lauren had been aware of each and every one. She'd known wearing her gray suit would make her stick out. Even so, she never considered wearing plain clothing to church. Playing a role for guests was one thing, but she wouldn't enter God's house pretending to be something she wasn't. If her great-aunt had sensed her uneasiness, she hadn't said a word about it. Instead she'd introduced Lauren to everyone in the nearby pews and acted as if nothing out of the ordinary was happening.

"*Ach!* Here you are," *Aenti* Sylvia said as she wheeled herself into the kitchen. Her face creased in a wide smile. "You've got company. Who is that dirty, little creature with you?"

"Not a cree-ter," Mary Beth said. "Me Mary Beth. I a girl."

"A girl who likes cookies, ain't so?"

The little girl's smile returned. "Me *loves* cookies. Gots some?"

"You know I always do. I've got snickerdoodles."

"Laurene said so."

Over the child's head, Lauren's great-aunt caught her eyes and arched her brows.

Lauren wanted to tell her nobody should put much stock into what a four-year-old said. Instead, she took the child to the sink and held her up so she could wash her hands. Because Lauren suspected the little girl got more water on the front of them than on her hands, she took out a cloth and washed Mary Beth's hands until they were clean.

"Sit and have a cookie and some milk," Lauren said, pointing to the table in the center of the room. "Meanwhile, I'll package cookies for you to take home."

With a toothy grin, the child scrambled up into a chair. She giggled with delight when Lauren gave her a plate with one of *Aenti* Sylvia's generous-sized snickerdoodles.

"Eat slowly," Lauren said. "If you eat fast, crumbs can escape, and you don't want to lose a single bite, do you?"

Mary Beth nodded and picked up the cookie. She turned it around, trying to decide where to bite first.

"I eat the outside before the inside," Lauren said as she set a glass half-filled with milk next to the plate. "Crunchy, then soft and gooey." She wasn't sure how to say the last word in *Deitsch*, so she didn't try. Not that it mattered because the little girl seemed to get the gist of her comment and nibbled on the outer edge of the cookie.

As Lauren put the milk into the refrigerator, *Aenti* Sylvia wheeled over to her. "You're very *gut* with her, Laurene. You should have *kinder* of your own."

"Someday maybe. When the time is right."

"My *mamm* used to say to me while you keep waiting for the right time, it may pass you by when you're not looking."

"This isn't the time to discuss such things."

"Because little pitchers have big ears?" *Aenti* Sylvia looked at where Mary Beth was focused on eating her cookie. "She's not paying any attention to us."

"It's not that. Until I know what's going on with my parents, I don't want to think about a family of my own."

"Have you spoken with them, *liebling*?"

"I thought I'd wait until I had a definite answer on the DNA test."

"You had that last week."

"They said it'd take about a week to ten days to get the results to the attorney." She didn't add she'd had them sent to Mr. Satterfield because she hadn't been sure if she would stay in Bliss Valley or go to her apartment or where she might be when they were ready.

"You'll call your parents once you've got the results?"

She faltered, not wanting to lie to her great-aunt, who had

given her a haven without making a big deal out of it. *Aenti* Sylvia was right, but she couldn't bring herself to make the call. She'd stared at the phone and the long list of unread texts and unlistened-to voice mails from her mother and her father for almost a half hour the night she'd gone to the lab and had her cheek swabbed. Then, she'd plugged it in to recharge and had gone to bed without calling.

"It's not simple, *Aenti* Sylvia," she said when she realized Mary Beth was finishing up her milk. Getting a plastic bag, she put five large cookies in it and sealed the top.

"Not simple?" asked her great-aunt, who'd followed in her wheelchair. "They're your parents, and they love you. All you need to do is get over your anger and open yourself to forgiveness."

"I don't know."

"Don't know what? How to forgive? *That* is simple, Laurene. All you have to do is offer it. Forgiveness is something you give. It says so right in the middle of the word."

"I need to take Mary Beth home before they start searching for her again. I'll be back soon." She went to the table, took the child by the hand and walked out.

It had been an argument she could never win. Not with her great-aunt. Nor with her own guilt that told her *Aenti* Sylvia was right.

Drawing in his reins as he reached the turn to the farm lane leading to his great-*grossdawdi*'s farm, Adam slowed his buggy. Two familiar forms walked along the road coming from the other direction. Lauren and his daughter. Had Mary Beth run away to visit her again? He climbed out of the buggy and watched as they paused to examine some wild daffodils that were ready to bloom.

Lauren noticed him when she straightened and said something to Mary Beth. He couldn't hear the words because of the steady breeze rising as the sun headed west, but his daughter's squeal of excitement rang out. Mary Beth started to run toward him. Lauren stopped her and took her by the hand again as a car came along the road.

It edged around them, but began to slow. Seeing a camera raised in the car, he turned away so his face wouldn't be visible. He didn't move until the car continued on. Most visitors to Lancaster County understood plain people didn't want their pictures taken, but a few rudely persisted.

By then, Lauren and Mary Beth had reached him. His daughter held up a clear, plastic bag filled with broken cookies.

"Look, *Daed*! Snickerdoodles!" Mary Beth crowed. "Want some?"

"After supper will be a *gut* time, ain't so?"

"One little bite now?"

"After supper," he said with a bit more sternness. "Take them and give them to *Grossdawdi* Ephraim. He'll make sure your cousins don't eat them before you can!"

"*Ja!*" As she spun to run up the lane, she paused and said, "*Danki*, Laurene. Don't forget!"

"I won't," Lauren said with a smile. "I'll let you know when the ducklings come. Don't come and disturb them, or Mama Duck and Papa Duck will hide them and we'll never see them."

"All right." Dismay crossed her face. "No cookies for a month?"

"*Aenti* Sylvia and I will make sure you get cookies, but only if you don't come to bother the ducks."

Mary Beth considered the offer, then nodded. "Bye, then!"

Adam watched her skip up the lane. "Did you drag her through the mud?"

"No, she came to the inn that way." Lauren laughed, but switched to English. "I asked her if she'd been wrestling piglets."

He wondered why she didn't keep speaking *Deitsch*. He halted himself from asking. Beneath her easy smile, he sensed she was upset as she looked everywhere but at him. "It would have been quite a feat because we don't keep pigs, but I can see how you thought that. *Danki* for bringing her home."

"It's a nice day for a walk, and I needed time away from the inn."

He almost asked her what was troubling her, but again stopped himself as another car sped over the hill and past the buggy so fast Sparks shied.

"These drivers need to remember they shouldn't take the crown of a hill at top speed." He frowned as he calmed the horse.

"Most people know."

"Too many people forget." He hesitated, then said, "I wasn't sure if you'd still be at the inn. Your car is working, ain't so?"

"Frank did a good job on it."

"Glad to hear it."

Why were they talking like strangers? Another question he had to keep to himself.

"Where are you headed now?" he asked. "Back to the inn?"

"Yes, but I'm taking the scenic route and going by way of the covered bridge."

"Why?"

"Why not? Other than the night I drove through it in the snowstorm, I haven't seen it in fifteen years, and I thought it'd be fun to take a look at it again."

She wasn't being honest with him, so maybe it was time for him to be honest with her about something he'd been thinking about for the past few days.

As she started to walk past him, he said, "Lauren, before you go…"

"Yes?"

"I'd like to talk to you about Mary Beth and how she's been running away to the inn."

The cool mask fell from her face, and her concern for his daughter reappeared. Just as he'd known she wasn't being truthful before, he could tell her worry about Mary Beth was real when she said, "Even though she made a mess of her clothes, I'm glad she comes through the fields rather than out here on the road."

"Me, too." He leaned one hand against the buggy to keep from moving nearer to her, drawn by invisible silken strings spun between them. "Lauren, you know why she's been coming to the inn, ain't so?"

"*Aenti* Sylvia's cookies and the ducks."

"They've been there for the past two years, and she didn't once go there on her own. She's going to see you."

"Me?"

"*Ja.* You're what she needs. She's been without female influence in her life for the past two years."

"I'm sure some other women in the community—especially young, single women—have offered to help with what she needs."

"What makes you think that?"

Lauren laughed. "Don't try an innocent look with me, Adam Hershberger! First, it doesn't fit on your face. Second, I was raised in this community. I saw how an unmarried man with his own business was of great interest to the unmarried women. It makes me think of a very popular book written in England more than two hundred years ago by Jane Austen. *Pride and Prejudice.* The opening line fits Lancaster County as well as it did England then."

"What's the opening line?"

Her eyes twinkled with lush purple fire. "The first line is, 'It is a truth universally acknowledged, that a single man in possession of a good fortune, must be in want of a wife.' You've got a good enough fortune, Adam, with your business and your family's farm. Therefore, it's assumed you are in need of a wife to oversee them and your household."

"A conclusion reached by several of the more eager match-makers in this county."

She laughed again and glowed with the amusement within her. It somehow made her even more lovely. Why had he spent so much time annoying her when he could have used that time to persuade her to laugh and let joy blossom across her downy cheeks and dazzling eyes? He'd been a fool. He wouldn't be any longer.

It took almost more strength than he had to focus on his daughter's needs again. "Lauren, I know I'm the last person in your life to ask you for a favor."

"Not the last, but close." That set off a new round of laughs as if she were no older than Mary Beth.

"This is serious."

She sobered. "All right. I'm listening."

"Would you consider—"

A bizarre sound, halfway between a buzz and a ring, erupted.

"My phone," Lauren said. "Let me check to see if it's some-one I've got to talk to." Pulling it from her pocket, she read the screen and blanched. She swiped one finger across the phone and said, "Hello? This is Lauren Nolt." A pause, then, "Yes, yes, I can come on Tuesday at three." Another pause, this one much longer. She shook her head, but didn't speak until she said, "All right. Thank you. Goodbye."

He said nothing when she lowered the phone to her side. She stared right through him.

"That was the lawyer's office," she said in a too-calm voice. "The DNA results are back."

"And?" he prompted when she didn't continue.

"Gina Marie Tinniswood is my birth mother."

He had no idea what to say or do. Some instinct urged him to open his arms wide. When she stepped closer and threw her own arms around his shoulders, he drew her into an embrace. She shook against him like clothes in a washing machine, and he leaned his cheek against her *kapp*. Though he hadn't known what to say or do, at least he got one thing right by offering her silent solace.

It seemed impossible to believe he'd never held her this way before. It felt so right for her to be in his arms, her cheek pressed against his chest. His heart faltered as her warm breath sifted through his shirt to warm the skin over his faltering heartbeat.

How long they might have stood there, in a place apart from the rest of the world and even time itself, he had no idea. The sound of a car coming over the hill separated them.

The devastation on her face told him she'd harbored the hope, no matter how ridiculous, that her being adopted was a hideous mistake. It didn't make sense, because even if the Tinniswood woman hadn't been her birth *mamm*, Ida Nolt had admitted she wasn't either.

"What will you do now?" he asked.

She took a deep breath and lifted her chin. "The attorney suggested I bring someone with me to meet Mrs. Tinniswood tomorrow. There's no way I can get *Aenti* Sylvia, her cast and her wheelchair into my car." She looked at him in the direct way he once had hated but now had to admire. "Will you come with me?"

He didn't know whether to be honored to be asked after all they'd been through together or horrified she didn't have anyone else to ask. He was certain of his answer.

"*Ja.*"

Chapter Ten

The attorney's office was the same as it had been during Lauren's previous visit, right down to the number of pink and red carnations on the receptionist's desk. Again, she was asked by Kai to have a seat until Mr. Satterfield was ready to meet with her.

However, the young woman stared at Adam as he followed Lauren toward the chairs in the waiting area. At first, Lauren thought Kai hadn't seen too many plain men before, though that seemed unlikely with the Central Market nearby. Amish and Mennonite vendors worked in the covered building, selling food and crafts and knickknacks.

As Adam walked away from the desk, Kai's eyes did an elevator evaluation of him. Quickly and then more slowly from head to foot and back again. When the phone rang, she flinched and reached for it, once again the professional administrative assistant.

Lauren wondered if Adam had noticed the appraisal, but she didn't ask as she chose a chair and waited for Adam to sit.

He remained on his feet, moving to look out a window that offered a view of the traffic on the street below. Holding his black hat, he became motionless. She wished she knew what he was thinking. He hadn't said more than a greeting when he arrived at the inn and had been even quieter on the drive into Lancaster. It hadn't taken much more than twenty minutes to reach the center of the city, but it had seemed like a millennium as silence had filled her car with so much tension she half feared that the roof would explode off.

While they'd walked from the multistory parking garage, he'd asked her opinion of Charlessatterfieldattorneyatlaw, though he called him Mr. Satterfield. She'd told him how the lawyer seemed to like the sound of his own voice and keeping tight control of interactions.

I see, Adam had said, then added nothing more.

She tried not to fidget. Was Adam looking for someone or something? Or was he mired in his anticipation of the meeting with her mother as she'd been since she got the call from Kai? Telling herself not to fret, she locked her fingers together on her lap and stopped her knee from bouncing with tension. It began its motion again seconds later.

As if this visit to the office was a play being performed a second time for the same audience, Mr. Satterfield emerged from the hallway to invite Lauren to come with him. She stood and looked at Adam, who gave her a silent nod. Her fluttering stomach settled as she realized instead of chattering as others might have and asking questions she couldn't answer, he'd offered her the opportunity to gather her thoughts before the meeting.

And to pray.

She knew without asking that Adam had been praying for her, and a sweet warmth eased the painful beat of her frantic heart. She stifled the urge to thank him. Not only would it embarrass him, because he wouldn't see what he was doing as extraordinary, it would also reveal how far she'd wandered from her childhood when God wasn't a distant figure to whom one should reach out only in times of the greatest need. She longed for the time when He'd been as ever-present as her own breath.

"This is?" asked the attorney.

"Adam Hershberger," Lauren replied. "He's a…my… That is, you suggested I bring someone with me, so I brought Adam."

Three sets of eyes blinked at her in near unison. She'd sounded silly, but she wasn't sure how to describe Adam. As a friend? Her feelings for him weren't that simple. There was an attraction, but a wariness, too, born of hard lessons. And even if she were drawn to him, there wasn't any future for any sort of relationship. Not when he had chosen to live his life plain, and her life was on the other side of the fence.

She wanted to say something else to fill the silence, but had no idea what. It was a shock to be speechless. She usually could make words do her bidding to persuade clients or the general public to buy what she was selling.

She didn't want to admit she didn't have anyone else to bring with her, that her life was filled with acquaintances but not friends. Only now was she realizing how much she'd lost when she moved away from Bliss Valley and the community she'd taken for granted. Her parents might have come with her…if she'd asked them. That door remained closed now, too.

You're a pitiful mess.

Mr. Satterfield introduced himself to Adam before motioning for them to follow him. He walked away as if the upcoming meeting wasn't about to change a lot of lives.

"All right?" asked Adam as he matched her steps along the corridor.

"I hope I will be," she whispered.

"I *know* you will be." He paused, then said, "Remember your *mamm* is sure to be as nervous as you are because she's facing the *kind* she gave away."

She nodded, no longer trusting her voice, when Mr. Satterfield opened the door to the conference room where they'd met before. He entered and motioned for her to take a seat at the table on the side closer to the door.

She was grateful for Adam's steady hand against her arm when she saw two women sitting on the other side. One was younger than Lauren, but the other woman was a generation older. They didn't wear plain clothes, which shouldn't have been a surprise because Tinniswood wasn't an Amish name. Yet, Lauren had let herself assume because she was raised by plain parents that her birth mother was Amish, too.

Lauren sat across from the older woman who stared at her. Searching the woman's very pale face, Lauren looked for something of her own. Their hair color was similar, though the woman's was shot with streaks of gray. She'd hoped her mother would have purple eyes like her own, something she'd been told was quite rare. Instead the woman had commonplace blue eyes edged by dark crescents as if she hadn't slept in weeks. Her face was longer than Lauren's, and her jaw more square. It reminded her of someone.

But not herself.

The other woman, a younger version of the woman across from Lauren except she wore stylish glasses and had a streak of bright blue in her hair, sat next to her and held on to her hand as if it were a lifeline.

Mother and daughter.

Was the young woman her sister? Or her half sister?

Lauren hadn't given any thought to meeting another of her biological mother's children here today.

Pulling out a chair, Mr. Satterfield said, "Before we go around the table and make introductions, I must make it clear—again—I'm here solely as Gina Marie Tinniswood's counsel. I can't act as anyone else's counsel. Do you understand?"

"Yes," Lauren said while the young woman on the other side of the table nodded.

"All right." The attorney sat and folded his arms on the table. "This is a joyous occasion, but I know it's also an uncomfortable one. Perhaps we should move right to the introductions. Gina Marie, would you like to start?"

The older woman said in a shaky voice as she began to point to herself, then halted, "I'm Gina Marie Tinniswood." She didn't add anything else.

The young woman's voice was barely audible. "I'm Skylar Lopez, and Gina Marie is my mother."

"I'm Lauren Nolt." The few words quivered as much as Mrs. Tinniswood's hand. She should think of the older woman as Gina Marie, but she couldn't. The woman was a stranger, and using her formal title kept a reassuring distance between them...at least, in her mind. "This is Adam Hershberger. He came with me."

It was lame, but the best she could do.

"I see," Mrs. Tinniswood said, though it was obvious she didn't. How could she when Lauren hadn't explained anything?

Mr. Satterfield jumped into the conversation before the silence could grip them again. "As I've mentioned to each of you, this is simply a preliminary meeting, so each of you can put a face to the names you have."

No one responded.

The attorney went on, "I'm sure you've got questions."

All eyes turned to Lauren, and she almost jumped up and

shouted she didn't want to be the focus for this meeting. But there were so many questions she yearned to ask.

Why did you give me up?

Why did you decide to look for me now?

Where are we supposed to go from here?

She didn't ask them. Instead she said, "The main question I had was if you're my birth mother. The DNA results confirmed that." She looked at Ms. Lopez. "Are you my sister or half sister?"

"Half." The younger woman's nose wrinkled as if the very thought of being related to Lauren was distasteful. "Mama never married your father. Unlike my late father, yours was a bum."

"Skylar..." The warning was quiet, but Mrs. Tinniswood's mouth had hardened as her fingers curled into fists. "I know you're upset, but please be polite."

"It's not easy when—"

"Skylar!"

This time the young woman subsided, leaning back in her chair and picking at a fingernail on her index finger.

Mrs. Tinniswood cut her eyes toward the attorney, who said, "I thought it'd be nice for you to have a chance to learn more about each other. Shall we do that, Gina Marie?"

"Yes." She looked at Lauren and splayed her hands on the table. "Thank you for agreeing to meet me."

"Of course." Again she felt as if she should add something more, and again no words formed in her mind as she gazed into her birth mother's eyes.

She'd thought there would be a moment of recognition, of some primal connection based on having come from this stranger's womb. There wasn't. If she'd passed Gina Marie Tinniswood on the street, she wouldn't have noticed any resemblance between them. Not in how they looked, not in how they spoke, not in their motions. Lauren seldom used her hands when she spoke, but the older woman seemed to move them to emphasize each word.

Realizing everyone was waiting for her to say something else, Lauren asked the most innocuous question she could think of. "Do I have other half siblings?"

"Two," Mrs. Tinniswood replied so quietly Lauren had to lean in to hear her. "Skylar has two brothers."

The younger woman looked up at her name but lowered her eyes before Lauren could discern what she was thinking. Her body language made it clear Ms. Lopez would rather have been crossing an erupting volcano than sitting in a room with an older sister she'd never met. It was the first thing Lauren felt in common with her birth family.

"Why did you give me up and keep your other children?"

"When you were born, I wasn't married. The midwife said she'd found homes for the children of other unwed mothers, so I agreed to let her find a home for you."

Didn't you want to keep me? She halted herself. The questions seemed too personal to discuss in an attorney's office. She wished she could ask everyone else to leave the room so she could speak honestly to her birth mother.

"Why aren't you dressed like he is?" Mrs. Tinniswood asked. "I was told you were going to be raised Amish."

"I was."

"You don't look it."

"I grew up as Laurene Nolt in Bliss Valley."

"So close?"

Ms. Lopez scowled. "If you were raised Amish, why aren't you dressed like *he* is?" She gestured toward Adam. "You don't look Amish to me. I'd bet your suit costs more than I make in a month."

Lauren smoothed her gray skirt and wondered what the two

women would say if Lauren was honest and said Mrs. Tinnis-wood didn't resemble her image of a mother. Surprised, she realized, no matter how upset she was with her parents, the images in her head of mother and father matched their loving faces.

She must have tensed because Adam placed a gentle hand on her sleeve. When she glanced at him, he gave her a slight nod. What was he trying to convey to her? If he thought she knew, he was mistaken.

There was, she knew, only one thing to say. The truth. It'd been concealed too long.

"My parents left the Amish when I was fourteen," she said.

Ms. Lopez gasped. "I thought if someone left, they got shunned."

"They did get shunned."

"Did they know that would happen before they went?"

"Of course. It's no secret." She looked at Adam again. "Adam can explain it better than I can because he's a deacon in his district. Deacons have many responsibilities, but one is making sure the members obey the *Ordnung*, the district's rules."

Adam copied Mr. Satterfield's motion of folding his arms on the table. "In most cases, a person who breaks the *Ordnung*'s rules isn't put under the *bann*—what you call shunned—right away. The person is counseled and given a chance to atone and ask forgiveness. If the person does, forgiveness is forthcoming and the matter isn't spoken of again. If the person doesn't, then, as a last resort, the person may be put under the *bann*. What you see as a punishment, we see as an act of love, a way to show the sinner what he or she will lose during their time on earth through their sins."

"She made it sound as if her family was kicked to the curb from day one," said Ms. Lopez.

"There would have been some contact with the Nolts. Visits from family and other members of the community, urging them to return. When that didn't work, Ida and Wayne Nolt, Lauren's parents, were put under the *bann*."

"But not my daughter?" asked Mrs. Tinniswood.

"She wasn't baptized yet, so she wasn't a full member of our congregation. As you may know, we don't have infant baptism as many Christian churches do. We believe a person must be of age to make the important commitment of living a life as Jesus taught."

Ms. Lopez frowned. "None of this explains why they left."

Lauren wished she had an answer. "They never discussed it with me. I do have another question. Can you tell me anything about my father?"

"I haven't seen him since the night I told him I was pregnant." Mrs. Tinniswood's lips tightened. "He didn't bother to check to see if I was okay after you were born."

"Maybe he didn't know."

"He knew. Trust me. He knew. He didn't check, though." She didn't add more, and Lauren suspected pressing would upset the older woman further.

She was surprised when Adam said into the strained quiet, "Lauren, I'm sure your *mamm* would be interested in hearing about what you do."

"Do?"

"For a living." He gave her a bolstering smile. "Isn't that what *Englischers* do when they meet? Talk about their jobs."

Ms. Lopez interjected, shocking Lauren even more, "What do Amish talk about?"

Adam's smile broadened to include the women on the other side of the table. "We talk about our relatives. Most Amish are related, some pretty distantly, to each other, so when we first meet, we try to figure where we sit on each other's family tree." He looked at Lauren and arched his brows.

"I work for a public relations firm in Philadelphia." As she began to explain her job and how it'd brought her out to Lancaster County, she grew calmer. She glanced at Adam, wondering if he'd known focusing on work would help her deal with the meeting.

Again, as she had that first night at the inn, she wanted to ask, *Who are you, Adam Hershberger? Who are you really?*

She would never have been able to imagine, fifteen years before, that Adam Hershberger would come to her rescue on one of the most complicated days of her life.

Adam had sent up a quick prayer of thanks to God when Lauren began to relax as she spoke about her job. Her serenity had seemed to rub off on her *mamm* and half sister as they told Lauren they'd lived in Strasburg for several years after Skylar's *daed* died, but had recently moved to Lancaster. They were renting an apartment near the hospital north of the city. Lauren's half sister had moved in with her *mamm* after Skylar's marriage ended in divorce.

The meeting lasted less than an hour, and at the end, the attorney advised they plan to meet again at his office in a week or two. Mr. Satterfield said his receptionist would be in touch with Lauren to arrange a specific date and time, depending on everyone's availability.

Adam was curious why there would be a delay in planning the meeting, and he saw Lauren was, as well. However, her *mamm* seemed pleased with the suggestion and agreed. He wondered how long Lauren would remain in Bliss Valley. Would she leave, or would she stay at her great-*aenti*'s inn even if she'd finished up her work with the casino developers?

He waited to ask until after they'd said their goodbyes, ridden the elevator to the ground floor and headed toward the parking garage.

"I don't know where I'll be in two weeks," Lauren replied as they entered the shadowed parking garage and walked along the ramp toward her car. "My boss wants me to stay out here until I get preliminary contracts signed."

"Will that be soon?"

"I don't know. I've got meetings set up with them, but these things always take time."

"I thought they were in a hurry to get the casino built."

"They are, but even in a hurry, things take longer than everyone expects."

He nodded, grateful for any delay in the project. "And once you get the contracts signed?"

"I don't know. I do have some vacation time coming. A lot actually. Though Patrick may want me back sooner."

"Patrick?"

"My boss," she said as she opened her car door and got inside to stretch across and open the passenger door.

Grateful she couldn't see his face at her explanation, he took his time getting into the small car that had far less room than his buggy. The last thing he'd thought he'd feel when she mentioned an *Englischer*'s name in passing was the whetted edge of jealousy. He was attracted to Lauren, but there was no future for them. If he walked out with a woman, she must be Amish. Lauren wasn't. Not any longer.

"That didn't go as I expected." He pulled on his seat belt and clicked it into place. "Are you okay?"

"I don't know how I feel right now."

"So you don't know if you'll see her again?"

"I don't know," she repeated.

She backed the small car out of the parking space and maneuvered through the garage. She paid before turning onto the street, which was busy with late afternoon traffic.

Not wanting to distract her while she drove through the narrow streets, Adam waited until they reached the highway, heading south toward Bliss Valley.

He broke the silence by saying, "This is none of my business, so you can tell me that and I won't say anything else, but I've got to say this one thing."

"All right." Her fingers tightened on the wheel, but she kept her eyes focused on the road.

Maybe it was for the best. If she'd looked at him and he saw the haunted void in her eyes, he might not have been able to say what he must.

"You need to be kind to your birth *mamm*."

"I was." She slowed to a stop at an intersection. As two cars went through, she glanced at him. "I was, wasn't I?"

"You were pleasant, especially with your half sister's hostility, but you didn't reach out to your *mamm* before we left."

"Adam, you of all people shouldn't be telling me I should have given her a big ole bear hug. Remember? I was raised Amish, too, and we're not apt to participate in PDAs." She shifted the car. "Public displays of affection, I should have said. It means—"

"I know what it means, and I never forget you grew up plain. All I know is if I'd been separated from Mary Beth for years and finally had a chance to see her again, I'd do or say whatever I could in an effort to heal the rift time had created between us."

"That's because you love your daughter."

"You don't think your birth mother loves you?"

"I don't know." She glanced at him with a sad smile. "I know I'm saying the same thing over and over, but it's the truth, Adam. I don't know what to think or what to feel right now. Nothing I've ever experienced has prepared me for this."

"I know." He wished he had words to ease her stress. The inspiration he'd hoped would come to him when he was ordained as a deacon was failing him again. *God, You chose me for these moments. Help me find the right words to ease her heart.*

"Right now," she said, "I'm family-ed out. I've got to take some time to decide what sort of relationship I want with any of them."

"Including Ida and Wayne?"

She nodded. "I'm still working on that."

"What about your great-*aenti*?"

Turning at a corner and taking a left, she said, "Isn't it peculiar the one relative I feel closest to is *Aenti* Sylvia whom I haven't seen in so many years?"

"I don't think so. She's made you feel welcome at the inn."

For the first time that afternoon, Lauren gave him a genuine smile. "She makes everyone feel welcome. Me, her guests—"

"Mary Beth?"

"*Aenti* Sylvia enjoys her visits." She glanced at him, then at the road. "I do, too."

"I'm glad to hear that because I need to ask you a favor."

"The one you wanted to ask yesterday before the phone interrupted? I'm sorry, Adam. I forgot all about it."

"You've had plenty of other things on your mind. I wanted to ask you if you'd be willing to have Mary Beth come over to the inn in the afternoon. If you don't have meetings, of course."

"You want me to babysit your daughter?"

"No." He sighed. "All right, maybe the answer is closer to *ja*. My great-*grossdawdi* can't be expected to keep an eye on her every day. It's too much for him, and you've seen how Mary Beth doesn't like being cooped up indoors. More important, she likes being with you, Lauren. When she comes home after seeing you, she doesn't talk of anything else but what you two did together. You give her something she can't get from us four guys. She needs a woman in her life." *So do I.*

For a frightening second, he thought he'd said those last three words aloud, but Lauren didn't react.

"Sure, I'll be glad to watch Mary Beth for you," she said, "as long as it's okay with *Aenti* Sylvia. I'm sure it will be." She lowered her eyes. "However, you've got to remember my work with the casino developers has to come first."

He wanted to assure her that fact was one he'd never forget.

Chapter Eleven

When a motion caught his eye, Adam looked up from the lawn mower that was in pieces on the worktable in his cramped shop. He'd been cleaning the blades before sharpening them. He tossed the grass-stained rag on the table and opened the door.

"Is it four o'clock already?" he called.

Beyond where the buggy was parked under a maple tree, Lauren and his daughter turned as one. Mary Beth waved, then ran to him to give him a hug. He listened to her excitement about how they'd spent the afternoon decorating cupcakes as if they were Easter eggs. His gaze settled on Lauren, whose hair was loose around the shoulders of the pink blouse she wore with a denim skirt.

"They tastes yummy, *Daed*!"

He smiled at his daughter. "Did you save me one?"

"Gots cupcakes for you and Simon and Dale and *Grossdawdi* Ephraim." She giggled. "And me, too." She touched the top of the foil on a plate Lauren held. "See? *Eens, zwedder, drei, fiah, fimf.* One for each of us."

His smile wavered. Who had taught his daughter to count to five? When Lauren regarded Mary Beth with a proud smile, he got his answer. He'd been hiding his inability to read from his daughter, and it'd become more difficult since she'd begun pointing out words she must have learned from *Grossdawdi* Ephraim. Now she was counting. How long would it take her to surpass his meager arithmetic skills?

Lauren held up the foil-covered plate. "We thought it'd be better for me to carry the cupcakes."

He hated the inadequacies flooding him as he walked around the buggy. Holding out his hands, he said, "I'll see they make it to the kitchen in one piece."

"Thanks." She handed him the plate before she bent toward Mary Beth, who'd trailed him across the grass. "*Danki* for helping me. I couldn't have done it the same way without you. I don't know if the kitchen will ever be the same, though it's pretty with frosting everywhere."

Mary Beth giggled again, then whirled to shout, "Dale, cupcakes!"

His younger cousin jogged to them. "Did you say cupcakes?"

"I didn't."

"Mary Beth did!"

"So she did." Adam held the plate over his head and out of his shorter cousin's reach. Not by much, he realized when Dale stretched up to grab it. He lowered it and gave it to the boy. "There's one for each of us."

"For dessert tonight," Lauren said. "Right, Mary Beth?"

"Right!"

Dale lifted the foil to look under it. He whistled. "Those sure are fancy. *Danki*, Mary Beth and…"

"Lauren Nolt," Adam supplied. "Lauren, this is my cousin Dale."

"Nice to meet you, Dale," she replied. "Mary Beth has told me about you."

"*Gut* things, I hope."

She arched her brows and smiled. "She does say you tease her a lot."

"Did she tell you she teases us, too?" his cousin asked.

"Not a word. I can't imagine a little sweetie like Mary Beth ever doing that."

His daughter giggled, and Dale rolled his eyes, then winked at Mary Beth.

Chuckling, Adam sent his daughter with Dale to the house. "*Danki* for watching the so-called little sweetie and bringing her home."

"I was glad to. She's a lot of fun."

"How are you doing?" He knew he should have patience, but he couldn't keep from asking, "Have you heard anything from Mr. Satterfield or Mrs. Tinniswood?"

"Not yet." Looking past him, she said, "Is that your shop?"

He took the hint she didn't want to talk about her birth *mamm*. "*Ja*. I fix small engines in there. Would you like a tour?"

If he could impress her about how much the farm meant to the whole family, maybe there was a way she might convince the casino companies to build elsewhere. He didn't know if she or her firm had that kind of influence, but he could hope.

She was about to answer when a black truck with a large cab rolled up the lane. It stopped next to the buggy.

"Just the man we wanted to find." Chip Weatherford got out of the truck, loosening his tie at the same time. Adam's friend from the fire department worked in an office at a retail distribution building about twenty minutes east past Kinzers.

From what Adam had heard, Chip was looking for another job, one where he didn't have to wear a tie.

"Well, that's *gut* because you found me." Adam smiled. "What's up?"

Chip Weatherford was almost as tall as Adam, but much heavier around the middle. Black hair curled along his forehead over his blue eyes. "Is *this* lady the Laurene Nolt you've told us about? She sure looks pretty enough to match your description."

Lauren's smile stiffened, and he guessed she was imagining him being a *blabbermaul* and telling his friends every detail about her and her past as well as her present difficulties and why she'd come to Bliss Valley.

"This is *Lauren* Nolt," Adam said with enough emphasis so he hoped his friend would take a hint. "She's Sylvia Nolt's great-niece and is staying at The Acorn Farm Inn."

"Nice to meet you, *Lauren*," Chip said with an identical stress on her name. He grinned. "Adam might have mentioned me to you a time or two. I'm Chip Weatherford."

"Nice to meet you," Lauren said in a cool tone. "I should—"

"Before you go, you need to meet my partner in crime." He laughed at his own words, then motioned to his fellow firefighter who was stepping out of the truck's passenger side. "Hey, Mahlon, come and meet Adam's new neighbor."

Mahlon had a long face and deep set eyes that brought a basset hound to mind. He didn't have a beard, but his status as a bachelor was obvious in another way. No Amish wife would have allowed her husband to leave the house with a safety pin taking the place of a button on his coat.

"This is Mahlon Miller, Lauren." Chip draped an arm over his friend's shoulders. "We're teaching Adam and Simon what they need to know to become full-fledged firefighters."

"I didn't know you were in training, Adam," Lauren said. "That's a big surprise."

He pushed down his annoyance at the tenor of her comment, hoping he hadn't taken it the wrong way. Or maybe she meant what she'd said exactly as she had. The kid she'd known, the one who'd done everything he could to push the buttons of anyone in authority, even the girl who'd been coerced into trying to help him study, wouldn't have sought out anything that required training by others.

"He and Simon," Mahlon said, "will be full members of the Bliss Valley Volunteer Fire Department soon."

"They've got a few more tests to pass," Chip added, "and, once they do, they'll be ready to fight fires without one of us babysitting them. Think you'll do better than Simon this time around, Adam?" He focused his smile on Lauren again. "Simon's gotten higher marks on the multiple-choice tests than old Adam here." Chip clapped Adam on the back. "Of course, Adam makes up for it with the practical exams where he's always the top of the class. He's going to be a real hero, this one."

"The department doesn't need heroes," Adam said as he had before when Chip piled on unwanted and often unwarranted praise. Knowing he sounded pompous, he wanted to keep the conversation away from his test-taking. Did Lauren suspect that he'd done so poorly on the tests because of his inability to read? "We need volunteers who'll save lives and properties."

"Isn't that the very definition of a hero? Hey, I understand. Mahlon's told me you plain guys don't want to be standouts when congratulations are being passed around." He turned to Lauren. "That's what makes these guys such great volunteers. They're in it to help the community. Got to say that's better than some of the young guys and gals who can't think of anything but getting a promotion and pushing the rest of us aside."

Lauren stiffened again, but hurried to say, "I get that."

"See you at the meeting tonight, Adam?" Chip reached for the truck's door. "Remember? You and Simon are bringing refreshments. That's what I stopped to tell you."

"We won't forget," he replied.

"C'mon, Mahlon. Let's get going so Adam can finish his chores. Hope to see you around again, Lauren."

Adam breathed a sigh of relief when the truck drove away. He'd been worried that Lauren would be curious about why he did so bad on the written tests. Just randomly marking the boxes on each exam had been far more successful than he'd dared to hope. Nobody at the firehouse seemed to notice how he missed questions he could easily answer, and he wanted to keep it that way.

When he heard the sound of his sigh echoed by Lauren, he said, "I know Chip can come on a bit strong."

"A bit? The man is a human bulldozer."

"He does have a way of rubbing people the wrong way. He sees himself as a comedian, and he'll say anything for a laugh."

"I noticed."

"What you can't tell from meeting him is he's an excellent firefighter. I've seen him risk his life more than once to rescue people and animals from burning buildings. He and Mahlon know how to balance being brave with being smart."

Was he apologizing for his friend or defending him? Adam wasn't sure.

"He has a way of sucking the air from the room," Lauren replied in the same chilly tone.

"Chip is a *gut* guy. He's been my mentor." He chuckled. "He's great at finding everything I do wrong during training, and he makes me repeat the steps over and over until I get them right. He's got eyes like a hawk, and I learned any attempts at a shortcut would be a waste of time."

"So he's not just a loudmouthed clown?" For the first time since Chip and Mahlon had stopped to talk to him, a hint of mischievousness glinted in her eyes.

He had to laugh at her description, which matched his own initial opinion of the man. "*Ja.* Like they said, Simon and I will be finishing our training in the next month, and, after our probation period, we'll be full members of the department."

The tension began to ebb from her taut shoulders. "So that's why you weren't fighting the fire the night my car broke down?"

"Simon went. They didn't want to go out of their way to pick me up."

"I saw vehicles with flashing lights coming from every direction. One of them must have come past the garage."

"Could be, but Simon said they didn't."

She glanced around the yard where the first dandelions were adding a bit of color to the grass near the fence. "I'm surprised you've got time to be a firefighter. You're running this farm and your shop, and I know a deacon has a lot of duties."

"That's true." He considered asking her to help him with those duties. A deacon was in charge of making sure the community supported one another financially. If someone went into the hospital, the deacon worked with the *Leit* to raise the funds to pay the bills. He'd learned whom to ask to help with a haystack dinner or an auction that would draw in *Englischers*. He kept a long mental list of volunteers for repairs in the wake of a disaster. He also knew which lumberyards to call for donations or a deep discount on materials.

What Adam couldn't do was add those figures to get a final total. Up until a few months ago, he'd asked his great-*grossdawdi* or Simon or even Dale to "double-check" his calculations.

Grossdawdi Ephraim was going to bed earlier, and Adam hadn't wanted to burden him. He'd had to turn to his cousins more, and they'd started asking why he couldn't check his own work. They were getting tired of his explanations, and he didn't blame them, because his excuses were getting sillier.

"Were you surprised when your name was put in the lot for the next deacon?" she asked. "There had to be at least three people who nominated you."

"Are you saying you can't figure out why anyone would add in my name?"

"In a roundabout way, I guess I am."

"I can tell you I was shocked to be called forward for the lot." He nodded, relieved for any change of subject that kept him from having to admit his inability to read or do numbers. "I guess folks figured there wasn't anyone better to do the job than a man who'd been brought before the deacon for discipline plenty of times when he was a *kind*."

"No more than Samuel or Joel."

His mouth tightened into a straight line. "Trust me. I got into plenty of trouble until Samuel and Joel jumped the fence. Samuel didn't stay in the *Englisch* world long. He returned after about four or five years."

"And Joel?"

"He hasn't come back. Rumor says he got in trouble with the law. I don't know if it's true or not. Nobody's heard from him in the past decade at least."

She glanced around the farm, then at him. "I thought you couldn't wait to get out of Bliss Valley. Why didn't you go with them? Didn't they ask you?"

"*Ja*, they did, and I planned to go with them. I had my license."

"And a car."

"You knew about that?"

"How could I have missed how often you talked about

that piece of junk you bought and hid out by the old hunting camp in the woods?"

He stared at her, shocked. She'd known about the battered car he'd bought with the few dollars he'd been able to save? Why hadn't she said anything?

When he asked her, she laughed. "I wasn't stupid. I knew you and Samuel and Joel would pay me back for telling anyone about that car."

"We wouldn't have—" He stopped himself as she shot him a disbelieving frown. "All right, maybe we would have made you sorry."

"There wouldn't have been any maybe about it." She shrugged. "I never thought you having a car would make any difference. Even I, who didn't know about anything with a motor, could tell you'd never get that old piece of junk running."

"You're wrong. I did."

"You did?" Her surprise was as sincere as the awe in her voice. "That's amazing."

He rested his hand on the buggy. "I had a lot of help. Though I'd been working on equipment on the farm most of my life, I didn't know that much about internal combustion engines. I went to Frank, and he gave me a bunch of pointers. The more he taught me, the more I wanted to learn."

"I guess you really did change."

He didn't have to ask her to explain. During their few lessons together, she'd believed he didn't care about learning what was on the pages of the schoolbooks. If she'd guessed the words and numbers printed there hadn't meant anything to him, she might have been more understanding. However, he'd done his best to ensure nobody knew his greatest shame.

On the other hand, he'd already discovered in one critical way Laurene Nolt hadn't changed. She was as persistent at getting an answer as a goat trying to escape its pen. The thought almost made him smile. He doubted she'd find it complimentary to be compared to a goat.

"Is that why you didn't go with Samuel and Joel?" she asked. "You decided to stay and work with Frank?"

"It was one of the reasons I changed my mind. Another was I'd learned how reckless my friends could be one day when they dared me to climb down one of the quarry walls near Paradise."

"Did you?"

"*Ja*, of course I did. I was a *dumm* kid. Too *dumm* to realize we could get caught, and the two of them would run off, leaving me hanging on the edge. I got back up, but just barely. That day, I realized God intended a different life for me. So I gave the car to my friends and stayed here. Samuel told people he and Joel had wrecked the car shortly before he came back to Lancaster County. I don't know if Joel was hurt, but Samuel messed up his right leg. He lives up north of Bird-in-Hand, or so I've heard."

"You don't know? You haven't seen him?"

He shook his head.

"But you were such good friends."

"I thought so, too, until I realized he was more interested in the car than he was in me." He drew in a deep breath and let it out slowly. "God was watching out for me the night he and Joel left."

She scanned the barns and the rambling farmhouse that was almost as large as her great-*aenti*'s inn. "This hasn't changed much."

"I hope it won't."

"You mean with the possibility of a casino being built in Bliss Valley?"

"What else? I don't want to see the beautiful view God created for us ruined by a garish casino."

"If you follow that line of logic, your ancestors were wrong to put buildings up here, too."

Adam frowned. Lauren had always been skilled with words, and too often, she made him feel even stupider. His voice grew sharp as he said, "Our farm isn't going to light up the countryside so it'll be impossible to see the stars at night like the casino will when it opens."

"It may not open."

Not open? Had he heard her right? Was saving his great-*grossdawdi*'s farm going to be so simple?

Lauren saw hope erupt on Adam's face as he asked, "Is there a problem with the casino being built?"

"You don't have to sound so hopeful at someone else's expense." She softened her scolding words with a smile. "Nothing has changed. Right from the beginning, it's been clear the casino might not be built in Bliss Valley."

His eyes widened. "I thought they'd decided to build it on Lehman's Road."

"That's one of the *two* possible locations being considered now. There were even more earlier."

"What's the other location?"

"North of Lititz, twenty miles from here. That's why I was planning to meet the development companies in Lancaster. It's about halfway between here and Lititz. Of course, the final decision of the casino's location will be made by the Pennsylvania Gaming Control Board. No matter which site is chosen, assuming one *is* chosen because the gaming control board could decide not to select either site, there are going to be unhappy people. The developers want to avoid letting

NIMBYs get out in front of the story, so that's why they're considering hiring us."

"What's a NIMBYs?"

"A NIMBY. *N-I-M-B-Y*. It means 'not in my backyard.' It's what people say when they want something built, but they don't want it near their home."

He grimaced. "Are you using English or some other language?"

"Every job has its own unique language. I'm sure when you're in Frank's garage if you started talking about carburetors and spark plugs and distributor caps, I'd be lost."

"You already are." His lips twitched.

"What do you mean?"

"Most cars don't have distributors anymore." A laugh burst from him. "I guess you're further behind the times than an Amish man, Lauren."

Something fluttered in Lauren's center as Adam's laugh rumbled through her, tickling her clear to the bone with his genuine humor. She almost gasped out loud. She recognized that quiver, though she hadn't experienced it in more than fifteen years, but she remembered the first time it'd happened as if everything had happened only moments ago.

The whole school had been at recess one fall day when she and Adam were about thirteen, and the scholars had been playing softball. She'd been playing first base, and one of the boys, far bigger than she was, although he was a couple of years younger, had run into her at full speed in an effort to beat the ball to the base. She'd been knocked off her feet. Hard. So hard her head spun, and she'd thought she was going to lose consciousness as everything fell into blackness.

Beyond the buzz in her ears and the cacophony of the players calling out in dismay, she'd heard a gentle voice say, *Open your eyes, Laurene. Open your eyes and look at me.* A large hand cradled her head, and another clasped her hand as the voice kept urging her not to move until she was steady.

That day, she'd looked up into Adam's dark brown eyes. They'd held an expression she'd never seen in them before or afterward. Instead of being crinkled with mirth at some prank he'd pulled on her and her friends, they offered compassion and care. For one second out of time, she and Adam had been connected in a way she'd never been able to explain. In fact, it'd been easier to push that memory into the back of her mind.

Like so many of those memories, it'd burst out, refusing to be hidden any longer. She couldn't forget the amazing delight that had strengthened her as much as Adam's calm words. For the first and only time, she'd believed he'd let her see beyond his nasty smile.

And now it was happening again.

This wasn't good.

Not good at all.

Chapter Twelve

The distant sound of the fire sirens reached Lauren as, three days after her conversation with Adam by his shop, she emerged from beneath the Bliss Valley Covered Bridge. Slowing her car on the otherwise empty road, she scanned the blue sky and saw a thin line of smoke.

Another fire?

There had been one yesterday. She'd been walking Mary Beth to the Weaver farm when Adam had raced past them to catch a ride to what turned out to be a fire in an abandoned springhouse. Now this one was blazing somewhere to the north and east. The smoke thickened into a cloud even as she watched.

Another fire in another building?

She frowned. This wasn't the time of year for barn fires. That happened more often later in the spring when an impatient farmer put hay into the loft before it had dried. This also wasn't the time of year for house fires. Those came in late fall or early winter when furnaces kicked on and caused an electrical short or, in one of the plain houses edging these country roads, a woodstove burned out of control. Again she shivered at the horrifying thought.

So why were there so many fires this spring?

She'd have to leave the answer to the firefighters. There wasn't anything she could do to help when she needed assistance herself. Less than an hour ago, she'd received a call from the office of Charlessatterfieldattorneyatlaw—and she'd stifled her laugh when the caller said it like that—to let her know a registered letter was coming to her at her great-aunt's inn. The person who'd called hadn't been the receptionist Kai and had refused to explain what was in the letter.

I was told to inform you it was on its way. I wasn't authorized to answer any questions, the stern female voice had said.

Lauren translated that to mean the caller had no idea what was in the letter. Thanking the caller, she'd tried to convince herself not to let curiosity consume her, but she couldn't keep from wondering what was so important the lawyer had sent it registered mail.

A restraining order to keep her from seeing her birth mother?

No, that didn't make any sense. When they'd been leaving the conference room, Mrs. Tinniswood had mentioned she hoped their next meeting would be soon.

Legal forms she'd need to sign?

That made more sense, but she couldn't imagine what forms would have to be mailed to her instead of her coming to the office where they could be witnessed and notarized as needed.

"Coming up with scenarios isn't going to make the letter get here more quickly," she murmured to herself as she shifted the Beetle and drove up the hill.

She couldn't keep from looking in her rearview mirror at the smoke plume. It had grown thicker while she was lost in her musings. A shiver coursed down her back. She didn't like knowing Adam and his cousin could be among the firefighters. Putting out fires was a dangerous business for volunteers who didn't have time for endless training as full-time departments did.

Keep them and the others safe. The prayer burst out of her. It once had been habit to reach out to God whenever she needed reassurance or guidance, but it startled her now each time it happened.

Following the road up and down several hills, Lauren took care not to take the crest of any hill too quickly. She saw only one buggy, and it pulled into a farm lane as she approached. She smiled and waved when two towheaded little boys peeked over the bottom of the rear window. They ducked, but their heads popped up again as she drove past.

She rolled down her window. For the past week, she'd become accustomed to walking in the spring sunshine, and she didn't want to shut out the warmth that was better than any freshener she could have used in the car, which had soaked up the damp and clammy odors of winter.

Lauren hummed as she drove. She was relieved when she learned her great-aunt had taken no reservations for Easter weekend, which was the week after next. She wasn't sure if *Aenti* Sylvia still followed the Amish tradition of praying and fasting on the morning of Good Friday, but knew her great-aunt would be attending Easter Sunday services at the Mennonite chapel in Strasburg. The Saturday in between had been, when Lauren was growing up, a day of furious activity to clean the house and make food for Easter Sunday. If Easter didn't share the same date as a church Sunday for their district, she and her parents had stayed home and spent the day reading the story of the Resurrection in the Bible and praying.

The days between Palm Sunday and Easter would also be filled with fun. No Easter Bunny had ever been spoken of in their house. However, Lauren and her mother had dyed Easter eggs in spring colors.

In addition to the holidays, she'd learned this morning there was a wedding to look forward to. Most marriage ceremonies took place in the fall when the harvest was in and people had time to spend celebrating with the bride and groom and their families. However, Diana Wickey, Lauren's third cousin twice removed, was marrying in April because her fiancé's maternal grandmother was very ill, and the family wanted the matriarch to be able to attend the wedding that had been postponed from the previous fall because the groom had needed to have his tonsils removed. *Aenti* Sylvia and Lauren had been invited to the wedding and the work frolic to be held a few days before it to help the family prepare for more than three hundred guests. The frolic would, her great-aunt assured her, be great fun and give her a chance to reconnect with relatives she hadn't seen in fifteen years.

The wedding was also a reminder Lauren's adoptive parents wouldn't be attending, even if they had any idea it was being held, because they were under the *bann.*

That was why she was driving on the far side of the Bliss Valley Covered Bridge now. She'd been told the district's bishop, Jonas Gundy, lived along the road parallel to the creek. His house was in his other district, because each bishop tended to two districts.

She discovered that Jonas's farm was at the top of a hill with a commanding view of the countryside. For a moment, she enjoyed the frivolous thought that God had chosen him as the area's bishop because he could literally oversee his flock.

As she pulled her car into what looked like a parking spot in front of the barn that needed repainting, as so many did at this time of year, she glanced at the white farmhouse. It looked in better repair, and she guessed, like many plain farmers, the bishop painted his outbuildings one year and his house a different one. As a bishop, he had to tend to his congregations as an unpaid leader, adding those duties to the work he must do on his farm. With so little time available through the warmer weather to do anything but tend the fields, the job of painting the house and smaller buildings was often left to the women. The bishop's wife was as busy as her husband because *Aenti* Sylvia had mentioned they had more than a dozen *kinder*.

Lauren parked and got out. She admired a small garden where red and yellow tulips mingled and bobbed in the breeze. She climbed the steps to the front porch of the meandering farmhouse set between two ancient maple trees. Nobody answered her knock, and she guessed the bishop's *kinder* were in school. No buggy waited in the yard, so his wife must be running errands or visiting.

As she walked toward the barns where she guessed she might find the bishop, she looked again at the smoke. It still rose in a straight column halfway up into the sky before high winds sent it spiraling. The fire must not be far from Paradise, which might prove to be a blessing, because there was a fire station right off Route 30 in the center of the village.

"Can I help you?" asked a pleasant tenor voice. "I'm Jonas."

Lauren flinched as she realized she'd been so caught up in thoughts of the fire she hadn't noticed anyone approaching. Turning, she saw a man who was a hand's breadth taller than she was. This was the bishop? He wasn't as old as she'd expected. The previous bishop, Dwight Reel, with his long, gray beard had seemed ancient to Lauren when she was a child. She wondered if she'd ever seen Dwight smile like Jonas Gundy was now.

"I'm Lauren Nolt," she replied and held out her hand.

He shook it, smiling. His heavy brows counterbalanced

the thick black beard on his thin face. "What can I do for you, Lauren?"

"Do you have time to talk?"

Hesitating, he said, "I've got a job I need to get done before supper. If you've got questions about the Amish, I'd be glad to answer them, but could we set another time to talk?"

"I don't have those questions." She took a deep breath. "You see, I was raised Amish in Bliss Valley."

"You?" He stared at her in surprise.

She didn't blame him. To make such a claim when she was wearing a business suit in her favorite shade of deep purple along with high heels and no *kapp* on her head sounded ridiculous. "My parents and I left Bliss Valley before you became bishop."

"Nolt, did you say?"

She nodded as he led the way into a small barn that he'd made into a woodworking shop.

"*Ja*, I remember now," he said. "You're right. You left before I was first ordained. I didn't live in your district, so most of what I heard was from gossip, not facts." He picked up a board and fed it into a planer. The loud passage of the board being smoothed made it impossible for either of them to talk.

Lauren waited with what patience she could dredge up while he did the same with a half dozen other boards.

He wiped sawdust off his trousers and faced her. "Nobody expected you to leave in the middle of the night."

"I certainly didn't."

His caterpillar brows rose at her answer, but his voice remained serene. "On the rare occasions when a whole family has gone *draus in da welt*—"

It took a moment for her mind to translate the *Deitsch* words he'd used. While most plain folks called leaving the community "jumping the fence," the bishop had used the more formal phrase which meant "out in the world." It made the decision sound even more momentous, and she knew it had been. Once they were living among *Englischers*, neither her mother nor her father had ever spoken of being under the *bann*. They weren't welcome to sit at a table with family or friends. They weren't able to accept something from an Amish hand. They were no longer in the community that had been a part of every breath they'd taken.

Yet they'd never complained. She hated the idea of them hiding their grief to make her transition easier.

Jonas must have taken notice of her distraction because he repeated, "On the rare occasions when a whole family has gone *draus in da welt*, the *kinder* aren't informed."

"Because kids have big mouths and can't keep secrets."

He smiled for a moment, then grew serious again. "I suspect parents don't want to burden their *kinder* with the weight of such a decision. If you've come to ask me about the discussions between my predecessor and your parents, there's not a lot I can tell you. Dwight's records are far from complete." He went to a shelf at the back of the shop.

Taking down a book, he began paging through it as he carried it to a table closer to the sunlight.

Lauren moved to the table and stood on the other side. She tried to read the tiny handwriting from across the table, but it was impossible.

When he paused on one page, he said, "Here Dwight notes your parents were taking his baptismal classes."

"That's about ten years before I was born," she said as she managed to read the date scribbled in the margin.

Jonas nodded. "Okay, let's look if there's anything ten years beyond here because Dwight was very careful about keeping birth and death records." Turning the pages, he seemed to find it much easier to read the handwriting than she did, because he didn't slow until he'd gone a third of the way through the notebook. "Ah, here we go. He made some notes about talking to your parents several times before you were born."

"Before I was born? Did he write what the meetings were about?" She tried to dampen the suspicion exploding through her head. Had the bishop played a part in her adoption? Her mother hadn't said.

Lauren recalled she hadn't given her mother a chance to explain anything. She'd ended the call quickly, unable to form a single logical thought other than she didn't want to discuss what seemed impossible.

"No," Jonas said as he continued to turn pages, "and I don't see any listing of a specific meeting with them until just before your family moved away."

"When I was fourteen."

"*Ja.* The dates match."

"So you have no idea what they talked about then either?"

"Dwight made a note of the meeting and nothing more. I'm sorry." He closed the book. "I wish I could help you."

"I appreciate your trying." She hesitated, then asked, "If my parents wanted to return, what would they need to do?"

"The first thing would be to meet with me so we could discuss the steps." His eyes narrowed. "You weren't baptized, ain't so? You'd be welcomed among the *Leit* on Sunday."

"Thank you."

He took her hands and pressed them, palms together, between his. "Listen for God in your heart, and you'll know when it's time to join us. Sitting with us while we praise our Lord might answer some of the questions I can see are plaguing you."

"Thank you," she said again as a yearning to accept the invitation washed over her. "I've been attending church at the Mennonite chapel with my great-aunt."

"I'm glad to hear you've kept your relationship with God. You're both welcome among us whenever you wish."

"I'll let her know."

"Gut." He didn't release her hands as he bowed his head and asked God to bless her and open her heart to His grace.

She left the shop and walked to her car. She hadn't gotten answers, but she felt more at peace than she had in longer than she could recall. That calm lasted as long as it took her to open her door and get into her car where her cell phone demanded her attention with a half dozen texts from her boss.

Since she'd come to Bliss Valley, she'd been caught between two worlds. The chasm separating them grew wider with each passing day. She wasn't sure how much longer she could straddle the gap without falling in.

The words on the computer screen in front of Lauren blurred. She sat back at the dining room table and rubbed her eyes. Glancing at her watch, she saw she'd been staring at the same page on the screen for a half hour. It was almost time to take the pie she and Mary Beth had made out of the oven.

In an upholstered chair in the corner of the room, the little girl was asleep and curled up with a gray tiger-striped kitten she'd found in the barn and insisted on bringing into the inn. The kitten was sleeping, too. It was an adorable sight, and Lauren was glad to look at the duo rather than the letter Patrick had sent her for corrections.

She sighed and stretched her arms over her head to loosen the tight muscles along her spine. Patrick had risen fast at Krause-Matsui-Fitzgerald, where perception mattered more than substance, but had reached a level where it was assumed he'd be able to compose a letter with diplomacy and basic grammar skills. He couldn't do either, and since he'd taken her under his wing, as he liked to say, he'd depended on her to be his editor.

Usually she didn't mind. She liked having each word perfect. Today the whole process felt demeaning and ridiculous. Not only did she find it impossible to summon the words she wanted, but she didn't care if Patrick's top account saw him use *their* when it should have been *they're*.

On top of that, she'd been fielding calls from Cassie Varozza all afternoon. Realizing Cassie was only interested in information she could use to advance herself, Lauren had turned off the ringer and let the messages go to voice mail and ignored the ever more frantic texts. She'd get back to Cassie before she went to bed, but she wasn't going to get caught up in silly games. It was more important Mary Beth got her nap and *Aenti* Sylvia's guests were welcomed as they arrived.

Lauren closed her computer. The problem wasn't either Patrick or Cassie. She hadn't been able to focus since the mail had arrived without the letter from the attorney's office. *Aenti* Sylvia had assured her that the mail sometimes could take a couple of days to come from Lancaster.

What was in the letter?

She heard the rattle of buggy wheels coming along the driveway. As she rose to look out the window, Mary Beth jumped up, sending the kitten fleeing with a howl.

"*Daed?*" the little girl asked.

"I don't think so. The horse doesn't look like Sparks."

"Oh." Mary Beth deflated.

Lauren hid her own disappointment from her voice. It would have been wonderful to have Adam stop by. Sparring with words would have kept her mind off that registered letter.

Pushing past her to peer out, Mary Beth cheered, "It's *Grossdawdi* Ephraim!" She ran to the front door with the kitten on her heels.

Aenti Sylvia rolled out of the living room. "Ephraim is here?"

"Looks that way." Lauren hid her smile at how her great-aunt sounded as eager as a teenage girl who'd been told a boy was on the phone.

"Go and invite him in. Mary Beth and I will wait here." She held her hand out to the child.

Mary Beth ignored it. "Me see *Grossdawdi* Ephraim. He see my cat."

"He will," Lauren assured her. "I'll bring him right in."

"No tell about my cat!"

She smiled. "I won't say a word. You can surprise him."

The child clapped her hands in glee, which spooked the kitten, who ran into the living room. Mary Beth gave chase.

"Go and get Ephraim," her great-aunt said. "He might as well enjoy the chaos, too."

As she walked out the front door, Lauren laughed. It felt so good to do so after such a frustrating day.

"I thought the time was long overdue for me to come and welcome you home to Bliss Valley," Ephraim Weaver said as he stepped out of the buggy.

"You did right after I arrived during the snowstorm."

"Did I?" He gave her a wink. "The only thing I remember was working on a curtain rod for Sylvia, who was looking to get out of the kitchen. I wonder why she was in such a hurry to flee a place she usually enjoys."

Lauren started to explain, then noting his twinkling eyes, knew *Grossdawdi* Ephraim was teasing her. He remembered seeing her that day and how her great-aunt had been trying to do a bit of matchmaking by leaving her and Adam together in the kitchen.

As they walked up to the front porch, she asked him if he'd heard anything about the fire yesterday.

"Adam told me a grass fire ignited a stack of wood behind the shops near the corner of Route 30 in Paradise." He slowed to climb the steps. "It was *gut* news because, for once, it wasn't a structure fire. We've had a lot of those this spring."

"I'm glad to hear that." She added, flustered, "Not that there have been other fires, but this one wasn't a building."

"I knew what you meant." He heaved himself up the last step to the porch.

Smiling, Lauren opened the door and stepped aside to let him go in first.

Aenti Sylvia was waiting in the hall as they came inside. "You must have some sort of pie radar, Ephraim Weaver. Lauren and Mary Beth are baking a snitz pie, and you come calling."

"The wind was in the right direction."

"There isn't a hint of breeze today," she scolded, but she was grinning like Mary Beth, who held up the kitten.

And he was grinning as broadly as she was, too, she realized. The elderly couple were adorable, and it was obvious their teasing was built upon years of friendship.

The distant ding of the timer sent Lauren into the kitchen. She took the snitz pie out. Apples and sugar bubbled through the slits in the top crust, sending sweet aromas of cinnamon and cloves through the room. After brewing coffee and pouring a glass of milk for Mary Beth, she carried the drinks to the dining room. She cleared her work off the table and piled it on the sideboard.

Lauren hid her disappointment when she looked into the living room and saw Adam wasn't there. Affixing a smile on her face, she said, "There's pie and coffee in the dining room."

"Now that," said *Grossdawdi* Ephraim, pushing himself to his feet, "is an invitation I'd be a *dummkopf* not to accept." Without asking permission, he gripped the handles on *Aenti* Sylvia's chair and wheeled her into the dining room.

Watching in silence, Lauren thought of how, on many occasions, she'd offered to maneuver her great-aunt through a tight space. *Aenti* Sylvia had insisted on handling her chair on her own, but not now with *Grossdawdi* Ephraim.

"Me help?" asked Mary Beth.

"I was hoping you'd ask." Lauren held out her hand. "I've got a job for you."

"For me?"

"For you!" She tweaked the child's turned-up nose. "I can't think of anyone I'd rather have help me."

As she took the little girl into the kitchen, she was glad Mary Beth didn't have the slightest inkling Lauren was being dishonest. There was someone she'd rather have help her.

Adam Hershberger.

Was she out of her mind? It was true Adam was handsome and hadn't been beastly to her, but there had been times when he'd been nice to her years ago. On each occasion, he'd reverted to his cruelty...and she'd felt like a complete fool. It was a feeling she didn't want to experience again.

Adam knocked on the door, but nobody must have heard him. Voices from inside the inn emerged into the afternoon. No words, just the rise and fall of conversation and laughter. Lots of laughter.

The sound drew him inside. He needed it after spending the past two hours making sure the last embers were out in the woodpile that had caught fire. Simon, as the other newest recruit, would have assisted him if his cousin had been at the incident. However, his cousin had been occupied helping their best cow with a difficult birth.

When Adam had returned to the farm, his cousin told him the calf had arrived safely and that *Grossdawdi* Ephraim had decided to drive to The Acorn Farm Inn to get Mary Beth.

Adam had taken time to wash up and change out of his stinking clothes before he crossed the field to the inn.

He put his hand to his waist. The chief had given him two beepers after the fire. One for him and one for Simon. It was a sign they'd almost completed their training. He'd been checking often to make sure he hadn't lost it.

"Out!" Adam froze before realizing his daughter had spoken. Nobody was ordering him to leave. Instead it was Mary Beth announcing she was coming into the dining room.

He paused, unnoticed, in the doorway as his daughter emerged from the kitchen. She carried a stack of small plates. Holding his breath, he didn't release it until *Grossdawdi* Ephraim helped Mary Beth place them on the table.

"Five?" his great-*grossdawdi* asked. "We're only four."

"So far. You never know when someone else might drop by," Sylvia said. "You know that, Ephraim."

"Not as much as you do because I'm not a lovely innkeeper." He grinned as Lauren's great-*aenti* blushed.

Adam smiled, too, as his great-*grossdawdi* continued a flirting game he and Sylvia Nolt had been playing for years.

"Out," Lauren called from the kitchen.

The luscious scent of streusel-topped apple pie tickled Adam's nose and reminded him how he'd skipped lunch. When his stomach rumbled, all four people turned to look at him.

His gaze focused on Lauren. With her cheeks flushed from being near the oven, her eyes seemed more lustrous. She should have appeared ridiculous with a plain-style black apron over her jeans and shirt, but she was as enticing as the pie's aromas. When she raised her eyes after placing the pie on a trivet on the table, they were caught by his. A softness he'd never seen in them before sent a powerful shock through him as if he'd grabbed a live electric wire. The sensation was *wunderbaar.*

Every inch of him wanted to cross the room and gather her into his arms so he could discover if her expressive lips tasted even better than the pie.

"See?" Sylvia asked, shattering the invisible contact between him and Lauren. "Didn't I say we'd need one more plate?"

His great-*grossdawdi* guffawed, and Mary Beth ran to give him a big hug. He bent to pick her up as if she were a toddler. When she leaned her head on his shoulder, he looked over her head at Lauren, again attempting to catch her gaze.

"Sit," Lauren said, avoiding his eyes, "and I'll get another cup of coffee."

He noticed how her fingers trembled. Was she fighting the yearning, as he was, to toss *gut* sense aside and surrender to the need for the kiss that had filled his dreams with torment for the past few nights?

Glad for *Grossdawdi* Ephraim's garrulous ways and Sylvia's quick responses to whatever he said, Adam watched Lauren vanish into the kitchen. If he followed, could they have a rare moment alone?

His great-*grossdawdi* gave him a knowing grin, and Adam cleared emotion from his face. Carrying Mary Beth to a chair next to her great-great-*grossdawdi*, he waited while she sat on her knees. She looked over her shoulder as Lauren returned with a steaming pot and a cup. She put them on the table along with a handful of forks before pulling some paper napkins from her apron pockets.

Adam drew out a chair for Lauren and was rewarded with a smile as she sat. Taking the seat beside her, he bowed his head when *Grossdawdi* Ephraim suggested they thank God for the delicious treat they were about to enjoy.

And enjoy Adam did, though when his plate was empty, he couldn't say whether the pie had been the best he'd ever had or the worst. All his attention was focused on the woman beside him. He couldn't remember the last time she'd laughed with such ease as she did when his great-*grossdawdi* told one story after another about their lives in Bliss Valley. Each time *Grossdawdi* Ephraim paused, Sylvia jumped in with a tale of her own.

Adam nodded when Lauren asked if he wanted more *kaffi* and hoped she'd offer him another piece of the pie. As she reached for the pot, her great-*aenti* let out a sudden gasp.

"Ephraim!" she cried. "Laurene! Adam! Help him! He's bleeding!"

Chapter Thirteen

When he saw crimson flowing down his great-*grossdawdi*'s face, Adam raced around the table. The blood was coming from *Grossdawdi* Ephraim's nose. The old man looked as startled as the rest of them.

"Tilt your head back," Adam ordered. "I'm going to pinch your nose, so breathe through your mouth. Lauren—"

"Gone, *Daed*," Mary Beth said, her eyes wide with fear.

Was Lauren one of those people who couldn't stand the sight of blood? A guy who'd started training with him and Simon at the fire station had washed out because even a single drop made the man pass out cold.

His great-*grossdawdi* mumbled something that sounded like a complaint, but Adam ignored him. They had to get the bleeding stopped.

"Move." Lauren's breath brushed against his cheek, startling him at how warm and sweet her breath was on his skin.

Focus on Grossdawdi *Ephraim*, he told himself, but it was futile as Lauren squeezed beneath his arm to get closer to the old man.

He was about to ask her what she was doing when she put a folded dish towel against his great-*grossdawdi*'s neck.

"Ice," she said.

"*Gut* idea." Sylvia steered her wheelchair over to where Mary Beth stood. "*Komm* with me. We'll get more ice."

Adam released his grip on his great-*grossdawdi*'s nose long enough to check if they'd halted the blood. He had to do it four times over the next few minutes before he saw it'd been stemmed.

Straightening, he said, "I think it's okay now."

Grossdawdi Ephraim nodded and reached up behind him to take the makeshift ice pack from Lauren. "I'm sorry."

"It wasn't as if you planned to have a bloody nose," she said.

Her great-*aenti* rolled into the dining room. "Don't be so sure. Ephraim Weaver likes to show off new tricks to anyone who'll watch."

"That's me," the old man said. "Got you to look at me, ain't so?"

When his great-*grossdawdi* chuckled weakly, Adam exchanged a smile with Lauren.

"Why don't you young folks enjoy the sunshine," urged Sylvia, "while I get this old *dummkopf* cleaned up?"

Lauren began, "We can—"

"Take Mary Beth for a walk. I'll keep an eye on Ephraim to make sure he doesn't get into trouble."

Adam wasn't surprised when Lauren nodded. Like him, she must have seen the steel in her great-*aenti*'s eyes. He'd heard the anxiety beneath Sylvia's jesting words. Letting his great-*grossdawdi* sit for another half hour would be a *gut* idea.

Taking his daughter by the hand, he said, "Let's go and see the flowers."

"See *bopplin!*" insisted the little girl.

"Bopplin?" He looked back at Lauren.

She smiled. "Ducklings. We need to wait another couple of weeks before they arrive, Mary Beth, but we can show your *daed* where the nest is. Okay?"

"Okay!" She released his hand and skipped toward the door. *"Komm mol!"*

Lauren hesitated as he started to follow, but caught up with him when Sylvia shooed her out of the house. Going out in the fading warmth of the late afternoon, he let her lead the way down the steps.

As they walked across the grass, Adam called to Mary Beth to slow down. She did, but skipped in a winding path that took her from one group of flowers to the next.

He didn't realize his sigh was so loud until Lauren asked him what was wrong.

"I can't keep from thinking on days like this how much Vernita is missing in Mary Beth's life."

"I never met Vernita."

"You didn't?" He answered his question before she could. "Of course you didn't. Her family didn't move to Bliss Valley until after yours had left."

"Was she like Mary Beth?"

"What do you mean?"

"Mary Beth cares about everyone around her, wanting to help even when she's too little to. She's all heart."

"She's like *Grossdawdi* Ephraim." This time he didn't make any effort to stifle his sigh. "I wish Vernita could have found joy in everything as Mary Beth does, but she didn't. Looking back, I'm not sure why she married me other than her two best friends were wed around the same time, and I don't think she wanted to be left out."

"Oh…" Lauren paused and faced him. "She must have loved you."

"She loved the idea of having a home of her own, but she wasn't happy living with *Grossdawdi* Ephraim. That's why I bought a house and a few acres near the covered bridge."

"You don't live there now."

"My great-*grossdawdi* needed help with his farm, and my cousins needed someone to make sure they don't cut corners. You know how teenagers can be." He tried to smile and failed. "I'm sorry. It's a nice day, and I shouldn't be talking about not nice things."

"You shouldn't blame yourself for Vernita's unhappiness."

"I should have never married her in the first place. I suspected something wasn't right, and *Grossdawdi* Ephraim was concerned, too. He suggested we wait a year, but when I spoke to Vernita about it, she cried and begged me not to listen. Instead of asking for time to pray on it, I gave in. She was overjoyed. I sometimes wonder if that was the last day she was happy. Her depression became worse when I was chosen by the lot to be the district's deacon."

"Hey!" she cried, looking past him. "Mary Beth, wait for us!"

His daughter skidded to a stop about ten feet from the pond.

"I'm sorry," Lauren began. "I didn't mean to interrupt, but fishing her out of the pond isn't anywhere near the top of my to-do list today."

"No, you don't need to apologize." He began walking again. "You're reminding me I can't wallow in the past. I need to keep my sights on the present and the future, mine and my daughter's."

"You're doing a great job with Mary Beth. She's a sweet girl."

"I keep reminding myself God doesn't give any of us more than we can handle."

"You've got it wrong, Adam."

Startled again, he asked, "What do you mean?"

"God sometimes does overload us with more burdens than we can handle on our own. However, He doesn't give us too much to handle if we accept help from others to hold us up during the worst times." She smiled as they reached Mary Beth, and he took his daughter by the hand. "Teamwork with Him and those around us."

His breath caught in the center of his chest when his daughter grabbed Lauren's hand, connecting all of them. Though he tried to keep his eyes forward, his gaze shifted to look over his daughter's head to discover Lauren was looking in his direction, too. He waited for her to turn away, but she didn't. Instead a slow, sweet smile drifted across her lips, lighting her face with a glow from deep within her. He knew because he was sure an identical expression was on his own face.

As his daughter babbled about the ducklings and the other animals she'd seen at the inn, he lost himself in Lauren's eyes. And found himself, because a part of him he'd thought he would never recover after so many losses emerged like a spring flower pushing toward the sun. The part of him that didn't belong to taking care of his family and working with the *Leit*.

He looked at the clouds gathering overhead. He was fooling himself if he thought Lauren Nolt was interested in him after everything they'd been through. *Ja*, she was helping watch Mary Beth. *Ja*, she'd asked him to come with her to the lawyer's office, but she'd been desperate not to go alone and couldn't take her great-*aenti*.

"Adam?"

He flinched at her soft and husky voice. Starting to answer, he paused and frowned. Those weren't clouds in the sky! It was smoke! He couldn't tell from where because trees blocked his view.

His beeper went off. As he reached for it, Mary Beth asked what it was. He didn't take time to explain. He'd leave that to Lauren as he had so many other things. He ignored his surge of guilt as he saw the smoke was growing darker with each passing second.

"I've got to go."

"Another fire?" Lauren asked.

"*Ja.*"

"How can there be so many fires this spring?"

He didn't wait to answer the unanswerable before he raced toward the fence and the field beyond it. He needed to get to the house where he and Simon would meet the other volunteers to go and put out yet another out-of-control fire.

The next morning, Lauren decided to distract herself by baking while she waited for the mail to be delivered. *Aenti* Sylvia's hired girls were working upstairs, doing a spring cleaning on the guest rooms, so she wouldn't be in their way. She took a round cast-iron pan from a cupboard. It'd been well seasoned already, so Lauren didn't have to add oil to it. However, the pineapple upside-down cake never tasted as good without a stick of butter melted into the brown sugar.

She put the butter into the microwave to soften. Everywhere else in the inn, her great-aunt maintained the illusion of it being a plain house. There weren't televisions in the guest rooms, and the electric lights resembled kerosene lamps and had bulbs that flickered like candles.

Illusion. That's what Lauren ached for now. She'd walked to the front of the inn too many times to count this morning to check the flag on the mailbox. The postal carrier would lower it once the letters her great-aunt had put in the box were collected and the mail delivered. Though she'd have to sign for a registered letter, which meant a knock on the door, she didn't want to chance missing its arrival and having to wait for it to be returned to the post office where she wouldn't be able to get it until tomorrow.

The microwave's beep interrupted her thoughts, and she opened the door to remove the melted butter.

"Ouch!" She released the hot bowl and reached for a pot holder. That's what she got for not focusing on what she was doing.

She added the melted butter to the pan and topped it with brown sugar and pineapple. The sweet and tart flavors combined to make her mouth water, but she turned her attention to preparing the cake.

"Here you are."

At Adam's voice, she flinched. Cake batter erupted out of the bowl to fly in every direction. Turning off the mixer, she frowned at the mess and then at Adam, who stood by the door from the dining room.

She wiped batter off her arm and grimaced at the bits on her apron. "Why didn't you say something instead of sneaking up on me?"

"I did say something, and you jumped out of your skin." Setting his straw hat on the counter, he went to the sink. He rinsed out the dishrag, wrung it and then handed it to her. "Looks like you need this."

She took it, biting back the words that she wouldn't have needed it if he hadn't startled her. Swabbing up the bits of batter sprayed around the bowl, she took the cloth to the sink and rinsed it before dabbing batter off herself. She didn't look over her shoulder as she said, "I didn't expect to see you this forenoon."

"Forenoon?" He chuckled. "You're sounding plain again, Lauren." Before she could respond, he added, "I stopped over to let Sylvia know *Grossdawdi* Ephraim hasn't had another nosebleed."

"I'm glad to hear that."

"I enjoyed not looking at the ducklings with you yesterday."

"Me, too." She smiled. "Being around Mary Beth is always fun."

"I agree." When he took the dishcloth, she realized it was dripping on the floor and the toes of her sneakers.

The buzzer on the oven announcing it had finished preheating was as loud as a clap of thunder, and Lauren flinched again.

As Adam turned to pick up his hat, she asked, "Where was the fire yesterday?"

"Same place as yesterday morning. In a field in Paradise. The chief is baffled. He was sure we got all the embers out, but we must have missed one. If Chip and Mahlon hadn't been driving past and seen it, the fire might have gotten out of hand and done some real damage." His face tightened. "As it was, a car parked nearby was burned."

"Good thing your friends were in the right place at the right time."

"*Ja.* That's what everyone's saying."

She paused as she was about to put the mixer back in the batter. "What's wrong, Adam? You don't sound happy."

"I'm happy—really happy—Chip and Mahlon spotted the flames. What I'm not happy about is I was sure we'd turned over every inch of the burned area and had put out every ember. We spent more than two hours going over that small area. I don't know how we could have missed one."

"Maybe you didn't."

His eyes narrowed as they aimed at her like two dark missiles. "Are you suggesting the fires weren't accidental?"

"I'm not suggesting anything. I'm saying you and Chief

Crofts believe you put the first fire out. Yet another fire popped up in the same spot."

"Almost the same spot. It started about fifty feet away."

"A long way for an ember to fly when it wasn't windy." She shrugged as his forehead furrowed with concentration. "I'm sorry. I don't know anything about firefighting, so I'm probably wrong."

He sighed. "You're not. Or, at least, you're not saying anything I haven't been thinking about since yesterday's fires. What do you think I should do?"

"Me?" She was astonished. The Adam Hershberger she'd known fifteen years ago had acted as if she didn't have a single worthwhile thought in her head.

"*Ja*, you. You said you've been wondering if the fires weren't accidental. You've got to have some thoughts about what the next steps should be."

She considered his words before shooting back she had other things on her mind. Like the registered letter coming from the attorney's office.

"Adam," she said as she turned the mixer on low, "you need to speak with the fire chief. If there's something to investigate, he's the guy to do it, right?"

"*Ja*."

"And possibly the police."

He shook his head. "You know going to the *Englisch* authorities isn't our way, Lauren. It's one thing to speak with Dean, because I'm already volunteering at the fire station. Going to the police is something else altogether. Dean can go if he feels he should. He may have already. But if I want to talk to the police, I'd need Jonas's permission."

"Then why don't you go and ask him?"

"That's a *gut* idea."

She gave him a cocky smile. "I have only good ideas."

"There was the time you and Naomi tried to get back at us boys, and you two ended up doused with water instead of us."

"Okay, okay." She switched off the mixer and set it on the counter. "I only try to have good ideas *now*."

"*Danki* for the advice." He took his hat off the counter and reached into it. "Oh, I almost forgot. Your great-*aenti* asked me to give you this."

When he held out an envelope, she stared at it. She could see Charles Satterfield's name on the envelope even from where she stood.

"Don't you want it?" Adam asked. "It looks important. Your great-*aenti* said she had to sign for it."

"Yes, it's…no… I don't know." Taking it with trembling fingers, she said, "I've been waiting for this, but now that it's here…"

"I can open it for you."

His gentle tone almost undid her. It was the one he used when speaking to his family. To hear it when he spoke to her shook her to her depths.

You're feeling too fragile. You can't judge anything now.

Listening to her common sense, she said, "No, I need to do it."

Neither of them spoke while she tore open the flap and pulled out a sheet of paper. Another one dropped on the floor near her feet. Adam bent to retrieve it. Without looking at it, he handed it to her.

"Oh, my!" Lauren breathed as she scanned the letter. "It's a request for me to have another test."

"A test? For what?"

"Being a possible bone marrow donor." She raised her eyes and met his gaze. "Mrs. Tinniswood has cancer. Non-Hodgkin's lymphoma. The letter says it's a blood cancer, and she needs a bone marrow transplant."

"From you?"

"If I'm a match." Her breath caught again. "What if I'm not a match? Then I can win the trifecta. I'll be a disappointment to all my parents." She laughed without a hint of humor. "Not that I've disappointed my birth father yet. He doesn't know I exist."

Adam's mouth hardened. "Are you done with your pity party?"

"It's not a pity party when it's the truth."

"What's the truth? You're a disappointment to Wayne and Ida? You know that's not true. They may not have said it—it's not our way to speak of matters that hint at *hochmut*—but I know they were proud of you when you lived here. Do you think they're any less proud of you when you've worked to make a *gut* life for yourself among the *Englisch*? They know, without your efforts, their transition from a plain life would have been harder than it was. From what Sylvia has said, so much of what they've accomplished in making a new home is because of *you*. What you learned from your new friends and their families helped your parents."

Lauren wasn't ready to give up because of mere facts. "My birth mother may have decided to look for me because she needs my bone marrow."

"Didn't the lawyer say she'd been looking for you for a long time? Even if that's not true, so what? Would that make her a bad person?"

Stuttering, she couldn't find an answer.

There wasn't any need because Adam went on. "Tell me, Lauren. What if the circumstances were reversed? What would you do if your life was in danger and there was someone out there who could save it? If a stranger had approached you and asked for help, would you have turned him away?"

"I don't know." She couldn't pull her gaze from the page she held.

"*Ja*, you do know. At least the Laurene Nolt I once knew would." He ran his fingers back through his hair. "Why are you angry with your birth mother? All she wants to do is to survive. What would you think of her if she'd given up and accepted she was doomed?"

"Those aren't fair questions." She pushed herself away from the counter, then realized she had no place to go. The pan she needed was right beside the bowl where she'd been working.

"Maybe they're not fair, but nobody ever said the challenges we face will be fair. We've been asked by God Himself to be honest with ourselves and others. In the twelfth chapter of Proverbs, the twenty-second verse states, *'Lying lips are abomination to the Lord: but they that deal truly are His delight.'* That's a pretty straightforward statement."

"Do you want the truth? All right, I'll give it to you." She wrapped her arms around herself, but the cold was inside her. "I believe if one of my half siblings had been a match, she might have given up looking for me."

"I believe that, too."

His calm answer startled her. She faced him and realized, though his voice had been composed, he was as torn as she was.

"You do?"

"*Ja*. She left you to your own life for almost thirty years. She didn't want to intrude on you and your parents. Don't you think she thought of you every day? Don't you think she missed you every day?" He frowned as she opened her mouth to reply. "Don't tell me you don't know. Sometimes you've got to look beyond what you don't know to figure out what you do."

"That doesn't make sense."

"Haven't you told me your job is about changing people's perceptions because what they perceive to be the truth is the truth for them?"

"It's not that cut-and-dried."

"Maybe not, but it's how you explained it to me." His expression eased from its deep lines of frustration. "There's one question neither of us have asked. What do *you* want?"

"I…" She halted herself from repeating *I don't know* as she had too many times already. That was, as Adam had told her, the easy way to put an end to questions reaching too close to her patched heart.

Lauren didn't answer as she put the batter on top of the brown sugar and pineapple. Smoothing it to fill the pan to the edges, she carried it to the oven and put it in. She twisted the timer to thirty minutes cooking time. Only then did she face him.

There was a simple answer. It was the truth she'd been trying to conceal, even from herself. "I want to know where I belong, where I'm at home." She flung out her hands in frustration. "Do you know what it's like to feel like an outsider everywhere you go?"

"No."

Tears rose in her eyes. The last thing she wanted to do was cry in front of him, so she blinked hard to keep the tears from coursing down her cheeks.

"Of course you don't," she said, her voice breaking. "You've always known where you belong."

He shook his head. "You know I considered jumping the fence before I was baptized."

"You didn't, because you knew where your home is supposed to be."

"I know now, but it took me a long time to figure out my home is where the people I love are."

"I wish it could be that easy. I wish I could know where my home is."

He cupped her chin in his broad hand and tilted her face up toward his. "You know already. Listen to your heart. It won't steer you wrong."

A raw laugh burst from her. "My heart has steered me wrong plenty of times. It led me to being stabbed in the back by a man I thought loved me more than his career. Boy, was I wrong!"

Adam hated the tears bubbling up in Lauren's eyes because he knew he'd caused them. She wasn't about to cry because of the man who'd treated her so badly. In fact, he'd heard only anger in her words.

God, I'm not the right person to be counseling her. We've got too much history between us, and I don't know if I'm forcing her to face what's in her heart because it's for her gut *or mine.*

After tossing the pages onto the table, Lauren turned to the counter. She gathered up the mixer and the bowl. She rinsed them and put them into the dishwasher.

Every motion was stiff, as if she'd been encased in plaster like her great-*aenti*'s leg. He wondered if he should leave her alone to decide what she was going to do, but every instinct told him that would be the worst thing to do. What if he called in Sylvia and added her advice to his? If Lauren wanted to discuss it with the older woman, she could have by now.

He wished for the camaraderie they'd shared yesterday on the way to the duck pond. No, not camaraderie. The emotion woven between them had been much, much stronger. He hadn't been able to put thoughts of that otherwise mundane walk out of his mind last night. When he'd gotten up to check on his great-*grossdawdi*, the first thought he'd had was of how it felt so right to be with Lauren and his daughter.

As he had so often since the night she'd walked into Frank's shop, he thought of the many ways he could have handled her reappearance better. He'd been shocked to see her and to learn she was in Bliss Valley to help with the future casino. That she'd stayed at the inn once the roads were plowed had astonished him even more.

She's hiding.

The fact was so clear to him he wondered why he hadn't considered it before. Lauren hadn't left once her car was repaired because she saw the quiet valley as a haven, a place connected to her past but not her present life that was whirling out of her control. He'd thought—no, he'd hoped—yesterday they'd turned a corner with their relationship.

Now everything was mixed up again. God had brought him to this moment. *But what do You want me to do?*

The answer was simple as he recalled the verse from Matthew that had been the focus of a sermon at a recent church service. *Give to him that asketh thee, and from him that would borrow of thee turn not thou away.*

Not moving from where he stood, holding his hat, he said, "It's a tough decision, but I don't know many who would be able to deal with it as you will, Lauren."

"Is that a compliment I'll make the right decision? Or is it an insult nobody else will mess it up as I will?" A wispy smile played along her lips. "No, the plain folk don't compliment one another, so it must be an insult."

"It wasn't either. It was a fact. You've always been someone who looks at the facts and makes a *gut* choice. I saw you do it when we were kids. I've seen you do it since you came back. I can't believe you won't do the same thing now."

He was glad when she began to list the pros and cons of doing the test. There were, in her opinion, he wasn't surprised, many more reasons to go ahead than not to. Not once did he hear another word of incrimination against her birth *mamm* for contacting her for a possible donation. As he'd expected, once Lauren began to think the situation through, she tossed aside emotion.

"It sounds as if you've made up your mind to do it," he said when she asked what he thought.

"I—"

The timer went off. A half hour was gone already?

Watching Lauren open the oven and lift the heavy cast-iron pan out, he stayed out of her way. She handled the pan with care as she placed it on a waiting trivet. Getting a large platter from a lower cabinet, she set it beside the cast-iron pan.

"You were right," Lauren said.

"Me? About what?"

"About why Mrs. Tinniswood looked for me. She wants to stay alive. If I can help, how can I say no?"

"So you'll do the test?" Adam didn't add he wasn't surprised at her decision. Knowing Lauren, he couldn't have imagined her making any other one.

Nodding, she asked, "Will you give me a hand here?"

"What do you need?"

"The pan is too wide for me to flip onto the platter on my own. Can you do it?"

"Sure."

"Without spilling sauce on the floor?"

"I'll do my best." He took the pot holders she held out to him. "No sense in wasting any of that yummy brown sugar sauce."

"How do you know it's yummy?"

"It smells delicious." He gripped the platter and the cast-iron pan together. Making sure his hold was steady and the platter wouldn't slip away, he inverted the pan and platter. As he put them on the trivet on the counter, he smiled as a trickle of brown sugar rolled over the edge of the platter. He tossed aside the pot holders and caught the sauce on the tip of his finger. He yelped as it burned.

"You should know better," she said. "It's just out of the oven."

He blew on his finger, then put it in his mouth. The sweet stickiness melted on his tongue. "I should know better, but your pineapple upside-down cake is so *gut*. I've waited a long time to taste it again."

"When did you taste it before?"

"You were making it the one time I came over to your house for you to help me with my arithmetic." He looked at his reddened finger. "Now that I think about it, I burned my finger that day, too, trying to sneak some brown sugar sauce when your back was turned."

"I don't remember that."

She didn't say anything else, but he could hear what he was sure raced through her head. She didn't recall that day because she'd tried to forget everything to do with him. Not that he could fault her. He'd dumped on her his frustrations with not being able to understand the letters and numbers printed on the pages of their schoolbooks. Too proud to admit he needed assistance, he'd seen everything she'd done to try to help him as pity.

It was too late to say he'd been a stupid, angry kid. Even if he apologized, it wouldn't ever change the memories of the anguish he and his friends had put her through.

He used to think marrying Vernita had been his biggest mistake. Now he wasn't so sure.

Chapter Fourteen

Adam's pager buzzed at 3:33 a.m. two nights later. He grabbed it from the nightstand beside the narrow twin bed where he'd slept from the time he'd come to live with *Grossdawdi* Ephraim, except for his short marriage. He stumbled out of bed and groped for his clothes. From the other side of the wall, he heard Simon thumping as he tried to get dressed, too.

He rushed out the door. He almost ran into his cousin, who'd burst out of his own room. Glancing at where Mary Beth slept, he was glad to see her door was closed.

"Another fire?" Simon tried to shove one foot into a boot even as he hopped along the hall. "These can't all be accidental."

"That would mean there's an arsonist in Bliss Valley." First Lauren, now his cousin had brought up the topic nibbling at his mind.

"I know." He gave up trying to walk and put on his boots at the same time. Stopping, he jammed his feet in. "I've been talking to other guys, some in the fire department and some not. They're sure these fires can't be happening on their own. I argued with them until the two fires in the field up in Paradise. Dean is exacting on things like making sure embers are doused. If the chief thinks something is going on, so do I."

"Dean hasn't said anything about arson."

"He wouldn't."

Adam nodded. "I agree. The guys you talked to are right. There have been too many fires. Someone may be setting them. Do they have any ideas who?"

"No proof. Not yet." Simon headed down the stairs. "Y'know, I can't help wondering what the casino companies would do to run us off our farms so they can buy them for next to nothing."

Though the same thoughts had played through Adam's head, something he hadn't admitted to Lauren, he said, "We've got to be careful about accusing someone without facts."

"Well, I'm sure someone is setting these fires."

As Adam reached the bottom step, *Grossdawdi* Ephraim came from his room on the other side of the living room.

"Another fire?" the old man asked.

"Ja." Adam opened the door.

"Where?"

"I don't know. We'll find out when we get to the firehouse. I need to get the buggy and—"

The blare of a horn interrupted him.

He ran into the chilly night and saw a truck at the end of the farm lane. Dew was thick on the grass, but the smell of smoke was unmistakable in the air. Adam rushed toward the vehicle. Simon raced past him.

As they climbed into Chip's truck, Adam wanted to ask why it'd come from the opposite direction of the fire station. Then he remembered Chip had a radio in his truck. He could have gotten a call from the chief along with the request to pick up Mahlon, Adam and Simon.

Tires squealed as Chip yanked the wheel. The truck spun. Chip hardly gave it a chance to stop before he slammed his foot on the gas pedal, driving Adam and the others back against their seats. Reaching up, he flicked the switch activating the flashers. Red and blue lights seemed to come into the cab from every direction.

"I love my siren," Chip said with a laugh as he hit another button.

"Our neighbors won't," Simon grumbled, trying to smother a yawn.

"The ones with the fire will. They'll be glad to hear us getting closer."

Adam shifted in the rear seat to look out the back window. He saw the silhouettes of their gear in the cargo bed. "Where are we headed?"

"Where to, Mahlon?" Chip asked. "You've got the directions."

Mahlon gripped the door handle as Chip swerved wildly around a corner. "Don't roll us before we get there. It's on Walnut Run Road. Chief said not far from Little Beaver Creek."

"Barn? House?" Adam felt sick even asking.

"Report said structure fire." Mahlon glanced across the cab. "Ain't so, Chip?"

"Let's hope," the driver said, "it's some outbuilding."

Simon leaned forward. "What do you guys think? Can all these fires be accidental?"

Chip glanced in the rearview mirror at them. "Arson is a big deal, Simon."

"I know." His cousin's lips pulled in a lopsided grin. "Adam said the same thing, but lots of folks are talking."

"Do *you* think these fires are arson, Adam?" asked Mahlon from the shadowed front seat. He half turned, and in the flashing lights on the truck, his face was alternately lit and lost to the darkness.

"The chief would call in the fire marshal if he thought these fires were suspicious," Adam said. "Isn't that right?"

"You see, Simon?" Chip's voice was filled with abrupt humor as he slowed for another corner. "You need to remember your lessons like Adam does. It isn't good for us volunteer firefighters to speculate on any fire. That's one of the first lessons, right?"

Adam tried not to rock into his cousin as the truck regained its speed along the road. Chip and Mahlon went on, reminding them of what they needed to do and not do when they reached the fire.

When Chip braked again, Adam groaned. He knew where they were. It was the Gingerich farm. Elvin Gingerich, the *daed* of Lauren's friend Naomi, used one of the outbuildings for his buggy shop.

Chip gunned the engine as they drove up the farm lane that was twice the length of the Weaver farm's and had three times as many potholes. The truck didn't slow for any of them. Skidding to a stop near other vehicles, Chip started to throw the door open.

"Incoming!" he shouted. He yanked the door closed as a ladder truck, a water tanker and the pumper flew past them.

And past the buggy shop, Adam noticed, relieved. As he jumped out and reached for his gear, smoke and heat struck him like a slap across the face. His lungs felt as if he'd swallowed an ember. Pulling on his gear, he squinted through the flashing lights to see the two trucks stop in front of a long, low building with big fans in its sides.

The chicken barn.

As far as he knew, there hadn't been any chickens kept in there since Naomi married and moved somewhere outside Bliss Valley. The chickens had been her job, and after she was married, her *daed* had sold off the flock. Was Elvin storing supplies in there? The smoke was acrid with a chemical taste.

Then he didn't have time to think, only act. His training guided him as he took up position on a hose. He lost track of Simon in the darkness and smoke and the crowd of firefighters. Shutting off his thoughts, he became an extension of the chief's orders. He shot the water where he was told to.

Within ten minutes, the fire had been beaten back. The windows glowed with its power, but flames no longer shot through the roof.

"Keep it aimed on the far end, Adam," Dean shouted to him as the chief walked from one side of the hoses, fanned across the ground, to the other.

Water pressure slackened for a few seconds as the hoses were switched, one by one, from the water truck to the pumper. Other hoses had been snaked across the ground to the pond on the far side of the biggest barn.

Adam smiled, knowing it was shadowed beneath his helmet. Mary Beth considered a pond only as a place for ducklings to be born. The wise farmer always had at least one pond nearby for water in case of a fire. He shoved aside those thoughts as the flames tried once more to climb above the roof.

An hour later, the darkness was thinning and the fire was out. In lights glowing from the house and the buggy shop, the skeletal remains of the chicken barn were encased with tendrils of smoke that drifted on the rising breeze.

The chief told Adam to turn off his hose. "We'll start raking the embers as soon as we can get close enough. Meanwhile, take a break."

"*Ja.* I—" He didn't add more as a cheer rose from a clump of firefighters to his right.

Seeing another crowd had gathered around an ambulance that must have arrived while he was concentrating on putting water where it needed to go, Adam walked over to his fellow volunteers. He saw Chip and Mahlon were in the center of the gathered people, standing next to a pair of buggies. They were being congratulated by their fellow firefighters for daring the fire to get the two valuable vehicles out of the chicken barn before they could be consumed by the fire.

Elvin, who once had been a tall, straight man and was now bent like one of the buggy wheels he mended, stepped forward to express his gratitude to the firefighters. He pumped Mahlon's hand, then did the same with Chip's.

"*Danki, danki.* I can't say it enough," the older man said. "If those buggies had burned, I would have been ruined."

Adam frowned. Ruined? Was Elvin having financial difficulties? If so, he should have come to Adam for help. No one in their community should have to suffer alone. Glancing at the destroyed chicken barn, he frowned. Unless Elvin planned to start breeding chickens again, there wouldn't be any reason to replace the barn. Instead, the *Leit* could raise money to help the old man with whatever money problems he was having.

He scanned the crowd, looking for Simon. Where had the boy gone? He wouldn't have left without telling Adam, and none of the firefighters would be leaving for several hours except those who had milking to do. Dale could handle the milking at the Weaver farm, so there was no reason for Simon to go.

He jumped when the ambulance's siren erupted. The vehicle raced along the farm lane, bouncing wildly. Its lights were flashing, and the siren sounded again when it neared the road.

Had someone been hurt? Why else would the ambulance

have its lights and siren on? Again he looked around him, but it wasn't easy to distinguish one smoke-covered face from another.

"Adam!"

At Lauren's voice, he whirled to see her running toward him, avoiding the maze of hoses on the ground. She wore a long, dark sweater over light-colored pants with some sort of design on them.

"What are you doing here?" he asked.

"It's Simon!" She grabbed the thick fabric of his coat. "They took him to the hospital, Adam."

"Is he okay?" That was a stupid question. If his cousin was unharmed, why would he be on his way to the hospital?

"The EMT told me he's got some burns. On his hands. They want a doctor to examine them. Just in case."

Just in case.

He reached out to God, asking for strength for his cousin and for himself. "Which hospital?"

"Lancaster, I'm sure." She pulled on his sleeve. "C'mon. I'll take you there."

It took almost ten minutes before Adam was seated in Ringo so Lauren could drive them to Lancaster. It had taken Adam that long to find the fire chief and let Dean know he was going.

On the way to the car, Adam had asked her again why she'd come to the fire. She explained how the sound of sirens had woken her and *Aenti* Sylvia. When they'd seen flames in the distance, her great-aunt had been certain the fire was at or near the Gingerich farm. She'd asked Lauren to find out. Because she couldn't sleep when Naomi's father's farm might be on fire, Lauren had agreed, throwing a sweater over her pajamas. She'd arrived to see the chicken barn ablaze as the firefighters got to work.

She'd stayed back and urged others to do the same. The crowd had grown while the fire was doused. Some had started to drift away before Adam's cousin had appeared out of the smoke and staggered to the ambulance, his hands held out in front of him as if they were something he'd never seen before. The EMTs had examined him and lifted him into the back. As they'd driven off, she'd gone to find Adam.

As she drove Adam through the night, she glanced at him time and again. He still wore his turnout coat and pants, and his helmet was on the back seat. The acrid odor of smoke had filled the car until she rolled down her window.

This was an Adam Hershberger she didn't recognize. Lost in his thoughts of his cousin, he gave her terse answers or none at all as she drove the Beetle through the dawn. It was far worse than when they'd gone to Lancaster to meet her biological mother. Then, they hadn't had any idea of what they might be facing in the attorney's office, but at the very worst, it couldn't be more than an uncomfortable situation.

As she raced along the same road toward Lancaster and the hospital, she didn't want to think of how badly injured Simon might be. She hadn't been able to see his outstretched hands.

There was more traffic than she'd expected in the city at such an early hour. She drove through the narrow streets toward the hospital. When she pulled in, she let Adam out at the emergency department doors. She followed directions to the parking garage on the other side of the hospital. She got lost twice on her way to the ER. Scanning the waiting area, she saw Adam sitting on a plastic chair that was almost lost beneath his smoke-stained turnout coat. The bright tape on it caught the light, blinding her as she went to sit beside him.

Again she sneezed as the smoke off his clothing tickled her nose, but whispered, "Have you seen Simon?"

"Not yet." He stared at his hands clasped between his knees. "This is my fault. I shouldn't have agreed for him to take the training when he's so young."

"He was well prepared, and the fire didn't care how old or how young he is."

"Maybe, but I should have insisted he wait when there were so many suspicious fires in the area."

She frowned, hating the self-accusations in his voice. For a moment, she was ready to remind him nobody could see the future. Then, taking a different tack, she said, "You're right, Adam. You should have thought it through before you let him sign up."

His head jerked up, his eyes snapping with abrupt anger. "How can you say that?"

When he started to stand, she seized his sleeve and rose along with him. She didn't let him walk away. "How can *you* think you have control over everything that happens? Aren't you the one who's told me to put my trust in God? That God is the One who knows the paths our lives will take. You didn't know what was ahead for Simon. You don't know what is ahead for yourself now or *Grossdawdi* Ephraim or Mary Beth!"

She watched his face, searching for any sign her words— *his* words—had reached through his fear and guilt. Taking his hands, she pressed them together between her own in a silent order to pray. He raised their hands up to his forehead, then leaned forward to press his brow against hers. She closed her eyes and reached out to God as she hadn't in years. Praying together in silence had always been something so special about a plain life.

He lifted his head. When she started to shift her hands,

he caught them in his far larger ones. She raised her eyes and found his still close to hers.

"*Danki*, Lauren," he murmured. "You're right. I need to put Simon in God's care and stop trying to find someone to blame."

"Especially yourself."

"My family is my responsibility, but they're in God's hands." He smiled fleetingly. "I was so happy when Simon wanted to be a volunteer. I thought it was a sign he was growing up."

"So you joined, too."

"Maybe I'm growing up myself. Is that what you're trying not to say?"

"No, that's exactly what I'm saying." She was rewarded by another of his smiles. "Wait here in case the doctor comes out. I'll get us some coffee."

"*Danki*. Get me the largest cup you can."

"I'd already assumed that's what you'd want."

Lauren glanced back into the waiting room before looking for a cafeteria or a vending machine. Glad to see Adam sit and bow his head in prayer, she hurried to find coffee. A nurse directed her to the cafeteria off a hall to the left.

Returning to the waiting room with two extra-large cups, she handed one to Adam before she sat beside him. "I brought creamer and sugar, if you want any."

"I need it black now." He took a careful sip.

She stirred some creamer into her own cup and then sagged against the hard plastic seat. "No news yet?"

"Nothing."

"I don't remember," she said, "there being so many fires before I left. Has there been an increase over the years?"

He shook his head. "The opposite. Now that most farmers leave their hay rolled out in the fields, we haven't lost a single barn to spontaneous combustion in more than five years.

There have been other fires, of course, caused by faulty diesel lines or equipment that wasn't maintained properly. There are always a few kitchen fires, but most of those are put out before we get there."

"So many so close together..."

"We were talking about that on the way to the fire. Simon shares my suspicions."

"And mine."

He nodded and took another sip of coffee. "Chip reminded me we shouldn't be speculating before the fire marshal has completed his investigation."

She had to admit that made sense, though she couldn't shake her first impression of Chip Weatherford. She hadn't liked him and how he treated everyone as if he were a bit better than they were. Mahlon seemed to jump to follow his friend's orders, and some instinct she'd refined during her work in public relations had warned her Chip didn't like Adam as much as he acted.

Drinking her coffee, she tried not to look at the clock that seemed to be moving too slowly. The sun rose to fill the room. Other people came in, sat and then left when they were called back to a treatment room to collect their loved one.

"Adam?" came a weak voice from the door.

Seeing Simon there, dressed in his turnout trousers and with his coat tied around his waist, Lauren smiled. Adam exploded to his feet and crossed the room with long strides. He reached out to his cousin, then halted and stared at Simon's hands, which were encased in thick bandages.

Simon held them up. "The *doktor* says I must come back each day for a week so my hands can be tended to. Adam, getting a driver is—"

"I will bring you," Lauren said.

The boy nodded. "*Danki*, Laurene. I guess you coming back truly is a blessing."

His words shocked her, so she nodded. Not that she would have had a chance to say much because a nurse appeared behind Simon.

She held a stack of papers, which she offered to Adam. "You must be his cousin."

"I am." Adam took the pages. "What's all this?"

"The doctor's report and a couple of prescriptions you need to get filled right away. Also there are instructions for burn care. Simon has second-degree burns on both hands. He must be careful to give time for his blisters to heal before he returns to any work."

"I'll make sure he does as the *doktor* orders."

The nurse blushed when Adam flashed one of his smiles at her.

Lauren pretended not to notice the woman's high color or her own vexation. She didn't want to be bothered when Adam made another woman flush with obvious pleasure at his attention. He was a free agent. Just because, when the sirens had woken her, she'd been in the middle of a dream of him drawing her to him and tilting her mouth beneath his and…

She stopped the replay of the dream before her own color started to rise.

Was she out of her mind? No, she was afraid she had let the truth out of her heart. She was falling for the last man on earth that she should.

Is this Your idea of a joke, God?

Chapter Fifteen

Adam teased his cousin about having to help him get ready
for bed, because Simon was struggling to do even the simplest thing with his bandaged hands. The salve the *doktor* had
used at the hospital helped deaden the pain. The worst of the
burns were on his palms, so his fingers had been spared. Even
so, the thick bandages made it impossible to undo a button
or feed himself.

"Danki." Simon sighed. "I hope I can get back to dressing
myself soon."

"You've been blessed with skilled *doktors* and nurses, Simon,
who believe, with work and time and God's help, you'll be
able to use your hands as you did before."

"I know I was blessed at the hospital, but before—"

"We don't have to get into that now." He smoothed out
the messy blanket and sheet on his cousin's bed. Simon had
thrown aside everything when answering the call to fight the
fire. It didn't seem possible that had occurred less than eighteen hours ago.

"There was something weird at the fire."

"There will be time enough to wait for the investigation. I'm sure Dean will want to talk to you, but not tonight."

"I want to talk about it tonight." Simon sat on the bed, then shifted so he could lean against the pillows Adam had propped on the headboard. A soft moan emerged from his taut lips when he brushed his hands against the bedding.

Adam wouldn't remind him being stubborn was a family trait. "What's so important it can't wait?"

"I didn't fall on my own. Someone shoved me into the fire."

Shock raced through Adam. He opened his mouth, but his cousin held up one bandaged hand to halt him.

"I know what you're going to say." Simon rested his wrists on his knees. "It was dark and smoky, and it's easy to bump into one another."

"Ja."

"It wasn't a bump like someone else's elbow or their equipment striking mine. It was a shove." He gulped. "It wasn't a mistake, Adam."

"Do you realize what you're saying?"

"Ja, I do. I'm saying the shove was on purpose."

Adam combed his fingers through his hair while he sorted out his thoughts. His cousin was adamant, and Simon was always honest with him. Sometimes too honest.

"Let me talk to Mahlon. I think he was working near where you were."

"He and Chip and the chief were nearby at one time or another."

"I was, too."

"I'm not accusing you of anything!"

"I know that." Adam reached out to put his hand on his cousin's shoulder, then shifted his fingers to the iron headboard.

"If there's another fire tonight—"

"Don't look for trouble where there isn't any."

"Yet."

"*Ja*, yet." Seeing Simon bandaged and in obvious pain made his blood hit a hard boil. "Do you need help with anything else?"

"I can manage." Simon gave him a weak grin. "You don't need to read me a bedtime story."

"Glad to hear that."

As he walked down the stairs, his cousin's words replayed through his head, and he prayed Simon was wrong about what had happened at the fire, but feared he wasn't.

Yawning two days later as he poured himself a cup of the strong *kaffi* he preferred first thing in the morning, Adam guessed he'd be drinking a bunch of cups before bedtime. He had morning chores, breakfast, fieldwork, supper and then a meeting to discuss the barn raising at the Gingerich farm within a month's time. A meeting with Elvin yesterday had been filled with surprises. The old man wanted to have the chicken barn replaced because he planned on hiring an assistant or two to learn buggy repair. The assistant would live in one section of the barn that would be set up with a couple of small rooms.

So now there needed to be fundraising to rebuild the barn. He had to have an idea of what the costs would be. Replacing such a structure in about four weeks was the usual goal, but the *Leit* had already put up money and time to rebuild a half dozen outbuildings and a springhouse in the past few weeks. They'd recruited almost a hundred men and boys to carry a shed from one corner of a neighbor's farm closer to the main barn to replace one that had burned. People were willing to give, but they were tired of fighting what seemed like a losing battle. Members who were usually among the first to step up now seemed less than happy when he appeared on their doorsteps to seek their help.

He was as weary of asking.

"It'll get better," his great-*grossdawdi* said as he walked into the kitchen.

"Better?" he repeated, not quite awake as he breathed in the fortifying fumes of the rich, dark *kaffi*.

"I've lived a long time." *Grossdawdi* Ephraim reached for a cup hanging on the sideboard. "One thing I've learned during my eighty years is tragedy and *gut* tidings come in waves. I try to think of life as a ride upon a vast ocean. Sometimes the waves try to sink me in despair. Other times, they lift me up in wonder and joy. I've learned the sinking times won't last forever, and neither does joy. So I need to ride out the bad and delight in the *gut*."

"That's pretty philosophical for this hour of the morning." He took a deep drink, ignoring the heat and the strong, bitter taste.

"I'm at my best when I'm half-asleep. My brain doesn't try to be reasonable. It thinks pretty much what it wants to. And mine isn't thinking about raising money to replace barns as yours is."

Adam turned to lean against the counter. "Are you a mind reader all of a sudden?"

"No." He poured himself a large cup and walked to the table, sitting in his usual seat. "I know what I'd be thinking if I were you. Assuming you aren't thinking about that pretty gal over at Sylvia's." He chuckled. "Why aren't you thinking of her?"

Dale walking into the kitchen saved Adam from having to answer his great-*grossdawdi*'s too insightful question. What would *Grossdawdi* Ephraim say if Adam told him the truth?

That he was focusing on rebuilding the Gingerich chicken barn so he didn't have to think about Lauren and how she filled his dreams every night along with his thoughts throughout the day.

"Ready to do chores?" he asked his younger cousin, who was rubbing sleep from his eyes.

"As ready as I'm going to be." His face almost split with a yawn. Opening the refrigerator, he took out the orange juice bottle and splashed some in a glass. He downed it with one gulp. "How's Simon?"

Adam shrugged as he opened the back door. "He was asleep when I looked in on him. He must be doing better."

"*Gut.*"

Dale waited until they'd reached the barn before he asked, "What do you think, Adam? Do you think someone is setting the fires?"

Turning on the lights and getting pails for the *millich*, Adam said, "I wish I knew one way or the other."

His cousin picked up another pail and walked to where the cows were ready to come into the barn. Opening the gate to let them in, he said, "It's hard to believe they all started on their own, ain't so?"

They didn't have time to talk more as they milked, fed the cows and the calves, and cleaned the barn. For once, his cousin did his share without a single complaint. His cooperation warned Dale was even more upset than he was letting on.

That was confirmed when, after they'd finished and were seated at the kitchen with the rest of their family for breakfast, Dale, who was helping his brother pour *millich* onto his cereal, again brought up the topic of the frequent fires.

"What have you heard?" Adam asked. "Anything to support your suspicions? If you've heard something, you need to take it to Jonas. I spoke with him yesterday, and he's heard lots of rumors, but no facts that he feels comfortable taking to the police."

"Nothing much." Simon picked up his spoon. Three of his fingers on each hand were now free of the bandaging, so he could handle something like a single utensil on his own.

"Nothing much," his younger brother echoed.

"Nothing much?" Adam shook his head. "Don't try to pull the wool over my eyes, guys. You may think I'm as old as Methuselah, but it wasn't long ago when I was as young as you are. I remember how curious my friends and I were about anything going on in the community."

"Because you didn't want to get caught?"

His hands tightened on his fork. "That's a fair question. *Ja*, my friends and I were often in trouble, but we also were curious about things others were doing."

"We haven't heard anything other than rumors, Adam." Simon sighed. "Honest. That's why I was asking Chip and Mahlon the other day." A flash of pain cut across his face at the mere mention of the fire at the Gingerich farm.

"Rumor isn't enough for any of us to do anything but speculate," Adam replied. "It's what Jonas said when I spoke with him." He stabbed a piece of egg on his plate. "Eat up. We've got to be at the hospital early today. Lauren should be arriving soon."

"Laurene is taking you and Simon to the hospital today?" *Grossdawdi* Ephraim frowned. "I thought she did that yesterday."

"She offered to take us as long as I need to go." Simon awkwardly lifted his spoon to his mouth. "She said it makes it easier for her to have some test or other today."

Adam saw his great-*grossdawdi*'s curiosity, but shouldn't speak about the request for Lauren to have the bone marrow donor sample taken. Not that he didn't trust *Grossdawdi*

Ephraim to keep the facts to himself, but she'd wanted to keep the request to herself until the results were back. Yet, he was curious, too, why she hadn't had the sample done before now.

"How will she manage taking you every day and still do all her work?" the old man asked. "Sylvia says she's on the phone half the day every day trying to get things done."

That could explain the delay, Adam told himself. He didn't want to give her a hassle about having the test done because he knew how uncertain she was about the whole process and its possible outcomes.

Dale interjected, "If Laurene's work gets delayed, isn't that for the best? Didn't you say, Adam, she's working for the people who want to build the casino here?"

"It may not even be built in this part of Lancaster County."

"No?" *Grossdawdi* Ephraim's brows rose in surprise. "I'd heard it was all set to be built on Lehman's Road."

"That's what I'd heard, too, but Lauren said it hadn't been decided." Adam smiled at his great-*grossdawdi*. "I've been praying the other site, one up north of Lititz, will be chosen so we don't have to fight to keep the casino from trying to buy our land as part of their development."

The old man took a reflective sip of his *kaffi* before saying, "I'm more worried about Laurene at the moment. She should take some time with Gina Marie and get to know her birth *mamm*."

"Birth *mamm*?" chirped Mary Beth, looking up from her attempt to get some apple butter on her toast rather than all over her plate.

Adam took it from her and smiled as he buttered the bread. "A birth *mamm* is the *mamm* who brings a new *boppli* into the world."

"I've got one?"

"Everyone has one." He handed her the toast. "Some get

to stay with us longer than others whom are called to God
very young."

"Like my *mamm*?"

"*Ja.*" He almost choked on the single word. Mary Beth
spoke of Vernita so seldom, he'd begun to convince himself his
daughter didn't remember—or want to remember—her *mamm*.

Grossdawdi Ephraim stretched to nab the bowl of apple butter. "Has she called Ida and Wayne yet? Sylvia is worried she
hasn't contacted them. They are her *mamm* and *daed*."

"Laurene's *mamm* is Ida?" Mary Beth frowned in confusion. "Ida or Gina Marie?"

Adam explained to his daughter about how Lauren had been
adopted and had reconnected with the woman who gave her
life. "So, you see, she has two *mamms*. Do you understand?"

"*Ja.*"

He was relieved she didn't ask another question, because he
heard Lauren's car pulling up the lane. Motioning for Simon to
finish his cereal, he grabbed another piece of toast and swabbed
it with apple butter. It was going to be a long, busy day.

Ending her call the next afternoon, Lauren lowered her
phone to her lap as she perched on the inn's porch swing. She
smiled at the sky that was embroidered with fluffy clouds and
gilded with sunshine. The discussion had gone better than
she'd expected. So much better, she had to suspect Patrick
had been relieved to hear her request for a leave of absence.
She'd considered asking to take vacation time, but everybody
at Krause-Matsui-Fitzgerald believed vacation and working
remotely were synonymous. The only way she could take a
break was to ask for unpaid leave.

By now, her boss had probably already called Cassie in and
dumped the whole project on her. In about fifteen minutes,
texts from Cassie should start filling up her phone because,

though the other woman wanted to be promoted, she'd never taken the time to learn how to do the job.

Lauren was fine with Cassie taking over. She'd offer the other woman what advice and help she could. Since she'd come to Lancaster County, she'd found she no longer wanted to play the endless games of one-upmanship. How had she forgotten the pleasure of doing something for another person without expecting anything in return? Looking back, she could see she'd already begun to tire of the blatant competition for attention and bigger paychecks. She'd continued to push herself in order to be able to help her parents.

Her parents... She looked at her phone again. Weeks had gone by since she'd last spoken to them.

The door opened behind her, and Mary Beth peeked around it. "All done with busy-ness?"

"I am." She smiled. "I was wondering when you'd get here."

"*Daed* worked too long." Her nose wrinkled. "I was sooooo hungry."

"When I take Simon to the hospital later this afternoon, I can ask your *daed* if it'd be easier for you to have your meal here at midday."

"*Grossdawdi* Ephraim and *Daed*, too?"

"Of course," she said, making a note in her head to let *Aenti* Sylvia know she'd invited the neighbors. Not that her great-aunt would mind, because she relished any opportunity to tease *Grossdawdi* Ephraim. Patting the swing beside her, Lauren smiled when the little girl scrambled up beside her. "How's Simon doing?"

"Itchy."

"Sounds like his hands are healing."

The child shook her head. "Itchy. Can't scratch."

Lauren laughed, though the situation mustn't be funny to Simon. Rocking the swing to the little girl's delight, she stuffed her phone into the pocket of her apron. She'd call her parents…

Later…

Sometime…

When she was ready…whenever that would be.

Mary Beth's chatter distracted Lauren as they sat in the sunshine washing across the front porch. It warmed the stones that still retained their winter chill. Her great-aunt had warned her the house wouldn't shake off its cold for another month. The child talked about everything and anything. She was intrigued by the world around her, and she wasn't afraid to ask questions. A sign, Lauren guessed, of an intelligent child. Though Mary Beth wouldn't start school until she was six, she talked a lot about books.

"Do you read them yourself?" Lauren asked.

"*Daed* reads, but me wanna read, too."

"You will." She tried to connect the memory of the boy who was reluctant to open a book with the father who read to his daughter.

"Read a book now?" asked the little girl.

"Okay. Do you have one?"

"Gots the kitties book." She jumped off the swing and ran into the inn. Moments later, she returned with a well-worn book. "*Daed* reads this. Will you?"

"Of course." As she opened the book, she smiled as the child snuggled close to her. The story of the three little kittens and their missing mittens had adorable illustrations. Each of the kittens was a different color, and their mother was a calico wearing a mobcap and a fluffy white apron over a polka-dot dress.

Mary Beth listened as if she'd never heard the story until Lauren turned the last page and read, "'The three little kittens they found their mittens, and they began to smile.'"

"No! No!" cried the child, sitting straighter. "That's not the way the story goes."

"Of course it does. See these words?" She ran her finger along the page. "They say, 'The three little kittens they found their mittens.' See? They've got them on their paws."

Mary Beth shook her head. "No, not story *Daed* reads."

"No? What does he read?"

"*Mamm* cat made them new mittens. The kittens won't lose these. They promised."

Lauren bit her bottom lip to silence her questions. She knew what was on the page in front of her. Why would Adam pretend the story went a different way? Maybe he'd wanted the altered story to teach his daughter a lesson he felt she needed. Once Mary Beth was able to read the simple words for herself, she'd know that he'd changed them.

"They're being good kittens," Lauren said, not wanting to argue.

Mary Beth, no longer interested in the book, rose to her knees and touched Lauren's *kapp* that had slid sideways again. "You gots lots of pins in your hair."

"I do." She pushed her *kapp* back into place. "My hair doesn't like to stay in place."

"Me neither." She giggled. "Not in braids."

"So I see." Wisps of soft curls had escaped Mary Beth's braids that were, as always, cockeyed. One was twice as fat as the other, and both were coming apart. "Would you like me to fix them?"

"Can you?"

"I used to braid my own hair when I wasn't much older than you."

"Teach me!"

"Today, I'll redo your braids. When you're six or seven…" She couldn't promise the child she'd teach her in a couple of years, because she had no idea where she'd be then. Yet, it was so nice to think about staying in Bliss Valley. She hadn't realized how much she'd missed the place she'd called home for almost half of her life. Since she'd left, nowhere had given her the same feeling. She'd kept herself so busy with studying and work that she'd been able to ignore the emptiness in her heart.

"Okay!"

"Get that stool over there." She pointed across the porch. "I'll get a brush."

When Lauren returned to the porch, Mary Beth was sitting on the stool and facing the swing. Lauren chuckled as she picked up the stool and the little girl and spun them so the child's back would be to her when she sat on the swing.

Mary Beth looked over her shoulder. "Can't see!"

"You don't need to see now." Drawing the stool back with a squeak against the porch floor, she put one knee on either side of the child so Mary Beth's head was centered. "This is the easiest way to braid someone else's hair."

"*Daed* doesn't do it this way."

"How does he do it?"

"He stands beside me. One side at a time." Her nose wrinkled. "He tugs lots."

"I'll do my best not to tug your hair. Did your *daed* braid your hair this morning?"

She shook her head, and the uneven braids bounced. "No, *Grossdawdi* Ephraim did. *Daed* had a…a…"

"A meeting?" She remembered Adam talking about getting the *Leit* together to discuss how they'd rebuild so many burned buildings.

"*Ja*. He gots lots and lots of those."

"He's a busy man, ain't so?" The Amish phrase fell easily from her lips as she spoke *Deitsch* with the little girl.

Loosening the braids, Lauren frowned. As she'd feared,

Mary Beth's hair was filled with snarls. *Grossdawdi* Ephraim was well-intentioned, but his gnarled fingers had missed the clumps of hair. She picked up a silken handful and began working on the snarls closest to the ends.

"Laurene?"

"What, sweet pea?"

Mary Beth giggled at the nickname. "Can I ask a question?"

"Anytime you want to." She worked on one snarl until it loosened and then moved on to the next. If she was pulling the child's hair, Mary Beth didn't mention it.

"Can I have one of your *mamms*?"

"What?" The brush stopped, caught in a snarl. "What did you say?"

"Can I have one of your *mamms*?" The child squirmed around so she faced Lauren. Hope glowed in her dark brown eyes that were so much like her father's. "*Daed* says you gots two *mamms*. Me gots no *mamm*. Can I have one of yours?"

"Oh, sweet pea, it doesn't work like that."

"Why not? *Daed* says share. Why won't you share with me? I gots no *mamm*. Not since mine went away. Miss her, and I wants a *mamm*. Can I have one of yours?"

Tears filled Lauren's eyes and blurred the face of the trusting, adorable little girl sitting beside her. "I wish I could say yes."

"Say it!"

"I can't. *Mamms* aren't something you can be given by me or anyone else on earth. She's something given to you by God."

"My *mamm* is with God. Why?"

"I can't answer that. Nobody can except God." She framed the child's face with her hands and held her gaze. "God knows what's in your heart, Mary Beth. He wants you to be happy. So have faith the path you walk with Him will bring you joy."

"And a new *mamm* all my own?"

The prayer came from her heart, deeper and more yearning than anything she'd offered up to God since she stopped attending services with the *Leit*. It was as if she'd thrown off a musty, old blanket, like the one over the boxes in her closet, and let fresh air into her yearning heart.

Lord, I know I'm not worthy of asking such a big favor from You, but I need You to find me the words to help Mary Beth and not hurt her even more. You see into our hearts, Lord, and I'm asking you to look into hers and show me the words I can use to ease her grief without breaking her spirit. She is a wunderbaar kind, *Lord, and we need Your help.*

Lauren stiffened as the prayer fell silent in her head. She hadn't expected *Deitsch* words to slip into her mind's voice, but they'd felt right when she was praying.

"If that's God's will, Mary Beth," she whispered. "Remember He answers all our prayers, but sometimes…"

"The answer is no." She sighed. "*Grossdawdi* Ephraim says that."

"He's right, but we need to remember God sees everything and we only see the here and the now. We need to trust Him to lead us to happiness."

"Maybe He'll give me one of your *mamms*."

"Who knows? God can do anything, ain't so?"

As the little girl flung her arms around her neck, Lauren prayed the child's heart would be healed soon. To do that, Adam must have a new wife, and the idea of him marrying someone else made her want to cry. She bent her head against the child's and added another prayer for help to heal her own heart, as well, because it must be broken to give Adam and Mary Beth the chance to be happy.

Chapter Sixteen

The reflection in the mirror no longer seemed alien, though Lauren had to admit the dress, in a deep shade of cranberry, looked better than the ones she'd borrowed from her great-aunt. *Aenti* Sylvia had surprised her this morning with a new dress and white apron to wear to their cousin's wedding. It was a gift from her cousin to thank Lauren for helping getting the Wickeys' house and barn ready for the big day that was being held on a Tuesday two weeks after Easter. However, she was sure the dress meant Diana didn't want her to appear at her wedding in *Englisch* clothing.

The wedding was being held in a barn at Diana's family's farm, less than a quarter of a mile up the road toward Strasburg. The marriage ceremony would be a small part of the service that would, like on any church Sunday, last almost three hours.

She settled the new *kapp* on her hair. Unlike the smaller, circular Mennonite ones she'd been wearing, it was a heart-shaped Amish *kapp*. She checked she hadn't loosened any pins holding her tiny bun in place. The *kapp* looked deflated because she didn't have a lifetime's growth of hair hidden beneath it.

How happy she'd been to have those long, heavy locks cut off before she attended her first day of school as an *Englisch* girl! The weight at the back of her head had vanished, making her hair bounce around her shoulders in the cute style other students her age wore.

She couldn't remember the last time she'd gone out without a bit of mascara and blush. Even the night of the fire at the Gingerich's, she'd dabbed on a bit. Her fear she'd appear half-dead vanished. Her cheeks held a soft, rosy glow, and her eyes weren't lost without eyeliner.

She felt more comfortable than she had in days. And freer. Not because of her new dress, but because her ensemble didn't include her cell phone. Yesterday, while helping at the work frolic, she'd had to excuse herself at least a dozen times to respond to frantic texts from Patrick and Cassie. She'd turned off her phone today and left it on the nightstand. She had disconnected herself from the outside world. She hadn't guessed it would feel so good.

"So *gut*." She laughed at her silliness.

Going downstairs, she saw her great-aunt waiting for her. *Aenti* Sylvia wore her best going-to-church dress, which was a somber dark gray that accented her hair, making it glisten with snowy fire. Her eyes sparkled, and she sat forward as if she couldn't wait to push her wheelchair down the ramp attached to the porch.

"See?" *Aenti* Sylvia said with a grin when Lauren stepped off the lowest tread. "You don't need that gunk on your face to look nice."

"Not when I'm in the plain world."

"Not when you're in any world. I've heard many *Englischers* talking about how beauty comes from within, but I don't think they believe it. Not with the cosmetics they wear."

"*Englischers* want to stand out in a crowd. Not like plain folk."

"I'm glad you understand that, Laurene."

She gave her great-aunt a wry smile. "I need to be able to understand *something* right now."

Though she thought *Aenti* Sylvia would ask what she meant, the older woman wheeled her chair toward the front door without another word.

Lauren followed, hoping she wouldn't make a big mistake and stand out today like a sore thumb—like a sore *Englisch* thumb—as she reentered the community she'd left so long ago and to which she'd assumed she'd never return.

Last night's fire at the hardware store in Paradise was the main topic of discussion as the men gathered outside the Wickey barn as they waited for the services to begin inside. Adam knew he needed to join the other ordained men for the prayers they shared while the *Leit* filed into the barn, men followed by women, for the wedding ceremony and worship service.

Yet he lingered as he listened to the talk about how nobody could guess what started the fire that consumed several wooden sheds along with the lumber stored near them behind the plaza containing the local hardware store. It had burned hot and fast, consuming the sheds made by a plain man who lived outside of Strasburg. The whole lumberyard might have gone up if the fire hadn't started close to the Paradise fire department's building. Even so, the firefighters hadn't been able to control the fire until volunteers from Bliss Valley and Ronks and the Hand-in-Hand Fire Company from Bird-in-Hand had arrived.

"That's the eighth outbuilding burned in the past three

months," grumbled Wyman Beachy, who had a farm on the other side of the Bliss Valley Covered Bridge. "Someone's behind all these fires. Someone with mischief on his mind. Mark my words!"

Adam paid the older man little attention. Wyman was the first person to point a finger of blame at someone else. His target used to be his own son before Joel had gotten tired of never living up to his *daed*'s highest expectations and decided to live down to his lowest ones. Maybe Joel would have had second thoughts about jumping the fence if his *daed* had—just once—taken his adopted son's side. Instead Wyman had declared the idea of adopting a *kind* had been his wife's idea, so he couldn't be held responsible for his son's mistakes.

"It *is* disturbing," *Grossdawdi* Ephraim said. Unlike Wyman, what his *grossdawdi* had to say was heeded. "We must be grateful to God nobody has been killed."

Excusing himself, Adam went to the bank barn's lower level and into the milking parlor where Jonas was talking with Gerald Hooley and Orus Hooley. The two ministers were first cousins and related to more than half the members of the district. They greeted him and began to discuss the upcoming service. By the time they'd prayed for God's blessings on the gathering and those attending it, the rest of the *Leit* had entered on the upper floor, which had been cleared of hay and equipment.

Adam followed the bishop and the ministers up the hill and into the barn. The *Leit* and the wedding guests were standing and singing. All the guests fit into the freshly swept barn, though a few of the young men remained in the doorway to seat anyone who arrived late. Someone handed him a hymnbook. He opened it as he walked between the two groups of backless benches where the men and older boys sat on one side facing the women and girls as well as the youngest children.

A few elderly guests had chairs close to the front, including his great-*grossdawdi*.

His steps faltered when he realized Mary Beth wasn't next to *Grossdawdi* Ephraim. Where was she?

He scanned the gathering and almost gasped when he saw his daughter next to Sylvia Nolt and… Lauren? What was she doing at the wedding service? In Amish clothes?

He forced his gaze to the songbook in his hands, though he knew every word of the hymn by heart. He should be rejoicing in the fact she'd come to the church service. It could be a signal she was considering a plain life again…and would give up pursuit of the development companies vying to build the casino.

Throughout the service, his gaze kept slipping to where she sat between Mary Beth and her great-*aenti*'s wheelchair. She kept his daughter from fidgeting by sneaking her little snacks to tide her over until the wedding dinner. He paid attention to the parts of the service that were his duty, but his mind wasn't on it. He sent a silent apology up to God and to the *Leit* when he made mistake after mistake. Fortunately he wasn't required to be part of the marriage ceremony itself, or he might have ended up seeing the nervous, young groom saying his vows to one of the cows from the lower level of the barn.

Adam waited through the long service. As soon as the last blessing was said and the final hymn sung, he congratulated the bride and groom. He headed toward the door where Lauren held Mary Beth's hand and stood by her great-*aenti*'s chair. On the other side was *Grossdawdi* Ephraim. His great-*grossdawdi* never was far from Sylvia's side when they could be together. Seeing several heads bend toward one another, he knew he wasn't the only one who'd taken note. Or were they looking at Mary Beth and Lauren, as he was?

"You're here," he said, forgetting every word he'd planned to say when he saw her.

"I am." She smiled at his daughter. "Didn't my cousin Diana look pretty?"

"So pretty." Mary Beth giggled as if sharing a private joke. "*Daed*, guess what? *Englischers* gots flower girls. They throw flowers at the bride."

"That's not *exactly* what they do." Lauren laughed.

"*Komm* along," Sylvia ordered from her chair. "The chicken and noodles smell *wunderbaar*. Let's find some seats."

"Sounds like a great idea," he replied, putting his hands on the back of her chair before his great-*grossdawdi* attempted to push it across the grass. He steered the chair out of the barn, being careful not to strike any of the guests on the lawn.

Having Lauren at the wedding was an unexpected pleasure, and he intended to take advantage of every minute he could spend with her today.

Was there a conspiracy among the wedding guests to keep Lauren and Adam apart? It was beginning to feel that way when, after the meal, each time they started to speak to one another, he was called away. He had many duties as the district's deacon, but she couldn't help wondering why everyone needed to speak to him at the exact moment he walked to where she stood.

Nobody seemed the least bit interested in intruding, though, when Mary Beth skipped up to her and took her hand. *"Bopplin?"*

"People *bopplin* or ducklings?"

"Duckies!"

"Let's let someone know where we're going, and then we'll check to see if the ducklings have arrived yet."

The little girl bounced on each step as they walked among

the crowd, looking for *Aenti* Sylvia or someone in Mary Beth's family. All of them seemed to have disappeared, because they weren't among the elders sitting on the front porch or with the men playing horseshoes or watching the younger kids' softball game.

Turning to head toward the house, Lauren gasped.

"Something wrong?" asked Mary Beth.

Lauren dropped the little girl's hand and rushed forward, not sure if she believed her own eyes. The woman in front of her was taller than she remembered, but the shape of her face and the pale streaks in her golden hair were the same.

"Naomi?" she called.

The woman, who was pulling a small wagon with two little kids in it, turned, and Lauren gasped again. This had to be her one-time best friend, even though she looked older than Lauren. Lines of strain pulled at her mouth and threaded across her brow beneath her sedate, black bonnet.

"*Ja?*" replied the woman in a leery tone.

Lauren stepped forward and hesitated before she could fling her arms around the person who'd been so dear during her childhood. "I'm Lauren. I mean, I'm Laurene Nolt."

Life seemed to rush into the woman's rich blue eyes, sweeping away the shadows etched into her face. She abruptly looked like the girl Lauren had called her best friend. Her gaze roved from Lauren's head to her feet.

"Laurene?" She gasped, then releasing the wagon's handle, threw her arms around Lauren.

As Naomi repeated her name over and over, Lauren said, "It's wonderful to see you."

"I can't believe my eyes." Naomi stepped back. "You're here? You're Amish still?"

"Yes and no." She considered explaining, but she was aware of the many ears that might overhear. Besides, she was more interested in finding out about her friend. "I couldn't believe my eyes when I saw you. I told myself you had to be Naomi Gingerich."

"I'm Naomi Ropp now."

Lauren's exuberance faded. "I've heard… That is…"

Naomi put a slender hand on Lauren's arm. "You're worried you're going to say the wrong thing. Don't. We once were closer than sisters, so how could you say anything to upset me when I'm happy to see you?"

"I don't want to say anything to remind you of your grief."

"It's something I never forget. Listen to me. I should be saying how *wunderbaar* it is to see you." Her smile wavered, but she squared her shoulders. Naomi had always spent more time thinking about making other people happy, even if she'd ended up miserable herself. It seemed that hadn't changed.

Lauren was grateful one thing hadn't because everything else in Bliss Valley had. No, that wasn't accurate. The places and people in Bliss Valley appeared the same on the surface, but subtle alterations had evolved in the past fifteen years. Her dearest friend must have become, through the challenges she'd faced of being widowed and losing her best friend without even a goodbye, a different woman. Lauren had changed a lot during her time away.

A clear memory of the night Lauren had left Bliss Valley burst into her mind when she heard her own younger voice arguing she couldn't go without letting Naomi know where the Nolts were bound. While she got dressed without even the glow from a single candle to help her, she'd begged her mother to stop at the Gingerich farm.

I can't just leave, she'd insisted.

How many times had she repeated those words as she went downstairs and out onto the porch, carrying two of her favorite books and a small grocery bag filled with what clothes she could stuff inside it? Her father had told her to be silent as they stepped out onto the porch, but she'd asked—one last time—to speak to her best friend before departing.

Now she was seeing Naomi again. There were so many things to say she couldn't think of a single one. When a small hand slipped into hers, she smiled as Mary Beth leaned forward to wave to the two toddlers in the wagon.

"I can see," Lauren said, "you've got a lot to keep you busy."

Naomi brushed the tops of the blond children's heads. "Busy and blessed. Marlin and I were married for almost ten years. We came to believe the *gut* Lord had decided not to bring *kinder* into our lives." She looked at the wagon and the toddlers in it. "When He changed His mind, He did so with enthusiasm. These are Jared and Jesse. They're two."

"Twins?"

"*Ja*, which was a surprise because there aren't any twins in my family or in Marlin's as far as I know."

"How many times have we heard people say God works in mysterious ways?"

For the first time, Naomi laughed, and the sound took Lauren back to sunny afternoons when they'd sat by the creek on her parents' farm and talked about everything and anything. Sometimes, they'd lain in the fragrant grass and watched the clouds sail across the sky.

Or they had until Adam and his friends had found their favorite spot and skulked around, dropping spiders, snakes and other creepy crawlies onto them.

Lauren pushed the memory away. She wasn't going to let the trio invade her joy today as they had in the past.

"Is this your daughter?" Naomi asked, smiling at the little girl.

"No, this is… Mary Beth." She felt odd telling her friend the little girl was Adam Hershberger's daughter. "She's—"

"Me this many!" Mary Beth held up five fingers, then nodded when Lauren folded her thumb down. "This many!"

"You're a big girl, ain't so?"

As Mary Beth squatted to play peekaboo with Naomi's twins, Lauren asked, "How's your father doing? It must have been quite a shock when the chicken barn caught on fire."

"He's doing fine." Her eyes shifted toward her children. "I've been trying to get him to move in with me and the boys."

"That would be good for all of you."

"He won't consider it." She sighed. "He was trying to get me and the boys to move in with him, but I'm not sure he'll have room for us. *Daed* has decided he should hire someone to work with him in his buggy repair shop. He planned on fixing up the chicken barn as living quarters."

"Don't be silly, Naomi! Your father would welcome you and the twins with open arms. I remember him saying many times how a full house is a happy house."

"I know, but…" She seemed ready to continue, then changed the subject. "Are you back to stay, Laurene?"

Every fiber in her wanted to share with her one-time dearest friend how her life had been turned upside down. She didn't as Naomi began to mediate between her little boys, who wanted the same stuffed fish. To dump everything on Naomi now, when she had the sole responsibility for two children at the same time she was mourning her late husband, would be cruel.

When her friend looked at her again, Lauren was able to affix a smile on her face. "I'm not sure yet. I've been helping my great-aunt. She broke her leg and is confined to a wheelchair."

"*Bopplin?*" chimed in Mary Beth. "Go now?"

Lauren smiled. "I promised to take her to look at the duck's nest by the pond."

"Go ahead. I need to check that my *daed* has located the district's deacon. He's determined to find out exactly when his chicken barn will be rebuilt." Naomi laughed. "One thing I can say for my *daed*. He doesn't give up when he sets his mind on something."

Should she warn her friend that Adam was the deacon for the district? Before she could decide, one of the twins let out a shrill cry, and Naomi's attention focused on her children.

"I hope we get to see each other again while you're here," her friend said without looking up. It was clearly a dismissal. A nice one, and a necessary one because the other twin began to howl, too. But a dismissal nonetheless.

"I hope so, too."

When *Grossdawdi* Ephraim told him that Lauren had taken Mary Beth for a walk, Adam was sure where they were heading. He thanked his great-*grossdawdi*, who'd been chatting with Sylvia, and left. Not quickly enough to miss the knowing glances they exchanged.

He strode along the road toward the inn, leaving the crowd's conversations and cheers for the games behind him. Birdcalls and the rustle of rabbits in the grass alongside the road filled his ears. He couldn't remember the last time he'd walked alone down the road.

Always in a hurry, I guess, Lord. That had been a problem for him his whole life. He'd always been in such a hurry to get to the next place. When everyone around him understood what the teacher was saying and it remained gibberish to him, he'd had a *gut* reason to want to skip to the next part of his life. Somehow, he'd let impatience become a habit.

It had allowed him to avoid dealing with things he couldn't

change. Like Vernita's death from an unknown blood clot that had taken her before anyone knew there was a problem. Like his parents' deaths. Like reading and arithmetic.

He looked across the inn's front yard and saw Lauren and his daughter walking toward the pond. He called to them and waved.

Lauren paused, telling Mary Beth not to get too far ahead of her. She waved back, and the day seemed sunnier when she smiled. She was beautiful in the plain clothing she once had worn. True, her hair tried to stick out from beneath her *kapp*, but the *kapp*'s heart-shape offered the perfect backdrop for her delicate features.

"Mary Beth had to check on the ducks," she said as he approached.

"That's what I guessed. You're spoiling her."

"It's impossible to spoil a child by helping them learn more about the world and its wonders."

He chuckled. "You always know the right thing to say. No wonder you're in the business you're in."

"No," she said, growing serious. "I don't always know that. In fact, when I was talking to Naomi Gingerich… I mean, Naomi Ropp. When I was talking to her and she spoke about her father wanting to talk to the deacon about his barn, I didn't know how to tell her you are the deacon."

"So what'd you say?"

"I didn't say anything."

"I don't—"

A heartbroken cry ruptured the quiet. Lauren's eyes widened in abrupt dismay. She'd recognized his daughter's voice, too. If she'd fallen in the pond…

He started to run toward the water, but Mary Beth burst out of the high reeds and raced toward them. Her face was stained with tears. When she tried to speak, he couldn't understand a thing she said.

"Take a deep breath, Mary Beth," Lauren said as she squatted in front of the little girl.

She tried to comply, but more sobs burst from her.

Sitting on the ground, Adam drew his daughter onto his knee. He cupped her elbows and nestled her against his broad chest. Within seconds, his shirt was spotted with her tears. He leaned his cheek against the top of her head.

"Did you fall, *liebling*?" he murmured.

She shook her head.

"No bee sting?"

Again she shook her head.

"Will you tell me what's wrong?"

"Bopplin!"

From beside him, Lauren said, "She means the ducklings."

Mary Beth sat up and looked from him to Lauren. "All gone. Broken to pieces."

He started to console her, but halted when Lauren said, "Look!" She pointed toward where the tall grass was quivering. "The ducklings aren't missing. There they are."

As if on cue, a duck emerged through the lush, green curtain and led the uneven line of her offspring to the nest.

Lauren held out her hand, and Mary Beth took it. As he rose to his feet, the duck steered her ducklings away from them.

"See?" Lauren asked. "There they are. Their eggs are broken because they hatched."

"No fox?"

"No. Their mother and father guarded them until they were old enough to push their way out of their eggs. Now look at them! They're walking around, and soon they'll be old enough to swim in the pond like their parents do."

"They can swim?"

"They will be able to," Adam said, "once their feathers are ready." He put his hand on her shoulder and turned her to where the ducklings were picking up pieces of twigs and grass before dropping each. "Look at how curious they are."

Mary Beth started to laugh, but he put a finger to her lips.

Lauren smiled. "If we make a lot of noise, the mama duck will take her babies somewhere else. She thinks she's safe here—"

"She is!" exclaimed the little girl.

The mother duck froze, swinging her head in every direction.

They held their breaths until the duck took another step toward the nest and began to herd her straggling babies into it.

"Eens, zwedder, drei, fiah, fimf." Lauren smiled at the little girl who was counting along with her on her fingers. "A full handful of ducklings."

"Lots of ducklings," Mary Beth announced, making the duck ruffle her feathers in consternation.

Putting her finger to her lips, Lauren whispered, "Actually there are six. One came late out of the grass when you were showing the number to your *daed*." She held up her other hand with a single finger raised and held it next to the child's pudgy fingers. "More than you can count on one hand."

"I can count on two hands." She demonstrated by counting to ten, raising one finger at a time. Then she lifted one foot. "I can count on my toes, too."

"So you can, but I've got something else for you to count." Lauren smiled. "Do you think you can count out three cookies? One for each of us?"

"Ja!"

Waving her toward the inn, Lauren smiled as she and Adam watched the little girl scamper toward the kitchen at the back of the house. He matched Lauren's steps while they followed at a much more sedate pace.

"She can already count to twenty?" he asked, hoping envy didn't seep into his voice. Danki, *God, that my daughter's brain works better than mine.*

"She's a quick learner. Though I was surprised she didn't know how to already. Most four-year-olds can count that high."

"There's a reason she can't." He stopped, waiting for her to do the same. Ignoring the part of his brain warning he was opening himself up to ridicule worse than he'd heaped on her years ago, he said, "She can't count because I can't."

"What?" Lauren's smile wavered, then vanished. "If this is your idea of a joke, Adam, it's not a good one."

"It's not a joke. It's a secret I've never told anyone. Not our teachers. Not my friends. Not even *Grossdawdi* Ephraim, though I'm sure he's figured it out." He closed the distance between them. Curving his hands over her slender shoulders, he said, "The truth is, Lauren, I can't do numbers and I can't read."

"You can't…" Her voice faded as she mouthed the words he'd said.

"I can't."

For a long moment, she stared at a button in the center of his shirt. When she raised her eyes, he steeled himself for what he'd see in them. Disgust with his lifetime of lies? Pity he was so incapable of learning what his four-year-old daughter had already mastered? Delight that the person who'd tormented her for so many years was himself tortured?

He didn't see any of that. He saw the clear light of comprehension in them. He'd given her the final piece to a puzzle that had remained between them for so long.

"That explains," she whispered, "what happened when I

read Mary Beth a story from her book. The one about the three kittens and their mittens. She insisted the words were different from what was printed on the page because of how you'd read it to her."

Shame hit him like a blow to the gut. "I made up the story as best I could by looking at the pictures."

"You got most of it right."

"I got enough wrong for you to become suspicious."

"Not suspicious. Just confused. You remember every word of the story you'd devised? You've got to have an amazing memory."

He sighed. "It wasn't hard when she wanted the same stories every night. At first, she was young enough so she didn't notice when I changed things. By the time she was older, I'd gotten my stories down pat."

"How can you be the district's deacon if you can't help people with their medical bills or figure out the cost of a barn raising?"

He explained how he'd developed ways for others to take over the sums he couldn't do on his own. "I ask them to check my work and give them the sheets without any answers on them. Nobody's guessed the truth."

"It would have been better if someone had."

"Maybe." A door slammed as Mary Beth emerged from the inn. "I don't want my daughter to be ashamed of her *dumm daed.*"

"You aren't stupid, Adam. You've learned to fix small engines and cars without being able to read a manual and figured out ways to hide your learning disability."

"Learning disability?" He laughed sharply. "Isn't that another word for *dumm*?"

"You're stupid only if you don't find someone to help you."

"Will you?"

"Me?"

He moved his hands until he held her elbows as he had his daughter's. The sensations racing through him as he touched her were nothing like anything he'd felt while he comforted Mary Beth. These were more powerful, more all-consuming, more intimate. When Lauren's eyes widened, he saw she was no more immune to the warmth than he was. His own gaze dropped to her lips, and he had to force it away while he asked her to do what he guessed would be the last thing she'd ever considered when she first drove across the covered bridge and into the pothole.

"Will you help me?" he whispered. "Will you teach me how to read and do simple arithmetic?"

"You want me to tutor you?" Disbelief heightened her voice.

"*Ja.*"

She turned away, and he didn't try to stop her. Was he asking too much? She'd forgiven him enough to make friends with his daughter, and she'd welcomed his great-*grossdawdi* to her great-*aenti*'s house. She'd driven his cousin to appointments with the *doktor* at the hospital. Most important, she'd forgiven him when she had every reason to hate him.

If only she had even one reason to love me. Was that a wish or a prayer or both?

"You want me to tutor you?" she asked with incredulity as she faced him. "Like before?"

"It won't be like it was fifteen years ago. Back then, I was an angry kid. Angry at my parents for dying. Angry at the world for not understanding how much I hurt. Angry at God. Angry at myself." He sighed and put his hands in his trouser pockets. "I inflicted that anger on you and anyone else who tried to help me. I needed help as much as I needed air to breathe, but I didn't want to admit it. I didn't want to admit I needed anyone or anything. To do that made me vulnerable to more pain, and I was determined not to feel anything else bad."

Her head bowed, and she clasped her hands. Was she praying for an answer? Would God help her see she could be the answer to Adam's prayers?

"All right," she said.

"All right?" He wasn't sure he'd heard her correctly. After all he'd put her through years ago, she was willing to help him now?

She nodded. "All right. We'll start tomorrow evening after supper. If you…"

She halted as Mary Beth skidded to a stop near her and held up a crushed cookie. Thanking his daughter, she listened as Mary Beth prattled about finding a chair and climbing on it to reach the cookie jar.

He said nothing but a silent *danki* to God. He'd been given a second chance he thought he never would have, and he didn't want to mess it up this time.

Chapter Seventeen

The next morning, Adam woke with a smile. The wind was howling under the eaves, and he could hear heavy rain being thrown against the window beside his bed. Dawn would be even later than usual with the heavy blanket of clouds concealing the moon.

He felt like the sun was shining on the most perfect day ever.

The burden he'd carried for most of his life no longer weighed on him. He felt as if he could challenge Sparks to a race and win.

He didn't realize he was whistling while he washed out the *millich* buckets until Dale asked, "What's gotten into you? You're not this cheerful early in the morning."

"Looking forward to a *gut* day," he replied. *And a better than* gut *evening having my lessons with Lauren*. He wasn't going to mention that to his cousin because he remained reluctant to share the truth until he'd learned the most basic skills.

"That makes one of us." Dale stomped across the concrete floor.

"What's bothering you?"

"Other guys are out with youth groups, and I'm not."

Adam should have expected such a reaction after hearing other younger teens talking at the wedding. The guests had come from eighteen different districts in four states. When young people got together, they were eager to compare *rumspringa* traditions in other areas. The so-called running around time varied widely. Some areas were lenient and allowed their young people to try aspects of *Englisch* life, including radios and cars. Others forbade it completely, having their *kinder* baptized in their teen years. Most districts, like their own, landed somewhere in the middle.

Dale, at fifteen, would soon join the older singles for youth singings and other gatherings. Most runaround groups in their area wouldn't accept anyone younger than sixteen.

"Choosing which events you want to attend," Adam said, "is something you're going to have to make up your mind on. Your sixteenth birthday is four months away."

"Seems like forever."

Adam couldn't silence his laugh. "You sound like Mary Beth when she's whining after having a second cookie and knowing she can't have another until the next day."

"Guess I do." Dale gave him a wry grin. "Sorry."

"I get it. Remember I used to be your age."

"About a thousand years ago."

With another laugh, Adam flung the soaking sponge at his cousin. Dale tried to duck out of the way, but water sprayed him. Picking up the sponge, Dale threw it back. Adam held up the bucket and caught it. They chuckled before finishing the chores.

When they stood in the barn's doorway, staring at the heavy rain, Lauren's Beetle drove up the farm lane. Adam smacked his hand against his forehead. He'd forgotten Simon's appointment this morning. It was important because the last of the heavy bandages were going to be removed. If all went well, his cousin would have gauze pads over his palms with a light wrapping for another week.

"Is that the car you helped fix?" Dale asked.

"*Ja.*"

"Can you teach me to fix cars, too?"

Adam was shocked into silence. He'd been helping both boys learn to repair the farm equipment, and Simon had shown promise. All Dale had revealed was indifference. Not that the boy wasn't capable, but his mind tended to wander and he ended up dropping tools and pouring oil on the floor.

"If you want to learn," Adam said, "I could start you on projects in the shop. Once you've gotten a feel for the tools and the work, I'll talk to Frank about you observing at his garage."

"Observing? I want to work on cars."

"In Frank's world, observing means doing everything to assist him. You'll have more hands-on work than you can imagine. Why the sudden interest in cars?"

Dale grinned. "One of my *Englisch* friends let me try driving his."

"You're not old enough."

"It was just around the barnyard."

"Okay, I'll help you learn, but only if you promise not to drive again until I say you're ready."

His cousin grinned, and Adam clapped him on the shoulder before raising his voice to tell Lauren to stay in the car. He'd clean up, and then he and Simon would be out. Smiling as he ran through the rain, he thanked God that Dale was showing an interest in learning something Adam could teach him. He prayed it would prove to be only the first great surprise of the day.

★ ★ ★

The lights in the large dining room were dimmed except for where Lauren sat beside Adam at one end of the table. Her laptop was between them, the screen displaying a website with the first lessons for working with an adult dyslexic. She hadn't been certain if Adam would be willing to use her computer, but he'd agreed for this first lesson.

"I'll have to check with Jonas before the next time," he'd said. "Under the circumstances, he may give me permission. Otherwise, he'll have to send me to be a scholar, and I don't think anyone wants that, especially Teacher Millie."

After they'd laughed together about their one-time teacher's horror at the idea of having Adam in her school again, Lauren had introduced him to the information on the screen. She used visual images like an apricot for the letter *a* and a baseball bat and ball for *b*.

C was represented by a curled up cat taking a nap. He struggled with the simple concepts, but unlike when she'd been asked to tutor him before, he made a real effort to grasp what she was explaining to him.

She stood and stretched her shoulders after going through three of the short lessons. "I think that's enough for tonight."

"Enough?" He got up, too, but his eyes remained on the screen. "I haven't learned anything useful yet."

"You've learned your ABC's."

"Just *a* and *b* and *c*." He pointed to each letter as he said it.

She smiled as his eyes grew wide when he realized what he'd done. "You've got to learn to walk before you learn to sprint, Adam."

He looked at her with entreaty. "I've waited so long."

"So be patient a bit longer." She leaned forward to exit the program.

"I don't know if I want to be." His voice roughened. "I don't know if I can be."

Were they talking about the reading lesson any longer? She raised her eyes and was caught in the power of his gaze. It was a flame overpowering the dim lights around them. And overpowering her.

Running his hands down her arms and sending a delightful frisson along her spine, he laced his fingers through hers. He drew her a half step closer. Could he sense her heart trying to beat its way out of her chest? It was louder than her uneven breath as he slanted toward her. When his mouth brushed her forehead, she gasped. Was *that* what he couldn't wait for?

As if she'd asked the question aloud, he smiled. His lips teased her eyelids and the very tip of her nose. Her gasp became a sweet sigh as he left dazzling sparks in a meandering path along her cheek. Then he found her mouth as he released her hands and pulled her into a powerful embrace. Her fingers clenched on his shirt, then softened to spread across his chest. Gently, persuasively, he explored her lips until her knees softened to jam.

Lifting his mouth from hers, he whispered, "Very nice."

Her fingers sifted through his hair as he sprinkled another shower of kisses across her face. When his mouth claimed hers again, it was gentle, so sweetly gentle, but she sensed the powerful longing behind its restrained caress.

When he released her, she heard a sigh. Was it his or hers or both in unison? Reality slapped her hard. He shouldn't be kissing her. Amish couples sometimes didn't kiss until marriage was proposed. He couldn't marry her, because she wasn't baptized into the *Leit*.

What if you were? She pushed aside that thought. Until she knew why her parents had left Bliss Valley and their community behind, she shouldn't think that way. *If she asked…* They'd never told her the truth. Would they now?

"I should go," he said, reaching for his straw hat. "*Gut nacht. Danki* for your help."

"Adam?" she called as he walked toward the front door.

"*Ja?*" He faced her.

Her feet ached to propel her forward into his arms again. She went as far as the dining room arch. Grasping the molding, she said, "I'm glad… I'm glad I can help."

He nodded before opening the door and leaving.

She slumped against the wall. Staring at the front door, she strained to hear his footfalls on the steps. They faded, and she closed her eyes. She'd sighed with regret when Adam walked away. Had his sigh been regret, too? Regret for having to let her go…or regret for kissing her when there was no future for them?

"How did the lesson go?" asked *Aenti* Sylvia as she rolled her wheelchair from the living room.

Lauren had the sneaking suspicion her great-aunt already knew the answer, but she said, "Using the dining room was great. I know Adam appreciates you letting us use the space, too."

"I'm glad the table worked for you." She smiled. "But you didn't answer my question. How did the lesson go?"

"As I told Adam, it's slow at first."

"Slow but sure is *gut*."

"It is."

Aenti Sylvia sighed. "I wish your *daed* had felt the same way when he decided to leave Bliss Valley."

"I didn't realize he'd discussed his plans to go with anyone." She didn't try to hide her surprise at how her great-aunt had changed the subject.

"Ida and Wayne came over one night to talk with me and Bruce."

"About what made them so unhappy they left?"

"They said they didn't feel like their opinions mattered any longer. They said they were looking for advice, but I think they'd already made up their minds and had come to tell us goodbye."

"They didn't have to cut themselves off from you and *Onkel* Bruce. You aren't Amish."

Aenti Sylvia shifted in her chair and grimaced as her leg moved. Pulling it to the center of the support, she said, "I'd hoped they'd join us as Mennonites, but your *daed* was insistent there was no life for them in Bliss Valley. They cut all ties, and now you're doing the same."

"Me cutting you off? I'm here with you, *Aenti* Sylvia."

Her great-aunt wagged a gnarled finger at her. "That's not what I'm talking about, and you know it. I'm talking about how you've cut off your parents. I know you're furious because they weren't honest with you, but can't you see the truth? They did what they thought was best for you."

"I wish I could believe that."

"You can. You do." She tapped the center of her chest. "You believe it in your heart."

Lauren couldn't argue.

All I know is if I'd been separated from Mary Beth for years and finally had a chance to see her again, I'd do or say whatever I could in an effort to heal the rift time had created between us.

Adam's words blared through her mind. They'd been speaking of her birth mother, but weren't the sentiments as valid for the two people she'd called Mom and Dad?

"Gut nacht," said her great-aunt before rolling her chair toward her bedroom.

Gathering up her computer from the dining room table,

Lauren went upstairs. She set her laptop on a chair, then went to the nightstand where she'd left her phone. Her fingers trembled as she picked it up and turned it on. A picture emerged on the screen. The waves washing up on the shore in Cape May were lit by the brilliant perfection of a sunrise searing the sky. Two small figures were silhouetted against that eye-searing crimson.

Her parents.

She'd taken that picture when the three of them had gone to the Jersey Shore to celebrate her high school graduation. It'd been for only three days in the middle of the week, because her parents couldn't afford more, but they'd filled those days with laughter and fun. For a short time, her parents had acted almost as young as she'd been. It'd been a special holiday and a reminder of how linked together they were.

She heard the phone ringing in her ear before she even realized she'd pushed the button to call.

It was answered on the second ring. "Lauren?"

"Hello, Mom." She thought of the words she'd planned for this moment, but none of them seemed sufficient. Piling on more fault for something she didn't understand wouldn't help. Nothing could change the past, but she might be able to salvage the present. "How are you and Dad?"

"Better now that I can hear your voice." Moving away from the phone, her mother called, "Wayne! It's Lauren! Pick up the extension!"

They talked until her phone battery died. As she lowered her phone away from her face, Lauren couldn't remember what they'd discussed other than her meeting with her birth mother. It didn't matter. They had reconnected. There were some big issues they must discuss, like why her parents had left Bliss Valley, and they would. She'd intended to ask, but the call had been all about putting aside the differences that had separated them for weeks. She'd bring up the question next time they talked, but for tonight, the broken link from their hearts to hers had begun to mend.

Thank You, God, she prayed with a bowed head. *Thank You for showing me what's important. Those who love me.*

Her head jerked up when Adam's image filled her mind. Did he love her? He'd kissed her. Didn't that mean something?

Adam set the wrench next to the chainsaw he was repairing. He'd gone to his shop after returning from The Acorn Farm Inn. Though he seldom worked in the evening, he needed time to sort out his thoughts about surrendering to his yearning to kiss Lauren. If he stayed in the house, *Grossdawdi* Ephraim was sure to start asking questions to get to the truth.

He didn't know what would happen now. Lauren might wear plain clothes, but her life was *Englisch*. She'd used her laptop as a teaching tool tonight, and she hadn't shown any signs of wanting to return to a plain life. Had he kissed her in hopes of bringing the issue to the forefront? If so, he should have stayed and asked her instead of running away like a scared rabbit.

Sniffing the air, he frowned. Smoke? Where was it coming from? He glanced around his shop, but saw nothing wrong.

He ran to the door and threw it open. The far end of the barn had flames shooting through its roof. Trucks with sirens and flashing lights raced up the farm lane. Someone had already contacted the Bliss Valley Volunteer Fire Department. He ran toward the closest truck. It was Chip Weatherford's. He didn't wait for it to stop before he grabbed turnout gear from the back. Pulling it on, he nodded when the chief jumped out of his truck and began issuing orders.

An hour later, Adam was thanking his fellow firefighters for knocking down the flames. The only portion of the barn destroyed had held the dairy tank. It would have to be re-placed, but he was grateful they hadn't lost livestock. Chip and Mahlon had carried the calves out. He needed to thank them, but a crowd of spectators were gathered around their truck, listening to the two relate how they'd shooed the cows away like a pair of cowboys. He'd let him bask in the hero worship before he intruded to express his appreciation.

His eyes widened when he saw Lauren walking toward him. He shouldn't be surprised to see her. The flames would have been visible from the inn, and her great-*aenti* would want to know what was happening.

"Are you okay?" she asked without a greeting.

"I'm fine. The barn will be, too. There's sure to be some water and smoke damage, but that can be taken care of while Dale, Simon and I rebuild."

"What do you think happened?"

The words he didn't want to say—the words he *had* to say—were bitter on his tongue. "I don't believe it was accidental. I think someone set it. Just like the others."

"I agree, but who?"

"That's the question, ain't so? Who? A farmer? That's ri-diculous. Even if someone was desperate for a new barn—"

"You're thinking of Elvin Gingerich." She shook her head. "He wasn't desperate. He had plans to fix up that chicken barn. Naomi told me."

"Even if someone was that desperate, replacing a barn after a fire means at least a month without a place to put animals or equipment. Assuming the animals and equipment survived." He held her gaze. "So who would profit the most from the destruction of these buildings?"

"I don't know."

"*Ja*, I think you do. I think you know very, very well because you know quite well the people who have the most to gain."

All color washed from her face, and she whispered, "You can't mean the casino developers."

"Why not? Don't they have the most to gain? If they build in Bliss Valley, they'll be interested in several of the farms that have had fires, including this one."

"Gingerich's is too far from the site, and the one the night I arrived was, too."

"Maybe the developers are trying to confuse us."

"You're confused. That's for sure!"

He went on as if she hadn't spoken. "They're trying to distract us from seeing them as suspects. If the farms they want have lost vital buildings, they aren't worth as much."

She stared at him. "You can't believe the developers are trying to frighten local farmers off their farms."

"It wouldn't be the first time."

"That's a big accusation."

"I know, but you've got to have considered it, too."

"I did."

He stared at her.

"The facts are the facts, Adam. I can see them the same as you can. I can also see there's a big hole in your logic. What good would it do for one developer to resort to those tactics when they might not even win the license? It doesn't make sense."

"Can't you find out? Isn't there someone you can trust enough to ask?"

She folded her arms in front of her. "No, not even if the project was mine."

"Not yours? What do you mean?"

"I told my boss I wanted a leave of absence."

"What does that mean? Did you quit?"

"No. It means I took some time off without pay."

He rubbed his smoke-blackened face, stopping when the grit cut into his skin. "I don't understand. Are you working on the casino project now or not?"

"Not. I thought you'd be happy I wasn't involved any longer."

"I am, but…"

Tears glistened in her eyes. "I don't have my finger on what's happening with the casino now, so you can't find out the latest from me."

"That's not it."

"It isn't?"

"No." His mouth worked before he said, *"Ja."*

"Is that all I've been for you, Adam? A conduit for the latest information?"

"You know that's not true. I haven't asked you about the casino, have I?"

"Other than the day we went to the attorney's office? No. Why did you ask me then? Did you think my defenses would be weak and you could get the lowdown?" She stepped back. "I'd thought you'd changed, Adam, but you haven't, have you? You'll still use anyone who helps you get what you want. It used to be laughs. Now it's more serious, but it's the same. *You* are the same."

She whirled and walked away.

He was prevented from giving chase by his cousins. They bombarded him with questions about where to put the calves overnight. As he answered them, he watched Lauren's slim shadow across the field. He didn't want to believe she was right about him.

But what if she was?

Chapter Eighteen

"I think this is what you've been waiting for." Mr. Satter-field held out a white envelope.

Turning it over, Lauren stared at the return address. She recognized the name of the lab that was testing her cheek swab to determine if her bone marrow would be a good match for her birth mother. The envelope trembled in her fingers.

She'd been trying to prepare herself since she received a call from the attorney's office before noon. Nobody had wanted to wait on the answer, so she'd jumped into Ringo and headed to Lancaster. This time, she hadn't had to sit in the reception area, but had been shown to the conference room where the lawyer, Mrs. Tinniswood and her daughter sat in the same chairs they had during their first meeting.

Only this time, Lauren was alone. She wished she wasn't, but she hadn't spoken to Adam since the fire at the Weaver farm five days ago. Mary Beth hadn't come to the inn, though Lauren had been sure the child would want to see the duck-lings taking their first jaunts onto the pond. Even *Grossdawdi*

Ephraim hadn't paid a visit to *Aenti* Sylvia. It was as if the world ended at the inn's back fence and nothing existed beyond it.

For Lauren, nothing did. She had to forget about Adam and his family and those sweet, sweet kisses. Telling herself she should be grateful she'd found out the truth before their relationship grew closer, she couldn't feel anything but numbness. The same numbness she'd experienced when she first learned she was adopted.

It wasn't anger. It wasn't hurt. It was having her heart betrayed.

"Aren't you going to open it?" Mr. Satterfield asked, jarring her out of her thoughts.

"Of course." She didn't move. Since everything else in her life had imploded, she'd believed God had had a single reason to bring her back to Bliss Valley. If she wasn't a match, then why…?

Mr. Satterfield handed her a letter opener. It was, she noted, some sort of commemorative gift.

She saw his name, a date and a few other words, but didn't stop to read them as she slipped one end of the pointed tool under the envelope flap. A quick motion slid the letter opener across its top. Setting the letter opener on the table, she reached into the envelope and pulled out a single folded sheet of paper.

Nobody in the room moved or even seemed to breathe as she opened the sheet and scanned it.

"Not a match," she whispered as her shoulders slumped.

She handed the letter to the lawyer, but didn't look at her birth mother. After all the uncertainty and second-guessing she'd endured, she wasn't a match. She'd been sure returning to Bliss Valley had been because she'd been meant to save Gina Marie Tinniswood's life. Had it been for nothing?

Two faces filled her mind. Adam's and Mary Beth's.

She'd been as mistaken about how they might have a place in her life as she'd been about being the one to save her birth mother's life.

It'd all been for nothing.

The hopes for happiness, the dreams of a future where she knew she belonged, the heartache she'd suffered as she tried to figure out who she was…every bit of it for nothing.

Ms. Lopez's soft sobbing broke into her self-pitying thoughts, and Lauren was horrified she'd been thinking only of herself. Her life would continue in the same messy way. For her birth mother, the report could mean any chances she had of a bone marrow transplant to defeat her cancer were gone.

"I'm sorry," Lauren said.

"It's not your fault." For the first time, her birth mother reached across the table and took her hand. "I appreciate you being willing to help me. Your parents raised you well. I'm glad we've had a chance to meet."

"Mr. Satterfield, you need to find the other one," Ms. Lopez insisted. "Right away! We've wasted too much time hoping this one would be a match."

"Other one?" Lauren asked.

"Your twin."

"I've got a twin?"

"Yes," replied her birth mother.

Lauren turned to the lawyer. "Is my twin the reason you ran into a brick wall with the court and contacted Teacher Millie?"

He looked blank for a moment, then said, "Ah, yes. We discussed that at our first meeting. Yes, that was a part of the problem in the search."

"So I've got a twin?" she asked again, focusing again on the women on the other side of the table.

"A sister." A troubled expression crossed her face. "At least, I think it's a sister."

"You don't know? How could you not know your own children?"

Mrs. Tinniswood glanced at Mr. Satterfield who said, "It's up to you, Gina Marie, but not telling her the whole truth has already led to misunderstandings I'd hoped we could have avoided. However, the choice, as always, is up to you."

"Mom," Ms. Lopez said, "it's long past time to stop being ashamed because of what happened. It wasn't your fault you were taken advantage of. You weren't much more than a kid yourself then."

Taken advantage of? What was her half sister talking about?

"You're right, Skylar," Mrs. Tinniswood said. "I should have listened to you from the beginning, sweetheart."

Something primal tugged at Lauren's heart. Would her birth mother ever use such an endearment when addressing her? From the depths of her memory came Ida Nolt's voice whispering what a precious gift Lauren was. In the midst of her anger and hurt at learning the truth, somehow Lauren had banished those special moments when she'd seen the truth in her adoptive mother's eyes. Lauren was beloved by her parents, someone special they'd adored as she'd loved them.

Mrs. Tinniswood squared her shoulders as she shifted in her chair to look at Lauren. "When I realized I was pregnant, I went to a midwife I'd heard about. Her name was Vikki Presley. She said she'd help me. I didn't realize she meant she'd take my babies before I even saw them. I was ill after the birth, and it took me a couple of weeks to get back on my feet. That's when I saw Vikki again, and she told me she'd found a home for my twins with an Amish family. She assured me, because you'd be raised Amish, you'd never come looking for me, and that was important to me when I wanted to put the whole pregnancy behind me."

"Did she tell you where?"

"In Baltimore."

"Baltimore?" Lauren glanced toward the attorney. "There aren't any Amish communities in Baltimore."

Mr. Satterfield cleared his throat. "There was one, but it was abandoned in the 1950s."

"Long before I was born."

"Me, too." Gina Marie sighed. "I know that now, but I was young and scared and grateful the problem of being an unwed mother was behind me. At the time, I didn't have any reason not to believe Vikki. She'd taken me in when my parents kicked me out, and she'd been kind to me. I didn't realize the extent of Vikki's lies until years later when I discovered she was selling babies."

"Selling babies?" Lauren sat straighter. "My parents—my adoptive parents wouldn't have bought a baby."

"They must have believed her stories of using the money to cover the costs of doctor bills and other out-of-pocket expenses to help the birth mothers. Those aren't unusual requests, Mr. Satterfield has told me, in private adoptions. However, Vikki asked for more than she'd paid, and she never gave any of the mothers a cent."

"She kept it all?"

"Yes, thousands of dollars. As for me, I was told one day to go home and forget I'd ever been pregnant. At the time I trusted her, so I did as she suggested. Five years ago, I decided to find you. We ran into a mountain of red tape, so I stopped looking. Then I got cancer, and with your half siblings not being possible donors, I had to take the chance of finding you, even if I disrupted your life."

"And I'm not a match either." Lauren didn't resist the impulse to reach out and put her hand over her birth mother's clenched fist. "I'm sorry I can't help you, Mrs. Tinniswood."

"Will you call me Gina Marie? I hope you will." She looked at Lauren's hand. "Can I ask you a question?"

"Of course. Anything."

"We were wondering if Vikki placed both twins in the same community. Was there another child who shared your birthday?"

"No. A few other kids had birthdays the same week as mine, but not the same day."

Mr. Satterfield picked up a pen and pulled a piece of paper out of the file. "Do you mind me asking you for their names?"

"I thought you said you were looking for my twin."

"Ms. Presley lied about other things," he said. "Why not a birthday? Anyone who went to so much trouble to get her hands on babies she could sell for ten thousand dollars each—"

"Ten thousand dollars?" Lauren gasped in disbelief. Focusing on the topic at hand, she said, "There were four of us who celebrated our birthdays the same week. One of those kids was adopted."

"His name?"

"Joel Beachy." She tried to repress her shudder at the idea Joel was her twin.

Mr. Satterfield's keen eyes caught the motion. "I take it you don't like Mr. Beachy."

"*Didn't* like him. I haven't seen him in more than fifteen years. He was a nasty bully when we were in school and got a lot of enjoyment out of tormenting me and my best friend, Naomi. Oh, Naomi has a birthday two days after mine."

"Her full name?"

"Naomi Gingerich…um, now Naomi Ropp."

"Do you remember Mr. Beachy's birthday?"

"No." She didn't add that she'd prefer to forget everything about Joel and his friends, especially Adam Hershberger.

"The fourth child with a birthday that week?"

"Edith Wickey. My cousin, but she's a year older than I am."

"Birth dates could have been changed to cover Ms. Presley's tracks."

"Not in a community as small as ours in Bliss Valley. Everyone would know when Edith was born."

"That leaves us with two possibilities." The lawyer turned to Gina Marie. "I'll start looking into each of them and get you an answer as soon as possible."

"I pray you find my twin," Lauren said. "And that he or she is a match for you."

"Thank you." Gina Marie's eyes filled with tears. "Thank you so much, my dear. By the way, where is your Amish friend?"

"Amish boyfriend," Skylar said with an acidic grin.

Ignoring the half sister she found impossible to like, she said, "Adam is busy on his farm."

Her birth mother gave a noncommittal reply as she listened to Skylar pepper the attorney with more questions about finding with whom the other baby had been placed. Her half sister pointed out Lauren didn't need to be there for the rest of the discussion.

As Lauren walked out of the office a few minutes later, she treasured the hug she'd shared with her birth mother. It had been a special moment, and the scowl on Skylar's face couldn't taint it. She sent up a quick prayer her twin could be the match she wasn't.

Her twin!

Wait until she told Adam…

She wouldn't be sharing the news with him. He was where he belonged at long last. Out of her life, once and for all.

Grossdawdi Ephraim pushed open the door to Adam's shop and strode in. His face was like a cloud about to erupt with lightning and thunder. Stopping on the other side of Adam's worktable, he jabbed a finger in Adam's direction.

"What's this I hear about you accusing Laurene Nolt about being in cahoots with whoever's behind these fires?" he demanded.

"I didn't accuse her of that."

His great-*grossdawdi* arched his snow-white eyebrows. "No?"

"Well, not in so many words."

"In what words, then?"

Adam cringed. This wasn't like when he'd been young and caught in some misdeed. The worst thing was knowing what he'd done after the fire was going to disappoint *Grossdawdi* Ephraim. Not even the threat of a thrashing out behind the toolshed was more horrible than facing the man he respected most in the world.

"I was stupid," he said. "I thought it was a reasonable question to ask if she knew anyone who might be behind the fires, someone working with the casino development companies."

"When she first arrived, you were leery of her connection to those companies, but did you ever listen to what she came here to do?"

"Of course."

"Really listen? She told Sylvia that she returned to Bliss Valley because her boss believed she would understand the best ways to work with the developers *and* plain folks. She didn't come here to build the casino. She came here to put the best possible spin on the development."

Adam's eyes widened as he heard his great-*grossdawdi* use a word like *spin*.

Grossdawdi Ephraim wasn't done. "Why do you keep thinking she's out to hurt us when you're the one who's hurt her?" He wagged a finger at Adam again. "She's forgiven you for more than anyone else would have. You made her life miserable when you were young."

"I know. I was a *dumm* kid."

"You aren't a *kind* any longer. You're a man, full-grown with a daughter of your own. Tell me, Adam, would *you* be as willing to forgive a boy who treated Mary Beth as you treated Laurene?"

He opened his mouth to say of course, he'd forgive the trespasser because it was their way to extend forgiveness to anyone who asked for it. Then he clamped his lips closed as he realized how difficult it would be to offer forgiveness to someone who'd hurt his beloved daughter.

"I don't know," he said.

"Laurene has forgiven you. Over and over. I can't help thinking of what Paul wrote to the Ephesians. *'Let all bitterness, and wrath, and anger, and clamour, and evil speaking, be put away from you, with all malice: And be ye kind one to another, tenderhearted, forgiving one another, even as God for Christ's sake hath forgiven you.'* She's learned well. Why haven't you?"

"I've tried."

His great-*grossdawdi*'s face eased from its anger, and his shoulders slumped. "I know you have, boy, but trying alone isn't *gut* enough when your efforts hurt those who love you."

Oh, how he wished Lauren loved him! He'd dared to believe she did while he'd kissed her, but the doubts had crept in again when he no longer held her close.

When Adam didn't answer, *Grossdawdi* Ephraim asked, "What's been eating you so much you can't think straight?" A swift smile washed across the old man's face. "Other than having your brain kicked off-kilter by Laurene's pretty smile and sparkling eyes."

"You."

"Me?" Any hint of a grin vanished.

Adam sighed. "*Grossdawdi* Ephraim, I didn't tell you. I've been contacted multiple times about the casino developers wanting to buy this farm."

"It's been rumored almost every farm in Bliss Valley is about to go on the auction block. The latest rumors centered about the Gingerich farm after the fire there."

"Why? Elvin's farm is too far away."

"From the casino, *ja*, but not the entrance road. If the casino is built on Lehman's Road, the county doesn't want that much traffic going through the covered bridge."

"That makes sense." He looked at the lawn mower he'd almost finished cleaning as hope surged through him. "So nobody's approached you about selling this farm?"

Grossdawdi Ephraim leaned his hands on the table, looking older and more exhausted. "I'd say I've had offers made to me by five different people."

"Five? Only two companies are bidding for the casino."

"From what they *didn't* say, I suspect the others were hoping to get the farm at a cut-rate price to turn a quick profit." He gave a shrug. "Can't fault a man for trying to make a nickel. However, no woman or man has ever been born who can pull the wool over Ephraim Weaver's eyes. Any profit is going in my pockets to be passed along to you and your cousins and your *kinder.*"

Shock swallowed his hope. "What are you talking about? Are you planning to sell the farm?"

"*Ja.*" Stretching across the table, he patted Adam's arm. "I've got diabetes."

"I know. You've been watching your diet."

Again his great-*grossdawdi*'s white brows rose.

"Okay," Adam corrected himself. "You've been watching your diet except for Sylvia's baked goods."

"And Laurene's. That girl is a *gut* cook, Adam. Even better than her great-*aenti*, though if you ever tell Sylvia I said that, I'll deny it. The truth is, Adam, I've developed kidney disease."

"What?"

"You've noticed the symptoms. The muscle aches, the rashes, the nosebleeds. The *doktor* believes within the year, I'll need to start dialysis. I don't want the costs of my treatment to be a burden."

"When did you see a *doktor*?"

"I went when you were busy with Mary Beth or your fire training."

Adam's head reeled. How could he have been so oblivious to what was going on with his great-*grossdawdi*? He knew the answer. He'd been too focused on Lauren. Guilt assailed him. "Why didn't you tell me before this? I would have gone with you."

"I'm a big boy, Adam. I took care of myself before you were born." He wagged a finger. "Now don't you start blaming yourself for not knowing. I didn't want anyone to know until I had to. I can't hide the truth any longer, but I'm far from dead, so don't start treating me as if I'm on my deathbed."

"But you've helped others all your life." He struggled to realize how serious the diagnosis was. "It's time for us to help you."

"Be that as it may, you don't have any interest in farming, Adam. You'd rather work in your shop than tend animals and the fields. Your cousins aren't interested either. I can sell most of the land and pay for my medical care. I've told those who are interested I won't sell the house or the barns or the five acres surrounding it. They don't care about the buildings. In fact, they're more than happy they won't have to demolish them."

"Why haven't you told me this before?"

The old man shrugged. "I didn't want to bother you with it until it became necessary. It has."

"You've never been a bother." He came around the table and hugged his great-*grossdawdi*. Shocked at how fragile the old man seemed, he added, "You never will be."

"Selling the farm's land is what I want to do and what I need to do. What about you, boy? Are you willing to go after what you need and want, too?" He gave a half chuckle. "Not just what you need and want, but what your daughter wants and needs, too."

"*Grossdawdi* Ephraim, making sure you're taken care of is what Mary Beth and I want."

"Don't act as if I'm a fool, Adam, and try to ply me with half-truths."

"You think I don't care about—"

"Close your mouth and open your heart, boy!" his great-*grossdawdi* said with rare vehemence. "Stop listening to what your brain is telling you and start listening to God's plan for your life. Search your heart, and you'll find the answers there. You've been hiding the truth behind a tough act for most of your life." He shook his head. "Such acting skills have served you well, Adam, when you were a boy. Now you're a man. You love Laurene. If you want my opinion, I think you have since the day you first saw her."

"You're right."

"Almost always am. So listen to me. Go tell that woman what's in your heart."

"What if she wants her *Englisch* life more?" *Especially now that I've made it clear I don't want her in my life?*

"Maybe she does, but how can you know if you don't ask her?"

"That's what you expect me to do? Ask her?"

"*Ja*," came the reply from the shop's doorway. Mary Beth walked toward him. "That's what you say, *Daed*. Don't know. Ask."

Grossdawdi Ephraim chuckled. "Out of the mouths of *bopplin...*"

Mary Beth leaned her head against Adam and gazed up at him with innocent eyes. "Me like Lauren. You like Lauren, too, *Daed*, ain't so?"

Hearing his great-*grossdawdi*'s smothered laugh, he didn't glance at the older man. He wouldn't put it past *Grossdawdi* Ephraim to have implanted such ideas into Mary Beth's head. When he saw the honest entreaty in his daughter's expression, he knew he was fighting the wrong battle as he had his whole life.

"All right," he said. "I'll ask her."

"'Bout time," grumbled his great-*grossdawdi*.

Chapter Nineteen

Lauren dropped her pen on her makeshift desk in her bedroom. Rubbing her aching forehead, she wondered why she couldn't muster the enthusiasm to finish the report she needed to put together and get into Patrick's inbox before start of business tomorrow. When she'd called earlier today, her boss had made her beg before giving her project back to her. That he'd eventually handed it over to her revealed how much of a mess Cassie had made. A quick scan of the files she'd received this afternoon had confirmed the other woman had alienated the representatives from both development companies. No doubt, even as Patrick had made Lauren plead for the project, he'd been promising those companies she'd be on the job right away.

Oh, she hated the games she'd been drawn into at Krause-Matsui-Fitzgerald, but the job was what she wanted, wasn't it? Yes! She couldn't wait to return to Philadelphia after *Aenti* Sylvia got rid of her cast.

Once Lauren had Bliss Valley in her rearview mirror, she

could put the complications of what was supposed to be a simple life behind her. What was simple about being stupid enough to trust a man who'd shown her years ago he didn't care about her? Hadn't someone said to trust what a person first showed you about himself? Instead of listening to common sense about Adam, she'd let her silly heart lead her astray, first by falling in love with Mary Beth and his sweet *grossdawdi*. If she'd been smart enough to stop listening to her heart at that point, then she would have been okay.

But no… She'd followed her heart right to his.

She'd gotten what she deserved for not heeding that small voice of caution about Adam.

She sighed and leaned her forehead on her upturned palms. From the moment she'd driven into Bliss Valley, almost every decision she'd made had been wrong. Now she had a chance to redeem herself in her boss's eyes and get the promotion that would allow her to help her parents. Not only her adoptive parents, but maybe she could find a way to help Gina Marie. It must have been expensive to search for someone after almost thirty years.

Coming to her feet, she reached for her keys. A drive on this nice spring evening might help her clear her mind. She stuffed the keys into her pocket and was reaching for her purse when a motion outside in the yard caught her attention. She switched off the light on the table. Everything went to black. She gave her eyes a chance to adjust. Again she caught furtive movement behind the inn.

Who? There weren't any guests tonight, and her great-aunt couldn't get out there alone in her wheelchair.

A faint smile tipped her lips. Was *Grossdawdi* Ephraim sneaking into the inn to see *Aenti* Sylvia? What a wondrous, romantic gesture! Just what her heart needed right now when it was battered.

Wait a moment! She saw a second form skulking toward the back extension of the house. Could it be Mary Beth? No, the silhouette was tall and wore pants.

Who was lurking in her great-aunt's backyard? If they were intent on mischief, she'd stop it immediately.

Glad someone had replaced the stone house's windows with ones that slid up easily and silently, she leaned forward to get a better look at where they were going. Their sibilant voices rose up to her, but they were speaking quietly so she couldn't catch a single word.

She gasped as she smelled an unmistakable odor. Gasoline!

A light flared, disappeared and then erupted into flame. Right next to the kitchen's propane tank.

"Stop!" she cried.

The two forms turned toward her, their faces distorted by the fire.

"Put it out! Put it out now!" she shouted.

They raced around the house and out of her sight.

Grabbing her phone, she called 911. "This is The Acorn Farm Inn. There's a fire."

"How many in the house?" the dispatcher asked.

"Two people, but one is in a wheelchair."

"I'm sending help. Stay on the line."

She didn't end the call, but shoved the phone into her back pocket as she raced down the stairs. She had to get *Aenti* Sylvia out. As she reached the bottom of the steps, she heard several voices. Guests? She ran toward the living room.

In the doorway, Lauren froze in shock as she stared at her adoptive parents.

Why did they have to come back to Bliss Valley *now*?

Mom held out her arms and started to speak, but Lauren interrupted. "Fire! Get out. Now!"

Her great-aunt and parents exchanged a puzzled glance, then as one turned to look at her.

"What are you talking about, Lauren?" asked her father.

"There's another fire," *Aenti* Sylvia said with a sigh. "There have been too many of them around here lately."

"It's not around here!" How could she get them to listen to her and understand? "It's here! The inn is on fire!"

Her great-aunt blanched and pressed her hand over her heart. Dad grabbed the chair.

"This way!" shouted Lauren, motioning for them to follow her.

She ran to the front door and threw it open. Flames danced wildly in front of her, skipping across the wooden floor along a river of gasoline. Within seconds, the whole porch was on fire. The heat drove her back, and she slammed the door shut.

"Out the back," Mom called.

"No! That's where they started the fire!"

Her great-aunt seized Lauren's hand. "They? You saw someone set the fire?"

She nodded, then pulled out her phone as she heard the dispatcher yelling her name. Hitting the speaker button so everyone could hear and could be heard, she said, "I'm listening."

"The fire trucks are on their way," said the dispatcher, his voice once again calm. "Are you out?"

"No! Fire is blocking both doors."

"Do you have a cellar bulkhead? Can you get out that way?"

"Not with a wheelchair."

Aenti Sylvia cried, "You go! The firemen will get me out."

"No," said Lauren and her mother at the same time. "We're not leaving you."

"Where's the closest window?" asked the dispatcher. "Somewhere where there's no fire."

Lauren ran into the dining room and discovered fire climbing up the bushes at each window. From the living room, she heard Mom call, "There's a break in the fire here!"

As she rushed into the front room, she conveyed that information to the dispatcher.

"It's where the old summer kitchen used to be," *Aenti* Sylvia said. "I never got around to planting anything there after it fell in on itself."

The dispatcher said, "I've alerted firefighters to the living room window. Stay right there. It may be the only chance for all of you to escape."

"I need volunteers to go in," shouted the fire chief. "They're going to need help to get Sylvia out."

Adam threw his hand in the air. From the moment he'd seen the fire surrounding the inn, he'd begun to pray he hadn't missed his chance to tell Lauren the truth about how he loved her. She was the only person who'd ever looked through the walls he'd kept in place since his parents' deaths to discover the hurt lingering in his heart.

He heard Chip call out he'd go in, too. When Mahlon raised his hand, as well, Adam hoped their run of successes as heroes would continue.

"Okay," Dean shouted. "Adam, Chip and Mahlon. Go in. They're in the living room. Do you know where that is?"

"*Ja,*" Adam called back. "I do."

"Then get in and get them and yourselves out alive."

Adam took a step toward the blazing porch, but Chip seized his arm. "Stay here. You're too wound up emotionally with your girlfriend in there. You'll make a mistake."

"I'm not going to stand here and do nothing!"

Mahlon settled his helmet on his head. "Listen to Chip, Adam! You're not thinking straight. That's the way to get yourself and others hurt or killed. We've got more experience than you do. You don't want to end up at the hospital like Simon did."

Were they right? Was he thinking too much with his emotions and not with his head? After years of repressing his emotions, he couldn't be sure how they were affecting him now.

God, show me the way.

Someone shouted, "There's a break in the fire on the porch. If you're going in, go now!"

Adam ran toward the house. Behind him, the chief shouted for water to be aimed at the edges of the fire, holding it back as long as possible. He had only seconds.

Throwing open the door, he held up his arm as smoke exploded over him. He ducked his head, glad for his mask and other protective gear. Pushing his way through the smoke, he didn't look back to see where Chip and Mahlon were.

He stepped into the hall and heard voices to his left. Hands jerked him backward as he turned toward the living room. Who...? He stared into Chip's face. It was distorted by his mask, but he saw his friend's fierce frown.

"Let me go!" Adam ordered. "I've got to get to—"

"You're not going anywhere," Chip snarled.

"What are you talking about? We're wasting time. They're in the living room."

"Tell him, Mahlon."

Astounded, Adam looked at the other man.

Mahlon released his grip, but said, "Listen to him, Adam. Get out! Now!"

"Not without Lauren." He yanked his arm out of Chip's hold and evaded the man's hand as it tried to grab his sleeve again.

Running into the smoke-filled living room, Adam didn't take time to wonder why his friends were acting weird. If it was so important for them to be the heroes at every fire, fine, but he wasn't stepping aside when Lauren and Sylvia needed help.

He couldn't believe what he was seeing through the smoke. There were two other people in the room.

"Mom, they're here to help!" he heard Lauren call.

Mom?

Adam stared into faces he hadn't expected to see again, most especially not tonight. Lauren's parents! They'd returned to Bliss Valley! Had she called them and asked them to come?

He ran across the room to the wheelchair. "Let's get Sylvia out of here."

"We don't want your help!" Wayne snapped. "Not after all you've…"

"No time now," Sylvia shouted. "We've got to get out of here. Now!"

Lauren picked up a wooden sculpture and hurled it through the window. Shouts came from outside, and she jumped back as an axe cleared the glass so they wouldn't be cut.

"Go!" shouted Sylvia over the increasing roar of the flames. The fire must be in the kitchen on the other side of the wall. "Wayne! Ida! Take Lauren and get out! Adam will help me."

Lauren's *daed* cupped his hands to give her *mamm* a leg up and over the window. He whirled and looked over his shoulder, motioning to Lauren. She was bent at the waist, coughing.

Lauren called through her coughing, "Adam, help us!"

"Wayne, grab my arm," he ordered. "We'll lift her out of the chair and through the window."

Her *daed* hesitated, "We're in the—"

"Don't be silly!" Lauren pushed past him to her *daed*. "Nobody will care about who's in the *bann* if we're dead. Let him help you."

He wasn't sure if her words or the coughs racking her convinced her *daed*, but her great-*aenti* put a hand on Wayne's arm and leaned into him. Locking their hands and forearms to-gether to make a seat, Adam and her *daed* lifted Sylvia and her heavy cast. They carried her to the window. Hands reached up to guide her out.

"Go, Wayne!" Adam shouted.

"Lauren—"

"I'll get her. Go! You know she won't go until you're out."

Wayne nodded and threw his feet up and over the window. He should be okay without help as the volunteers carried Syl-via to safety.

Adam didn't wait to see him climb out. He whirled. Where was Lauren? The smoke was thick and searing his lungs. There! Right behind him.

He grabbed her arm and pulled her forward. "Go!"

For once, she didn't argue. She shoved something into her pocket. Her phone, he realized as he heard a voice calling her name from it.

Bending, he offered his cupped hands to lift her out the window. She carefully balanced herself on the window with-out touching any of the broken glass. He started to lift her up.

Something hit him hard, knocking him off his feet. Lau-ren screamed as she fell. Not out the window, but back in-side. She struggled to get up. As soon as she did, a form in turnout gear shoved her back into the smoke. He heard her hit the floor hard.

With a roar to challenge the fire's, he ran to where she'd disappeared. Strong hands caught him. He tried to break the hold, batting aside arms trying to drag him out of the house. He whirled, and the grip loosened enough for him to discover who was trying to stop him from getting to Lauren.

Chip! Had the man lost his mind?

"Let me go!" he shouted. "Lauren—"

"Forget about her. We've got to get out of here. You don't want your kid to be an orphan, do you?"

He ignored the words that cut him to the quick. He fought to escape his mentor's hold. Mahlon was tugging on his other arm. He tripped over something, and they took advantage of him being off balance to pull him toward the door.

Mahlon said, "We're not really leaving Laurene—"

"Do you want her to pin this fire on us?" Chip snarled.

Adam didn't want to believe his ears, but as the two men continued arguing, he knew the answer about the frequent fires was right in front of him. He couldn't ask why now. He had to save Lauren. Using their arms to pull himself to his feet, he gasped as both men collapsed on him.

At the same time, an explosion ripped through the smoke. The concussion slammed him into a nearby wall. Was he dead? Not yet. Pain claimed every muscle as he began to crawl to where he thought Lauren had fallen when Chip pushed her away from the window.

He found Lauren by discovering her hand sticking out from beneath a flipped-over couch. Shoving it off, he drew her into his arms. He didn't try to get to his feet because the smoke was growing hotter by the second. He held her tight to his chest as he struggled toward the front door.

Where were Chip and Mahlon?

He didn't have the strength even to call out to them as he crossed the room and the hall, inch by torturous inch. When hands reached out to him, he shoved them away.

"Hey, Adam!" shouted Dean. "What's wrong with you? We're trying to help you. You guys, get them out of here."

The chief continued to bellow orders as Adam was guided to the door and onto the porch, which was scorched, but strong enough to hold him. He looked at Lauren's face, contorted as she struggled to breathe. Two things fell from her pocket. Her phone and a ring of keys. He gasped when he saw the screen was lit. A voice shouted at him.

The person helping him—a guy he knew as Phil—bent to retrieve the phone and keys. He started to stuff them into the pocket of Adam's coat, but paused as the voice asked, "Are they out? Hello! Can you hear me? Are they out?"

"It's the 911 dispatcher," Phil said. Holding the phone to his ear as he dropped the keys into Adam's pocket, he listened before saying, "Yeah, they're out. We're— What? Are you sure Chip and Mahlon...? Yeah, I get it. You heard everything." He listened a moment longer as he began to guide Adam down the steps. "Gotcha. I'll get him now." Lowering the phone, he asked, "Can you manage on your own? I've got to talk to the chief. Right away."

Adam nodded, though the simple motion almost buckled his knees. As Phil raced away, Adam lurched to the ground. He staggered backward as a black truck roared toward him. He couldn't make it up the steps, so he put the risers between them and the truck.

The truck suddenly spun in the opposite direction and tore across the yard. It rolled over the hoses as if they weren't there.

Chip should know better, some random part of his brain announced in slow motion.

Chip!

His friend was driving the truck trying to run them down? No, not his friend. Chip wasn't his friend and never had been. Chip and Mahlon had tried to leave Lauren to die in the house.

A huge explosion rattled the house and knocked him forward to his knees. He clung to Lauren, not wanting to drop her. An orange fireball climbed into the air. The propane tank by the pool must have erupted. He tried to turn in that direction. In disbelief, he watched the detonation hit Chip's black truck. It left the ground, its tires still spinning, and flew into the mud at the edge of the pond.

His ears rang, and he could barely hear the shouts as people ran toward the pond. Fighting his way to his feet, he couldn't keep from noticing the truck had landed at the opposite end from the ducklings his daughter adored.

"Dean!" he called as the chief ran past him.

"Get her to the ambulance!"

"I'm on my way." When he took a single step, he reeled.

The chief grabbed his arm and steadied him. "Have them check you out, too."

"Don't let them get away."

"Who?"

"Chip and Mahlon." He coughed, his throat aching with the smoke. "I'll explain after I get Lauren to the EMTs. Don't let them get away until I can explain."

The chief stared at him for a long minute, then nodded. The chief must be furious Chip had driven over the hoses and risked other equipment. Loping to where the two men were being pulled out of the truck, Dean stopped when Phil raced to him and handed him Lauren's phone and gestured wildly toward the pond.

Adam took a single step on the wet grass. His knees almost collapsed beneath him. He adjusted Lauren in his arms. He choked when he realized she was motionless.

"Breathe!" he begged. "Breathe!"

"Let us take her," a woman said.

He looked up, recognizing the two EMTs who worked with the fire department. Their names were a fuzzy memory, but he grasped on to it. Bebe Bolton and her husband, Buddy.

"She's not breathing," he whispered. He couldn't speak more loudly.

"She is," Bebe said. "Just not deeply. We'll get her on oxygen. Let's get her to the truck."

When Buddy lifted a gurney over the hoses, Adam set Lauren gently on it. The EMTs pushed it away at a speed he couldn't match. He was only halfway to the driveway when they put the gurney in the back of the ambulance.

Buddy turned to motion to him. "C'mon, Adam. We need to give you the once-over, too."

He took a single step toward Buddy, then paused as his name was called. He turned carefully, so he didn't end up on the ground. When he saw who'd shouted to him, he forgot all about Buddy.

Adam couldn't help being astonished at how much smaller and older Wayne and Ida Nolt were. He was being *dumm*. Time had passed for them as it had for everyone else. While he'd gotten taller, they hadn't, but the years had cut lines into their faces. Those wrinkles were deepened by what had happened in the fire and their worry for Lauren.

"They've got Lauren in the ambulance. They'll take *gut* care of her," he said as the Nolts edged closer to him.

Why were they so tentative? Living among the more crowded villages and towns where *Englischers* congregated close to Philadelphia, they must have seen an ambulance many times before. They acted as if they didn't want to get any closer to the vehicle.

No, he realized, as they stopped more than an arm's length from him. It wasn't the ambulance they wanted to avoid. It was Adam Hershberger.

"Stay out of our daughter's life," Wayne said in the coldest tone imaginable.

"What?"

"Haven't you done enough to ruin our daughter's life, Adam Hershberger? And ours, as well? You tormented our sweet

Laurene to the point we couldn't stay here and endure seeing her pain any longer."

"Are you saying *I* am the reason you left Bliss Valley?"

"*Ja.*"

The simple answer almost rocked him off his feet again. He blurted the first thing he could think of, "Why didn't you come and confront me before you ran off?"

"Why would we speak to a boy who wouldn't stop hurting our daughter? We know she tried her best to convince you to treat her better."

"Why didn't you try your best?" Adam retorted. "Why didn't you step in to help your daughter?"

Ida spoke, startling him because she'd let her husband take the lead up until then. "We did. We spoke with the bishop, and he said it was a matter for the deacon. We spoke to the deacon, and he said it was a school matter."

Adam clasped his fisted hands behind his back. The Nolts were far from the first people he'd heard about who'd gone to the previous bishop and his own predecessor seeking help and guidance and who were turned away with nothing, not even a prayer for a resolution of their problem. Some had moved to other communities, but several other families had also left the Amish during Dwight Reel's tenure, too disillusioned by their leaders' indifference to stay. Why hadn't he seen that before now?

"So we went to the schoolteacher." Wayne's slow, steady voice couldn't hide his fury. "She told us we were making something out of nothing. That we needed to stop being overprotective. Protecting Laurene is something we'll never stop doing. Now, all these years later, you've endangered her so you can play hero."

"I didn't—"

He refused to listen as he jabbed a finger in the center of

Adam's turnout coat. "I don't want to listen to your lies. Stay away from her. If you don't…"

"Wayne, we've got to go," Ida said, glancing toward the ambulance.

The threat went unsaid as Wayne took his wife's arm and led her toward a late model car. The intent of his warning was clear.

A siren split the air, and Adam looked over his shoulder to see the ambulance racing up the road toward Lancaster. The Nolts' car followed close, leaving him at the inn not knowing how Lauren was. He slammed his hands into his pockets, then pulled out the ring of keys. Seeing one with a Volkswagen logo, he headed toward Lauren's Beetle.

His younger cousin burst out of the crowd of spectators and headed him off. Dale held out his hand as he said, "You can't drive, Adam. You can barely stand."

"You don't have enough experience driving, and it's a stick shift."

"I can handle that."

Deciding not to ask for the details, because he suspected he didn't really want to know, Adam handed Dale the keys. "Get us to the hospital in Lancaster in one piece."

"I will."

He opened the passenger door and sat heavily. He knew he would infuriate her parents, who'd become even more resolved he not see her, but it was the price he must pay to make sure she survived the treachery of two men he'd trusted so unwisely.

Chapter Twenty

Adam sat in a hospital waiting room that was empty, other than a television broadcasting the morning news, including regular updates on the fire at The Acorn Farm Inn. He'd been sitting alone all night after being checked for smoke inhalation. He'd asked everyone in the emergency room, but he hadn't been allowed to see Lauren.

Only immediate family, he'd been told by a nurse who gave him a sympathetic smile as she took in his turnout gear and smoke-stained face. She'd pointed out a restroom where he could clean up while he waited.

His cousin had gone in search of the cafeteria after surrendering the car keys to Adam. Dale had done a *gut* job getting them to the hospital, where they'd turned the car over to a valet service because his cousin wasn't sure if he could navigate a parking space.

Bending his head in prayer, Adam thanked God for guiding them safely to the hospital. The rest of his prayers were for Lauren. Nobody would tell him if she'd been seen. He didn't know if she was breathing better. Was she conscious?

Losing one's self in prayer was a cliché, but he was grateful God had kept Adam's thoughts focused on requests for Lauren's healing instead of his fears for her. The hospital was skilled, for they'd been keeping his great-*grossdawdi* alive as well as helping Simon's hands heal.

His jaw grew taut at the thought of his cousin. Why hadn't he listened to Simon when the boy said someone had bumped into him on purpose when he was fighting the fire?

It wasn't a mistake, Adam.

Simon's words exploded out of his memory. Adam hadn't wanted to believe his cousin's assertion someone had shoved him forward so he'd fallen into the fire and scorched his hands badly. Now he knew Simon hadn't been imagining anything.

His anger now burned as hot as the fire at the inn. How could men he trusted—men he'd called friends—have done such horrible things? He wondered if Simon had been hurt because he'd shared his suspicions about the fires with Chip and Mahlon. Lauren must have witnessed them starting the fire at the inn. Why else would Chip have been so insistent it would be bad if she could identify them?

The only answer he didn't have was why the two men had gone from fighting fires to starting them.

"Adam? Adam Hershberger, is that you?"

He raised his head. "Mrs. Tinniswood, what…what are you doing here?"

"I'm here for an appointment with my doctor." Lauren's birth *mamm* came into the room and glanced around at the unused chairs. "Why are you here? I didn't know you are a fireman. My late husband was a firefighter, too. Right here in Lancaster."

He motioned for her to sit. He couldn't let himself forget, even in the midst of his misery, she wasn't well.

"Thank you." She lowered herself with care to the chair beside him and settled her purse on her knees. "Ah, much better. So why are you here?"

He told her about the fire and how Lauren had been overcome with smoke while helping her parents and great-*aenti* escape. Mrs. Tinniswood's face drained of what little color it had.

"Is she going to be okay?" she asked.

"That's what I'm waiting to hear. They won't let me go in because only immediate family is allowed back there." His eyes widened. "You're her birth *mamm*. You can go and see."

She shook her head. "Her adoptive parents are with her, and that's how it should be."

Instead of annoyance that she was tossing aside the opportunity he craved, he was suffused with understanding. She didn't want to meet the Nolts until Lauren gave her permission to become part of their lives.

"Mrs. Tinniswood—"

"Call me Gina Marie. Lauren does." Tears fell down her cheeks. "I hope she'll be all right."

"I've been praying she will."

"Thank you, Adam. I can understand why Lauren trusts you. You're a good man."

"Not *gut* enough, I fear."

Gina Marie's brow threaded with confusion, and he saw more of a resemblance to Lauren in her expression than ever before. "Has something happened between you? You're Amish, and she isn't now. Has that created problems for you?"

Though he shouldn't have been surprised by Gina Marie's insight, which was as quick and incisive as Lauren's, he was.

"It's my fault she's in the hospital," he said.

"Did you do something to cause the fire?"

"No."

"Did you help her escape?"

"*Ja.*"

"You did all you could, but I see the guilt on your face and hear it in your voice." She astonished him again by taking his hand between hers.

As his own *mamm* had when he was an unhappy *kind*. The gentle motion sent cracks spiraling along the stoic walls he'd raised from the moment he'd regained his senses in the hospital and discovered he was an orphan.

"I don't know you well," she said, "but I can tell you care about my daughter."

"Very much. It's been tough watching what she's gone through in the past few weeks."

"With me?"

"With you and finding out she was adopted and then seeing how it hurt her to think you only wanted to find her because you need a bone marrow donor."

Her eyes narrowed. Had his words been too blunt?

He realized his mistake when she asked, "Didn't Lauren tell you she's not a match?"

"No. We... That is, I..."

"I get it." Gina Marie shifted her purse to the chair next to hers and half turned to face him. "My daughter is a strong-willed woman. I wish I'd been more like her when I was her age, but God had a different plan in mind for me. Not that I realized that. God and I weren't exactly on speaking terms then, but He's opened my heart to Him, and all things are possible with His help."

He looked at her in amazement. He hadn't stopped to think, until now, how she, too, must feel as if God had deserted her.

"Don't be shocked that I believe in God's forgiveness," she said softly. "I'm not evil."

"I never thought you were." Or had he? Had he judged Gina Marie the same way Lauren's parents had judged him for mistakes made long ago?

She gave him a sad smile. "Yes, you did. You care so much about my daughter you're willing to defend her, even against a person who has never wished her anything but happiness."

"I wasn't seeing you as a person, Gina Marie. I saw only your choice."

"Everyone makes mistakes."

"I can't argue with that," he said, trying not to think of the long, long list of misdeeds he'd tried to forgive himself for.

"What matters," Gina Marie went on as if he hadn't spoken, "is what we learn from those mistakes and how we change so we don't make the same mistakes again." Her sunken eyes caught his gaze and held it. "What have you learned through all of this, Adam?"

What had he learned from the many mistakes he'd made? The answer danced on the tip of his tongue, but he didn't speak. He'd learned he loved Lauren. Maybe he had since he was a boy and she'd agreed to help him, even when he was at his most terrible to her. Looking back, he had to wonder if he'd acted out around her to prove to his friends he didn't have a crush on pretty Laurene Nolt.

Remembered voices filled his head. Joel's voice chiding him for hanging out with a girl instead of sneaking away on some mischief with them. Samuel's voice taunting him when he made the mistake of mentioning he wasn't dreading having to study with Lauren.

With his teenage heart uncertain about many things, Adam had listened to his friends. He'd thought if he showed anything but contempt for Laurene Nolt and her attempts to be kind to him, he'd be a laughingstock and belittled by his friends. How could he be angry at them? They'd been kids, also scared of the strange new feelings adolescence was bringing.

Just as his cousins were. He should have had more sympathy for them, and he would try to from this point forward.

"Adam?" urged Gina Marie quietly. "What *have* you learned?"

The answer was simple, he realized. "To trust God knows the best path for my life, especially when I don't have the slightest idea what it is."

She stared at him for a long moment, then a slow smile spread across her face. "A lesson I need to learn, too. I've spent almost thirty years being angry at God because of the mistakes *I* made. At the same time, I expected Him to fix the problems I'd created for myself. I acted as if the gifts of love and grace He'd brought into my life didn't exist. Or if I admitted they existed, I acted as if they didn't matter, that I didn't need them."

"It sounds like we're more alike than I'd guessed."

Her laugh startled him. "Something we both need to think about, huh?"

Adam started to reply, but halted when he saw two other people entering the waiting room. Their gazes slammed into his, and as one, Lauren's parents turned to leave.

Jumping up, he crossed the room in a pair of long steps. "Don't go. We need to talk."

Wayne Nolt shook his head. "We don't have anything to say to you."

"All right." It hurt him to say those words, because saying them forced him to realize that he might never be able to make amends for the pain he'd caused Lauren and her family. "You don't have to talk to me, but you need to talk with Lauren's *mamm.*"

The Nolts exchanged a glance, then looked past him. When their eyes widened, he heard a chair scrape against the tile floor and knew Gina Marie had come to her feet.

When nobody else spoke, he said, "Wayne and Ida Nolt..." He turned to look at Gina Marie who had her hands up over her mouth. Did she want him to introduce her to Lauren's parents? When she gave a faint nod, he said, "This is Gina Marie Tinniswood, Lauren's birth *mamm*. Gina Marie, these are Lauren's adoptive parents."

He waited for the others to say something. Moving aside, he watched as Ida and Gina Marie each took a single step forward. They both paused at the same moment, their eyes locked onto each other's. He held his breath. Had he been wrong to introduce them? *God, show me what to do now.*

He got his answer when both women whispered at the same time, "Thank you."

Gina Marie motioned toward the chair beside hers, and Ida scurried over to sit, gripping the edges of the seat as if she feared the floor was going to drop out from beneath her. When Gina Marie lowered herself to her own chair, they continued to stare at each other.

When they both said, "You're welcome" at the same time, they gave unsteady laughs. The sound might not have signaled an immediate friendship, Adam guessed, but it was a beginning for the two *mamms* who obviously wanted to put aside their assumptions about each other and learn the truth. There was an undeniable, invisible connection between the two women, a connection that was moored deep within their hearts.

"How is Lauren?" Gina Marie asked, cutting her eyes toward him.

He wanted to thank her for posing the question the Nolts might not have answered if he'd asked, but he remained silent.

"The doctors are with her now," Ida replied. "She still hasn't regained consciousness, and they said it might be a while. But they're hopeful. They told us to go and get coffee because, I'm sure, they wanted us out from underfoot." She tried to smile, but failed. "They're sending someone here to alert us when she's moved to a room."

Scowling, Wayne stepped between the women and Adam. He pointed a gnarled finger at Adam. "Don't you have any decency? It's time for you to leave. Can't you see this is a private family matter?"

He didn't have an answer for that. Not one that wouldn't risk starting an argument. Lauren's family was already on edge, worrying about her and having this unexpected meeting. He didn't need to compound their stress. There would be time later…

His heart cramped when he realized that there might not be. If Wayne and Ida had their way, Adam would never speak to their daughter again.

"No, let him stay," came a soft request from the other side of the room.

In amazement, he realized Gina Marie had spoken. Why would she risk getting off on the wrong foot with her daughter's adoptive parents by contradicting Wayne?

Slowly, looking at each of them as if she could weave them together with her eyes, Gina Marie went on, "You need to know that when Lauren first came to meet with me at the attorney's office, she was told to bring someone with her. She brought Adam."

"She did?" Ida whispered, her voice breaking on each word. "But why would she do that?"

"I didn't ask, but I assumed she'd decided to bring someone she could trust. Your daughter is a smart woman."

"Our daughter." Ida held out her hand, and Gina Marie put hers on it.

Gina Marie's eyes must have been caught by the face of her watch, because she suddenly said, "Oh, I've got to go. I can't be late for my appointment."

"You've got an appointment here?" Wayne asked, his tone gentler than when he spoke to Adam.

"Yes." Gina Marie again glanced at Adam. When he nodded, she went on, "I'm being treated for non-Hodgkin's lymphoma. That's the reason I intruded into your lives. I was hoping Lauren might be a match for me as a bone marrow donor."

"And is she?" asked Ida.

"No."

She folded her hands over Gina Marie's. "I'm so sorry."

"Me, too." She smiled weakly. "I hope we can talk again."

"I do, as well."

Reaching into her purse, Gina Marie pulled out a small notebook and a pen. She tore out two pages, jotting a phone number on each. She gave one to Ida and held out the other to Adam. "Can one of you call me and let me know how Lauren's doing?"

"I will," Adam said at the same time Ida did. He took the slip of paper and folded it into his pocket next to the car keys.

He didn't say anything else as Gina Marie walked with slow, careful steps from the waiting room, but he prayed the *doktors* would find a way to save her life. Lauren needed to get to know her birth *mamm* while she had the chance.

That was another thing he'd learned. Second chances didn't come along very often. He wasn't going to let his own with Lauren slip away without making one more attempt to heal the hurts he'd caused.

"Wayne?" he asked, looking at Lauren's *daed*.

"I told you. I don't have anything to say to you," the older man said.

"Then listen to what I've got to say to you."

"You don't have anything to say that I want to hear."

Ida interjected as she came to stand beside her husband, "Let him say what he feels he must, Wayne."

"Why?"

"Didn't you hear Gina Marie? Lauren trusts him. We need to believe Lauren has a good reason to trust him."

Adam waited for Wayne to object again, but the man simply muttered something before waving for Adam to speak.

Praying that God would help him select the right words, Adam said, "I understand how you must think me bold and heartless to ask for your forgiveness. I understand, as well, how painful it must have been for you to watch while your daughter was hurt by my thoughtless words and cruelty."

"How can you understand any of that?" demanded Wayne.

"Because I've got a daughter of my own now. She's suffered pain, too, by losing her *mamm* so young. I would do almost anything to keep her from feeling that pain. Just as I know you did for your daughter. You gave up your plain lives in order to try to free her from the anguish I inflicted on her. I haven't had to make the same sacrifice because Lauren has been helping my daughter come to terms with her sorrow."

"How convenient for you!"

"*Ja*," he said, refusing to take umbrage at the sarcasm, "and I'm more grateful than words can say how God provided for Mary Beth by bringing Lauren into her life." His own voice cracked as he went on, "And back into mine. I'm asking for your forgiveness, Wayne, Ida. Not because the boy I was deserved it, but because I'm no longer that angry boy who was so desperate to fit in with his friends that he was willing to do whatever he had to in order to keep their friendship."

"So you're blaming the other boys?" asked Ida.

"No. I take full blame for what I did and what I urged them to do, but I'm not a boy any longer. I think 1 Corinthians 13 says it better than I can."

"'*When I was a child,*'" Ida said, "'*I spake as a child, I understood as a child, I thought as a child: but when I became a man, I put away childish things.*'"

Wayne shook his head. "That's easy to say."

Ida put a hand on her husband's arm. "God has urged us all to repent and to be forgiven. And we're urged to let others repent so we might forgive them. That's at the heart of our beliefs."

"I know," Wayne argued, "but I don't want to see Lauren hurt again."

Adam sighed. "Neither do I. In fact, if it were within my ability, I would want to insure that she's never hurt again."

"Like I said, words are easy," Wayne grumbled. "Actions are harder."

"I agree. I can't change the past, but I want to assure you that I have changed. Lauren has forgiven me and offered me another chance. Will you?"

Where am I? It was such a clichéd question, Lauren wanted to laugh into the gray haze surrounding her.

She couldn't. Her throat felt too tight to make a sound. Not that it seemed to matter. She was floating in a fantastical dream. Something tickled her cheek, but she couldn't reach up to discover what it was.

Nothing was connected. Not voices. Not flashes of light. Not strange sounds she couldn't identify. A steady beep-beep-beep. No, two beeps at different pitches. What were they?

Then, abruptly, everything sped up until Lauren thought she must be in a movie gone amok. Hands came out of the confused montage around her, lifting her. Why was she lying down? Hadn't she been standing when…? She couldn't remember what she'd been doing before this moment when she heard deep voices urging caution.

Words floated around her. Not even complete words. Syllables. She strained her ears, but couldn't hear anything like the powerful wind that had torn words apart the night of the freak blizzard. There was an odd puffing sound, but it wasn't steady or very loud. So why couldn't she hear properly?

Or see?

Or taste anything but acrid ashes coating her tongue?

Even something as simple as breathing was hard. She realized the unsteady sound was herself gasping for breath. It hurt each time she tried to inhale, and she shuddered when she exhaled. A strange wheeze reminded her of an oboe followed by a deeper bleat from a bassoon. Every time she breathed out, it was as if a pipe organ was playing a multitude of notes deep within her lungs.

What was going on?

She wanted to ask, but her brain seemed to have forgotten how to order her lips to form the words. Could her thickly coated tongue move to make the sounds?

Why wasn't someone telling her what had happened?

"Let him try."

Mom? Was that her mother speaking? Let who try what?

"I don't know if we should." That was her father.

"Let him try. Please, Wayne."

"All right, but if this doesn't work, he leaves now. Agreed?"

Her mother must have agreed because suddenly another voice drifted into her bizarre dream. Her heart identified it immediately as Adam's and bounced a couple of times before beating even faster.

"Lauren." His voice broke. "Lauren, *liebling*, open your eyes."

She fought her eyelids, which didn't want to rise. Her heart soared, and the beep-beep-beep became more rapid.

Then her eyes opened. She looked up at Adam. His cheeks were darkened with a low mat of whiskers. Gray arcs underlined his eyes that were reddened as if he hadn't been sleeping... or he'd been crying. Odors of smoke drifted from him as he grasped her left hand between his.

She tried to say his name. Her lips formed the words, but no sound came out.

"It's all right," he said, a smile creasing his exhausted face before he turned away from her. "She's opened her eyes."

He stepped aside as her mother and father came to the bed, touching her hair and her cheeks as if she were made of fragile porcelain. Mom was crying, and Dad wiped his eyes to hide his own tears.

Why?

"What do you remember?" Mom asked, using *Deitsch* with an ease that suggested she'd never stopped.

"Remember about what?" Was that her voice? It sounded as scratchy and rough as a crow cawing.

"The fire at the inn." Adam hadn't left. He stood close to where she was lying.

Looking past him and her parents, she realized she was in a hospital room. The tickle across her cheek was an oxygen hose. As she raised quivering fingers to touch it, memory slammed into her like a train.

"The fire," she croaked. "Chip and Mahlon set it."

"I know," Adam replied. "Do you want something to drink?"

She nodded, and he raised the head of the bed up enough

so she could drink water from a cup with a straw. After she'd taken several sips, she said, "That's enough for now."

Her mother used a tissue to dry her face, but tears kept coming. "Don't you ever do anything like that again! Next time, you're the first one out the window."

"Let's hope there's no next time." Her dad's words were both a vow and a jest. "Ida, I think I could use some *kaffi*. How about you?"

"I don't want…" She glanced at Lauren, then nodded. "It sounds like a *gut* idea. Can we bring you any, Adam?"

She saw his shock at the ordinary question. What had been said between him and her parents while she was unconscious?

"No, *danki*," he replied. "I'll wait here with Lauren while you go to the cafeteria. If you see an Amish kid there, tell him I'll meet him back at the car in an hour."

Her mother squeezed Lauren's hand before leaving with Dad.

"Car?" asked Lauren.

"Ringo. Dale drove us here."

"You let…? He's only fifteen!" Her vehemence made her cough, and when Adam asked if she needed something to drink, she nodded. She held out her hands for the cup, but he held the straw to her lips. "Is *Aenti* Sylvia all right?"

"*Ja*. I saw her interviewed on the news after the fire was out. She said she plans to open again no later than two months from now. That's pretty ambitious with the kitchen extension completely destroyed and the rest of the house having fire and smoke damage, but if anyone can do the impossible, she can."

She smiled.

"Your great-*aenti* is a lot like you." Adam pulled a chair closer to the bed and sat. "You helped everyone out the window."

"Not you and not…" She shuddered as she felt again how two strong hands had shoved her back into the smoke.

"Everyone is out and safe." He put a hand on her shoulder. "You need to rest and let them take care of you."

Though his advice was good, she had to ask, "What about *them*? Chip and Mahlon? Oh, I need to tell you about what—"

"I know. Simon called Dale on his cell phone early this morning and brought me up to date on Chip and Mahlon."

"I didn't know your cousins had phones."

"Neither did I, but today I'm glad they did. Chip and Mahlon have been arrested. Apparently, your call to 911—"

"I never hung up. He said stay on the line, so I did."

"The call was recorded, and their voices can be heard incriminating themselves."

"But why?"

"Simon said the fire chief thinks they wanted to be lauded as heroes, so they started fires in a way that allowed them to save the day by rescuing anyone inside." His voice held no emotion, but she wasn't fooled as she once might have been. He was calm, not because he felt nothing about how two men he'd known and trusted had tried to kill them, but because he felt too much too strongly.

She sank into the pillows and drew in a sigh of relief. The hit of oxygen threatened to choke her, but the sensation went away when she began breathing more slowly.

"I'm glad you're here," she said.

"I am, too. I wasn't sure if your parents would let me see you." Not giving her a chance to ask why, he related what they'd said to him as the ambulance took her to the hospital and the conversation in the waiting room with her adoptive parents. "I'm sorry, Lauren. I never once guessed *I* was the reason your family left. If I'd known…"

"You would have felt guilty all these years."

"That's what Gina Marie said."

She sat up straighter again. "She's here?" Her scratchy voice rose an octave and broke. Grimacing, she reached for the pitcher on the table across the bed. She hated how her hands trembled as she raised it to pour more water into her glass. It splattered on the table, little of it getting into the glass.

Without a word, Adam gently took the pitcher and filled her glass. He went into the bathroom and returned with some paper towels to wipe up the puddles on the table and blanket. As he tossed the wet towels into the wastebasket, she took a slow, appreciative sip of the water.

"Gina Marie isn't here now. She was at the hospital earlier to see her *doktor*, and we talked. Not only did we talk, but she spoke with Ida and Wayne. She convinced them, as she did me, that mistakes of the past need to be forgiven so they can remain in the past. Her advice convinced me to speak with Ida and Wayne. I can't say they've forgiven me. That won't happen in a single day. However, I believe they're willing to let me show them that I'm not that boy any longer."

Lauren rested against her pillows and gazed at the ceiling. *Thank you, God, for bringing my families together when I was afraid to.* She knew the way ahead for her and her birth mother wouldn't be smooth, especially if her half sister had anything to do with it, but she wanted to try to have a good relationship. For many years to come, if Lauren's twin could be found to give the bone marrow donation to save Gina Marie's life.

"She got me thinking," Adam said with a lopsided grin. "Thinking about some things I hadn't thought about in years."

"What things?"

"About how I was determined my friends never guessed—" He shook his head. "No, it was more than making sure my friends didn't guess. I didn't want to admit to myself that I would have rather spent time with you than them."

She stared at him. "You mean when we were in school?"

"*Ja.*"

"You never showed anything but contempt for me."

"I know." He picked up her hand again and folded it between his. "I was a stupid teenager who was frightened by the strong feelings I had for you. Feelings that are even stronger today. I know I haven't given you any reason to believe me, but if you never believe me again, know I'm being honest when I say I love you, Lauren."

"I love you, too."

Joy glowed in his smile and lit his eyes as he pressed his lips to her palm. "I want you in my life for the rest of my days. I know what I'm asking you to give up, but think about the life we could have together."

"I want that life."

"Enough to become Amish?"

She tapped the center of her chest. "In here, I've always been plain."

He sat on the edge of the bed and gathered her into his arms, taking care not to jostle her or the tubes and monitors connected to her. Switching to *Deitsch*, he said, "*Ich liebe dich.* I love you with all my heart. Will you marry me, Laurene Nolt?"

"*Ja.*"

As his lips found hers for a tender kiss, she knew her most precious wish was coming true with the man she'd loved for longer than she'd known.

Epilogue

"I'm putting in two doors to the kitchen," *Aenti* Sylvia said as she pointed to the architectural drawings on the table in the middle of the inn's front lawn. She leaned on the crutches she'd be using for another couple of months until her leg healed. "No more having to call 'in' and 'out.' Brilliant, ain't so?"

"Absolutely brilliant." Lauren smiled at her great-*aenti*, then almost laughed aloud at how she'd begun to think in *Deitsch* again after a month of helping *Aenti* Sylvia oversee the cleanup of the stone house and its contents.

The house had weathered the fire well, though scorch marks still hadn't been completely removed from the stones closest to where the kitchen once stood. The furniture on the first floor had been ruined by water and smoke, but *Aenti* Sylvia had sent the dining room table out to be rebuilt. The rest she was replacing along with ordering extra furniture for the three additional bedrooms she was having constructed over the new kitchen.

With the casino being built closer to Route 30 by a developer that hadn't even been under consideration until the land abruptly became available, the inn would need to be ready to host guests who didn't want to stay at the busy hotel connected to the casino. Krause-Matsui-Fitzgerald had created a big public relations campaign based on the ideas Lauren had proposed before quitting her job, subletting her apartment and moving in with her great-*aenti* into the small house behind Frank's garage.

Her parents were moving, too. Not to Bliss Valley, but to Florida with the money Lauren had gotten as part of the severance package she negotiated with her former boss's boss. She'd been shocked to discover Patrick's boss had been well aware of how Lauren was the creative heart of the team. Before Dad and Mom relocated, however, they'd made arrangements to meet with Jonas to begin the process that would lift the *bann* and allow them to attend their daughter's wedding and continue to be a part of her life.

Short arms clamped onto Lauren's waist. "*Gute mariye*, Mary Beth."

"Visit the *bopplin* ducklings?"

Smiling, she faced the *kind* who would be her daughter after Lauren finished her baptism classes and could be married in another six months. Her smile broadened when she saw Adam standing behind the little girl. As he walked over to look at the plans for the rebuilt inn, she wondered if she'd ever tire of seeing his handsome face with the grin that was just for her. Even though she knew the answer already, she was willing to take a lifetime to prove she wouldn't ever take his gentle, sensual grin for granted.

"I like how you've arranged these bedrooms," he said, tapping the word on the plans. He winked at Lauren, who smiled back. He'd conquered learning to distinguish between *b* and *d* the previous week, so could read the word *bed*. "They'll have a nice view of the pond and the ducks."

"*Bopplin* ducklings," his daughter corrected. "They're little like me."

"The ducklings," Adam said with a chuckle, "are getting almost as big as their parents. Just like you are."

"*Bopplin* ducklings," Mary Beth insisted.

"Go and see the ducks," *Aenti* Sylvia said. "I've got a couple of things to check."

"Don't go inside," Lauren said at the same time as Adam did.

When they all laughed and her great-*aenti* agreed not to go inside as she'd tried before, Lauren held out her hands. Adam took one and Mary Beth the other while they walked toward the pond. She looked up at him, and he smiled as he gave her *kapp* string a teasing tug. Leaning her head against his shoulder, she knew she had the reason at last for why God had brought her back to Bliss Valley.

She'd come home.

★ ★ ★ ★ ★

Don't miss the uplifting follow-up to
A Wish for Home.
Look for the second book in the
Secrets of Bliss Valley series
from celebrated author

JO ANN BROWN

A PROMISE OF FORGIVENESS

Every little secret is a chain to the past...

"Jo Ann Brown's writing is both powerful and charming. She
provides a respite from the cares of the day and gives the invitation
to join her for a journey of peace that lingers in the heart."
—Kelly Long, bestselling author

Coming soon from Love Inspired!

LOVE INSPIRED
loveinspired.com

LIJB0421BPATR

LOVE INSPIRED

INSPIRATIONAL ROMANCE

UPLIFTING STORIES OF FAITH, FORGIVENESS AND HOPE.

Join our social communities to connect
with other readers who share your love!

Sign up for the Love Inspired newsletter
at **LoveInspired.com** to be the first
to find out about upcoming titles,
special promotions and exclusive content.

CONNECT WITH US AT:

 Facebook.com/LoveInspiredBooks

Twitter.com/LoveInspiredBks

Facebook.com/groups/HarlequinConnection

Grace found Nicole had pulled herself up to the front door and was high-fiving none other than Adrian Schrock. He'd squatted down to her level. Nicole was having a fine old time.

Grace picked up her *doschder* and pushed open the door, causing Adrian to jump up, then step back toward the porch steps. It was, indeed, a fine spring day. The sun shone brightly across the Indiana fields. Flowers colored yellow, red, lavender and orange had begun popping through the soil that surrounded the porch. Birds were even chirping merrily.

Somehow, all those things did little to elevate Grace's mood. Neither did the sight of her neighbor.

Adrian resettled his straw hat on his head and smiled. *"Gudemariye."*

"Your llama has escaped again."

"Kendrick? *Ya.* I've come to fetch him. He seems to like your place more than mine."

"I don't want that animal over here, Adrian. He spits. And your peacock was here at daybreak, crying like a child."

Adrian laughed. "When you moved back home, I guess you didn't expect to live next to a Plain & Simple Exotic Animal Farm."

Adrian wiggled his eyebrows at Nicole when he seemed to realize that Grace wasn't amused.

"I think of your place as Adrian's Zoo."

"Not a bad name, but it doesn't highlight our Amish heritage enough."

"The point is that I feel like we're living next door to a menagerie of animals."

"Up, Aden. Up."

Adrian scooped Nicole from Grace's hold, held her high above his head, then nuzzled her neck. Adrian was comfortable with everyone and everything.

"Do you think she'll ever learn to say my name right?"

"Possibly. Can you please catch Kendrick and take him back to your place?"

"Of course. That's why I came over. I guess I must have left the gate open again." He kissed Nicole's cheek, then popped her back into Grace's arms. "You should bring her over to see the turtles."

As he walked away, Grace wondered for the hundredth time why he wasn't married. It was true that he'd picked a strange profession. What other Amish man raised exotic animals? No, Adrian wouldn't be considered excellent marrying material by most young Amish women.

Don't miss
The Baby Next Door *by Vannetta Chapman,*
available April 2021 wherever
Love Inspired books and ebooks are sold.

LoveInspired.com

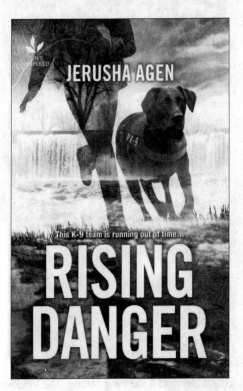

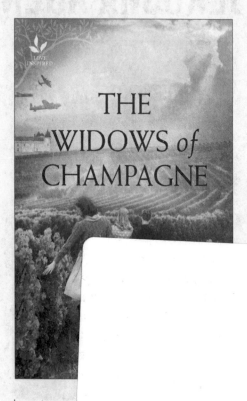